Desert of Fire

Across Time & Space series

The Eternity Stone
Mountain of Glass
Desert of Fire
Desert of Ice
The Hidden Door
Whiter Than Snow
City of Light

Fairytale Memoirs series
The Mostly Forgotten Memoirs of Rose Red
Viola Sends Her Regrets
Gifted

Standalone books
Breaking the Glass Slipper
Unshakeable
Tyger
Take Me Home
Hereditary

For information on new and upcoming books,
go to **mmarinanbooks.com**

Desert of Fire

ACROSS TIME & SPACE

BOOK THREE

M. Marinan

First published in New Zealand in 2018
This edition published 2023
by Silversmith Publishing

A catalogue record for this book is available from the National Library of New Zealand

Original cover paperback ISBN 978-0-473-43502-8
This cover paperback ISBN 978-1-99-001422-2
This cover hardcover ISBN 978-1-99-001423-9

Dedication

This book is dedicated to David,
for no particular reason.

Also thanks to Kate and Anne-Marie
for the time and energy you both
put into this story.

Contents

Prologue

The Borderlands, 2590 AD

The small chest had been found buried deep in the forest, its wooden sides worn and dirty from neglect, but its precious contents still mostly intact. The locals all crowded around the open box, feeling the shared excitement, but most of them not entirely sure why.

"This is a momentous discovery," their leader announced proudly. "Here we have two of the three emblems that make up the Anima Chest, one of the most valuable objects of power in existence."

"It's more like a group of objects," a preteen boy pointed out. He had brown hair, brown eyes and brown, slightly damaged-looking skin, and he'd not yet learned that proud people didn't like being corrected. "Anyway, it just looks like a rock and a flower."

And indeed, inside the chest was a fist-sized rock: mottled brown with a thick streak of crystal through its centre. Beside it was a flower: a fresh yellow blossom that sat unwithered in its carved compartment, although it must have been there for many years. There was also a third, empty compartment.

The leader glared at the boy. "The emblems," he repeated, "make up two-thirds of the Anima Chest, which is one of the most valuable objects in existence. The *rock*, as you called it, is called the spirit's bone. The bloom is called the spirit's flesh, and the last, missing piece is a small golden flask, known as the spirit's blood. Together, they create-"

"Fire!" somebody shouted from behind them. "Fire on the hill!"

The leader rolled his eyes. "Someone's been smoking in the scrub again. Go deal with that, Trennan," he told the preteen boy. "Take a bucket."

The boy took two, because the smoke was starting to look significant. It was up on the nearby rocky hilltop, the low, neatly-shaped peak that they called 'the volcano' because of its shape rather than any actual volcanic properties.

This area was on the border between the normal and the Other realm, ever since the split a few centuries earlier that had created a direct entryway into the Other, but it boasted nothing except rocks and trees.

Except when he finally reached the origin of the smoke, he found it wasn't a fire at all. It was a split in the rock, belching out thick, white, sulphurous clouds from some unknown point beneath the surface.

He studied it warily, and then – not wanting to displease the leader further – dumped the first bucket of water right on top. For a bare second the smoke died back…and then he felt the ground shudder.

That was his only warning for what happened next.

The Mountain of Glass, time irrelevant

Somewhere outside of the normal realm there was a vast round room, one unreachable by any human means. It had football field-sized walls covered in an elaborate grey tapestry, or what *looked* grey but was instead made of very fine black and white threads, carefully woven together to create the illusion of tone.

One man, Amaranthus, hovered in the centre of this enormous tapestry. He was halfway up one of the enormous swathes of fabric, his attention focused on the threads themselves.

He noted several fine white threads that were sewn back and forth across more distance than most covered. He wanted them to go further still, but he couldn't pull them. That was the best way to damage the tapestry.

So instead he just created several little loops in the cloth, and waited for the threads to move themselves…

GLAD TIDINGS

The Mountain of Glass, time irrelevant

"Elspeth!" Anne scrambled up the shining peak of the inner Mountain, feeling light with excitement and expectation. "Bethie! I have the most wonderful tidings!"

But even though Anne knew her younger sister was within hearing distance, the girl did not respond. Anne scowled, then lifted herself off the ground and flew the last few feet to the Mountain's summit. This was a plateau of about ten feet across, perfectly circular, with a small pool of water at its centre.

From here one could see the tiny streams of water trickle from the pool down the sides of the Mountain, turning into streams that flowed through the vast Garden surrounding them, then into mighty rivers that ran underground throughout the Other and the normal realm, if only one knew how to look for them.

Sitting next to the pool was Anne's half-sister Elspeth, staring into the water as though enthralled. Next to her sat a handsome, pale boy in plain white garb. He was talking quite closely into Bethie's ear whilst gesturing at the pool, and neither of them had noted Anne's presence.

Anne coughed loudly, and finally the two of them looked up. "Did you not hear me calling?" she asked irritably.

"You were calling?" Jon replied blankly.

Anne scowled again. "Indeed I was, sirrah, although I sought my sister rather than you. I now see you have held her attention instead. And what might you have been saying that required you to sit so very close?"

"Anne!" Elspeth blushed deep pink, gazing at her reproachfully, although she did shuffle just a little distance from the boy. "You need not glare at him so, for we were merely speaking. We've been watching your two odd friends, Ashlea and George, and 'tis the strangest thing! They are together."

Anne pondered that a moment. She had not laid eyes on those two since their sudden expulsion from the Mountain some weeks before, but Bethie's news surprised her not at all. "Of course," she replied. "There are gateways between their times left by the Eternity Stone, so any separation would be from their own choice. Although I note they have not attempted to return *here*. But I did not climb this Mountain merely to discuss the lives of others!"

"You didn't climb it at all," Jon pointed out. "You flew."

Anne waved a hand dismissively. "Nevertheless. I have most glad tidings to share – Amaranthus has offered me immortality!" She waited with bated breath for their excited congratulations, but Elspeth merely looked confused. Jon looked bored, as was his fashion.

"'Tis a very good thing," Anne persisted. "I could become one of the everlasting People, and live here in the Mountain, and never have to return home to the stinking sixteenth century! And if *I* might, then you might too, Bethie!" She paused. "Oh, and you too, Jon. If you must."

The other two exchanged a glance that Anne did not understand. Elspeth said, "That would be a fine thing indeed, sister, although Amaranthus has already told me I do not have to return home."

"Did he promise immortality?"

"Well, not in such terms–"

"Then 'tis not the same," Anne finished decisively. "But he has given me tasks to perform on behalf of the Mountain, anywhere across time or space by use of the remnant gateways. Oh, I am most excited! He said I may go at once if I wish. There is a gateway open at the south end of the second vineyard. I merely wished to advise you before I left."

"Oh," Elspeth said. She smiled, looking very pretty with her light green eyes and dark hair, and Anne realised why Annoying Jon insisted on spending so much time with her. Oh, Anne did hope that she protected herself. Even in this place, the life of a bastard could not be a good one.

"Then I do wish you the blessings of the Eternal One, dear Anne," Elspeth continued. "We shall await your return with interest."

Anne nodded, ignoring Jon's half-hearted shrug. "And you two, stay in public places!"

"Sister!"

Elspeth watched her sister's red head disappear over the steep side of the inner Mountain. At this moment she felt that her own cheeks must match that colour.

"My apologies for her insinuation," she said to Jon. "She is only six months my elder, but does think herself my keeper also. I know you are most honourable."

He shrugged, smiling at her. "Never mind Anne. She's off to have an adventure, and she's welcome to it."

"Indeed." Elspeth felt a pang of anxiety at the thought of her petite sister braving the wilds of the world all alone, but then recalled that with Amaranthus, no one was ever truly alone. If he had sent her, then he would also protect her. "But I confess I'm surprised at her. I would have thought she'd want to watch the wedding."

Jon shrugged again, then turned back to the pool, waving a hand over its surface. "Then we'll watch together, shall we?"

The reflection changed from the ever-blue glass dome above them to an image of two familiar figures, standing hand in hand in an unfamiliar setting. The dark-haired girl wore a long white gown, and the fair-haired boy… ah, who cared? No one ever looked at the groom.

"Oh yes, let's." Elspeth did so love weddings.

The registry office, Whiteside, Leicester County,
Angland, mid 2013 AD

"I do solemnly declare," Ash repeated after the Registrar, "that I know not of any lawful impediment why I, Ashlea Jane O'Reilly, may not be joined in matrimony to George William Seymour."

Whew. She'd got through those old-fashioned words without stumbling. Her fingers tightened on George's, and she smiled at him. He was smiling back, as he had been through the whole short ceremony. Oh, he looked so handsome in his formal wear borrowed from 1818, although a little out of place in this modern registry office.

As if anyone cared beside the two of them.

As if anyone else mattered.

"I call upon these persons here to witness," the Registrar continued, and Ash repeated the words, ignoring the sound of sobbing in the background. They had as witnesses one of her co-workers from her old administration job and a neighbour they'd become quite friendly with. *They* weren't the ones sobbing.

Then the bride and groom said the last few binding words, put on the rings, kissed, signed the documents and were congratulated by the witnesses and Registrar, and their time was up.

"By Jove," George said as they exited the building, laptop in one hand and her hand tightly in the other. "That was an odd thing, wasn't it?"

"Do you mean my mother sobbing over the webcam because she couldn't be at the ceremony? Or the Registrar in her pink suit? Or your birth certificate being forged? Or the fact you just married someone two centuries younger than you are?"

"Lecherous old man that I am," George agreed happily, leaning in to give her a brief kiss, public be damned. "All of the above, never mind the documents. But I say, your parents *do* like me, do they not? They always said they did, but it's difficult to tell when one can't meet face to face…"

"They like you," Ash assured him. "They're always saying how lovely your manners are. Besides, Mum would have cried even if Dad hadn't just had his knee surgery and they'd been able to come. She always cries at weddings." Or christenings. Or the sad bits in children's films. "If only your family liked me as much."

"They like you," George said staunchly. "Or once they know you, they'll like you. How can they not?"

Ash's hand tightened on his, and her smile faltered a little. Judging by the cool reception she'd had from his brother and sister-in-law just before they'd left, the Viscount and Viscountess Morley hadn't found it *that* hard to dislike her.

It was a time-travel thing, she'd decided. When George went forward to her time, everyone found him delightfully old-fashioned (or stuffy, but she wasn't going to tell him who said that). When she went back to 1818, she came across as uncouth. Or so she'd been told.

"At least we've got our finances sorted," Ash said instead, changing the subject. "Isn't it great how you can just bring things from your own time and sell them as antiques online? Along with my contract work, we'll do just fine."

She had another month on her current landscaping contract, then she'd agreed to go back to Regency Angland for a 'visit'. Hopefully they could keep it short. Hopefully she wouldn't screw up too badly.

"Don't let it be said I live off my wife," George said a little less cheerfully. Her working was one of the few things they'd disagreed about. In his time, ladies did not perform menial labour. "But when we go to my time, we'll live off my allowance until my business proposal takes off. But never mind that now, *Mrs Seymour*. We're on honeymoon, and finally we're morally entitled to…"

Ash coughed as he whispered in her ear, feeling her cheeks turn pink. That was one of the reasons they'd got married so quickly. Not the only reason, but for him it was a big one. One did not become intimate with a lady outside of marriage, and he'd decided she was a lady. It was rather nice, actually, especially compared to how things had been when they'd first met.

"Oh alright, if you insist," she agreed happily. Now, off to find that hotel they'd spent a week's wages on…

…and the rest of it would sort itself out. Right?

*The Chosen Compound, The Secular Republic of Lile,
Eastern Europa, 2597 AD*

The night was starless and still, the surroundings lush and green, and the half-dozen huge bonfires lighting the whole area flickered orange onto the hundreds of people surrounding them. The crowd was quiet, but there was a strong sense of expectation, of excitement.

Then the Elder said his piece just like he did every Summer Solstice, and the enormous cauldrons of cold water held just for that moment were tipped over the bonfires. There was a *hiss* as water turned to steam, screams or squeals from people who'd been too close to avoid the flood, and general laughter as the lights switched back on and the real fun began.

"Party! *Wahoo!*"

Coryn Regindotir leaned back just in time to avoid being run over by her younger brother Ladon in his hurry to reach the centre of the steam – where all his friends were, and where they'd all get a lovely steam burn if they weren't careful. She'd learned that the hard way in her younger years.

Just then a teenage boy came up beside her. Trennan was the same age as her – seventeen – but where she was fair, he was brown. Brown hair, brown eyes, brown skin with a vaguely bark-like pattern that spoke of his half-inhuman heritage, and the loveliest smile…but perhaps she was biased.

"And the Fire Lord is defeated yet again," he said dryly, slipping his hand into hers. "Gotta love the symbolism."

Trennan referred to the whole reason for this celebration –

that some ancient Fey tyrant had been destroyed aeons ago before he burned the whole world to a crisp – as if it mattered here and now. Coryn squeezed his hand and beamed at him, uncaring of who could see. Displays of open affection weren't encouraged here in amongst the Chosen, since they said singular romantic attachments were bad for the soul.

Eh. Whatever. If Coryn could have felt her soul, she would have said it was in excellent shape. "I'm just happy we're here. You've qualified for your knight's trial, and once you pass the endurance test…"

He squeezed her hand back. "I'll apply to handfast with you."

And they could finally be together as they'd planned all along. The thought made her giddy with joy, but she also felt trepidation, since the knight's trial was dangerous, and not everyone made it. Trennan would have to spend thirty days in the cold darkness of the Other realm, unaided by human or Fey. The things that happened in that place…

But he *would* make it. He had to.

Since Coryn was a girl, she didn't have a knight's trial. She only had to make it to seventeen without dying or being kicked out of the Compound – which she'd done – and now had to stay on the good side of the Elders so that when Trennan made his application, it would be accepted.

But there'd been another application that had been accepted, and she'd barely got out of *that* one. The reminder had her scanning the crowd anxiously. "Do you see Aras?"

Trennan shrugged a shoulder towards the other side of the bonfires. "There, with the other handfasted couples. But you're not scared of him, are you Cory?"

Well yes, actually she was, just a bit. He was so big: tall and muscular, with the scars that came from his years as a soldier. And while other, older girls might think his longish blond hair and silvery prosthetic arm were appealing, his grimness had always made Coryn want to run a mile. And the way he'd always watched her with that cold intensity made her so nervous.

Still, she hadn't expected him to apply to handfast with her on the eve of her seventeenth birthday, right after she'd pre-applied to handfast with Trennan! And then the Elders had approved it…

By the Fey, if it hadn't been for her dear friend Kamile stepping in and making a cross-application for Aras, and the Elders changing their mind…well, she might have been stuck with *him* for the next twelve months until the handfast period expired. Talk about a lucky escape.

But all she said was, "I hope he doesn't think I tricked him."

"Eh. Probably." Coryn glanced at Trennan in shock, and he just grinned in that Trennan-like way, slightly lopsided and with a dimple in one cheek. "He might feel that way, but it's legal now, him and Kamile. At least until next Solstice. So if he's mad about it, he should just be mad at the Elders, not you. Oh, and himself for agreeing to handfast with Kamile instead. No one forced him."

Coryn bit her lip, not reassured. She'd spotted them now, sitting in the half-dark along with the other newly handfasted couples. Kamile was so much smaller than her temporary partner, slim and delicate enough that she looked younger than Coryn even though she was several years older.

Although Coryn couldn't see it from here, she knew they'd have one hand bound together with red ribbon, so everyone could see that for the next year each was off-limits to anyone else. That was the point of handfasting. Well, that and making babies, of course.

Coryn made a sidelong glance towards Trennan. She sure wasn't ready to be a mother, even if the Chosen laws would allow it, but she couldn't mind *trying* with Trennan. Ha, ha.

Just then Kamile saw her looking and smiled ruefully, waving her free hand. Coryn waved back – but then Aras looked up. His light blue gaze was as cold as ever (did the man even *have* emotions?) and Coryn let her hand drop awkwardly, dipping her head and turning away. Trennan might say that she hadn't tricked Aras, but she would still always feel like Aras was angry with her.

"Of course he can't complain," she agreed with Trennan, deliberately turning away from the couples lined up alongside the glowing coals. "He just needs to wait out the year. Be faithful to Kamile for that time, and then…"

"And then we'll be handfasted already," Trennan vowed. "And that'll be the end of that."

For a year, anyway. But they'd deal with what came after *after*.

Coryn glanced over his shoulder to where some older men were preparing horses, their ceremonial black armour gleaming in the firelight. "It's just about time to go," she said wistfully. She wanted to kiss him goodbye, but everyone was watching and they were at least *pretending* that they weren't together.

"Oh, wait, I have something for you." Trennan fumbled in his pocket and pulled out a tiny cloth bag. He tipped a small silver object out into his palm, holding it out to her. "For you. If you wear it, I'll always know where you are."

It was a ring, simple and pretty with three almond-shaped light blue stones set neatly on top. Coryn felt a tingle of alter-power as she touched it, and knew it must have been created by one of the Chosen. None of the Sec society outside of this compound would have known how to imbue an object with alter-power like this. When Trennan said he'd always know where she was if she wore it, he meant it.

"It's so small because you wear it on your fourth finger," he quickly explained, "rather than your thumb like most rings. It's an old tradition, or so the maker told me."

Coryn's eyes almost filled with tears, and she slipped it carefully onto that little-used finger, trying to show through her expression how much she appreciated the gift. "Thank you," she whispered. "It's beautiful."

"Not too strange?" he asked with a crooked grin.

She waggled her fingers, watching how the ring caught the light as she moved. "Not at all. It's perfect." Then she said loudly for the benefit of those around, "Good luck with your knight's trial, Trennan Halfling. We'll see you in thirty days."

"Thirty days," Trennan echoed, and then after a final glance he turned to head off with the knights. They'd accompany him across the border into the darkness of the Other, making sure he went all the way in and didn't simply duck back into the normal realm once he was out of sight.

Coryn watched him go, heading away through the Compound's old buildings until they reached the forested Borderlands. Even though it was dark here anyway, she knew once they'd reached the Other. They all blinked out of sight….and it was up to fate whether she ever saw him again.

Trennan felt the change as he moved into the Other proper, trading his normal horse for a hardier (and smellier) Fey one. The greenery disappeared off the trees, replaced by a clinging, wispy black fog, and the tingle of power and potential in the air made him shiver even through his thick trial gear. The Other could be icy cold, but it had to be mind over matter.

Hard to believe that just a few miles away, the cities of Lile didn't even know these places existed. That was probably a good thing. The government was very Sec, very anti-alter-power or anything that hinted of religion or the supernatural, and they'd bomb the Borderlands to shreds if they knew about them.

Next to Trennan the three older knights had barely registered the change. Jan, Meric and Evers had been with the Chosen for longer than Trennan had been alive, and they were greatly respected for their wisdom, skill and courage, even if they were a little past their prime physically.

They rode silently for what might have been an hour – time was hard to tell in the Other – and it grew darker until Trennan could barely make out what was around them. But that was the Other for you. Always dusk, and full of fantastic and terrifying beings.

Then they stopped.

"You know what you have to do, boy," Meric said gruffly. He was a solid man with short grey hair and a friendship with the Elders that seemed to be faltering lately. Still, here he was, guiding the boys through their coming-of-age trial.

"Not die?" Trennan suggested, then winced a little as he realised it had sounded flippant. Always one of his flaws – taking things too lightly. "Last for thirty days," he corrected.

"Thirty days," Jan agreed. He looked older than Meric, and was lean with long lines on his face, his jowls sagging like a bloodhound's. "But what are you going to do with those thirty days?"

Not die, Trennan wanted to say again, but it seemed as though they were waiting for something. "Is there something I should be doing?"

The men exchanged knowing glances.

"You can do whatever you like," Meric replied. "Seek out the Fey cities. Search for treasure. Simply try not to die. But if you want to see something *really* interesting, you'll need to go deeper."

"Go right in," Jan added. "Deep into the Other until it's colder and darker than you could imagine. Go in until you see light, then find what's hidden beneath the ice."

"Ice?" Trennan echoed curiously. "I know it gets cold, but since when does the Other have ice?" It would need to have *water* to have ice, and they all knew there was little of that to be found.

"It does," Meric confirmed. "But you'll have to go a very long way, further than anyone has ever taken you before. If you're going to have thirty days, boy, do that."

Trennan considered it. "But how will I know what you're talking about?"

The older men smiled, even Evers who barely said anything except for 'pass the salt'.

"Oh, you'll know it when you see it," Meric replied.

And that was all they'd tell him. They just left him there, alone with his Fey horse, in the cool air of the Other. Well past the Borderlands, he had only just enough light to see his surroundings of rocky desert plains and mountains off to the side. It was perpetually dusk here, but the further in he went, the darker it looked. Not very appealing.

But Meric had told him to go in far, farther than he'd ever been, and Trennan would have been neglecting the tenets of courage and wisdom (listening to his elders) if he had ignored him.

So he sighed, picked up his reins, and started riding.

The market town of Eldre Clair-well, Frencia, 1322 AD

Anne stood at the edge of the bustling market crowd, her nose scrunched up in distaste. Forsooth, this whole place reeked like a privy. When Amaranthus had given her a mission, she'd not expected something so plain and…*stinky.*

Her gown had changed as she'd stepped through this gateway, and while she'd regretted appearing in this servile brown garb, now it made sense. Who would risk befouling fine fabric in such surroundings?

She stepped sideways to avoid being trampled by a couple of oxen – *splat.* "Ugh!" She'd stepped in their droppings.

Anne wiped her shoe on a cleaner patch of dirt, resolving to dispose of these boots as soon as she was able. But for now, to complete her mission. She took a deep breath – oops, too deep! – choked a little, then stepped towards the merchant as she'd been directed. He was a small, skinny man with leathery, sun-tanned skin, and as she watched he grabbed a squawking fowl by the neck, held it down over his wooden bench, then…

Chop.

Anne swallowed, pausing mid-step. While a lady might enjoy the occasional bite of cockenthrice, one didn't want to *see* the original creature disposed of.

Why not a gold merchant, or even one who sold cloth? Why a fowl merchant, Amaranthus?

She could do this. She could. Clenching her fists at her sides, she steeled herself to move forward and stood before the merchant.

He paused mid-pluck, smiling up at her with a grin that was more gap than tooth. "'Ow can I 'elp you, miss?"

The Frencine words translated effortlessly to low Anglish in

Anne's mind, and she barely had to bite her tongue to stop correcting him, *my lady*. Although she was the widow of not one but two earls of Longford, she'd chosen not to use her title while outside her own time of 1556. "Good day, sir. Might you be Perrin son of Guarin?"

The man's hands flew over the now headless fowl, plucking fluffy feathers by the handful. "That's me. 'Oo's asking?"

And here was the rub. Anne leaned in closer, lowering her voice. "Amaranthus sent me. He says you have something for me."

Perrin froze mid-pluck, and his brown eyes widened. "Wot?"

Mayhap he had not heard aright the first time. Or mayhap she had spoken in Anglish by mistake; 'twould not be the first time. "Amaranthus sent me," Anne repeated more loudly. "He said-"

"'Ere, that's enough of that," he said in a low, hoarse voice, releasing the fowl and stepping around his bench.

He moved so fast she didn't have time to step away; jostling and shoving her away from the stall, pushing at the front folds of her voluminous servant's garb. Anne shrieked a little at the contact, stumbling backwards, then *thud*. She fell onto her backside on the hardpacked dirt.

"Now you go away," he hissed at her, stepping back into his booth and picking up his cleaver. "Go and bother some other poor soul."

Poor soul! Anne scrambled to her feet, eyes pricking with furious tears. How dare he! How dare he treat her in such a manner! She took in a deep breath to berate him as he deserved, but then noticed the curious eyes of those around her. *Stay quiet, stay unnoticed*, Amaranthus had said.

"Reeking drate-poke," she muttered in Anglish, then turned and headed back for the gateway she'd come in by. Z'wounds, but she'd have to admit failure. Her very first mission, and she'd ruined it.

But when Anne returned to the quiet corner of the market that held the gateway, she found that the whole thing was blocked off by a very large cart full of straw. No, not just straw – pigs and straw. She could see the gateway there, shimmering faintly like the air above a hot cauldron, but 'twas clear she could not use it until the cart was gone.

"Saints' teeth," she said desolately. "Now I shall have to stay even longer."

Letting out a sigh of dismay, she slipped through the doorway of what appeared to be a tavern. It was dark, crowded and smelled of sour ale, but at least no one was insulting her in here. Now if only she might find a seat, mayhap she'd even buy a drink.

"You there! Wench! Bring us your finest ale."

Ha, pity the poor barmaid that wretch spoke to. 'Wench' was only a step above 'slag', and Anne knew how insulting both terms were. But there were no seats to be found, so she leaned back against the rough wooden walls, letting out a heavy sigh.

Mayhap 'twas not for her to be immortal. Or mayhap Amaranthus would give her another try…

Anne felt a sharp pain on her skirt-clad rear, and she squeaked, spinning to face her assailant. "I beg your pardon!"

The youngish man leered down at her, the richness of his garb denoting a higher social station than many of the others here. Behind him stood another man dressed in the same fashion, and with an equally stupid smirk on his face. Both men were armed with swords. Nobly born, or mayhap just wealthy. "Hey, slag, didn't you hear me? Two ales!"

She glared at him, stunned. "I heard you. I don't-"

"No excuses," the first man cut in. "Get on with it, girl, before I have you cast off for shirking your duties."

"So sorry, milords," Anne said sarcastically, giving a deep curtsey. "I'll get that for ye right away."

They didn't note her tone. "See, Roland," the louder one said to his friend. "The lowborn are naturally lazy, but they will be appropriately servile if you simply use a firm tone."

Anne's mouth tightened in a thin line. Lowborn, lazy and servile, was she? She'd planned to walk out, leaving them waiting for drinks that would never arrive, but now she'd show them just how servile she could be.

She quietly took two empty tankards from a nearby table, then headed out the front door where she'd come in. A few seconds later she saw a horse's water trough, currently being used by a small donkey. The water was muddied and pale brown, and smelled sour.

Perfect.

Two minutes later she set the tankards in front of those two noblemen, her head bowed meekly to hide her smile. The taller man went to flick some coins at her, but she just said sweetly, "Oh, no, milords. 'Tis a gift, for my slow service."

They shrugged and turned to their drinks, and Anne ran for it. She'd almost made it back to the door when she heard a roar of disgust. But there was no time to escape without being seen, and she doubted she could outrun them.

Ducking down behind another table, she heard the man shout, "What kind of swill is this?"

Horse swill, she could have answered, but she heard the tavern keeper's startled reply that he served only the finest ales. But they all said that, didn't they?

"You call this fine?" the noble roared, and she watched

through the gap under the table as he shoved the tankard in the tavern keeper's face.

The second noble sniffed his tankard's contents and grimaced. "This isn't ale," he said. "This smells like horse piss."

"Where did you get it?" the bewildered tavern keeper asked.

"Your damned red-haired tavern wench, that's where!"

Anne heard the tavern keeper's confused reply of, "But I don't have a red-haired tavern wench…" just as one of the *real* tavern wenches walked by, carrying half a dozen empty tankards in her arms, and spotted her.

"Oi," the girl said in surprise, and that was enough for Anne. She sprung up out of her hiding spot and sprinted for the door. The nobles spotted her and ran after her, and it might have gone very badly indeed had not a strong brown hand grabbed her just as she ran through, pulling her aside.

She met Amaranthus's dark eyes and he lifted one finger to his lips. *Stay still, stay quiet.*

Anne obediently did so, and the rude nobles ran out, followed closely behind by the tavern keeper. They ran right past the two hiding in plain sight, looking around in clear anger for the 'wench who dared trick them thus'. The taller of the men had drawn his sword.

"I swear this was not my doing," the tavern keeper babbled. "I'll give ye all the ale ye wish for, free, of course, to make up for this disgrace!"

Unable to find Anne, the men grudgingly gave up the chase, turning and walking back into the tavern.

When they were gone, Amaranthus turned back to her. Today he wore his taller, younger form rather than the old man she'd first met him as, but either way he was unmistakeable. "Was your day so bad that it could only be improved by feeding horse urine to strangers?"

There was no condemnation in his tone, but Anne felt it nonetheless. "'Twas not horse urine," she mumbled defensively. "'Twas only water, from the trough."

"Any liquid from a horse's trough that looks like that is never just water," Amaranthus said reprovingly, and Anne couldn't stifle a giggle as she realised what he meant.

"Oh. I see. Well, mayhap I should have been more self-controlled, but they were so *rude* to me! You should have seen it."

"I did," he said frankly. "I was in there the whole time."

"Oh," she repeated. So he'd done what they just had, what he called 'hiding in plain sight'. If one didn't move or speak, then somehow people's gazes would slide right past… "But 'twill not kill them. They deserved it."

"Perhaps they did," Amaranthus agreed mildly. "But they wouldn't have been the ones to suffer, would they? You saw that one of the men had drawn his sword. Don't you remember what that meant? This place is much like your own time in that aspect."

Suddenly Anne understood, and a wave of guilt swamped her. She'd forgotten how life was for the different classes. Here only the upper classes could carry swords, and they could use them freely on the lower classes with very little consequences. If the tavern keeper was blamed for the incident, the nobles could do anything to him and not be punished.

"Forgive me," she blurted out. "I thought not of his welfare. Will he be harmed?"

Amaranthus poked his head around the corner of the door briefly. "They'll all be fine. They're a fair way to drinking themselves stupid already. He's brought out the strong stuff."

Anne sighed in relief, then suddenly remembered why she'd been in the tavern in the first place. "It all went wrong!" she wailed. "The fowl merchant you sent me to was most unkind, and he shouted at me, and pushed me! Just because I said who had sent me!"

"He pushed you, did he?" he asked mildly. "What's that in the pocket of your skirt?"

She looked down in confusion. One of the things which made this gown so hideous was the enormous pocket in the front, since presumably servants needed that sort of thing.

She slipped her hand into the pocket, not expecting to find anything, but her hand touched a small, hard item. Pulling it out, she saw 'twas a little flask made of plain, cracked leather, stoppered at the top with brass. "What's this doing here?"

Amaranthus smiled. "Congratulations on fulfilling your first task. The merchant is a long-time friend of mine, but hides it for fear of reprisal from his neighbours. He doesn't dare let anyone know of our friendship."

Feeling a mix of pleasure and irritation, Anne muttered, "Well, he need not have been so rude about it."

"I agree. But it's funny how sometimes the people who are supposed to be on your side can insult you the loudest, hmm?"

Anne didn't think 'twas very funny at all. "So what shall we do with the flask?" she asked. "Return it to the Hall of Treasures?" That was assuming 'twas a treasure. It looked like nothing at all, but she was learning that often the plainer the object, the stronger the power.

"This one," Amaranthus explained, "is like the Eternity Stone, in that it must remain in the normal realm. My people and I must not touch it, for it would cease to exist." And then he produced something from his pocket that looked rather like the flask, only its stopper was a brighter shade of gold, and the whole thing glowed a little. 'Twas most impressive. "Here."

Anne looked down at the two flasks dubiously. Barring the slight hint of gold on one, they were identical. "Do you wish me to give them to someone?"

He just grinned in response: a wide, somewhat roguish grin. "A bit more of a challenge than that. I want you to *hide* them, separately and so well that they won't be found for many lifetimes, and through any gateway you can find. Will you do that for me?"

Anne's jaw dropped. Now *that* was a challenge she could happily take on. "I won't let you down!" she vowed. "Er…for what purpose is this task?"

But Amaranthus just tapped the side of his nose, smiled again, and disappeared into thin air. Anne was left there in the quiet shadow of the tavern, musing on where on earth she might hide such a thing – then realised she needed not one but two such places.

Then she had an idea.

The road between Whiteside and Little Meadswell,
Leceister County, 2013 AD

"By Jove, it's hard to fathom that we've been married two months," George mused as they walked along the gravel road, suitcases in hand. "Feels like mere days, doesn't it?"

"Mm," Ashlea agreed. "The honeymoon in Eirland was my favourite part, even if that *was* only for three days."

George would have to agree with that. They'd driven Ashlea's decrepit old vehicle to the west coast of Angland, whereupon they'd taken a 'ferry' to the neighbouring island. It had been quite an experience for an Anglish lad like himself, who hadn't gone far from his place of birth. Barring the time-travel, of course, but that hardly counted.

But the being-married part? *That* had been quite, quite

lovely.

"And while I've enjoyed my time here rather more now I know it's not forever," he continued happily, "I *am* looking forward to going home. No one makes cream cakes like my mother's cook. Did you ever get to try them, Ashlea darling?"

Ashlea didn't answer, and he glanced sideways to see her pretty face was creased in a frown and her gaze fixed blankly on the road ahead of them. They'd left her car some distance behind in a place it wouldn't be immediately broken into (her words, not his) but that meant the walk to the remnant gateway was considerable. Perhaps she was finding it difficult in her nineteenth-century day dress and boots.

"Ashlea?"

She jerked to attention. "What? Were you saying something?"

George tried not to take offense and only partially succeeded. "Nothing of importance. How are you finding those cases? Might I help you?"

Ashlea looked down to where he held a large case in each hand, then raised her eyebrows, smiling. "With what, your teeth? No, it's fine. I'm just tired from the work week, that's all."

A pang of guilt went through him at those words. "Then thank the Eternal One you shan't have to work again."

"What do you mean?"

"We'll live off my allowance in 1818," he explained, "and if my investments pan out, with two hundred years' worth of interest we can live more than comfortably here too. You needn't work."

Ashlea was quiet a long moment. "But I like to work, George."

"Don't be silly. No one *likes* to work. One does it because one must."

She huffed out a sigh, but didn't stop walking. "Then *one* ought to find a job that one likes! Look, it'd be great if your investments work out. I really hope they do. But I'm not the sort to sit at home staring at the wall. You know that."

"Naturally." George *did* know that, but he also knew she'd never truly experienced life as he had. Now was her chance to do so. "We'll stay at the country estate for a week, then go to Lunden to enjoy the Season. I know my mother will be most obliging and will escort you wherever you need to go if I'm not able to do so. Oh, and Olivia too, no doubt."

"Great."

Ashlea's tone was flat, but when he turned to look at her, her expression was neutral. She was tired, he reminded himself. This time in *his* time would be good for her. Very good indeed.

THE MISSING PIECE

"That's a pretty bonnet," Lady Eleanor Seymour said. "With a nice wide brim to protect your face from the harsh sun. Do try it on, Ashlea dear."

George's mother's words were kind, but to Ash, trying on hats wasn't exactly thrilling. "I already have a bonnet, thank you," she replied politely, refraining from pointing at her head where the darn thing sat. She'd made a point of wearing it non-stop, having heard that sort of comment on her last visit. Here, if your skin wasn't fish-belly white, then you were getting too much sun.

Lady Eleanor's arched eyebrows shot up. "A lady usually owns more than one bonnet. Even those of the lower classes might have several."

Behind her in the milliner's store Ash could just see the slender form of her blonde sister-in-law Olivia, also known as Lady Morley. Her pale, pretty face was twisted in an expression Ash took to read 'you uncouth weirdo', but she remained silent. She'd barely spoken to Ash the whole time they'd been here; somewhere along the way Ash must have offended her.

Join the club, Livvy.

Ash sighed almost silently, forcing a smile onto her face.

"Then I shall certainly try it."

She allowed them to remove her current bonnet – rather like an Amyrican pilgrim's wagon, only covered in flowers and stuck on her head – and replace it with the new, wider brimmed bonnet. Her reflection in the small mirror looked much the same as it had before, but why argue? "Very pretty," she said a little too heartily. "It'll match with, er…"

"We shall need to find you a new pelisse also," Lady Eleanor said decisively. "Directly after we've finished in here."

No, not more shopping! *Darn you, George, for escaping into a bookstore when she had to come into this place of torture!*

Ash freed herself from the new bonnet then sidled over to the front of the shop. Through the small glass windows, she could see the bookstore across the street. Its own display window showed a dozen different books, all leather-bound in blue, green or red. None looked very interesting – and in truth she found the old-fashioned language irritating – but at least you didn't have to try on books with a judgemental audience.

A small boy dressed in brown ran past the window, almost hitting a well-dressed couple, the woman carrying a parasol. Ash watched them idly. Parasols *did* look pretty, she had to admit, and you could probably use them as a weapon as a last resort.

A shimmer of light bounced off the metal tip of the parasol as the woman swung it, and Ash blinked. But the light was still there. It wavered and sparkled at the edge of her vision, rather like the air above tar seal on a hot summer's day, or a heat vent from an underground train.

But there were no subways here, not yet.

Three seconds went by, and Ash finally realised what she was looking at. A whole new remnant gateway, right in the middle of Axford Street.

"Excuse me," she said, even though no one was listening. "I'm just going to take a breath of fresh air."

George would *so* want to hear about this!

Ten minutes later Ash and George sat silently on opposite sides of the carriage as it jostled its way along the cobbled streets. His mother and sister had stayed out shopping, but they hadn't argued when she'd asked to go home. Not after *that* interaction.

After the silence had become drawn out and awkward, Ash said, "I really didn't expect that response."

"It's a *men's* bookseller," George replied, studying her with raised eyebrows. "What else could you expect? That the proprietor would welcome you?"

She hadn't really thought about it at all. She'd seen the sign reading 'Tolliver's Gentlemen's Bookseller', but that hadn't translated in her brain into 'no girls allowed'. Hades, the colour of the shopkeeper's face when he'd seen her standing there – who knew a man could turn that shade of purple? "But I had something to tell you. Something really cool."

"Was it life or death?"

"Well no, but-"

"Then you should have waited, Ashlea," George said gently. "It's not socially acceptable to do otherwise."

Ash sighed heavily. And right there, that was the problem with this society. Who on earth thought *segregated bookstores* were necessary? "I understand, but I still think it's unfair."

There were a few more seconds of silence, then he asked, "So what was it that you wanted to tell me? Did you find a new bonnet?"

Ash's jaw dropped. "George," she said flatly, "even if I found a bonnet made of pure gold and studded with eyeball-sized emeralds, I probably wouldn't bother to tell you about it. The only thing more boring than bonnets would be…" She struggled to find the right description. "…I don't know, lace or parasols or something equally useless."

"But you said you liked the lace parasol I bought you last weekend!"

"Of course I did," Ash said quickly, scrambling to cover her misstep. She'd forgotten about that, and really, the parasol *was* quite pretty, if useless. Not sturdy enough to be a weapon; no good in the rain. "But now I've got one, I hardly need to look for another, do I?"

"You were supposed to look for *bonnets*, not parasols," George retorted. Then he sighed. "When will you stop being surprised that females here don't have the same freedoms as they do in the twenty-first century?"

Ash didn't answer, mostly because she didn't know the answer. When they'd got married, she'd known she was signing up for a challenge. Cross-cultural relationships were never easy, or so she'd been told, and their situation was more cross-cultural than most.

But she and George had been riding high on the excitement of newly discovered love, and she'd not even worried about how fitting into his time might mean more than just wearing the right clothes. Love would conquer all, right?

Or maybe not. She loved George – his solid character, his sense of humour, their shared experiences that no one else could understand – but darn it all to heck, these restrictions were driving her crazy!

After a few seconds of silence, he sighed again then came to sit beside her, putting his arm around her shoulders. She leaned into his neck.

"Ashlea, you know life is different here. You knew it before you married me. It's not a question of whether it's fair or not, it's about fitting in for my sake, if not for your own. I strive to fit into your society when we're there, so you need to at least attempt to fit into mine." Then George added more gently, "Please."

Ash wanted to argue more because she was feeling quite out of sorts, but instead she echoed his sigh. "Fine. Sorry. Even though having men's-only stores that aren't even for dodgy stuff is just another way for the pigheaded, sexist males of this century to assert their power… But not you, George," she added belatedly.

"So you'll wait at the townhouse for Mother or Olivia to come home? I'm supposed to meet Edward at Whyte's. That's a *men's* club," he added, emphasising the second-to-last word.

"Yes, I *know*. And yes, I'll be fine."

George took her at her word and left her at the front door of the family townhouse, which was a generous 'new' building made of white stone. In her own time, it would be over two hundred years old.

Ash went in and wandered down the carpeted halls with their too-high ceilings towards the suite of rooms she shared with George. Yes, a suite – two bedrooms separated by small dressing rooms and a parlour. There were fireplaces in each bedroom, and the maids insisted on keeping George's lit even though she'd told them they shared a room every night.

There was also a small lock on her door. Ash stared at it briefly, then shook her head. She'd save that for if they had a proper fight. She just needed to get a handle on her mood, which hadn't been great since they'd arrived here in 1818.

It was probably because she felt out of place, like everyone was judging her and thinking she wasn't good enough. Thinking she was an imposter in her frilly Regency dresses and wagon-style bonnets.

Well, she *was* an imposter – a time-travelling one. But even imposters wanted to feel accepted by their in-laws.

Feeling a little glum, Ash sat down on the small, high-backed couch in the shared parlour, then turned her mind to the remnant gateway she'd seen. The only other ones she knew of were back in the 'country', AKA George's family estate, and that was a long carriage ride away.

But where did this new one lead? It could be anywhere at all, any *time* at all, and just going through it without checking it first would be a terrible idea. Ash knew that much.

But oh so tempting…especially if she left before Lady Eleanor and Olivia the Ice Queen got home.

Hmm. She could just go quickly, confirm it really was a gateway, then come back, she decided. No one would even need to know. *George* wouldn't need to know. Or she could tell him about it after she'd checked, and they could have a look together later.

"It'll be like a date," Ash said aloud. Wow, she'd almost convinced even herself.

Two minutes later she was hurrying back down that same hallway, a plain brown cloak thrown over one arm. "Don't mind me," she told the startled butler. "I'm going for a walk."

Prowd's eyebrows lowered to a more normal position, although remained higher than usual: his sign of disapproval. "Your maid, madam?"

"Will not be required."

The eyebrows shot up again.

The Chosen Compound, Borderlands, 2597 AD

"What has you so worried, Coryn? Wait, I can guess. It starts with a 'T', and ends with 'rennan'." Kamile set the tray of food on the long table in front of them, then plunked herself onto the bench next to Coryn. "Try not to wear your heart on your sleeve, Sis. It does you no favours."

Coryn scowled. She'd made a real effort to look serene and unconcerned, just as the Chosen taught, especially out here in the communal dining room. "What are you talking about? I'm not worried."

Kamile tapped her between the eyebrows with one slim finger. "You've a furrow here like you're about to plant corn, and you keep twisting that ring like it's the only thing keeping Trennan alive. If that isn't worry, then I don't know what is."

Coryn thought about arguing, then finally shrugged a shoulder, sighing. "It's been ten days since the Solstice, Kam; and no word from him. The Other is a dangerous place. What if something's happened to him?"

"Seriously, you're asking me that? Sure, anything could've happened to him. He might've been eaten by a feral Fey, or burned into ash in what's left of the Fire Lord's pits. Or he might've made friends in the Fey cities, or even found an object of power. We *don't* know. That's the whole point of no contact."

Coryn glared at her friend. "Kamile Greenskin, that does *not* help." Her shoulders slumped. "Do you really think he might've been eaten?"

Kamile sighed heavily. "I think it's unlikely. I bet he's wandering around in the desert reciting Chosen tenets and trying not to think of how hungry he is. And in another three weeks he'll come back out with marvellous, no doubt exaggerated tales, and he'd *really* like to think that you respected him enough not to show fear for him. That's what I think."

"Oh." Coryn paused, thinking about it. "You're probably right."

"I usually am when it comes to males," Kamile agreed loftily.

Speaking of males... Coryn turned to study her friend's face and neck, trying to detect any signs of pain or harm under her shoulder-length dark hair, but she looked much the same as ever.

Kamile paused halfway through devouring a rolled pancake. "What are you doing?"

"Um..." She couldn't admit what she was *really* doing, but she didn't stop pulling back the girl's shirt and checking down her back. "Nothing."

"Really? Because it looks like you're trying to see if I'm bruised or something. You can stop, because I'm not."

"Because you're a Halfling, and you don't bruise easily."

"Because I haven't been *hurt*," Kamile retorted, pushing her hand away. She smiled ruefully. "By the Fey, you really do think Aras is a monster, don't you?" Coryn made a mumbling noise that really meant nothing at all, and Kamile continued, "He's not that bad, he's just a bit cranky. Besides, I haven't seen him since the Solstice either."

Coryn's head shot around to stare at her friend. "Really? Why?"

Kamile shrugged carelessly. "Dunno. He didn't tell me. I figure he's taken off in a snit over the whole handfasting thing, and he'll come back when he's ready."

That just made Coryn feel worse, because it was Kamile who was stuck with the man-beast for the next twelve months, not her. "Maybe he went into the Other," she ventured hopefully. Maybe he'd never come out again.

Kamile shrugged again, still chewing. "Maybe," she said through her mouthful. "I don't care either way."

Coryn wondered how her friend had got so hard, and what it would take for Coryn herself to ever be that way. She decided she'd rather not know, and changed the subject. "I'm going to meet Brosca soon," she said, referring to her Fey mentor. "What are you doing for the rest of the day?"

"Mm." Kamile swallowed her mouthful. "Patrolling the Borderlands. Elder Starbright wants to see how far they've extended. She thinks there might even be a few miles of new land."

Once upon a time the two realms had been entirely separate, and the Other could only be reached in brief moments through the mind, or through intense bursts of alter-power. But then a few centuries ago the Great War had done more than just carve up the landscape of this small, green nation. It had created a connection between the Other and the normal realm; an actual entrance where humans could walk right in and experience a world of power and beings they'd never known existed.

The Chosen had sprung up from a few of those first humans who'd met with the Other's inhabitants – the wise and powerful Fey – and they'd lived here in the centuries ever since. And year by year, the entrance had grown and it had become a realm of its very own. The Borderlands.

They were lush where the Other was barren, and they moved without warning. They also tended to hold the most dangerous Fey who liked to come right up to the barrier between the realms...and who didn't always treat humans with kindness.

Which was why Coryn said with some alarm, "Elder Starbright sent you by yourself? Really?"

Kamile shrugged, then smiled ruefully. "As you said it, Coryn, I'm a Halfling, or at the very least a mixed-blood. You know they prefer to send us for these types of jobs. I don't really mind. At least it's a challenge."

Yes, it was a challenge, and there was no point in Coryn contesting it further. If an Elder had decreed it, then that's what would happen.

And yes, they did tend to choose the few Halflings living among them for those most difficult, risky jobs. They said it was because the Fey would treat the Halflings with more respect, being that they were related, but Coryn thought it was because Halflings were dispensable. They weren't common, because Fey and human didn't breed easily, and the outcome wasn't usually half as pretty as Kamile or Coryn's own Trennan.

Halflings were often freakishly tall or long-limbed, with warped facial features and unusual strength. They were treated with wariness by humans, and ignored by the Fey. Kamile might have only been a quarter Fey – they never found her parents, so no one knew – but the small, slender brunette that sat here next to Coryn looked very different in the Other. There was a reason Kamile was called 'Greenskin'.

"Of course," Coryn said, forcing a smile. "Be safe, will you? Carry a big stick."

Kamile rolled her eyes, then gave Coryn a quick hug. "Back at you. Now you'd better hurry up, or you'll be late meeting Brosca. It's already midday."

"Ah, swine-spit!" She hadn't realised how much time had passed. "I'd better go."

As Coryn briskly walked her usual route towards the true Borderlands, she realised that her delayed visit had been somewhat intentional: she'd *wanted* to forget the time.

She'd felt…odd…around Brosca lately. That was weird, because she'd been meeting with her Fey mentor in the Other ever since she was a small child, and had never thought twice about the visits. Yes, the Other was dangerous, but Brosca had always protected her from any harm; had given her knowledge and power; had specially chosen Coryn out of all of the humans living here.

As Coryn's mother often said, Coryn was truly honoured to have such a position. She knew that, and she *was* grateful. It was just...

Just nothing. Swallowing back the whatever-it-was, Coryn picked up her pace. She strode towards the ever-changing border between the Compound and the Other, heading past the Compound's outer buildings and towards where the trees grew thick and green. She didn't slow at all, because it was here that some the nastier Fey would linger, as a few humans had found out the hard way – including Trennan's mother.

She went through the lush greenery, and suddenly the few remaining trees were bare except for clumps of dark fog clinging to their branches like old leaves. She'd reached the black-clouded forest: the true border.

Then even the black-clouded trees and the sunlight was gone, and Coryn stood in the desert and the perpetual dusk of the Other. Dusk, dusk, always dusk, no matter what time of the day it was outside.

Brosca had explained that here in the Other, one day took many thousands of years. Once night hit, the world ended and then was reborn. Coryn had once asked if that meant the end of the world was soon, then? Brosca had just laughed and said that every end was a beginning, and not to fear it. That hadn't really helped.

Coryn shivered in the cool air, wrapping her arms around herself. She'd worn her long-sleeved cloak, but the cold here could cut through half a dozen layers. And Brosca hadn't yet shown up from the distant Fey city, even though Coryn was the one who'd been a little late.

Coryn looked about nervously, checking for movement that

might have belonged to someone else, but all was still and empty. She knew better than to call out, not wanting to attract the wrong attention. Once her mentor arrived, she'd be fine, but now? She felt remarkably helpless.

Yes, the Fey were pretty, and might seem friendly, but unless she was Fey herself, she should never go over the border without Brosca there to meet her. Some of them had a rather cruel sense of humour, especially the Wood Fey who lived just on the border.

She squinted into the darkness where the black-clouded forest clustered, wondering if she saw a sylphlike shape move…

"I am here."

Coryn barely contained her jolt of surprise and turned to greet Brosca with a respectful bow. She felt the Fey's cool, firm hand on her head for a moment – their usual greeting – and then stood, head still partially bowed in respect.

"You are late," Brosca said. She was a small female, only as tall as Kamile, and appeared slender under her long robes. Her silver hair looped gracefully over her pointed ears, and her face usually held an ageless, peaceful beauty. But today, she looked…annoyed?

Coryn opened her mouth to say *no, you are late*, then realised that she'd been late first, and Brosca had no doubt held off showing herself just to make a point. "Forgive me. I was distracted."

Brosca studied her, those orange-ish eyes unblinking. "And what might cause my prize student to think of lesser things? A boy?" She barely paused. "But of course it was a boy. Soon to be a man, if the Other does not claim him first. But just a boy, Coryn of the Chosen. His destiny is not intertwined with yours, and if you try to make it so, you will find nothing but pain."

That thought pricked at Coryn's heart. *His destiny is not intertwined with yours.* She instinctively wanted to reject it, but she said what Brosca was expecting to hear. "Yes, Brosca. I understand."

"And then you also understand," the Fey said gently, "that it does not matter who you handfast with. One male is much the same as another in that aspect, if you wish for children. *Do* you wish for children, Coryn?"

No. Not yet. Really, really, really not yet. But if Coryn said as much, then she'd have to admit that any desire to handfast was so she could be with Trennan, not be a teenage mother. "Eventually," she mumbled. "Most people do."

"And this was why you did not handfast with Aras."

Coryn nodded, head still down.

"And yet you would have handfasted with another?"

Caught out, of course. Coryn paused, carefully considering her answer. "I don't like Aras," she said finally. "Kamile does. She wants children."

Brosca walked close enough to Coryn that she could see the orange flecks around her pale irises, and tilted her head contemplatively. "Kamile has been trying to breed for years, unsuccessfully as we all know. She is unlikely to ever succeed, and that is the universe's way of saying that she should not. You, however, Coryn..."

She reached up one slender hand to touch Coryn's cheek, and long used to this, Coryn didn't flinch. Even though Brosca's skin looked smooth, it felt cool and harder than it ought; like polished wood or bone. "You have a greater purpose, when you finally stop letting your fear keep you from it."

"Yes, Brosca," Coryn whispered, not knowing whether she agreed or even understood, but knowing what she was expected to say.

"Good," the Fey said briskly. "Now, tell me of your dreams, Coryn. What have you learned?" She meant night-visions rather than secret hopes, of course.

As Coryn had done many times before, she closed her eyes and thought back to the previous night. She felt Brosca stand behind her, hands pressed gently to Coryn's temples to help her clarify her thoughts, and those thoughts came to mind; those dreams she barely could remember when she woke all rushed forward, as clear as if she was living them out herself now.

She saw herself in previous lives, moving in different bodies and different scenarios like an actor playing out a character, and perhaps even seeing glimpses of future lives. Any unease Coryn felt had long been squashed down, and she simply watched.

She was weak and hungry, scrabbling in the bowels of a city for scraps to eat… She was in a room full of screaming people, all being shot down one by one and dissolving into ash… She was an underdressed bride, weeping at her own wedding…

Superimposed over all those scenes was a golden glowing flask, and a giant snake winding its way around her legs and up her body, tightening as it whispered-

"What?" That last part shook Coryn out of her dream-slumber, and suddenly she was back in the chill darkness of the Other. "What did you say?"

For a moment Brosca didn't reply, and her hands tightened on Coryn's temples. "You've broken the vision." She sounded displeased.

"But you said…" Coryn petered off into silence as she realised how very silly her next words would sound.

"I was silent, as always," the Fey said impatiently. "Anything you heard was from within the vision. What did you see, my dear?"

Her voice had gentled again, and Coryn dismissed what she'd thought she'd heard. It made no sense anyway. She recounted the images she'd seen, and Brosca nodded sagely with each one.

"Your past lives have contained pain in accordance with your deeds. They make you a more powerful and compassionate soul, and lead you ever upwards."

The part about the bride had seemed quite medieval. It had taken place in a castle, so Coryn was happy to dismiss that as taking place in a past life. But the part about the people dissolving into dust sounded alarmingly modern.

"Alter-power," Brosca said briskly when Coryn asked. "It could have happened any time. Did you see anything else?"

Well, there'd been the snake, but Coryn had had that nightmare ever since childhood, and neither the Chosen nor Brosca had any patience for it. Coryn was supposed to have dealt with that fear years ago, especially considering how it had come about. "A flask," she blurted out instead. "It glowed. I don't know what it was for."

Brosca's eyes lit up – literally, glowing as brightly as the flask had. It meant she was pleased, or at least interested. "Did it look like this?" She waved one long-nailed hand in the air, and a little image appeared. The flask was only as large as her palm, square and narrow, with a tiny neck and a clear, shining cap.

"I think so. What was it?"'

"Now that," the Fey replied with an audible sense of interest, "is something extremely precious to my people, something that's been missing for thousands of years, and which I know that you have heard of. The spirit's blood."

It sounded hazily familiar, but Coryn couldn't think why.

"The Anima Chest," Brosca snapped. By the Fire Lord, she'd been impatient today. "You remember several years ago your people discovered it in the woods not far from here. It contained two of the three emblems, but was lacking the flask that would give it its full power." When Coryn still looked blank, she added icily, "The same day the volcano went off. You should remember that, as your Trennan was partly to blame."

Now Coryn remembered, although it wasn't at all fair to say it was Trennan's fault. It had been an alter-power thing, something to do with the borders shifting and changing the scenery near the Compound, and when the child that he'd been had innocently poured water over a smoking hole in the rock, the whole hill had exploded.

It was a miracle he hadn't been killed. No one had, but the hill they'd jokingly called 'the volcano' had *become* a volcano in truth, complete with underground lava pit and a deep chasm running between much of the Compound and the Other.

It was a completely supernatural thing since there wasn't even a fault line in this part of the world. The government would have been all over it had it not been explained away as an exploding heating device far past its use-by date. If only Jurgis hadn't sent Trennan with a bucket of water, thinking he was dealing with a scrub fire…

"We feared the Fire Lord had come back," Brosca said with a distant expression. "We feared that in spite of all we'd done, his defeat thousands of years ago had not been final. But it was just the inconstant joys of the Other realm meeting the normal. And the spirit's blood is what matters, girl. If you saw it in a vision, then it'll be in your future. When you find it – or find out about it – you come to me, understood?"

"Of course." Coryn paused. "What does it do?"

"Never you mind what it does," the Fey replied briskly. "Now go on. You've spent enough time in here. Go, and meet me again as the sun dips towards the horizon on the fourteenth."

That meant about four pm. Dismissed, Coryn bowed to her mentor and headed back towards the dark, clouded patch she knew led to the Compound. As always, the walk out took much longer than the walk in. She moved quickly and with her head down, focussing on the exit and thinking of what had just happened.

The fourteenth. That was a couple of days after Trennan was due to come back from his knight's trial, and it wasn't uncommon for Coryn to see her mentor once or twice a month. But the Fey had been different this time: harsher and less pleasant than usual. Her appearance had seemed harsher too, and Coryn had wanted to shrink away from her.

But that made no sense, because nothing had changed, and she'd always felt very comfortable with Brosca in the past. This particular Fey was known for being wise and gentle, and Coryn had been very honoured to have been chosen at all.

Or so she was told.

So Coryn dismissed that thought (*You don't like to think deeply on things, do you?*) then dismissed *that* thought, because what could she do? And no, she didn't think deeply, and she didn't challenge the status quo. It wasn't her job to do so.

But even as she stepped out of the black-clouded forest, she couldn't stop thinking about that golden-bright flask, and what she *thought* Brosca had whispered to her at the end of the vision. But surely, surely she wouldn't have said *that...*?

But still Coryn found herself rubbing an itchy spot on the side of her neck, and wondering.

Lunden, 1818 AD

It was worth braving the disapproval of the butler, Ash thought triumphantly as she trotted along the paved street back to the shopping district, her hooded cloak hiding her face. *Just another lower-class girl minding her own business...*

Deias, she shouldn't be enjoying this so much! The sneaki-ness of it, of going out on her own for the very first time in Regency Angland – she could hardly keep herself from smiling at every person she passed.

She smiled at the couple walking their little lapdog. She smiled at the man dashing past with soot on his face and a big load under one arm. She smiled at the-

Oh, no. She wasn't smiling at *that*.

"Hey! What do you think you're doing?"

But the stout, well-dressed man didn't even pause, still whaling away at the small, ragged child with what looked like a riding crop. "Thief!" he shouted. *Whack. Whack.* "Vermin!" The child cringed but was unable to escape, with one thin arm caught tightly in the man's grasp. As busy as the street was, no one even tried to stop him.

Almost trembling with fury, Ash stormed over and grabbed the crop right out of the man's hand, then shook it at him angrily. "You should be ashamed of yourself – a grown man like you abusing a helpless child!"

Just then that helpless child proved herself ungrateful as well by disappearing like smoke, leaving Ash alone with one furious, expensively dressed gentleman. Except judging by his expression, he wasn't gentle at all.

His face flushed even redder. "How dare you!"

"How dare *you*?" she snapped right back, but even as the words came out, she realised people were staring. Even worse, she was holding his riding crop in her hand. She surreptitiously dropped it behind her, hoping no one noticed. "It's wrong to hurt those weaker than yourself. And very unchurchian," she added in a more normal tone, since that was what the people of this time strived to be...or at least to *look* in public, which was unfortunately quite different.

"Unchurchian," the man snorted. "What would you know about that? You're not even Anglish!"

Darn that Southern-Isles accent which came out when she was upset. Ash could fake a snooty Anglish accent along with the best of them, but once she stopped concentrating the signs of her homeland would come right out, unable to be hidden. Two dozen accents in this small country alone, and the locals could always pick that hers didn't quite fit.

To make it worse, she *could* speak any language in existence (long story) but she couldn't hide her accent for any length of time when she spoke Anglish.

Unfortunately having it pointed out that she wasn't, in fact, Anglish, wasn't the worst to happen to Ash that day. The angry man managed to attract the attention of a watchman (since the Anglish hadn't yet got 'round to having a proper police force) who strolled over, looking mildly concerned. "Is there a problem, sir?"

"This *person* assaulted me!" the man announced, face reddened to almost boiling point. "She aided a thief in picking my pocket, then struck me with my own riding crop!"

"That's absolute nonsense!" Ash burst out defensively. "I didn't hit him, just shook the crop at him, and only because he was beating a defenceless child! Who I didn't know was a pickpocket, by the way."

The watchman scanned her up and down, and then her accuser, and she could see him drawing his own, incorrect conclusions from her very plain clothing, and the man's air of wealth.

Which was why she said, "I happen to be the wife of the Honourable Mr George Seymour, brother of Viscount Morley. He'll vouch for me."

The angry man laughed derisively, and the watchman

looked unimpressed. "Where's your maid then, ma'am? Or your husband? Ladies don't walk the streets alone."

Ash lifted her chin, trying to look both honest and upper class – a bit of a challenge. "I'm hardly walking the streets, simply *walking*. And ladies require time alone too, you know."

"If she's a lady, then I'm a pig's uncle," the angry man said with a laugh.

"We already knew your genealogy," she retorted. "And I'm a lady by marriage, not by birth, as you've been so kind to point out. But this conversation is wasting my time. I have somewhere to be."

Maybe the snooty tone was overdoing it, because the angry pig's uncle just about blew his top and insisted that she be arrested.

And the watchman listened. "You're going to need to come with me, ma'am."

Ash considered running off, but thought better of it. "If you must. But I require a message to be sent to my husband immediately."

"We'll get to that ma'am, at the station. Come on now."

And so she went, secretly regretting not bringing her maid after all. But one good thing came out of it – she stepped on the riding crop and 'accidentally' broke it.

Ha.

The Honourable Mister George Seymour finished his cigar with relish. He deeply appreciated Whyte's smoking policy, (as in 'feel free to smoke anywhere') because it was most useful when one had been forbidden to do so by one's new bride. He could just say that the smell on his clothes came from *other* men's cigars.

Yes, George knew thanks to his outspoken, *extremely* modern wife that smoking caused cancer, but once in a while? Not to worry. Besides, what Ashlea didn't know wouldn't hurt her, and he wouldn't touch a cigar once they returned to her time.

He found himself frowning at that thought. Not because of the cigar; because of the time-travel. The problem with all this back-and-forth was that instead of fitting in both times, he was beginning to feel like he fit in neither. By Jove, they should choose a time and stick with it, for the sake of their sanity and any children they might have.

And it should be here, naturally. Here, George might have made his mistakes, and society wasn't perfect, but at least they respected marriage! They respected *him*, as the brother of a viscount, and he had good social standing and steady income-...*somewhat* steady income, which should increase if his new, carefully made investments panned out well. Fingers crossed.

But in Ashlea's time they always had to work, work, work, and there weren't any servants. She might claim that appliances made servants unnecessary, but he said it was always nice to have someone who never complained about bringing you a cup of tea because they were paid to do it, even if they didn't have the benefit of an electric jug and teabags.

Stubbing out the cigar in a conveniently placed ashtray, George headed for the door. The footman handed him his coat and hat, and he stepped out onto the street with a sigh of content-ment, then spent the half hour walk home planning how to convince Ashlea to stay in 1818.

"What do you mean, she's not here?" George repeated in surprise. "She specifically told me she was staying home for the afternoon."

The butler, Prowd, bowed apologetically. It looked wrong on the man – Prowd by name, proud by nature. "I'm sorry, sir, but she left almost an hour ago."

George pushed back his irritation. "Not to worry," he said casually. "She must have changed her mind, and I think I know where she is."

At least, where he *hoped* she was. Less than ten minutes later, George was back at Tolliver's bookseller. But when he asked the merchant about Ashlea, the man had no idea what he was talking about.

"You should keep better control of your wife, sir," he said.

"Indeed," George bit off acerbically. "What would you suggest, a leash?"

"If that is what it takes."

Then George told the man precisely what he thought of him – and that was how he was banned from Tolliver's.

Outside, the feeling of wellbeing had entirely dissipated. He'd known Ashlea had been unhappy earlier today, but it wasn't like her to say one thing then do another. And really, where could she have gone?

He quietly stepped into a nearby alley and pulled out his second-favourite possession from the twenty-first century. It looked like a plain metal snuff box, but jammed inside was an old mobile phone that Ashlea had given him. He kept it for emergencies, and the only number it held was hers.

He pressed his thumb against the old, stiff lid in that particular way that made it pop open, then tapped the couple of buttons to call her. They'd discovered that the phones would work a considerable distance from the gateways, as though the cell reception went far further than expected. Never as far as this, though; and if she'd gone tried to return to her own time...

But after a minute of ringing, Ashlea still hadn't answered. George considered that she might not have heard it, or might be too far from a gateway to have reception, or might be in a place where talking to oneself would be socially unacceptable…i.e. in the company of almost anyone.

Cursing under his breath, he put the phone back in his pocket and kicked desolately at a pebble. No doubt she'd come back in her own time, but would he ever have something to say to her.

But he was no longer alone.

George looked up to see a couple of roughly dressed men blocking the end of the alley. One lifted his jacket aside just enough to show the long blade hidden there, then nodded at George. "Alright, guv'ner. Hand us yer goods and we'll let ye go."

"Oh, dear," George moaned pathetically. "Don't hurt me. Let me just get out my valuables…"

As the men waited impatiently, he slipped his hand into his pocket, feeling the familiar (but little-used) shape of his *most* favourite possession from the twenty-first century. He pulled out the taser, aimed, and fired.

Bullseye. The man with the knife fell to the ground, convulsing impressively, and his friend fled with a shriek.

George waited until the fallen man looked incapable of movement, then released the trigger, unhooked the electrodes from the man's dirty shirt, and carefully put the whole thing back in his pocket.

Ashlea had insisted that he carry some form of defence with him at all times, and while she'd likely meant something more era-appropriate, he just loved the feeling of the taser. It handled like a gun, but was far less lethal. Marvellous. He didn't think Ashlea knew he still had it, or that he quietly recharged it every time they returned to the twenty-first.

Glancing down at his assailant one more time, George wondered briefly what brought a man to be robbing strangers on the street. He was rather thin, and he couldn't just be evil to the core… No more than George, anyway: because he'd really enjoyed using that taser far too much.

Back out on the street George was approached by one of the interchangeable street urchins that you'd find everywhere in Lunden. The child had to be ten or so – it was hard to tell since lack of food made them small – and had the world-weary look of one who'd seen a lot, and stolen most of it. "You lookin' for someone, sir?"

"Why, yes I am," George replied. "Have you seen a tall, dark-haired lady with a slight accent? She might have been wearing a brown cloak."

He thought he saw a flash of guilt in the child's face, but then it was gone. "I might 'ave. There's lots of ladies wot 'ave brown 'air."

"Dark hair," George corrected with a sigh. He pulled out the miniature portrait of Ashlea that he carried around with him. It was actually a photograph, edited to look like a little painting. "She looks like this, only bigger."

The child didn't get the joke. "I might 'ave seen 'er. What's it werf to me?"

George fished out the appropriate coinage, but held it out of reach. "Tell me first."

"Coin first."

What could be so bad that the boy wanted to be paid upfront? They settled on half, and then the child said, "The watchman took 'er."

"I beg your pardon?"

"If that was yer lady, then I'm tellin' ye, the watchman took 'er straight to gaol, 'cos she got on the wrong side of the toff what was hittin' my sister before."

Ashlea. In gaol. George froze as a series of horrific possibilities ran through his head. "How do I know you aren't lying?"

"Arsk someone else, then. They'll all say the same. Was quite a buzz."

George sighed and scrubbed his hand over his face. "When?"

"Not 'arf an hour ago."

Oh, *no*.

Three
BORDER PATROL

The Mountain of Glass, time irrelevant

Anne stepped through the final gateway back into the lush, fragrant garden, her heart light with satisfaction. She'd found magnificent hiding places for the flasks. 'Twould be impossible that anyone found them for many, many years.

She headed towards the Mountain's peak once more, intending to find her sister, but in the manner of these things they found her first.

"Anne, you have returned," Elspeth called. She sat off the side of the path with Jon, under a weeping willow next to one of the many streams that ran through the garden. "Come, tell us of your journey. Where did you go?"

Anne settled herself on the grass beside them, fluffing out her wide skirts to sit comfortably. Her plain brown gown had reverted to the more usual dark green upon entering the Mountain, her colour of choice as it contrasted prettily with her red hair. "Where didn't I go, is more the question."

She told them about inadvertently retrieving the flask from the fowl merchant, and about being mistaken for a tavern wench. Elspeth and Jon both laughed, thankfully, for Anne also thought it rather amusing. But then when she had to hide the flasks…

"In a boot full of rocks, down at the fork of a mighty river," she announced proudly. "I know not where, but 'twas as hot as a midsummer's day. Mayhap South Amyrica or Afreca? And then the *other* flask I also hid inside a boot full of rocks, but in an underground cave. I'd vow that not a single soul has visited that place, except that the gateway led there."

Z'wounds, it had been so dark and isolated she'd begun to fret that she wouldn't find the return gateway. She hadn't dared to take more than two steps from *that* particular gate, and there'd been the dreadful but faint sound of slithering in the dark…

"Whose boots?" Elspeth asked. Anne tucked her bare feet under her, blushing a little, and her sister shrugged. "Well, I vow that the flasks won't be found in an age, and neither will your boots. Well done."

Jon looked rather less impressed. "But we don't know what the flasks *do*, do we? If they're objects of power then they'll be found sooner or later, no matter how well hidden they are. What's that saying – that everything done in the dark will be brought out into the light?"

"Not these ones," Anne challenged, but her bubble of happiness had deflated somewhat. The boy was most irritating, and lately he'd been dreadfully glum about something. But he wouldn't say what bothered him so, or even where he was from. The mystery made Anne itch with curiosity.

"Never fear," Elspeth assured her. "I'd vow you completed the mission most satisfactorily, as you will with all those you are set. 'Tis a most noble cause, that of becoming one of the People."

Anne cheered a little upon hearing those words. Indeed, Amaranthus *had* promised her that she might become one of his own immortal People and live forever in this blessed place.

He'd said 'twould be a most difficult change, and would require much compromise on her part, but so far it hadn't been so dreadful, had it?

Except for the foul-tempered fowl merchant, and being chased by men with swords (the latter possibly caused by her own actions) and losing her boots, again.

She thought longingly of her own dearly missed sparkly purple slippers, abandoned in the twenty-first century, and how she'd not yet had a chance to return for them. She hadn't seen Ash or George since their brief visit a few weeks earlier, and regrettably hadn't any chance to ask for the slippers to be delivered to the Mountain either. Anne knew that Ash wouldn't fit the things (as the girl had colossal feet to fit her colossal form), but she surely wouldn't have disposed of them in such short time?

Anne said as much to the other two.

Jon scoffed, getting to his feet. "Time-travels differently outside of the Mountain, Anne. Who knows how long it's been for them?" Then he turned on his heel and left.

Anne stared after his receding form in amazement. "What has him so foul-tempered, I wonder?"

"'Tis his fear for his friends," Elspeth confided. "I hear they are all in most dreadful danger. Jon was snatched away from it by Amaranthus, but he fears they will be lost while he's gone."

"Friends back home?" Anne asked, trying to keep her tone light. "And where might that be?"

"Friends in Frencia," Elspeth corrected. "He stayed there for some time, I understand, but 'tis not his true home."

"And his true home is…?"

The younger girl shrugged, getting to her feet. "I know not. Oh, and by the way – Amaranthus requested your presence anon. He's in the tapestry room."

Anne watched her sister follow after the moody boy, and felt her own mood drift upwards again. When was Amaranthus *not* in the tapestry room?

Lunden, 1818 AD

The carriage ride home from the gaol was quiet and tense. George had tossed around his brother's title shamelessly, but it had taken a substantial bribe to get the charges against Ashlea dropped.

He was morally opposed to bribes, and financially opposed to paying for anything he didn't consider good value…which meant that his wife's freedom was probably worth the price. Probably.

As for the girl in question, she sat stiffly in the carriage, her face still flushed pink and her eyes wide. She kept watching him with a hopeful expression on her face, as if waiting for him to burst out laughing and it would all be alright.

He wasn't laughing.

"So," Ashlea said into the heavy silence. "That was clever, how you told them I was raised by missionaries in darkest Afreca, and that was why I didn't know how to behave appropriately. They seemed to accept it. That, or the money you threw at them."

He didn't speak.

"George?" she prompted several seconds later. "Are you OK?"

He just looked at her. "Ashlea. I just retrieved you from gaol. GAOL. How am I possibly meant to be 'OK', as you put it?"

She lifted her chin. "It's not the first time we've ended up locked up, or in trouble with the law. Think of future Iversley, or the Other, or the Reman soldier near those crosses…"

"That wasn't our life," George cut in, suddenly weary. "That was…a diversion. But this is *my* time, Ashlea. *My* life! Ours now. And if anyone knows what happened here today, even our grandchildren will suffer the damage to their reputations as a result."

Ashlea's face fell. "But there was a child," she said in a small voice. "The man was hitting them with a riding crop. I *had* to do something!" She looked up at him beseechingly. "Wouldn't *you* have done something?"

Oh, Hades. What to say to that?

"I likely would have intervened," he replied finally. "But I'm a gentleman, Ashlea. And you…you're a woman, and one without even the benefit of a maid. You know the expectations here. Why did you go out alone today?" *And after you'd said you would stay at home?*

She sat in mutinous silence for some time. Then she said, "I thought I saw a remnant gateway outside that sexist bookstore. I wanted to check if it was real or just my imagination."

George jolted in surprise. "A new remnant gateway? By Jove, what a thing! I wonder where it leads?"

"Me too! That's why I was looking. And *you* were out," she said a little accusingly.

He could have said, *but* you *said you would stay at home*, but didn't want to get into that argument. "Well then. We should take a look, should we not? That would be quite an adventure."

Ashlea seemed to perk up at that. "Yes, let's! How about now?"

"Er…don't you need to…recover?"

"What do you mean?"

"From the harshness of gaol," George explained. "It would be a new, and no doubt most unpleasant experience."

"Oh." Ashlea looked bemused, then shrugged a shoulder. "Well, I suppose the one back home *was* much nicer. Smelled a bit better, too."

George's jaw dropped. "You've been in gaol before?!"

She shrugged again. "Just for trespassing when I was in high school, before they realised I was under eighteen. It's no big deal."

"You've been in gaol before, and you didn't tell me?" He was stunned, appalled even. By Jove, he had married a criminal!

"Like I said, it's no big deal. I was under eighteen at the time, so it's not even on my record. It was a youthful prank. Forget about it."

He'd sooner forget his own name! "How can I forget about it?! It's not a small thing, Ashlea! Not here. And you'd better hope no one finds out about that, or about today."

"I guessed that from your reaction," she said sarcastically.

"Aren't you even a little sorry? You married me and didn't say a word?" He couldn't say why it was bothering him so much, but it did. He didn't know her half as well as he'd imagined he did.

"There are a lot of things you haven't told me," Ashlea snapped back, "and that I don't want to know. So let it go, alright?"

"*Let it go*," he repeated in a falsetto. "What else is there that you haven't told me? Robbery? Prostitution?"

"Don't you talk to me about that sort of thing!" she burst out. "I *know* what you men are like here, and you have no moral high ground, none!"

"That's because you're always comparing me to the supposedly perfect men of your time who treat all women like mistresses?! Well, I'm not one of them, and I don't want to be!" he exploded.

She went silent. Then she said in a small voice. "They're not perfect. I thought perhaps you were actually better, but I see I was wrong. And you know what? I don't want to be a woman of your time, either."

Unspoken as they walked up the stairs to their townhouse were the painful words, *I don't want to be* your *woman, either*, but

George heard them nonetheless. He took off his coat and hat and handed them to the waiting footman, then moved to the quiet lower hall, servants scattering as they approached.

"How unfortunate," he said roughly, careful to keep his voice low. "You have to be, at least half the time. You vowed you would when you married me. And just this morning you promised you'd try to conform to this culture, at least while you're here."

"How am I supposed to do that?" Ashlea asked quietly.

It seemed a reasonable question. "By doing what ladies of my class do, of course."

"You mean nothing. They don't do anything, George. You need a shake up, all of you do. You need the women and the men of your class to actually *do* something differently."

"Like beating a gentleman with his own riding crop?" he asked in frustration.

"I told you, I didn't beat him! I just waved it at him a little. He lied!"

"You shouldn't have intervened at all!" The argument was going around in circles, but George couldn't seem to stop himself.

"Well, I'm sorry, but I couldn't stand by and watch such a terrible thing!"

George threw his hands in the air in frustration. "Then don't go out! You cannot change the world, and this sort of thing happens all the time, terrible or not! You need to accept that this is normal, and stay *away* from places where it happens!" On a roll now, he continued, "In fact, while you are here in my time, you should stay at the house. There's plenty to do here, and if you must go out, make it with my mother or Olivia."

Ashlea went quiet, dangerously so. "What is there to do here?"

"Well I don't know. Embroidery. That's what ladies do, isn't it?"

Her eyes bugged out. "Embroidery? You know I don't know how to sew!"

"Then now's the time to learn," George said triumphantly. "You're always saying you can do anything you put your mind to."

Ashlea's face went red. "George! I am a functional, intelligent person, and I am not going to waste my time with something as useless as embroidery or flower arranging, or charity works which are more about making me feel superior than actually helping anyone, or instructing servants to do things I could just as easily do myself. I need a real purpose! I need to make a difference!"

"You need a job," he countered flatly. "Because it appears you are unable to entertain yourself. However, you cannot get a job here. Not without humiliating our entire family."

Too late he realised that he'd practically told her to go home and get a job – which wasn't at all what he'd meant.

But she shook her head. "It's not about a job, George. It's about feeling needed. Like before we went to the Mountain of Glass. We helped people. I felt *useful*. Amaranthus thought I was useful."

He almost laughed at the reminder of the man who'd basically set them up, except he was too frustrated to laugh. "Amaranthus could have used anyone, Ashlea. And don't you remember that the last time you were 'useful' as you called it, you hated the whole thing. It was scary and tiring, you'd said. You *wanted* this life! Just…just forget this nonsense of being 'needed' and having a 'purpose'. *I* need you, as a wife and mother. Well, as a mother eventually, I suppose, but that's a very good purpose to have, and you shouldn't belittle it."

"George."

He continued, "And while I'm sure that embroidery is a very worthwhile occupation, if you don't like it, Mother can find you something else to do-"

"I can't believe this."

"What?" George stopped in his tracks. "What's the matter?"

Ashlea shook her head, her whole body slumped in a posture of defeat. "I'm going home."

"No, you're not," George said flatly, looking shocked that she would even suggest it.

"Yes, I *am*," Ash insisted. She was so angry that she could hardly get the words out to explain herself. If she'd been a cartoon character, there would've been steam coming from her ears.

"Ashlea, you agreed to stay at least a month this time, to fit into the culture. I stay in your time for you, and if you leave now, people will ask questions."

"Oh, for goodness sake." Ash wasn't leaving him; she just wanted some time to herself. She felt so confused and upset, and George wasn't helping *at all*. She tried to step around him to get to the exit, but he blocked her.

Looking a little panicked, he commanded, "Don't go near that library, Ashlea. I mean it."

"Oh, for goodness sake," Ash muttered again. She wasn't actually going to ride all the way from Lunden to Leister County, to the library in George's family manor, just to have an hour to herself in her own kitchen in the twenty-first century. She just wanted to get *out*.

Just then Edward, George's older brother and Viscount Morley, wandered in. "Why mustn't she go near the library?"

Knowing he thought George had meant the townhouse's library, Ash replied snarkily, "Because George doesn't want me reading and broadening my mind. He wants to keep me ignorant and decorative."

"Oh, don't be ridiculous," George exploded. "No one would call you ignorant and decorative!"

At least he wouldn't call her ignorant. But… "Are you saying I'm not attractive enough to be decorative?"

"You're intentionally misinterpreting my words!" he argued. "This isn't about books *or* looks!"

Ash laughed, but without humour. No, it was about how he'd just told her to forget being important for anything except bedding and breeding, and to ask his family (who hated her) for help entertaining herself…? "I'm going to my room, and I don't want to see you there." She stormed off, and this time the men didn't try to stop her.

And the worst part was, after all of that fuss, she hadn't even gotten to check that remnant gateway.

The Mountain of Glass, time irrelevant

Anne wandered along one of the myriad halls in the city of glass, humming pleasantly to herself. She'd spoken with Amaranthus-…about nothing much, in truth, but it had left her feeling rather good about the world.

"Ooh!" She stumbled over something, landing hard on her hands and knees. It didn't hurt, but it startled her.

"Watch out," Jon said grumpily, for 'twas him she'd stumbled over. He was sitting on the ground in a little alcove off the hall, his long legs extending just enough to trip unwary passers-by.

Anne was annoyed enough to smack him hard on the leg. "Who's the one sitting in the hall like a numpty?"

Rather out of character, Jon let out a sigh. "You're right. I'm sorry I tripped you."

She stared at him, stunned. "Oh, my. You truly are out of sorts, for you have never before apologised for anything."

"I apologise."

"Not to me."

He shrugged, waving a hand in defeat.

Anne could have left then, but her insatiable curiosity came to the fore – and mayhap just a little compassion. "You fear so much for your friends, then? What is their danger?"

Jon paused. "Have you heard of the Frencine Great Terror?"

It sounded somewhat familiar. "Something to do with rats?"

"No! What's so terrifying about rats?"

He'd not seen the same ones that Anne had, clearly. "Plague?"

"Not rats, not plague," Jon retorted, but there was no bite in his voice. "Revolution."

"Ah, yes," Anne said with a nod. "Angland shall have one of those, although after my lifetime. I believe we shall execute our king, briefly attempt a republic, and then reinstate the monarchy. Is that what is happening in Frencia?"

Jon's jaw dropped. "You know your own country's future?"

"There were history books in Ash's time," she said defensively. "Was I not to read them? Besides, I did not learn anything about my own future."

"Revolution," he said slowly, "is somewhat different when one is living it. They're killing all the Frencine upper class, Anne. Locking them up in their castles, and then chopping off their heads one by one. *That's* what Amaranthus pulled me out of, and that's why I'm worried about my friends."

"Oh." Anne was silent for a long while, the image of chopped-off heads running through her own upper class head rather unpleasantly. *Chopping off their heads one by one.* Well, it could hardly be done in synchronised fashion, could it? "Why did Amaranthus not take all of them away?" she asked finally. "Why only you?"

Jon shrugged again, and this time she saw the weariness and defeat in it. "Because he took me from my own time in the first place, I suppose. We mustn't think that time-travel is the usual solution to problems, because it isn't. You, me, Bets – we're exceptions, not the rule. And who knows how much time has passed outside the Mountain? They might all be dead now."

"Or they might not," Anne retorted. "Have you ever gone back to see?"

"Of course not. I only arrived here a few weeks ago, barely before you did. And I haven't been given permission to gallivant around the gateways as you have."

She hadn't known his time here had been so brief – he'd greeted her and Elspeth when they'd first arrived. "But were you instructed *not* to use them?" she challenged.

Jon was silent. "No…but I wouldn't know which one to use. I don't see them like you seem to, Anne, maybe because I never used the Eternity Stone like you did. How would we find it? Where would we *take* them?"

She pondered the question. 'Twas true that upon first arrival she had noticed only a few of the remnant gateways. They sat like shimmering patches of heat in the air, only seen once very close.

But the longer she stayed here in the Mountain, the more clearly she saw the gateways. Not only the ones left behind by the Eternity Stone, but the ones left behind every time Amaranthus and his People moved through time…

So, so many. Thousands, mayhap, and now Anne would see them standing like faint doorframes in the middle of a garden, hall, tree…

"Verily, there are gateways everywhere," she said finally. "And if you recall where you first arrived here, we ought to be able to find the right gateway. I can test it first, see if 'tis the right one."

"How would you know if it was?" Jon challenged. "You wouldn't know my Frencia from Iron-age Briton."

Anne intelligently refrained from asking what an Iron age was, but he did have a point. "Then we shall go together, and we shall find a way to take your friends to safety."

"But Amaranthus-"

She rolled her eyes. "He *lives* for such deeds, Jon. He'd never say aught. We shall start with finding the point in which you entered. You do recall it, do you not?"

"Of course I do." And now Jon had regained a little of his customary Frencine snootiness – but then he wasn't Frencine, was he?

"Well, come along, then. We shall save your noble froggy friends, never doubt that!"

"Froggy?!"

"I heard George say it once," Anne explained as they got up and walked along. "It refers to the Frencine diet of frogs, I believe."

"*I* never ate frogs!" Jon said indignantly. "Although there were some extremely small chicken legs…" He faltered into silence, turning a little green as he realised what that meant.

Anne patted him on the arm comfortingly. "As I said. We shall save your froggy friends, never you mind."

And so they headed towards what appeared to be the peak

of the inner Mountain, new excitement growing inside of Anne with every step. She was *finally* going to see where Jon had come from.

Wouldn't Elspeth be jealous?

The Borderlands, Lile, 2597 AD

Kamile followed along the edge of the Borderlands in her two-seater vehicle, jolting every few seconds as she hit a pothole deep enough to be felt through the vehicle's hover function.

The roads were poor, scattered generously with such potholes disguised by leaf litter from the surrounding trees. But even with the full foot of air space that the hover function gave her, she could see it wouldn't be long before she'd have to stop the vehicle and walk.

She wondered who built the road in the first place. If Elder Starbright was right, then it was simply the remains of the old road that was here before the Borderlands had extended well past Compound territory. No one had used it for many, many years, she'd said, but Kamile could see she'd been wrong about that.

The road had been rediscovered. She could see the distinctive trails of other vehicles, including the double tracks that the old-fashioned bicycles left. By the Fey, who would *cycle* all the way out here? Couldn't they sense the danger of the place?

"Clearly not, because otherwise they wouldn't *be* here," Kamile muttered aloud, the words whisked away in the wind left behind by her vehicle's movement. "Probably someone with thighs of iron and no sense of self-preservation."

She turned the corner, and just ahead saw the two cyclists

parked at the side of the narrow road, their double-cycle upright next to them. One was glaring at a holo-map in a way that suggested they hadn't expected it to lead them here, and the other stood sipping at a water bottle and studying the surrounding trees with wide eyes. Perhaps not so clueless after all.

She sighed with relief. If they were here, then there was still a chance for them. She pulled her vehicle to a halt, ignoring the shriek of the air-brakes on the loose leaf litter, and leaned across towards the cyclists with a smile. "Hello there," she called. "Were you aware that this is private land?"

The cyclist with the map set it down, grimacing. "Just followed the map, love, and it took us here. We're trying to get to Silver Falls. Is it close?"

"Not really." As they groaned in disappointment, she added, "If you go back for about ten kilometres, you'll find a junction in the road. Take that, and you'll end up back on the main path."

"Ten kilometres," the other cyclist muttered. "That's a fleecin' long way. Are you sure there's no more direct route? Besides, there was no sign marking this as private property."

Kamile kept her smile. It was imperative that these two believed her, because if they kept going they'd find themselves in the Other without a clue – and would probably never make it out again. "The maps are supposed to warn people off. We still get the occasional lost hiker, though. And no, there's no more direct route. This road stops not too far from here."

It seemed like they accepted that, because the first cyclist let out a sigh, then smiled back. In late middle age, the man probably had a wife and two kids back in the city, and this was his way of 'getting back to nature'. "Alright love, we'll be off. Thanks for the advice."

"No problem." Kamile waved as she drove on, but she still checked the rear sensors for some distance to make sure they hadn't followed.

Unfortunately with places like this, people simply didn't know what they were getting themselves into. Even she couldn't see where the Other began and the normal stopped; she was going by sense alone. Oh, and that her appearance changed once she was truly in the Other. But she could *feel* where the Fey were, she had always been able to, and so she would stay away from them.

The rutted road grew narrower and more overgrown until it was impassable, and Kamile drew the vehicle to a halt, climbing out with some reluctance. The vehicle was open-sided and small, but she'd still felt safer in there. Now there was nothing between her and whatever was out here.

Why, oh *why* did it have to be the nastiest Fey who lived on the borders?

As if proving her point, a mere few metres ahead she could see a set of footprints: heavy, so likely male, and stopping abruptly at the edge of a large, soft area of grassy moss. Likely he'd seen something in the trees, a beautiful face perhaps, and had gone in to investigate and never come out again. Or maybe he'd been taken by something that wanted a bit of fun and games, but chances were if they ever sent him back, he would have lost months of his life…or his sanity.

The Fey didn't mean to be cruel, Kamile often thought, but they were anyway. They couldn't help themselves, the way a small child trying to play with a butterfly couldn't help but cause injury.

But maybe that was giving them too much grace – after all, the Wood Fey in particular were known for being beautiful, wild, and unpredictably violent. Trennan's mother had strayed into the Borderlands and had come out again pregnant, unable to say what had happened. Trennan didn't seem any worse off, except for his odd skin, of course.

Not that Kamile could talk about odd skin…

By now the road was completely gone, and the fallen trees seemed arranged in piles, the logs covered in green moss, and their broken ends pointing the way further in. She had never walked this far before, and had no idea where it led.

But within ten minutes she started to see others up ahead. Both male and female, at least half a dozen of them and mostly young, walking along the border to wherever the not-road led. More hikers, no doubt; and perhaps even with the same group.

Bad, *bad* choice of destination.

"Hey!" Kamile shouted, trying to catch their attention. "You shouldn't be here; this is private property!"

No one seemed to hear her, so she picked up her pace, wishing her legs were longer. "Hey! Stop walking right now!"

She may as well have been shouting at a rock. They just kept walking further, further in, as if they were drawn mindlessly by whatever lay there. It was the power of the Other. There was a certain sort of person who was susceptible to its pull, and they were usually the ones who ended up fascinated by mysticism or spirituality or magic or the occult – alter-power in all its forms.

So Kamile followed along, burning with frustration and anxiety as she studied her surroundings for where the Border-lands ended and the Other began. This whole place was unfamiliar. It *was* new land, and no doubt mere weeks ago it would have been perfectly safe. Now? Not so much. She could *feel* the danger, not see it.

Then the land beside the muddy dirt path was replaced by green, murky water. It was so still and perfect an insect could have walked on its surface, but that just made her even more nervous. If she fell in, whether she could swim or not would be irrelevant.

Up ahead she could see that the land ended entirely. But out on the water the logs continued, floating on its surface in a rolling bridge that disappeared into the mist. As she watched, a young man – a boy, really – stepped out onto the first set of logs, swaying dramatically as the log rolled and he barely caught himself.

Then Kamile saw the first tendrils of black cloud curling around a nearby tree. She cursed, then called out to the boy. "Hey kid, stop! Don't go there! It's not safe!"

But just like in a bad dream, he carried on forward as if he couldn't hear her, and several others began to follow him.

"Ah, *no*. No!" Kamile ran to the edge of the water, reaching out as if to grab them and pull them back to solid ground, but of course it was no good. They were out of her reach, both literally and metaphorically. And she certainly wasn't going to follow. Halfling she might be, but that just made her more of a target for some of the Fey. *No one* liked half-breeds.

"STOP!" she shouted again desperately, knowing her efforts were probably pointless. When the pull of the Other had you, you were deaf and blind to all else. "Don't go any further! It's very, very dangerous here! You go onto that water, you won't come back out!"

But then somehow, miraculously, one of them paused where they balanced on a log, turning back to look at Kamile apprehensively. It was a girl; probably in her mid-teens and with a head of ginger-brown hair. She tapped her shorter brunette friend on the shoulder, and the second girl paused too.

Encouraged, Kamile called out again urgently, "Come back off the logs! There are things in there, things that'll catch you and maybe even kill you! If you can hear me, turn around!"

The first few didn't turn. She knew they wouldn't, because she knew the hold the Other could have over some people.

But the two girls *did* listen. The redhead took the other's arm and began pulling her back towards the land, step by careful step, even as the greenery around them faded and was replaced by clinging black fog.

Kamile waited until their feet touched ground, then turned and began to briskly walk in the direction of her vehicle. "Hurry up," she tossed over her shoulder. "The sooner we're out of here, the better."

"But what about the others?" the brunette asked timidly.

A pang of sorrow twisted in Kamile's belly. "Who knows. They might come out again, they might not. It's not our problem." There was silence at that, and when Kamile glanced back over her shoulder, she saw they'd both stopped in the middle of the path, white-faced. "You got a death wish? Come *on!*"

"How can you just leave them?" the redhead choked out.

Kamile stopped, just for a moment, gesturing down at herself. She knew what they'd see – a small, slim brunette plainly dressed in the brown tunic and loose, calf-length trousers typical of rural communities. "Do I look like I could throw them over my shoulder and carry them back out here? Force them to stay when they'd want to turn back?"

"Um," the brunette replied. "No."

"Good, because I can't. And even if I *was* strong enough to get them, it's too late now." That wasn't the only reason Kamile wouldn't bring them back. The Chosen stance (as dictated by the Fey) was that if anyone felt drawn to the Other, they'd be granted entrance. It wasn't her place to stop anyone from going in, never mind how she felt about it. "It's not safe for me, or for you, and I'm certainly not going to stand around talking about it."

She began walking again as fast as her legs would take her. There was definitely a path underfoot now, but the surrounding trees still hung with dark fog. The black-clouded forest had crept up the way it always seemed to, and it would take far longer to get out than it had to get in.

Kamile heard footsteps behind her, and a moment later the

girls drew alongside. Even though she'd just been talking to them, had watched them follow, she experienced a moment of panic and wondering if some clever Fey was playing a trick.

But her internal alter-power sensors didn't go off, and she knew they were just two girls: kids, really, and younger than she'd first thought. The redhead's baby-face implied that in spite of her height she might not be more than thirteen or fourteen – *far* too young to be out here alone.

"I'm Poli," the redhead said, a little breathless from their walking speed. "And this is Magdalene, or Mags."

"Kamile."

"Kamile," Poli echoed. "So why do you think it's unsafe?"

"I've been here before," Kamile replied shortly. "Why did you follow me?"

"Because..." Poli paused. "Because we saw shadows in the water, and faces in the trees. And because I've never felt so unsettled in my life."

Next to her, Magdalene shuddered dramatically and wrapped her arms around herself as she walked. "*I* didn't see the faces, but I saw the shadows. I believe Poli, and we believed you too. What *were* those things? And why didn't the others listen?"

Smart girls. "Long story," Kamile replied without missing a step, "and the answer is going to depend on you. Are you good citizens of the Secular Republic?"

There was a long silence, and finally Poli answered, "I don't know. Does a good citizen of the Secular Republic see how your skin changed before?"

"Yeah, it was *green*," Magdalene added. "Like a leaf. Weird. Was it a hologram?"

Oh, Fire Lord. A hologram? Kamile tossed up her options – giving the girls the full truth, or lying and protecting herself from the possible wrath of the Sec government if anyone ever found out

– then decided to take a risk. "Let's get to my vehicle, then I'll tell you about it."

"Alright," Poli agreed finally. "But if it's got something to do with the Other realm or the River of Life, you don't need to hide it from us."

Oh, Fire Lord! "Fine. I'll tell you what I know. But if you tell anyone..."

"We won't," the girls agreed in unison.

Kamile couldn't predict what the girls would or wouldn't do, but by the time they were finally free of the black-clouded forest, they'd told her about the journey they'd taken from the city to reach this place, and the hiking group they'd met up with just this morning.

Good thing they weren't too attached to those others, Kamile thought, or they'd be pretty upset by now.

They **were** both thirteen.

On the other hand, she'd told them what she was, what they'd almost walked into, and the risks involved. "The Fey aren't all like that," she finished. "Some go out of their way to share knowledge and power. But you should *never, ever* go wandering into unknown places like that without an invitation, because you never know who you'll run into."

They turned a corner on the road/path, clambering over fallen trees and lush greenery, and finally Kamile could see her two-seater just ahead. *Finally.* She felt like she'd walked for miles.

"But you could," Magdalene offered. "Because you're one of them, and they wouldn't hurt you. You could take us in."

"A Halfling is not a Fey," Kamile corrected. "Didn't you just say that I was one of them, even though I just told you I'm at least half human? They feel exactly the same way. And as for going into the Other – why do you want to do it so much? I just told you how dangerous it is." She approached her two-seater, dismayed to see that it was covered in trailing vines. She aggressively pulled them free, checking that there was nothing else wrong with the vehicle.

"Wow," Magdalene exclaimed. "How long have you been here?"

Kamile checked the vehicle's calendar. "According to this, only two days." Although it had felt like only a few hours. "But things can grow fast on the Borderlands of the Other."

"Two days!" Magdalene exclaimed. "It didn't feel anything near that!"

Exactly.

Kamile shrugged. "Time gets weird in the Other. Consider yourselves lucky to still remember your names. But you never answered my question. Why do you want to go in there so badly? You're not drawn towards it like some people are, surely. You just told me that you found it unsettling."

The two girls, so different in appearance, exchanged almost identical wary glances. Then Poli straightened her shoulders. "We're looking for the River of Life."

"What!"

"We know it's in the Other," Magdalene continued her friend's words in a rush, "and we heard that there's an entrance around here. That's why we came all the way out from the city."

"Oh." Kamile focussed on starting the vehicle, her head turned away so they wouldn't see her smile. The River of Life, really? How sweet, and how foolish, and how remarkably dangerous their choice was. "Then I'm sorry you've wasted your time. Now, I can take you back to the nearest town, as long as one of you doesn't mind sitting on the other's lap. But do your parents know about this?"

"We don't have any parents," Poli replied. "We're orphans."

"Oh." Kamile didn't have any parents either. Even with the

Chosen's refusal to use the names 'Mother' and 'Father', she didn't know who hers were. Mother was human, presumably, but Father…likely somewhere across the border, not that she cared. "Well, where can I take you then?"

"To the Empty Zone," Magdalene blurted out.

Kamile stopped halfway through climbing into her seat and stared at the girl. "Why on earth would you want to go there?" The radiation from the Great War centuries before had meant that nothing grew there, and while levels were supposed to be safe now, the city's population had moved well away.

"They say the River might be there, too."

"Do they." Kamile was getting irritated at the girl's persistent stupidity. "I don't know who this 'they' is that you keep speaking about, but they steered you wrong about this place, didn't they? And why are you so all-fired certain that the River even exists? Maybe it did once, but it's gone now. I've seen the Other many, many times, and trust me, once you get past the trees it's dead. Dark, desert, and freezing cold."

"Dark?" Magdalene echoed.

Kamile nodded firmly. "Yes, dark. So this river of yours-"

"I've seen it," Poli cut in determinedly. "I found it by accident when I was six. It's not dark, it's beautiful, and I drank some of the water, and I never forgot it, never. And I'm going to find it again." She put her hand on her friend's arm. "We're going to find it, and we're going to live forever."

This time Kamile couldn't help it; she laughed aloud.

Poli scowled, clearly insulted. "Don't laugh at us just because you haven't seen it!"

"I didn't mean to insult you," Kamile soothed. "I didn't mean to laugh at all, it's just that you were so solemn... But Poli, there are all sorts of rivers out in the world. How do you know it's 'The River', and not just a random river that your memory's made into something magical for you?"

"I went there," Poli repeated. "You don't have to believe me, but I know what I drank. You can muck around with your deserts all you want, but we're going to find it."

Kamile put up her hands appeasingly, deciding it wasn't worth the argument. "If you say you went there, who am I to argue? There's always more to find out in this world, that's what I've learned." She found herself smiling a little wistfully. "If you ever find this River of Life, you let me know, alright? I wouldn't mind living forever myself."

"You'd have to drink from it every day," Poli said, still mutinous.

Kamile shrugged. "I'd do it."

The redhead watched her for a long moment, then nodded. "Fine. When we find it, I'll tell you where it is. But you have to be quiet about it! I don't want to get into trouble for sharing non-Sec stuff, or whatever they call it."

"I believe they call it sedition," Kamile corrected. "And I've got my own reasons to stay silent, as you've seen already."

Magdalene let out a long, dramatic sigh. "Oh, the perils of living in a secular republic."

Kamile laughed, and the others laughed with her. "So, how would you get the information to me?"

Poli smiled. "Do you have access to VR?"

"Not at home, but I can come into the city." The Chosen didn't ban their people from using it, but they didn't have any access on site. But in the city virtual reality was cheap, and it seemed like there was an emporium on every corner.

The taller girl *hmmed* to herself thoughtfully. "No, that's not good enough." Then a wide, rather naughty smile curved her freckled cheeks. "What do you know about hacking?"

In a small ordinary apartment, in a small, ordinary suburb of Lile City, Mortimer the god of death hummed as he prepared for his VR session.

He put on the specially made headset and twiddled a few dials, listening in until he heard the right tone. Then he checked the block-like interceptors, noting its green lights. On.

He checked then double-checked the other device that would tell him if anyone was listening in on *him*, but that too was clear.

Excellent, he thought in satisfaction. Hacking into someone else's VR session really wasn't difficult, as long as one had the right equipment. It almost felt like mind-reading, except without the use of alter-power, unfortunately.

Back in the good old days with Seyen (far too brief, and cut dramatically short) he and the others in her pantheon had so much power that they could just dip into other people's minds, taking what they wanted, planting what they wanted. Here, VR really wasn't so different. Naturally it was more about manipulating technology than using alter-power, but he was happy to do either as long as it achieved his goal.

Godhood, of course. Why settle for ordinary humanity when you could have so much more?

Once upon a time he'd been simple Tomas Grey, born in this area a century or so earlier, and unusually gifted when it came to collecting alter-power. The lack of – what was that word? Ah, *empathy* – helped with that. Others called him a sociopath, but Seyen Johannis had seen what he really was – a visionary. She'd styled herself a queen, and had led him and others out of their own time periods and into a near-immortal life.

And then she'd lost the Eternity Stone which gave her that power, and then he'd lost most of *his* powers except for his ability to burn with his hands, and then he'd been tossed back into his own time which he'd left so long before...and so on and so forth. Boring, *very* annoying, and in the past, he thought. Chaos, except he *did* miss being able to create illusions...

Ah, well. Now he had a fresh start in this slightly unfamiliar world of twenty-sixth-century Lile. It wasn't too far from what he remembered from before he'd begun time-travelling. Some technology was better, some was worse, and some was merely different.

Society was much the same, although the aggressive Secular Republic was a new thing. It would mean that if found out, he would be in *big* trouble... But then so would he be if his 'harvesting' was discovered. This government disapproved of human sacrifice, hence the need to keep his activities quiet.

And nothing was as quiet as a secretive hack into VR, all the better to have those quiet conversations that would lead to success.

Or at least they had in the past.

Click. And then he was watching from the edges of a new VR session.

Perfect.

Four

DESERT OF FIRE AND ICE

"What do I know about hacking?" Kamile repeated. "Like…illegally accessing someone else's virtual reality session? Absolutely nothing."

Except she *did* know that you were basically piggybacking on someone's fantasies, in their mind, and it was as illegal as alter-power or religion. That didn't mean it never happened, though.

Poli smiled again very mischievously, exchanging a knowing glance with Magdalene. "That's alright. We can show you."

"But how can this help us get in contact?" Kamile asked in confusion. "We can't exactly *meet* in VR. It's not possible."

"Actually it is," Magdalene corrected. "It's just not very safe. Multi-player technology might not exist according to the government, but there are other countries that have it, even if it's not very good yet. The government's just too scared that people will use if for…well, sedition. Secret meetings."

Kamile's eyebrows shot right up. "So we could meet in VR?"

"If you don't mind things getting a bit crazy, and that you wouldn't really be able to control it," Poli said. "But it's a perfect place to talk about secret stuff, because the government can't listen in, not like with links. We'll teach you how to do it."

"For our secret spy network, run by teenage girls?"

Poli shrugged a shoulder. "Close enough."

Kamile grinned, both impressed and a little disturbed. She had to admire their confidence, but she hoped that they *didn't* get caught out. Although they were no doubt doing nothing but gossiping, the government wouldn't see it that way.

Well, the current Premier was kind of lenient on that sort of thing – religion or Other related, she meant. Compared to previous Premiers, anyway. Even though it was illegal, his attitude seemed to be that if you did it in the privacy of your own home, he didn't care. But they'd be better not to call it 'spying', just in case.

With the girls safely in the other seat – Magdalene on Poli's lap – Kamile revved the engine. The vehicle rose gently into the air, and then they were off.

That evening Kamile left the orphanage with a frown on her face. It was one of those that took the title just to get government benefits rather than out of any accuracy: there had to be about two dozen children aged from about six to sixteen, all living in a three-bedroom house. The rooms were stacked to the ceiling with bunk beds, a cracked vid-screen filled one wall of the house, and the whole thing screamed of squalor and neglect.

There wasn't even an adult living on site! Apparently one just turned up every morning to make sure the children hadn't killed themselves, as Magdalene aptly put it, which was why they could be gone for two days and have no one notice…or be hacking into strangers' VR sessions, and also have no one notice.

Kamile was tempted to contact these girls more often just to see if they were alright. They didn't seem to know that this kind of life wasn't normal, and that was *her* saying that.

Kamile had grown up in a culture where parenting was done by the community at large (translation: no parents) but at least she'd always had good food and adults around if she needed anything. Not that she had, of course. Past the age of ten or so, Kamile had been entirely independent. But it was the principle of the thing!

She looked over her shoulder once more as she drove away. The orphanage looked very small, and she completely understood why they wanted to find something better. Their fixation on the River made much more sense now: they wanted their lives to be more than just a struggle to get by, unnoticed and unwanted.

Kamile had managed to talk them out of visiting the Empty Zone today. That place was vast, and she had no idea how they thought they would find anything there besides rubble and the occasional squatter. But she'd made them promise that if they wanted to go, they would contact her first.

A part of her was looking forward to it.

The Other

Trennan trudged along through the darkness, his arms wrapped tightly around himself against the cold, and his sword hitting him painfully in the knee with every step.

Meric had told him to go far into the Other, farther than he'd ever been, and so he had. And now it was almost completely dark, the landscape lit only by faint light from behind him, from the Fey cities.

But Fire Lord, it was cold. So freezing that even his Fey horse had refused to go any further and he'd had to leave it behind. So freezing that the earth beneath his feet had become hard as ice, hard as metal, and had formed strange distorted sculptures all over the landscape. And it was black, all black, because there was no light here at all, except for a strange glow in the distance…

"Stupid Fey horse," Trennan muttered, his teeth chattering so it sounded more like 'hooorrrse'. "Stupid *me* for coming out here."

Extra stupid him for not turning around now. But he couldn't, not until he found out what that strange glow was. Fingers crossed he didn't just die first!

"Oof!"

He tripped on an unseen obstacle, falling forward and landing hard on the ground. His gloved hands hit the frozen surface with a crack, and he forced himself back to his knees, grumbling all the way.

But then he saw the glowing crater his hand had left in the ice.

Suddenly excited, Trennan punched at the crater a couple of times with one fist. It cracked further then finally broke through, revealing a narrow ravine just big enough to set his hand in, and glowing faintly orange as if there was light beneath it. The ice hadn't melted, though.

"By the Fire Lord," he murmured, sitting back on his haunches to stare at it curiously. Light beneath the ice? He'd never heard of such a thing! For that matter he hadn't known it got so very dark here in the Other, or so very cold.

You'll see something interesting, the old knights had told him.

Trennan looked up into the distance where that faint orange glow lit the ice. Suddenly he didn't feel so cold anymore.

Full of new energy, he began to run towards the glow. That lasted until he tripped over again. Then he settled into a fast walk, his sheathed sword extended in front of him like a blind man's cane. But he needn't have worried. Within minutes the lights were around him, shining under the ice in bright, round patches. He sidestepped them carefully, not wanting to fall through, and kept going.

Then after *that* the fire pits began. Craters or cracks in the ice, some as wide as his handspan, some as wide as his forearm, and all of them casting flickering orange and red onto the surrounding landscape. And yet the ice didn't melt…

'Interesting', Meric had said. It should have been impossible!

"Let's figure this out," Trennan muttered as he walked along. "Fire under the ice. Alter-power, not real fire, because otherwise it would have melted. No one seems to know about it, or at least they didn't say anything to *me*. This doesn't make sense…"

He stopped abruptly in place as a horrible thought dawned. The Fire Lord. The ancient Fey tyrant who was supposedly destroyed millennia ago in an event that split the normal and the Other apart. Or so the Fey said…

"I could be mistaking this," he mused. "These fire pits might be just leftovers from his rule, right?"

That sounded good, except the Fey had said the Fire Lord's fire was destroyed along with him.

"Then they're illusion," he argued with himself. "Illusion is easy to make in the Other. There's a Fey somewhere nearby playing a trick on me."

But his hardy Fey horse had balked and refused to come any closer, hadn't it? And these pits didn't have the characteristic tingle of illusion that he as a Halfling could sense. They seemed real.

Trennan moved forward more cautiously, noting that the fire pits were closer together and larger here. Where before they had only been about a foot wide, or cracks in the ice, now they were big enough to fall into if he wasn't careful. He gave them a wide berth.

Then through the darkness he heard fragments of conversation. "Youuu missseeedd ittt…"

What?!

Trennan took a few more steps and saw others in the distance, silhouetted against the flickering light from the fire pits. They looked like men, and they were…playing football?

He just stopped and stared, but the tiny illuminated figures kept moving, calling to each other, and sending a tiny spot which *had* to be a ball sailing between them.

It was so surreal that he had to pinch himself before he realised that yes, they were really there, and yes, they were really kicking a ball around. In the Other. Amongst fire pits, possibly caused by the most evil being that had ever existed.

Closer, he saw that they'd made a camp and a fire of their own, although next to the pits it looked feeble and pale. Closer still, one of them turned so the light shone off his face, and Trennan recognised him immediately, then recognised all of them. The three knights who'd sent him here in the first place were *playing* on the Fire Lord's doorstep. How had they beaten him here?

Strike that. How had they known about all of this, and yet said nothing? How had they sent *him* here, as if he'd see something 'interesting'? He watched their foolish, grinning faces as the most tremendous sense of betrayal came over him. Then finally one of them noticed him.

"Trennan!" Meric called. "You made it!"

"Yes, I made it," he gritted out. It was an effort not to draw his sword. "You'd better have a bloody good explanation for all of this. How did you get here so fast? Do the elders know about this place?"

The knights exchanged glances, and as one they moved towards him.

Trennan stepped back, setting his hand on his sword, and Meric rolled his eyes. "We're not going to hurt you, boy! Put that thing away."

"Then what!? This *is* the Fire Lord's land, isn't it? A desert of fire and ice?"

The men exchanged another glance, then Evers shrugged. "Maybe. We don't know. That's why we wanted you to come here."

"We took a shortcut," Meric added. "We wanted a second opinion."

"What? From *me*?" Trennan asked in disbelief.

"You're a Halfling," Evers explained. "You can see through illusion in a way that others can't, and you won't side with the elders just out of loyalty or fear. You ask questions, and you like things to make sense, right?"

Trennan stepped forward cautiously, his fury subsiding. "Of course I like things to make sense; everyone does. What kind of second opinion do you want?"

"Illusion," Meric said flatly. "Take a look in those pits, and tell us if what you see down there is illusion. Because we've looked and looked, and we don't see any fire, and we don't smell any brimstone. Instead there's-" But he didn't finish his sentence.

"I'm not going to lean over the side so you can push me in," Trennan said mutinously.

The three older knights exchanged weary glances, then as one, stepped away from Trennan, leaving a substantial distance between them.

"Go on," Meric encouraged. "Take a look for yourself."

"Take a *smell*," Jan muttered.

Still suspicious, but now very curious too, Trennan shuffled up to the nearest pit, which was one of the biggest he'd seen at more than two metres across. It might have been deep too, but he couldn't see the bottom – it was filled with an orange haze, like smoke or light from about an arm's width down. A gentle warmth emanated from the pit, like the sun in summer.

Just then a slight breeze arose from inside the pit, ruffling his hair. He sniffed. Flowers, but no tingle of illusion. "Have you been down there?" he asked numbly.

The men looked at each other sheepishly and shook their heads.

"We didn't know if it was real or not," Evers replied. "So, what do you think?"

"It's not illusion," Trennan said. He stared down into the orange haze, frowning and trying to make out *something* through it, anything. But it was like staring at the sun, and his vision grew spotty. "Maybe it's a portal of some kind. There's something down there, that's for sure."

"Right," Meric said definitively. "I'm going down. Give me a hand with my armour, will you?"

Evers began to unclip the heaviest pieces of armour from his friend's back, and Jan pulled out a piece of rope, using the alter-power around them to make it grow unnaturally long. He hooked its looped end around one of the distorted sculptures of frozen earth and began to feed the loose end into the fire (or not-fire) pit.

"You actually mean to go down there?" Trennan asked in disbelief. "And without your armour? *Anything* could be down there!"

"Could be," Meric agreed grimly. He didn't stop what he was doing though, moving to grab onto the rope and clamber over the edge of the pit. The orange glow lit him from below, making him look a bit sinister with his sword now strapped across his back. "But it could also be the answer to everything we've ever wondered about, so I'm taking the risk." He nodded at the other two. "Tell the boy, will you?"

They watched in silence as the old knight descended then was finally enveloped by the fiery haze.

There was a long silence where Trennan waited for the sound of screaming or perhaps a sudden burst of flame, but there was nothing. The pit stayed empty except for that rope, and the three of them finally looked up at each other.

"What did Meric mean when he said for you to tell me?" Trennan asked. "Tell me what?"

Jan and Evers exchanged a glance. "About the man we met out here," Evers replied. "And the dreams, and the volcano, and the big gaps in what the Fey've been telling us about their past. That's why Meric risked going down there."

It didn't make sense to Trennan that such experienced knights of the Chosen would have questions about *anything*. Weren't they supposed to have all the answers already?

He knew that he was a curious type, perhaps even a little too curious, and not entirely happy with his situation amongst the Chosen. But he also knew that no one outside of the Chosen would understand why he looked the way he did. They would see him as deformed or damaged. Besides, like many Halflings, he couldn't stay away from the Other for more than a few days. It made him sick.

But there was something here, some vast mystery that he hadn't noticed before now, and it had to do with the scent of flowers down a pit of fire.

"Tell me," he said. "Tell me everything."

The Chosen Compound

Come on, the guide said, flashing Coryn a bright white grin. *We'll swing across the stream. It'll be easy.*

They were surrounded by verdant jungle, the sounds of birds and other creatures filling the warm, damp air. The guide looked strong and capable in his light brown uniform, but still a niggle of unease shook her. She looked down at the opaque surface of the stream before them. It was narrow, but did she see a shadow moving under the surface?

I'm not sure, she replied. *What if you fall in?*

He just smiled, winding the rope tightly around one wrist. *I've done it a hundred times. There's nothing to be afraid of.* He pushed out across the stream, still grinning as he held his weight with one arm. *See? It's so easy-*

Suddenly a colossal snake shot out of the water and enveloped his entire body before disappearing back under the surface with barely a splash. It had swallowed him whole.

Coryn screamed and screamed and screamed and-

…woke up. She was in her own bed, her small room dark, and the sheets damp from sweat. She was trembling, but her jaw was clamped tight shut. It had been a dream. Just a dream…

She tapped the bedside light on, listening carefully, but there was no sound of approaching footsteps. *Good.* The elders wouldn't be pleased to know that she still had these nightmares a decade after the original, disaster VR session.

She'd been a kid, not long after her mentoring sessions began with Brosca. She'd gone into the city with a couple of other children including Kamile, and their first stop had been a VR centre. For Coryn, coming from the restricted technology of the Compound, it had felt like a wonderful treat.

She'd walked through the entrance, feeling the spray of the tiny sensors that created the feeling of virtual reality, and then she had chosen the 'Amazone Adventure' programme. It came complete with lush green jungle, waterfalls, and an impressively muscular guide she'd been too young to appreciate at the time.

At first everything had been fine. VR sessions were moulded by each person's mind, and Coryn had wanted an exciting adventure with lots of interesting animals. Well, she got them.

Coryn had screamed like a banshee and wished furiously to undo the nightmare, but the snake had turned and come after her, and no matter what she'd tried she hadn't been able to change it. *She* was supposed to be able to control the VR session, so she'd focused desperately on the VR centre. Within seconds, right as the massive snake roared through the jungle towards her, the scenery had changed and she'd been back in the building's lobby along with Kamile and the other children from the Compound.

She'd started to cry, saying that the snake had eaten her guide, and Kamile had turned to look at her. But *Kamile's* eyes had turned yellow, and a moment later she was the snake, chasing Coryn through the halls of the building…

Not too surprising that Coryn had had nightmares, right? She'd finally made it out of VR and back into reality, but she'd been terrified, unable to look at Kamile for several days without trembling. As for going back into VR? It had taken her a full four years before she had the courage to try again.

Everyone said it was bad luck, just a glitch, and that they happened once in a blue moon. *Don't worry about it, Coryn.* But she still had these dreams night after night, where every person she spoke to, everyone she knew, turned into the snake and chased her with jaws wide to swallow her like it had swallowed that guide, or twisted its way up her body, squeezing tighter and tighter until she couldn't draw breath. Its goal was always the same: to kill and consume her.

It was so *stupid*, she told herself as she stumbled out of bed and to the bathroom. The guide hadn't even existed, but she could still see the look of surprise on his face as the snake ate him.

And if Coryn's mind had come up with that, there was

something seriously wrong with her.

Years ago Brosca had told her the snake symbolised fear, the fear in her life that kept her from being truly great. Coryn was sure she was right, but it felt more like the snake had brought fear with it, and it was responsible for many a bad night's sleep.

She frowned at her reflection in the mirror. Shadows under her eyes, lank, mousy-blonde hair, pale skin, a nagging bruise on her neck… It was a wonder that Trennan thought her pretty. It was even more of a wonder that Aras did, for that matter. She'd always thought she could do with some more meat on her bones, but that was down to genetics rather than appetite.

"Oh Coryn, you're awake."

Coryn turned to smile blearily at her mother. Regina had done her best to take on the Chosen tradition of communal parenting, but in Coryn's mind, the woman would always be Mama. She was like an exaggerated version of Coryn: taller, slimmer even, if that was possible, with hair that was almost white blonde and wide-set pale eyes. Unlike Coryn, she looked peaceful and attractive this morning.

"Good morning, Regina."

Her mother studied her briefly. "Coryn, you look dreadful. How much sleep did you get?"

Coryn shrugged, long accustomed to her mother's brusque manner. "Maybe twelve, fourteen hours. I'm trying to keep up with all the time I've been losing in the Other with Brosca."

When she'd returned from her most recent trip where Brosca had shown her the golden flask (and had been quite short-tempered and unpleasant) she'd found that ten days had passed in the normal. That was a more than a week ago, and Trennan was supposed to be coming back this afternoon. It had been a full month since the Summer Solstice.

"It's the price you pay for the knowledge you gain," Regina

said sharply. She'd always been hyper-sensitive to the way Brosca had chosen Coryn, when she herself (who was more qualified, she felt) had been largely overlooked by the Fey.

"I know, Regina."

In the mirror Coryn could see her mother watching her, and the thoughts that were flickering through Regina's mind were clearly reflected on her face. Suspicion. "Have you seen Kamile lately?"

Coryn shook her head. "No, not for a few weeks, since right after…" *she handfasted with Aras*. Coryn stopped herself, because she knew how Regina felt about *that* too, but her mother had already picked up on the missing words.

"Some kind of friend she is, to allow you to indulge your fear of intimacy rather than face it head on," Regina said with a sniff. "Aras is so highly respected! And handsome, too. I bet she thought it was her lucky day."

"Kamile was being a good friend," Coryn said calmly. "You know she found him attractive, even if I don't. And I don't have a fear of intimacy. I'm just not ready to have children yet." And not with someone ten years her elder, who she'd never seen display a single emotion, let alone a smile. Was 'grumpy' an emotion?

"But what about the insult dealt to Aras? I wouldn't be surprised if he wanted revenge for that."

Coryn turned and gave her mother a pat on the cheek, and a smile. "Don't worry about it. We deal in non-violence, remember? Besides, don't you need to let me be free to follow my own path?"

"Yes, but I'm your-" *mother*, Regina was about to say, but then obviously realised she would be violating their tenets as well, the ones she'd tried so hard to adhere to ever since they'd arrived. "Very well," she said neutrally. "I'll leave you to follow your own path. And make your own breakfast. I just thought you might like to know that you have a visitor."

Trennan! Coryn's heart leapt and she felt her lips curve into a wide smile, but fortunately Regina had already turned to leave and didn't notice. Coryn dressed at high speed, brushed her teeth (because morning breath was never a nice greeting) and headed out to the visitor's room, wishing that the Chosen believed in makeup. She could have done something for the shadows under her eyes.

But the person waiting in the visitor's room wasn't Trennan, back early from his trial. Instead he was blond, about ten years older and five inches taller, with twice the muscle and covered in scars. His left arm was a silvery Fey-made prosthetic, and rumour went that although he was naturally right-handed, the prosthetic was so good that now he used it for everything.

He turned to greet her, and as always the scowl on his face made her think that everything she'd heard about his violent reputation must be true. Quaking inside (and really, really disappointed that it wasn't Trennan) Coryn forced a smile. "Good morning, Aras. Are you here to see me?"

Aras stared at her, the narrow scar across his left eye catching her attention as always. "Didn't Regina tell you?"

Coryn gulped. "Ah…she said it was someone. I didn't know who."

"Well, it's me."

"So I see." And unfortunately for her, it looked like he wouldn't be spending the next eleven months out of sight, out of mind. She waited for him to confront her about the 'trick' she had played, but instead he just watched her face for a long moment, until she grew so nervous she had to look away. How could Regina and Kamile consider him handsome?

Then he spoke. "I've heard a rumour."

What rumour? That she and Trennan were together, and that was why she'd asked Kamile to help her avoid an unwanted handfasting? Oh dear. "Have you?"

"A rumour that you and Trennan Halfling…"

(And Coryn froze with fear: he knew about them!)

"…know the whereabouts of the spirit's blood."

For a moment she thought she'd misheard. "The spirit's blood?" she echoed. "Do you mean that golden flask, the third emblem from the Anima Chest?"

"Yes. I hear that Trennan knows where it is, and he might have told you about it."

Coryn shook her head vigorously, giddy with relief. "I have no idea where you heard that, but I swear I don't know where it is. Trennan and I have never even discussed it. I didn't even know what it was until Brosca told me about it last week!"

"Brosca?"

"My Fey mentor."

Aras seemed to believe her. "I've been misinformed then." Then studying her with those cold blue eyes again, he asked, "Who did you think I was going to be? When you came in, I clearly wasn't who you were expecting."

"Oh. Ah, Kamile, or…um, Trennan." Coryn braced herself for anger and recrimination, but Aras didn't show any reaction at all. That bothered her more than a display of anger might have.

"I haven't seen Kamile since the ceremony," he said. "As for Trennan Halfling, he's still out in the Other, last I've heard."

"What? But he was supposed to be back this morning!"

Aras stared at her dispassionately. "It's not even midday yet."

"Then he's hours late!"

The big man shrugged. "Even if time wasn't different there, things happen in the Other. Being a Halfling won't save him from all danger."

That sounded like a threat. "Are you saying he's dead?"

Coryn whispered.

"I don't know," Aras replied flatly. "If he was dead, his body would have shown up somewhere on the borders. You know the Other doesn't keep such things, and I haven't heard of such."

She was silent a long while, and Aras finally nodded at her. "That's a pretty ring. Where did you get it?"

She glanced down at the small, silvery ring on her fourth finger. She'd worn it without fail since Trennan had gifted it on the night of the Solstice, a quiet symbol of their commitment. No one else had noticed that she'd been wearing it. "Trennan gave it to me."

Aras had nothing to say to that, instead turning to leave the room. She barely noticed him go.

Lunden, 1818 AD

Ashlea haughtily walked up to her room, leaving George and his brother Edward looking at each other awkwardly. A moment later George saw that Olivia, Edward's wife, had also been standing behind him, and had caught at least the end of the argument. How mortifying.

"By Jove, she's difficult sometimes!" George exclaimed in frustration. "Why can't she be like other women?"

"I thought that was why you married her," Edward replied, frowning. "But what did she mean about going home? Her home is months away by ship in the Colonies, you said, and you just came from there."

Feeling very tired, George answered dryly, "Well, the truth is that she's a time-traveller from two hundred years in the future, and there's a portal to her kitchen in our library back at the manor in Iversley."

Edward and Olivia didn't laugh. They stared at him wide-eyed, and George laughed awkwardly. "Oh, come now. I wasn't in earnest."

"Yes, you were," his brother said, shaking his head slowly. "I've heard you talking to her about this before."

Cursing his own lack of discretion, and wishing he was a better liar, George insisted, "I was *joking*, Edward. It's merely a game we play."

Olivia spoke up, her pretty face creased with concern. "I know your wife *is* different, George, and you know that I believe in the presence of alter-power in our world. But time-travel? Come now."

George sighed heavily and rolled his eyes. A moment of losing self-control had led to his brother and sister-in-law thinking he was mad. "It was a foolish joke. Please, forget I said anything."

They left it, and that seemed to be the end of the discussion. George went back out to his men's club for the evening, trying to avoid Ashlea, and only returned when he was certain she'd be sleeping, having had a few drinks with old acquaintances to fill the time. But then it occurred to him that his wife had been known to actually *wait up* for him, and he decided that his time would be better spent relaxing in the library.

The townhouse library was rather limited in terms of actual books, but it did have an excellent supply of Frencine brandy, something he missed when he was in Ashlea's time. He poured himself two fingers of the golden liquid, then sat to enjoy it.

"Drowning our sorrows, are we?"

George choked as the brandy went down the wrong way. His brother Edward, who was more than a little tipsy himself, chortled and slumped back in his chair. He'd been so quiet that George hadn't even noticed him sitting there.

"That's what you get for choosing a foreign wife instead of a good Anglish one," Edward declared. "Trouble. She doesn't know what's what; that's the thing. Mark my words, you need to show her who is head of the household." And then he ruined his fine speech with a belch.

George barely noticed. "I keep trying to show her," he said glumly, "but she doesn't listen. Sometimes I might as well be just spouting hot air."

"Oh, surely it's not as bad as all that?"

"It is. I keep telling her to stay out of other people's business, I don't care if she thinks it's morally reprehensible. Then next thing I go for a quiet cigar at Whytes...you were there, were you not?" – his brother gave a grunt of assent – "...and then she's been taken to the slammer for interceding for some purse snatcher. Gaol, I mean, Ned."

But Ned didn't seem to notice his slip of speech, so George kept talking. "She speaks wrongly for our class. Everyone we introduce her to sees that right away, and if it wasn't for our connections then she would be completely shunned. As it is, people think I'm a fool, or at the very least eccentric for marrying beneath me."

"Why did you then?"

"Well, I love her, of course," George said matter-of-factly. "But sometimes it doesn't seem enough."

"You should have loved a lady like I did," Edward told him. "Much easier that way."

He gave his older brother a look of annoyance. "Yes, I would think so. But you don't always choose who you'll love."

"No, but you choose who you'll marry. You should have just kept her on the side like I do with Alice." Edward frowned. "Like

I *did* with Alice. I broke off with her months ago after Olivia found out, not that it's done me any good. Livvy still hasn't forgiven me, and as for Alice, the dem girl went and got married, would you believe it? Whoever it was didn't seem to mind my leavings, but I was quite put out when I heard that."

George rolled his eyes. Alice had been Edward's mistress; Olivia was his wife. He knew that mistresses were very normal for the upper class of this time. He had never questioned the morality of them until he'd spent six months in the 21st century and discovered that there, women did not overlook infidelity. In fact they took it so seriously it was grounds for a divorce.

So now he was inclined to forgive those like his brother who did commit adultery, since really they didn't know what they were doing, but his own personal perspective had changed. Marriage vows were made before the Eternal One, and to casually break them was showing disrespect both for the Eternal One and for himself, as if his words were worth nothing.

Oh, and it would really bother his wife. Happy wife, happy life…whoever said that had been a wise man.

But George didn't mention any of that. "Have you replaced her yet?" he asked instead, turning to look at his brother.

"Who?"

"Your *mistress*, Neddie. You said that you sent her off when Olivia found out, and that she's married since."

Edward had the same curling, dark blond hair as George, but his complexion was paler and his face narrower. He'd always been considered the more handsome of the brothers, but when George had said that to Ash, she had laughed and called Edward a pretty-boy, whatever that meant. *No offense to your brother, George,* she'd said. *But you're much more my type. You're a* man.

Well, his pretty-boy brother stared into his mostly empty tumbler of brandy, swishing the amber liquid around the sides of the glass. "Oh. No, I haven't." He sounded as surprised by that as George was. "I promised Olivia I wouldn't, and that was months ago, right when your Ashlea first turned up. But…well, getting rid of the mistress hasn't exactly smoothed things over with the wife, if you know what I mean. I think she's still angry with me."

"Would you be angry with her if she'd been unfaithful to you?"

"It's not the same thing," Edward said, but even he didn't sound like he believed that. Then he sighed. "Enough about my disaster of a marriage. What about yours?"

"Who says my marriage is a disaster?" George asked defensively.

"We heard you arguing in the hall earlier, remember? And then you made that foolish joke about her being a time-traveller." Edward wasn't as far gone as George had thought, if he could still think that clearly. "Where is she from again?"

"I told you, the Colonies."

"Obviously," Edward agreed. "But *where* in the Colonies? Greater Britannia has more than just two or three, and when her accent slips it doesn't sound Amyrican. Besides, I asked a few people I know from over there, and they've never heard of a Miss Ashlea Hamiltyn."

"She's not Amyrican." But if George said where she was *really* from… At this point in time, that little group of islands on the other side of the world didn't even have an Anglish name.

"I wouldn't have thought this of you, but you've been a little strange over this past year. You didn't pick her up in Monaster's Garden, did you?" Edward said jokingly, referring to the infamous square known for its nightwalkers.

George gave his brother a long stare. "Suggesting that my wife was a prostitute isn't going to endear you to me, Ned."

"I wasn't…" Edward began, then sighed deeply, using a pet

name he hadn't used in years. "Look, Georgie. We know there's something you're not telling us about her. It's evident that she's not like anyone we've ever met before, and if she's not of a lower class, then what is she?"

"Her society is classless, or so they like to think," George murmured, suddenly feeling sorry for himself. Too much drink, down in the doldrums, and he was so tired of hiding this enormous part of his life from a person who had been so close to him. "But it's mostly about money. It always is."

"Well, what is she then? George?"

Suddenly sober, George stared solemnly into his empty glass. "What I said earlier today was true. I met her in Angland, hundreds of years in the future."

Edward gave a loud guffaw. "You are funny."

George looked him right in the eye. "It would be funny, if it weren't true. But it is."

"Is that what she told you?" Edward asked, his speech slurring slightly. "That she came from the future just to meet you and your money and connections? Demmed convenient of her."

"No, that's where I met her. In the future."

His brother nodded solemnly. "Naturally. And you were time-travelling because…?"

"Because someone in about four hundred years thought it would be clever to kidnap a whole lot of people from different times, put us together and see if we killed each other, basically. I was chosen because apparently no one would notice if I disappeared."

Why hadn't he said this before? It was so easy to admit, and look how well Edward was taking it!

"Oh, come now Georgie," Edward cajoled. "You know that's not true. Perhaps months ago when you'd had that difficult spell and went off, but not now."

"It *was* months ago, and I spent six months in the early twenty-first century with Ashlea. That's where she's from. Oh, and a Tudar lady called Anne of Covington came too. Tudar brat, more like." They'd also met a man who lived in the clouds and probably wasn't human, but George kept that part to himself. He wasn't feeling quite that honest.

Edward laughed again. "Is that the one who was burned at the stake for witchcraft?"

George shook his head vehemently. He'd wondered the same thing when he'd first met Anne, but had dismissed the idea. Amaranthus would never *ever* allow such a thing. At worst, some historian had noted Anne's sudden absence in 1556 and had confused her fate with that of some other medieval redhead.

"No, it must be another Anne, although I recall hearing the same thing once upon a time. I believe there are – oh, at least five or six Annes from Covington in the medieval period. Besides, it wasn't witches who were burned at the stake, but heretics. That's a common misapprehension."

"No, I'm certain it was witches," Edward argued. "Witches burn. Isn't that the way of it? And if you don't believe me, Olivia has some book or another with a history of alter-power in Angland. *That* would tell you the truth, indeed." He stumbled to his feet then wandered over to the nearest bookshelf and peered at it at length.

"Witch or heretic, it wasn't my Anne," George said with certainty, taking another sip of his brandy. A sudden, dreadful thought occurred to him, and he gave his brother a gimlet glare. "And you'd better not tell a soul that I've said all of this. I'll be sent to Bedlam insane asylum within the week."

Edward scoffed, still studying the shelves with the careful fascination of the drink-addled. "Bosh. Angland's full of eccentrics; you'd be just one more. Ah, here it is." He pulled out a substantial tome, then ambled over to drop it in George's lap before slumping back in his own seat. "See if I'm right."

George was still recovering from the book's sharp corner stabbing him in an awkward place, and he didn't answer at first. Then he realised Edward hadn't called him mad, or a liar. "Do you believe me? About the travelling through time?"

"Oh, but you were joking, weren't you?"

George shook his head.

"Oh." There was a long silence as Edward watched him cautiously. The effects of the drink seemed to have faded. "Georgie," he said finally, "If there's any way you can prove the truth of this tale, show me now. Otherwise I want to pretend this was all a great jest, and never speak of it again."

George knew he'd said too much. Both he and Ashlea had vowed that they'd never speak of it to others. In fact, when they supposedly went 'to stay with George's family' for weeks at a time, Ashlea had explained the lack of emails and phone calls by saying that they were very rural, and had no electricity. But now, with his brother, he could pretend it had all been a joke, or he could do what he'd always wanted and tell the truth.

So he laid all his cards on the table, so to speak, and did it.

George told Edward everything, right from the time he'd been taken by Dr Walker in a stomach-churningly confusing moment. He told him what had happened in that other Iversley, and about how he had met strange people who weren't quite people, and about Amaranthus – in truth, everything seemed to come back to that man.

Then he told about how he'd been shown a new, easy way to travel through the remnant gateways without needing the Eternity Stone, and about how he and Ashlea moved between the two times, but now they both seemed to fit in neither.

"Odd that I should think of that now," he said absently. "No,

Ashlea doesn't fit here. But I've changed too. I don't seem to fit either. I can't overlook the things I used to, Edward."

But his brother was fixated on something else. He didn't ask George if he was crazy, instead he said, "This…*Other*. It sounds like celestials and dark spirits to me. You know, in the Holy Book it says that some of the celestials were thrown out of the heavenly realms for mutiny…?"

"I've never thought of that before," George said in surprise. "I suppose it does. But it can't be the same, or else that would make Amaranthus…well, the Eternal One."

Which in truth wasn't as much of a stretch as he might have thought. The longer he knew Amaranthus, the more he marvelled at what the man was capable of. He had a mind that could take in the whole of human history, and an incredible interest in individual lives. Surely there couldn't be two such beings in the universe? But while that thought had some merit, George couldn't think on it too much now, so he mentally filed it away for later.

All the strange talk and imbibing of spirits had put Edward into a contemplative mood. "I always feel guilty whenever I think of the Eternal One," he mused. "So gen'rally I try not to. Not very good for a Churchian, is it?"

"That's the thing," George said thoughtfully. "I don't believe being a Churchian is actually about following all the rules and being afraid of the Eternal One. Rather it's about…a relationship, you know? Knowing that because of the Christos dying on the cross for us – and crucifixion is about the most appalling thing you ever saw, trust me, I've seen it – that you're all right with the Eternal One, and he's not mad at you, and you don't need to feel guilty.

"But I don't know if Amaranthus is. I always thought the Eternal One would be…mighty. You know, scary. But he's sort of…humble. Simple. Not frightening, but very likeable."

"You speak strangely," Edward commented.

"Dem, you're right." George had been lapsing into a strange accent that was a mix of his own and Ashlea's. "But he doesn't make me feel guilty, but instead like I want to be better. Does that make sense?"

"I suppose so."

They sat in the quiet for a while, and then overcome with appreciation for his brother (and perhaps the six standard drinks he'd had that evening), George said, "I never thought it would be so easy to tell someone. And you just listened, didn't you Eddie? Didn't even call me mad or anything. Demmed fine of you, Ned. Nedward."

Nedward smiled blankly at the guttering fire. "Yes, I am a fine fellow, aren't I?"

"And a good brother." George felt almost tearful.

"And a *very* good brother," Nedward agreed.

"I'm going to go find my wife," George announced. "It's late, but I think she'll still be up."

His brother shrugged. "Maybe she'll have gone off time-travelling again." His tone was slightly mocking, but George answered seriously.

"She can't have. The gateway's all the way back in Leister County. If she has gone…well, I'll have to go and get her, won't I?" George stood and headed for the door, wondering why the world seemed to be moving slightly. Earthquake? No, it was more likely that he'd overindulged. Oops.

"Hey Georgie," came the plaintive cry from the armchair.

"Yes, Neddie?"

"May I come with you?"

"Er…I don't think it would be a good idea for you to just disappear. You are a viscount, after all."

There was a silence which meant Edward was thinking about

it, then he said, "You're correct, of course. I am a lord. You are a mere mister."

A drunken lord, that was, and a tipsy mister. "Perhaps you should go to bed," George suggested.

More silence, then a snore. Edward already had.

George walked very carefully up the stairs to his bedroom suite, holding onto the polished wooden handrail so he didn't stumble. He was halfway up before he realised he was still holding Olivia's book about alter-power in Angland, but going back seemed far too difficult, so he just took it with him. He and Ashlea had separate bedrooms connected by a small sitting room with a tidy couch. He made it through his room, across the sitting room, then tried his wife's door handle.

Locked. By Jove, that was the first time Ashlea had dared to lock him out of her room!

"Ashlea!" he whispered loudly. "Ashlea, let me in!"

There was silence, and George leaned his head against the door tiredly. "Ashlea," he said again. "I don't want to fight. I love you. We'll…" He struggled to think of something that would please her. "We'll go to the gateway tomorrow, darling. Together, first thing in the morning, yes?"

He listened for a response, but none was forthcoming. Now he was too tired (and a bit too squiffy, in truth) to try any further, so he stumbled over to the small couch and slumped into it, the book still clutched tight under one arm. He'd wait for her to come out, that was all. Then they'd talk, and all would be well.

He'd just wait right here and rest his head on one of these cushions. Just for a few minutes.

Zzzzzzz…

Ash had woken up in time to hear George's apology, as well as his promise that they'd check out the gateway tomorrow. That'd do, she decided, because she didn't like fighting either.

So she quietly crept out of bed and unlocked her bedroom door. But when she opened it, it was to reveal her husband sprawled on the tiny, uncomfortable couch between the two rooms, his head thrown back and his mouth open in a snore. Fast asleep.

She smiled, then gently kissed him on the forehead. "Tomorrow," she vowed.

As long as he didn't forget what he'd agreed to.

UNEXPECTED PORTALS

The Mountain of Glass, time irrelevant

"This is the place," Jon declared. "I'm sure this is where Amaranthus brought me through." He stood with Anne on the very top of the inner mountain, next to the pool of water where he'd so often sat.

Anne studied the small space, noting not one but four patches of shimmering air marking remnant gateways. Each of them would lead to a different location across time and space, without any indication of what lay on the other side. "Do you recall what view you beheld upon arriving?"

Jon just shrugged. "Green. Lots of green."

Which meant it could be any one of these gateways, as the whole inner Mountain was surrounded by verdant garden. She sighed heavily. "Very well. What did it look like, the place you left?"

"A hall with a marble floor, and paintings with gilded frames on the walls. Dark blue velvet curtains."

"That should be simple enough to find," Anne said decisively.

She grabbed Jon's hand and promptly stepped through the first gateway. There was a brief tingle, then they were standing at the bottom of a rocky ravine with cold water running over their feet. Hers were bare.

"What-" Jon said.

"Z'wounds, 'tis the wrong one." Anne stepped right back through the same gateway, returning to the Mountain of Glass with Jon stumbling behind her. "We shall try again."

"Wait," he began, but she'd already moved through, wet feet and all.

Now they stood in a lush forest with sunlight shimmering faintly through the high canopy. No, 'twas not the right gateway either.

Anne went to move back to the Mountain, but Jon dug in his feet. "Where are we? This place is beautiful."

"'Tis, rather." She took a moment to appreciate it, then tugged on his hand. "Come. I know not what kind of people and animals would be around here, and 'tis not the right location."

Jon reluctantly allowed her to pull him back to the Mountain, and then just as she would have tried the third gateway, he dug in his heels again. "Do you really move so quickly?"

"Of course," she replied in surprise. "What sense is there in delaying?"

"Don't you need to, I don't know, prepare mentally?"

Anne stared at him blankly until he shrugged, sighing. "Oh, alright then. Let's go."

Finally. Anne grinned, taking his hand again and moved into the shimmering space that marked the third remnant gateway. As she did so, there was the faint sound of the wind, or someone calling her name-

"This is it," Jon said a moment later. "This is Chamborde castle."

And indeed 'twas as he had described: a luxurious hall with marble floors. There were no paintings on the walls, though; nor were there velvet curtains – or curtains of any kind. Anne commented on it, and he frowned.

"It's changed since I was last here. The revolutionaries must have taken them." His expression grew even more anxious, and Anne tried to distract him.

"Your garb has not changed, though. Mine has." 'Twas once more the simple servant's garb that her velvet gown changed to upon her last visit to Frencia, although the waist was a little higher and fuller, and the bodice and sleeves were made of a plain, billowing white fabric. Her shoes had reappeared: small and brown and ugly. *Sigh.*

Jon looked grim. "I suppose we'll have to find out how much time has gone by, and if they're dead or alive."

He began to stride down the hall in his fancy silver and white courtier's costume, and Anne skipped to keep up. "Did you hear a noise as we were leaving the Mountain?"

"No, not at all."

Must have been her imagination.

"Anne! Jon!" Elspeth called at the top of her voice, but 'twas too late. The two had already vanished from the top of the inner Mountain even before she could reach them, and she stood dejectedly at the peak for a few moments.

There was no doubt that Anne had taken Jon to find his own home, and it only bothered Elspeth that she had not been invited.

"By the Rood," she muttered to herself. "Would it have been truly so difficult to wait for me?"

She'd just come from the Hall of Treasures, bursting with excitement at the gift she'd been given, and *they'd left her behind.*

'Twas a dreadful betrayal, although one common to younger siblings. To make it worse, they could have gone through any of three or four doorways that she could see shimmering there.

A tiny black bug buzzed past her ear, flickering green and gold as if 'twas a little light from the heavens. Elspeth ignored it – she'd seen one or two insects down in the Garden, although at least they did not have the nasty tendency of landing in one's food here – but it buzzed past her face once more, its shining carapace glowing an even more intense shade of green, bright enough to make her squint. 'Twas hovering in front of one of the gateways, she realised finally. But even as she understood that, it vanished through the gateway.

How very curious. For not only were there seldom insects here in the Mountain, but Elspeth did not know of any that could come and go at will.

Straightening her shoulders, and armed with the knowledge of her new, wonderful gift, she followed the bug through the gateway.

'Twas the right one. In fact, Elspeth could see a jewel-toned skirt disappearing around the corner of the long hallway even as she arrived, and she knew that Anne's garb changed to fit wherever she visited. Indeed, Elspeth's own plain tunic and loose breeches had been replaced with a perfectly lovely black and white gown with a very full skirt, and little leather slippers on her feet – by far the nicest garb she'd ever worn. How marvellous.

As if to confirm, the little bug alighted upon Elspeth's shoulder, its colour fading to the more usual black and gold.

"Why thank you, little gate-bug," she told it. "How very helpful you have been."

But when Elspeth finally caught up to the woman she thought was Anne, a stranger turned to look at her in confusion. 'Twas an older woman in a deep blue dress, and most certainly not her sister.

Elspeth swallowed back the nerves that she felt every time someone clearly upper class looked at her, waiting for their scorn. But this woman did not know she was base-born, and there was no reason to tell. "I'm dreadfully sorry," she said politely. "I seek a short, red-haired girl about my own age, and a tall, fair-haired boy. Have you seen them?"

The woman looked at her in startled dismay, babbling something unintelligible. Elspeth realised after a moment that 'twas another language.

"I beg your pardon?"

"Aengleesh," the woman enunciated. "No…Aeengleesh."

Oh. So she didn't speak Anglish. How very awkward. Elspeth might have tried to ask again (mayhap speaking very slowly; did that not help in such situations?) but the woman nodded briskly at her then trotted away.

Elspeth turned to retrace her own steps, but realised that in her eagerness to catch up she'd quite lost her way.

Oh, rotten cabbages.

The Chosen Compound, Lile, 2597 AD

Kamile could tell something was different when she arrived back at her small room in the main housing block that evening. She could hear someone, something; but couldn't see anyone. "Hello?"

No one answered, and she sat down on her bed with a sigh. She was still tense after the run-in on the borders with those girls, and the thought of those people walking mindlessly towards their possible doom made her feel ill. But what could she have done?

Something moved against Kamile's hand, and she took a moment to realise what it was: a small, dark green snake slithering past on its way to hide under the pillow.

With more self-control than she knew she had, Kamile slowly pulled her hand away from the bed, then stood. She pulled back the cover and saw that she had not one but four small snakes wriggling around in her bed.

"What in Hades?" she exclaimed in disbelief. She wasn't afraid, since she recognised the two types of snake and knew that neither was particularly dangerous – just grass or garden snakes. It was their location that bothered her more.

Just then, as if called up by Kamile's desire for an explanation, Irena popped her head through the door. She had the room across the hall and could be counted on to know most things gossip-related. "Oh Kamile, you're back. Did you see the snakes?"

"Yes," Kamile bit off. "I saw the snakes. Why are they in my bed?"

Irena shrugged. "I suppose they crawled in there for the warmth. Some guy dropped them off earlier, except they were in a bag. He said they'd been left to him by a relative, and he didn't want them."

Kamile frowned. "What guy? What did he look like?" She didn't know anyone who would leave her *snakes*.

"Um…Asien, kind of good-looking? Wore glasses."

"Oh." She knew who that would be. In this day and age of easy, government-funded laser surgery, the only people who wore glasses did so as an affectation, to look cool. It would be Leonas, a guy who she'd handfasted with once in her late teens, and who she'd barely spoken to since the day their year ended. "And I thought we were on good terms," she muttered.

"He said that you had a snake, so you might want a few

more," Irena chirped. She flicked her long brown hair over one shoulder, then frowned at Kamile. "I didn't know you had a snake."

"I don't. He's talking about the python that belongs to our whole block. You know, Harry?"

"Oh." Losing interest, Irena left Kamile alone in her little room with a bed full of reptiles.

Damn that Leonas. He could have just put them in the container with the python! Or given them to anyone except her. Anyone at all.

Kamile found the thick cloth bag they'd originally been in, and slightly repulsed, set about picking them up by their tails and dropping them back into the bag. The last one, a very small, thin black thing, reared up and stuck its little fangs in her arm as she did so.

"Ouch," she muttered. "Little beast." She was pretty sure it wasn't venomous, but even so, she should get that seen to. Any bite could be harmful if it festered.

She dropped the last snake in the bag with a grimace, then headed out to the common room where Harry the python lived. He filled up the whole of his thick plastic container, but sat in the small space placidly as if he had not a care in the world. Kamile wondered briefly if he'd view the other snakes as snacks, but decided she didn't care. They were just snakes, and besides, one had bitten her.

She rubbed the sore spot on her arm ruefully. She'd thought that black garden snakes in this area didn't have fangs, but perhaps she'd been wrong. The thought occurred that perhaps it wasn't a garden snake at all, and she determined again that she *would* get it seen to.

Kamile quickly pushed off the lid and dumped in the smaller snakes, then replaced the lid. Or tried to anyway – it was flimsy and had clearly been broken a few times, and getting it to stay on was a hard task. It was balanced over the gap rather than actually clipped on.

"Why do we even have you, Harry?" she asked aloud. "This is like a disaster waiting to happen." He was too small to eat a human, but still…

Peep.

The quiet chirp caught her attention, and she looked around in confusion. Where had that come from?

Peep.

"They're the new birdies," a childish voice said. It was a little boy, perhaps about five years old, standing and watching her with interest. Now Harry wouldn't be too small to eat *him*.

"Why aren't you in the crèche?" Kamile asked.

He shrugged. "Wanted to see the birdies."

"What birdies?"

The little boy pointed, and she realised why the lid was so distorted. The actual lid, a thick, sturdy affair, had been taken off and altered, and was sitting on a shelf near Harry's cage. Someone had changed it so that it was a long, low cage of its own, and sitting very quietly inside were about half a dozen little birds. Most of them resembled sparrows, but one was very slightly larger and red-feathered. There was no room for them to walk around, let alone fly, and for them to be so close to the snakes was the worst kind of cruelty.

"It goes on top of Harry," the boy said helpfully.

"Why on earth would anyone put a birdcage directly on top of a python's cage?" Kamile asked in disbelief. The small size of the cage was bad enough, but the location…?

"To test the belief that fear is inbuilt in small prey," Aras said from the doorway. "The snake can't reach them. The plastic is too thick, but as you see, the birds are quiet and still even so."

"So they're scared to death," Kamile retorted. "Whose brilliant idea was this?"

He walked over to stand next to her, picking up the bird section of the top of the cage, and sitting it over the lower snake section. It clicked shut, and the birds barely stirred. The snakes, on the other hand…

"Not mine, if that's what you're asking," he replied casually. "It was Jurgis's idea."

Feeling a bit like a little bird next to a snake, Kamile noted that she barely reached his shoulder. "Oh." If Jurgis had put them there, then there they would stay, no matter how cruel and unnecessary she thought it.

She turned to take the child back to the crèche, but he had vanished as soon as Aras had come in. It was almost funny, she thought, that most people responded to Aras in fear the same way Coryn did. There was something about him that was menacing, even though he didn't shout or swear or hit. It was like his next move couldn't be predicted, like he could go from placid to furious in a single second and she just hadn't seen it yet.

"When are you coming to my rooms?"

Kamile's eyes widened. She thought he'd made it pretty clear that he wasn't interested in her (judging by his fixation on Coryn, she figured blondes were more to his taste), but apparently a man was still a man. "Ah…later."

"Tonight?"

She didn't really want to, but they *were* handfasted, and at her request. "OK."

Their conversation apparently done, Aras turned to leave. Kamile watched him go with something like regret, even though she wasn't sure what she regretted.

Once he had gone, a little dark head popped out from behind the chair, staring after his retreating figure with wide eyes. The boy hadn't left at all, he had just hidden, and Kamile almost laughed. "Come on," she said. "I'll take you back to the crèche."

"OK." They began to walk, and the boy asked, "Why are you going to his rooms? Is it to see the ponies?"

Kamile looked at him in surprise. "What ponies?"

"The little talking ones," the boy replied. "I saw them there last week. One black, and one white, and very friendly. They came out from behind the drawers."

Ponies behind furniture… From any other child at any other place, Kamile would have immediately discounted that as imagination. But she had a particular relationship with two small horses fitting that description. Some of the smallest, sweetest Fey she'd ever met, the two had turned up sporadically through her childhood: in dreams, in the Other, in VR even, but never before at the Compound.

They shouldn't have been able to, since the borders were far from the sleeping areas. The buildings had been built that way on purpose. Not even the Chosen wanted to wake up to find a Fey over their bed.

Surely the borders hadn't moved again? It was possible that they had, and behind that set of drawers was a little doorway right into the Other. Possible, but unlikely.

"What's your name?" Kamile asked the boy. "What were you doing in Aras's rooms?"

She must have sounded too sharp, because instead of answering, the boy turned and ran ahead towards the nearby crèche. "Don't go near Harry's cage again!" Kamile hollered after him, but he didn't respond.

"Huh." Technically all property was communal, so the child wouldn't have been forbidden to go into Aras's rooms, but he would have to be pretty brave to risk that scowl. Unlike Kamile, who had been invited…

Well, she could just have a look right now, couldn't she? And when Aras missed her, she'd apologise sweetly and say that they got their wires crossed.

Aras's rooms were a part of the knights' complex across the way.

Aras was a special case here. He hadn't had to go through the years of study before his knight's test as most did. Instead, since he had spent several years as a soldier in the most intense environments that the normal realm could offer, the elders had voted to give him the knights' test straight away, and if he survived he'd be given special dispensation.

He survived, naturally, and so he wasn't given just one room as plebeians like her were, but a set of rooms. Lucky him.

There were people moving in and out all the time, and no one spared Kamile a second glance as she casually sauntered in, checking the names on the doors. She found Aras's, gave a light knock – which luckily went unanswered – then sidled in.

The first room consisted of a small kitchen and table, with two doors leading off into other rooms. There were no drawers in sight in either the first room or the second, which turned out to be the bathroom, so she went right into the last room.

It was dominated by a large bed in the centre (long rather than wide, as Aras was so tall) with a built-in closet and a set of drawers off to one side. A sword, still in its sheath, sat propped against the wall next to a long-range rifle. The latter had clearly been used many times, and Kamile wondered at it still being here. The Chosen didn't use projectile weapons, not even arrows.

More disturbingly, next to the weapons sat Aras's prosthetic arm. It looked just like a human arm, dipped in silver, and it sat on the floor as if it had been discarded. She frowned at that, because she knew he had been wearing it when she'd spoken to him not twenty minutes before. Perhaps it was a spare?

Crouching down in front of the drawers, she closed her eyes, trying to sense the presence of the Other. It was one of the benefits of being a Halfling (or a quarterling, whatever) and it worked this time as well. She felt the faint tingle of alter-power close by, and then she heard the sound of a drawer being opened.

She opened her eyes as the wide middle drawer was pushed out and fell with a crash to the floor, revealing two sets of eyes hidden in the darkness within the furniture. Beyond them she could see a tunnel that seemed to lead right into the wall. "Hello?"

"Greetings, Kamile Greenskin," the first little horse said in its childlike voice, unchanged since she'd last seen it more than five years before.

There was a clunk, and then the lowest drawer came out as well, and the wee black beast ducked underneath and pranced into the room, followed by a shyer white pony.

She smiled at them. She couldn't help it; they were just so cute. The boy had been right when he said they were small, since they were only the size of a large dog, with disproportionately big heads. And she hadn't seen them in such a long time.

"Greetings, my lord Fey," she said, using the proper title for a Fey whose name hadn't been given. Yes, over eighteen years, and she still didn't know their names. "What brings you here?"

"A new border; a new gateway," the black pony replied sweetly. "New things to explore; new people to meet."

How charming. "Has the border extended all the way out here?" Kamile asked, although she knew it hadn't. When the border moved, the black-clouded forest moved with it, and *that* was hard to miss.

"Not the border," the white horse whispered. "A conduit."

"A conduit?" Kamile echoed in surprise. A conduit was an object which had been imbued with large amounts of alter-power so that it became a doorway of sorts for the Fey to use. It enabled them to move outside the Other, although they lacked a true physical presence, they were still attached to the object, and their powers were severely limited. She came to the obvious conclusion. "Is it the set of drawers? Who would bespell a set of drawers, and why in *here*?"

More to the point, who would bespell it for her ponies? Usually a conduit meant a link for only *one* Fey. Or in this case, two, since the ponies were different halves of the same entity. But it took no small effort to achieve such a thing.

The black pony shook his head playfully, and the white one shied back as if afraid. "You've been turning away from our counsel," the black one said gently, not answering her question. "We had to go to such lengths to talk to you again."

Kamile frowned. The only counsel she could think of was something they had said to her as a young girl which still affected her to this day. And it seemed unlikely that they would build a conduit in *Aras's* room to see *her*. Unless Aras had prompted her to come here for this very reason. That almost made sense, but not quite.

"I don't understand," she murmured. "What counsel have I ignored?"

"The most important counsel," the white pony continued where the black one left off. "That of not just the Fey and the Chosen, but of the universe, and the fates of those to come. Do you not remember, child?"

Kamile was twenty-four, but yes, she remembered. Feeling that same old tug of shame and disappointment, she lowered her head. "I remember. Fey and human shouldn't mix. And I haven't been trying to!"

"And yet you have handfasted once more. Why handfast if not for the desire for young, Halfling?"

The black one continued gently, "We have told you out of a

genuine kindness and sense of what is right. Humans are a good, natural race," and now the white pony joined in, and they spoke in unison from their place just outside the open drawers, "and the Fey are a good, supernatural race. But the offspring of the two is unnatural and unwanted, and comes into this world to suffer nothing but pain and rejection until the kindness of the universe destroys it. Why would you risk this fate upon a yet-to-be conceived child?"

"I'm not going to have children, OK?" Kamile burst out, overwhelmed by those same feelings of shame and perhaps a little anger, although she squashed down the last part. No one else knew about this. She'd never mentioned the reason that she'd been taking infertility injections for years – not to help with her infertility, but to make her that way. "And I didn't handfast with Aras for children, I did it for – for a friend, and whatever my reasons, I have to follow through. I made an oath!"

"And what of the oath you made to us as a child?" the black one asked. It had stopped gambolling about and was standing stock still in the middle of the room. The white one was hiding half behind it, even more timid than usual.

Kamile shrugged. She'd realised as a child that she was different. Weaker in some ways, stronger in others. Left on the fringes of even their fringe society. And then she'd made friends with the ponies, and they'd told her why. "I've kept that oath. I've never conceived, and I won't this time either."

"And what of your handfasted partner?"

"I doubt he'd care." Until he'd seen her earlier today, anyway. But that reminded her of another question. "Why did you come to Aras's room to see me?" she asked curiously. "Did you send the child to come get me?"

Just then, Kamile heard the outer door being opened. Her heart raced as she realised Aras must be home early. But more surprisingly, the ponies shuddered as if afraid. The white one turned and ran back inside the dark tunnel to the Other, and after a moment, the black one followed it. "Hide us," it whispered. "That one means us harm."

"Aras can't hurt you," she argued, shocked. "You're immortal."

The pony shuddered, shaking its mane in fear. "Distract him. There are worse injuries than death."

What on earth could it mean?

Just then there were loud footsteps outside the bedroom door, and she hurriedly pushed the drawers back into place, hiding the Fey's entry point. But she hadn't even got the second one in when the door opened to reveal Aras. He stared at her coldly, then his gaze turned to the black space visible behind the empty drawers. His Fey prosthetic clenched its shiny fist. So the other was a spare after all – and there was no way he hadn't seen what she'd been doing.

"You're early," he said.

She smiled at him as sweetly as she could manage, feeling her heart pounding. He was attractive, of course he was. She'd always thought that. But now all she could think was that the ponies were scared of him.

The immortal Fey, scared of Aras? *Why*? Perhaps she'd been wrong when she'd assured Coryn that he was harmless. Perhaps Coryn had seen what she had been too careless to see… "Yes. You don't mind, I hope?"

He didn't answer, turning to stare at the now closed drawers where the Fey ponies had disappeared. "I told those little bastards not to come back," he muttered, causing Kamile to jolt in surprise at his disrespectful tone. "Tried to remove the conduit, whatever it was." He turned back to Kamile, those blue eyes cold and narrow. "Did you bring them here?"

Her jaw dropped. Not only had he known about them, but he thought *she* brought them? "Of course not!"

"But you knew them. Otherwise why would you hide them?"

Because they had asked her to? Kamile smiled again to hide her nervousness, lounging back on the bed. "I met them as a child. I think they're cute. Anyway, I didn't hide them; they wanted to go."

Aras just kept staring until she felt uncomfortable. Finally he sat on the soft bed next to her, the whole thing sinking with his weight and making her fall into him. She'd bet he literally weighed twice what she did. She lifted a hand against his chest to stop herself falling, but he grabbed it. His hand *was* twice the size of hers.

"What did you think I was going to do to them, Kamile?" he asked coldly, cutting through her pretence that she hadn't been hiding the ponies. "What kind of man do you think I am?"

"I really have no idea," she replied lightly, determined not to show how scared she was, and making a concerted effort not to pull her hand away. She didn't know if she was scared or just really, really attracted to him, but either way her heart pounded so hard she could hear it in her ears. "I don't know you at all."

He regarded her emotionlessly for a few long seconds, and she felt a chill of fear run up her spine. Bur instead of quailing, she smiled seductively and leaned back on the bed. "We're only handfasted for these short months. What do you say we make use of the time?"

Aras obviously wasn't satisfied in regards to the ponies, but he just stared at her assessingly for a few long moments before shrugging. After all, they *were* handfasted.

A few minutes later he stood to leave. He stared at her again for a long moment, then turned and left. The whole interaction had taken less than three minutes, and without even a kiss. They'd made use of the time without emotion or even kindness, but Kamile supposed she could count herself lucky he hadn't been rough considering how she'd tricked him in the first place.

"Let yourself out," she murmured to herself. He hadn't even thought it necessary to say that much.

She sat in the same place on that bed for untold minutes. Not thinking, really, just absorbing what had happened. It hadn't meant anything. That sort of thing never did. But unlike the other times, where at least she'd had a bit of fun along with it, this time she felt so very, very used, like a tissue that someone had sneezed into and then thrown away. As if she had no value at all.

"What does it matter?" she asked herself. "He's just another guy."

And whether her heart had been in it or not, she'd need to go into the city to stock up on her supplies of contraceptive. She'd taken the last lot two – or was it three weeks ago? Hmm, considering they only lasted two to four weeks, she'd better get onto that. Couldn't have any unwanted, unnatural mixed-blood babies in the world, she thought bitterly. (Although if they were so unnatural, why did the Fey and humans keep breeding them, hmm?)

Kamile leaned forward on the edge of the rumpled bed, feeling unwanted and ashamed and everything that she'd always hide, and everything that the ponies had claimed Halflings were. She glared fiercely at the now ordinary-looking drawers, thinking that as cute and sweet as those Fey were, she really hoped they wouldn't come back.

Little bastards, Aras had called them with more emotion in his voice than she'd ever heard from him. He had gall calling Fey such names, though.

And they'd been scared of him…

Kamile sighed, leaning her head in her hands. What was she even doing here? Entertaining cold, violent men; wandering along the Borderlands as if to give herself a purpose? She hadn't changed a thing. Barring those two girls, she hadn't helped *anyone*.

Abruptly she stood and left the room without even a glance back. She was going to contact Magdalene and Poli right away, she decided, and they were going to look for the River. And maybe, just maybe, they'd find it, and she'd see if there was more to life than what she'd found so far.

Because the way she'd been living…it really didn't seem like it was worth the trouble.

Lunden, 1818 AD

George woke up on the couch outside of Ashlea's room, a painful crick in his neck and his mouth dry as dust. He lay there for a few moments feeling sorry for himself, then finally heaved himself onto his feet, stumbled down the hall until he reached one of the servants' bells, and tugged on it heavily. For some reason there weren't any up in his rooms.

A few minutes later no one had arrived, so he grumpily stomped down the stairs until he reached the kitchen. Prowd saw him and barely blinked an eye – but then the butler was very well-trained. "How might I help you, sir?"

"No one answered the servants' bell upstairs," George said crankily, then more graciously added, "Some kind of drink, I beseech you."

It was tea, naturally, and he'd seated himself in one of the alcoves that came off the kitchen (gaining a few nervous looks from the staff, who seemed like they'd rather he wasn't there) when he finally realised he was still holding the book under one arm. There'd been a reason why he was holding it, he mused. Something about heretics…?

Oh, that was right. He'd been arguing with Edward over whether it was witches or heretics that were burned at the stake, and Edward had insisted it was witches. George, on the other hand, was sure it was heretics, and thought that the witch thing was perhaps relegated to the Colonies.

He recalled a moment later that he'd done rather more than argue technicalities with Edward. He'd also seen fit to tell his entire time-travel story from start to finish. George felt briefly awkward about it, then shrugged it off. Edward had taken it well, and George hadn't yet been bundled off to Bedlam, had he?

George began leafing through the pages of 'A History of Alter-Power in Angland', and it took less than ten minutes to find what he was searching for.

"Heretics," he announced happily, startling a nearby scullery maid. "They were burned in Angland, not witches."

"Me, sir?" she squeaked.

"Are you a witch or a heretic?"

"No, sir!"

The girl looked terrified, and George sighed heavily, realising his joke had fallen flat. He dismissed the girl, then took himself up to one of the parlours along with some toast – he certainly didn't feel up to a full Anglish breakfast with the nagging headache he still had. He settled himself in a comfortable chair, then kept reading.

By Jove, history was violent, especially the way people were dealt with when they crossed the line of whatever society considered acceptable. Witchcraft being one of the main culprits, although as far as George could see there was very little actual alter-power in use (nor mention of communication with the dreadful Creatures, which was perhaps closer to *actual* witchcraft). It seemed as though people simply wanted to find a scapegoat for their problems. Someone to punish, whether for religion, politics, unapproved abilities or actual crimes committed.

The book was a little disjointed, skipping through different subjects as it rigidly adhered to the chronology of Angland. Then George reached the Tudar period, and his heart skipped a beat as he saw a familiar name. *Anne of Covington.*

"There are half a dozen by that moniker," he said aloud. "Our ancestors were most uninventive with names – half the girls were called Anne or Mary, and half the boys were called John."

But he kept reading.

Anne of Covington, famed for wedding both the second and third Earls of Longford, was ostensibly executed for heresy as was her first husband. However, it is likely that her death can be attributed just as much to the suspicious disappearance of her second husband. She is worthy of noting in this book because of the legacy of supernatural power she left behind...

And then it listed off several ridiculous feats that this Anne was supposed to have accomplished, such as healing the sick, flying on a broomstick, and calling upon the spirits of the dead.

But George had gone cold when it had specified her two husbands. His Anne had been only sixteen when he'd met her, and he'd *known* that the second marriage was about as passionate as a bowl of porridge. (It had also ended decisively when they'd left that second husband in the distant past along with some enormous, hungry predators. Oops.)

But while there were several women called Anne of Covington, there couldn't possibly have been more than one who'd married two Earls of Longford.

George leapt to his feet, spilling the book and tea onto the floor, then fumbled and turned back for the book before running out of the door. He slammed full-force into Prowd, then bounced back and almost hit the wall.

"In a hurry, are we sir?" Prowd asked politely. He didn't seem at all shaken by the collision, except that his neatly folded cravat was now askew. "The Viscount has requested your presence in his office at once."

"Not now," George said distractedly, trying to step around the man. "I have to find my wife."

"He was most insistent, sir, and said it was a matter of the utmost importance. Perhaps you might at least acknowledge his request?"

George didn't want to. Never mind Anne's predicament, he didn't want to be ordered about like a child, especially by his slightly older brother, but the politeness was ingrained. "Two minutes," he told Prowd.

He'd tell Edward to wait for later, then he'd find Ashlea, and together they'd find Anne and make demmed sure she never returned to her own time.

Her life depended on it.

Ash slept badly. Funny how she'd only shared a bed with George for three months, but not having him with her for one night just felt *wrong*.

After finally drifting off near dawn, she woke well into the day. The grandfather clock down the hall chimed eleven times, and she dragged herself out of bed to find that the little couch in the room next to hers was now empty. So was George's room, and his bed didn't look like it had been slept in.

He'd better be waiting for her down at breakfast, that's all she could say.

Ash got dressed in her modern-made regency gown, complete with frilly blue fabric and cunningly hidden zip, washed her face with scented rosewater (yes, really), pinned her wavy dark hair into a loose, era-appropriate bun, and headed downstairs for breakfast.

But George wasn't down in the breakfast room, or the library, or the quiet parlour where they'd spent a few comfortable moments together. There was no one else around either. Even the servants had disappeared, not counting the housekeeper who had brought her a re-warmed breakfast.

Growing increasingly irritated and perhaps a little concerned, Ash finally bumped into Olivia in the hall. The petite, slender blonde was in her mid-twenties and was rather pretty in her pale, lacy morning gown, but her greeting was as cold as ever.

There was no love lost there. In fact, Olivia insisted on calling Ash 'Mrs Seymour' and on Ash calling her 'Lady Morley'. Ash had now spent enough time in Regency Angland to know that between family members, this distance was a real insult. She couldn't stomach calling Olivia Lady anything, so simply didn't use her name at all.

"Good morning," Ash said warily. "I'm looking for George. Have you seen him?"

"I'm afraid Mr Seymour has already gone to his club," Olivia replied, but her gaze slid away from Ash's.

"His club," Ash echoed in dismay. "Already?"

The other woman raised her eyebrows but didn't comment, and Ash realised he must have forgotten about his late-night promise to go with her to the gateway. Or perhaps he'd changed his mind. "Did he say when he'd be back?"

"He's instructed the servants not to hold him a place at supper."

That was the evening meal, usually eaten as late as ten pm or even midnight: a real struggle with Ash's nine-to-five lifestyle. "But it's not even midday!"

Olivia shrugged in a very ladylike way. "Nevertheless."

She may as well have held up a sign saying 'You're not wanted' and Ash slumped in disappointment. She made a sudden decision. He didn't want to go with her? Fine. "Very well. I do believe I'll go out today too."

"Will you be wanting a maid? I've given them the day off."

Ash frowned. She didn't have a maid of her own because she found it weird having someone else choosing her clothes and helping her bath. She wasn't *infirm*. But there was a girl who'd help her with her hair and so forth every time she came to George's time. It felt like Olivia had stepped over the line by giving *Ash's* temporary maid the day off.

"No," Ash said finally. "Maids need time off too. I'll go on my own."

"Of course you will." And while there was nothing overtly rude in Olivia's tone, Ash knew she was being judged.

"I'm sure I'll enjoy the freedom all the more," she snapped back in her frostiest upper-class accent. "So don't hold a place at supper for me either. Perhaps you might stay home and embroider with the dowager viscountess, or whatever brings you pleasure. Good day."

She stiffened her back (easy in this horrible corset) and returned to her room, sitting down on her bed with a sigh and thinking of Anne. Anne had been far ruder than this when they'd first met, but she hadn't left Ash feeling small and worthless like some of the people here did.

That thought made Ash miss Anne even more. She hadn't seen the girl in a good three months, not since they'd had that time-travel mess where they'd ended up in the Mountain of Glass briefly along with Anne's sister Elspeth…except for one odd little meeting a month or two ago.

It had been early one Saturday morning right after she and George had been married. Ash had heard a sudden noise in the lounge room as though someone had turned on a television, and she'd come out to find Anne there along with a bunch of strangers in poofy old fashioned dress – oh, and a little yapping lapdog.

Anne had hugged her, apologised for the brevity of the visit, then vanished along with the rest of them, leaving behind only a puddle of wee in Ash's potted basil…hopefully from the dog. And that was the only physical proof Ash could show George that the encounter had actually happened. She hadn't seen Anne since.

Ash pushed that thought aside with a pang of regret. There were very few people who could understand what it felt like to be a time-traveller, to belong nowhere at all. Anne was one of those people, and Ash could only believe that one day they'd run into each other again. In the meantime, she'd try to have some fun.

Ash pulled out the outfit she kept hidden under her bed. The simple men's clothing had been a joke between George and herself, a reference to their first meeting where he'd mistaken her for a boy. She'd never had cause to wear it, but now seemed as good a time as any – as long as she could get out of the house without being caught. Otherwise, they'd really think she was perverted, or even mad. In her time a woman wearing trousers meant nothing much, but here it was *just not done*.

Ash rearranged the corset to create a different, flatter body shape, then slipped on the comfortable trousers and loose shirt and set the cap over her head, knowing that if anyone looked closely they wouldn't be fooled. But she wasn't trying that hard. She just wanted to get to that bookstore and take a good look at the remnant gateway in the street outside its front door.

And if there wasn't a gateway after all, and she'd been mistaken? Ash grinned. Perhaps she'd give Tolliver's bookseller's a visit after all.

Getting out of the house proved far easier than Ash expected. Again, there was a decided lack of servants, so she walked right out the house's back entrance without even being challenged. Then it was the matter of a brisk walk back towards the shopping district, taking care not to catch anyone's eye.

And there it was. The remnant gateway, about as high as her shoulder and shimmering like a heat wave even though the sky was grey, unseen by anyone except her. It was just on the street outside the bookstore, and it wasn't hidden by any meaning of the word. Ash knew that meant that someone had used the Eternity Stone to travel across time and space in that very place, as if they didn't care if anyone saw them.

Well, neither did she. She had a definite urge to see what was on the other side of that gateway, and who was to stop her? George didn't care, and his snobbish family certainly didn't either. She'd just make sure she wasn't gone too long, and who knew? Perhaps someone on the other side would find her a little more useful than anyone here.

Walking as though she had not a care in the world, Ash wandered towards the gateway. As she reached it, she took a deep breath and thought of *travelling*…

…and she was gone.

Checking that George's charlatan wife had truly left the house, Olivia quietly walked back to Edward's study where the two brothers were closeted with the doctors they had called in.

She and Edward had paid to bring them in urgently and in the utmost secrecy. If anyone found out that George was as mad as the Anglish king, it could ruin the reputation of the whole family and of whatever children she and Edward might have one day.

That last event seemed increasingly unlikely. The way she was feeling, she'd happily clobber her husband with a brick before letting him touch her again.

The servants had all been given the day off, except for the housekeeper, who Olivia trusted implicitly. She had said that Ashlea had left…dressed as a man, apparently. Olivia shook her head in disgust. That just confirmed they were doing the right thing, regardless of how she felt about it.

On the other side of the door, George sat in a comfortable chair at Edward's sturdy desk, twitching with agitation. Also at the desk sat two men: well dressed, but not extremely so, and both with an air of intelligence and self-importance. Doctors Farthing and Pennysworth, an excellent combination of names. Edward stood at the other side of the room, looking wearier than Olivia had ever seen him.

"I told you already," George argued. "This is my idea of a silly joke. Ashlea and I have joked about it many times, saying that she's so different from other women that she may as well be a time-traveller. I was short of sleep; I was angry and upset…I just said it for effect. I didn't expect to be taken seriously!" The last sentence was said with a roar and a sharp glare at his brother.

"What about last night?" Edward asked wearily. "You told me all this nonsense about meeting Ashlea in the future, and about evil queens or something or other. Don't tell me that was all a joke too."

George stared at him incredulously. "We were both drunk! I still have the headache to prove it, and even the sound of my own voice is causing me pain. How can you take anything I've said while in my cups as truth?"

He sounded sincere, but Olivia wasn't convinced. There was something wrong with his wife, something wrong with their relationship, and she wanted to find out what it was. But she didn't speak up. This was a men's thing, and she was fortunate to even be allowed in the room. Edward had allowed her in because he was still trying to sweeten her up, not that it was working.

The senior of the two, Dr Farthing, was a distinguished-looking gentleman with a lush grey moustache. He coughed to clear his throat, then said to Edward, "My lord, I do believe-"

But the rest of his words were drowned out by the strangest noise. It reminded Olivia of a mix of birdsong and a demented horn, and it was, quite frankly, impossible to miss.

Peep peep PARP peep peep PARP peep peep…

It started quietly, then grew steadily louder and louder…

"What on earth is that?" Edward exclaimed. "It sounds like it's coming from right inside this room."

"Don't be silly," George countered. "Do you think someone's hiding behind the bookshelves, blowing a whistle?"

The noise continued, growing louder to the point that no one could focus on anything else.

"I think it's coming from the desk," Dr Pennysworth suggested.

"What, a marching band hidden amongst the inkwells?" the older doctor scoffed.

Dr Pennysworth flushed, but then asked, "Is there a music box around here somewhere?"

"If there is, it isn't mine," Edward replied. "Is it yours,

George?"

George scowled. "No, of course not. I'm not in the habit of carrying around music boxes on my person, and if I was, I'd carry something that sounded less horrendous."

Finally the noise ceased, and everyone breathed sighs of relief. Olivia noted that the younger doctor still looked curious, though.

"As I was saying before," Dr Farthing began, "I do believe this investigation is at an end. I have no fear of saying this in front of you, my lord, my lady, but I am certain as can be that your brother is quite sane. He is certainly eccentric, but that is hardly anything to be concerned about." He gave George a nod. "I would recommend you mind your jokes in future, young man."

White-lipped and glowering, George nodded back.

Olivia couldn't help herself. "But what about his wife? I've heard her saying the strangest things…"

Dr Farthing scowled at her, and Edward shook his head. "We'll leave it be, madam. I do believe we've done enough harm for today."

The doctors stood to leave, and George stood with them. To Edward he said, "Might I have a word with you privately?"

"I'll see the doctors out," Olivia said quickly. "After all, the servants are off today."

She walked with them to the hall, closing the door firmly on what looked to be a rip-roaring argument.

As the three moved towards the front door, the younger doctor fell back to talk to her. "Naturally I didn't want to speak in front of the others," he said in hushed tones, "since my colleague doesn't seem to share my opinion. But I believe your concern is well-founded. When someone knows their beliefs will be considered mad and is intelligent enough to try to conceal them, then they're particularly difficult to treat. I believe that your brother-in-law is in imminent danger of a turn for the worse."

Olivia gasped, moving a hand to cover her mouth. "Is there anything we can do?"

Dr Pennysworth looked intently into her eyes. He wasn't unattractive, Olivia noted, although he was trying – and failing – to grow a moustache to rival his colleague's. "With situations like this, we need to use…stealth."

She listened as he outlined his plan, then nodded. "How soon can you do this?"

"How soon do you want it done?"

Not two minutes later George came storming out of the study, Edward trailing behind him. The latter wore a look of such dismay that Olivia felt her heart soften, just a little. He *did* care for his brother, but most people would never have to face such a situation as this.

George saw Olivia, then lifted his chin and walked straight out the front door where the doctors had only just exited. He closed it after him with a slam, making both Edward and Olivia cringe.

"Where did he go?" she asked.

"Who knows. His club, most likely, but he seemed in a dreadful hurry." Edward sighed in despair, scrubbing his hand over his face. "Well, it looks as though we got that one wrong, didn't we? I'll be lucky if he ever speaks to me again."

"Wrong?" Olivia echoed in disbelief. "Edward, the man rambled on at length about his adventures in the future. You told me what he said. He's clearly trying to cover for himself, but he can't take it back. He *does* believe it."

He looked at her with sad, irritated eyes. "He was deep in his cups, Livvy. I don't know what's going on with him; he's certainly been strange enough lately. But we clearly haven't helped. We need to let this go."

"You've always said that people speak the truth when drunk," Olivia argued. "George was just savvy enough to lie when he was confronted today. If we can explain to him that this is for his own good, that we mean him no harm…"

"I don't understand. You yourself believe that alter-power is far more widespread than most people realise. You've got your little club where you all meet to talk about it. Why does it bother you so much that George said what he said?"

"I haven't attended in months," she countered. After a while she'd seen the group for what they were – sad, hopeful eccentrics who wanted the world to be more than what it truly was. "What does that have to do with anything?"

Edward sighed. "I've really no idea. But I have the most dreadful headache, so I'm going to bed."

Olivia thought about what Dr Pennysworth had said, and she smiled gently. "Very well, Edward."

Then, after he had stumbled miserably to his bedroom, she quickly wrote a note, sealed it closed with a blob of wax, and set about finding a messenger to send it.

It read, *He's at Whytes. Go ahead as planned.*

A FRESH START

Anne studied her new surroundings in fascination. Now they'd left the narrower hall, they'd come out into a wide space where the walls were built of clean white marble, just a little sullied by time. 'Twas finer built than Anne's home of Renwick Castle, and certainly newer judging by its unfamiliar style.

But the greatest marvel was the open staircase filling the centre of the room, with ornate carved bannisters of the same white marble. It seemed to spin around and around on itself, like a picture of DNA Anne had seen in Ash's time.

"Clever, isn't it," Jon said flatly. "Two staircases winding around each other, and never meeting."

"What has you so sour?" she asked in surprise. "We are here, are we not?"

"We are here, yes, but I've no idea how much time has passed…and I haven't seen a single soul."

He had raised a fair point. But even as Anne pondered that, a young girl swept into the open space. She wore long, full skirts in a pretty white and floral pattern, and she had enormous, elaborately curled grey hair. 'Twould be a wig, Anne thought self-righteously, for the girl's lips were also redder than nature would allow, and her whole appearance was one of artifice.

Her kohled eyes widened in her powder-white face. "Jean-Louis! Our Jean-Louis, where have you been all this time?" she exclaimed in Frencine, the language automatically translating in Anne's mind.

Jon brightened a little. "Hello, Sophie-Ange," he said in some of the most mangled Frencine Anne had ever heard.

There was a slight silence where Anne waited for Jon to say something further, but he didn't, and finally Sophie-Ange reached forward and looped her arm around his. "I shall take you to the comtesse at once," she announced, and they swept away, Anne trailing behind and completely ignored.

Comtesse. That was Frencine for countess. *But I'm the countess too*, Anne thought whinily, then sighed. She did not appear a countess now, but just another of the no doubt numerous servants required to upkeep such a large building. The girl had not so much as looked at her.

They turned only a few times amongst the numerous halls before they reached a room. This one gave the impression of being more ornately decorated than the others, but upon closer inspection Anne realised 'twas simply those inside that made it seem so.

There were mayhap a dozen folk inside; nobles by the look of their ornate garb. They wore towering grey or white curled wigs adorned with every kind of decoration, frills from neckline and bust and sleeves, and every available colour of cloth.

A dozen sets of eyes turned to stare at them from a dozen powdered, beauty-marked faces. These men and women were all dressed in more splendour than Anne had seen since she'd visited the court of Queen Henrietta the Eighth as a child.

But she didn't see the arrogance she would have expected from such a crowd. Instead they seemed fearful, and Anne noticed the slightly soiled, worn nature of their garb, as though it had not been changed in some time.

Everyone began to speak at once in rapid Frencine, and a young woman climbed to her feet, gracefully shifting her wide, silvery skirts. She looked to be several years into her third decade, with an innocent beauty emphasized by her white wig, pale clothing and powdered skin. "My angel!" she cried, silencing everyone else. "Where did you go? We thought you were dead!"

"We thought he'd found a way of escape," a middle-aged man muttered next to her. "Either that or turned traitor."

"He can't answer you, my lady," Sophie-Ange said in exasperation, proving that the woman in silver must be the comtesse. "You know he doesn't speak Frencine."

As if to prove the point, Jon said again, a little awkwardly; "Hello. I am well. Hello."

Anne had been silent, almost hidden behind the other two, but now she exploded. "Jon, you do not speak Frencine? How can you possibly have known what's going on?"

"Who is *that*?" an older lady asked cattily. She held a small, half-hairless dog cradled in her arms like a babe. It reminded Anne unpleasantly of her sister-in-law Blanche's pet – good only for biting ankles and relieving itself in inappropriate locations.

"I don't know, she came with Jon and appears to be Anglish," Sophie-Ange said impatiently. Then to Anne; "He can't understand you. He barely speaks Frencine."

In truth, Anne had not realised she was speaking Frencine. The others had spoken; she had replied in the same manner.

"I do actually understand some of it," Jon countered in another language, his cheeks a bit red with embarrassment. The words tumbled through Anne's ears, quickly making sense as her marvellous translation device processed them. "I just don't speak much Frencine, that's all."

"Oh," Anne replied to Jon in the same language he'd just spoken. "What language are we speaking now, then?"

"It's Mesianth, the language of Erus Province. It's the only one I know." He looked exasperated. "How can you speak it and not know what it is?"

Anne lifted her chin. "I speak any language; 'tis a gift. I'm certain I've said that before. And how can *you* have lived in this place – if you truly did live here – and not speak the native tongue? You called these people your friends-"

"They *are* my friends. They looked after me in one of the darkest times in my life, and I owe them everything. But I didn't choose to come here, just as you and Bets didn't choose to leave your own time, and I'll do the little I can to help. Even if they don't understand me." Jon folded his arms, pink with embarrassment but looking very decisive.

"What are they saying?" the comtesse was asking the others. "Who is that person?"

That was when Anne made a decision of her own. "Very well," she told Jon in Mesianth. "I shall be your spokesperson, and we shall save your friends." Then to the room at large, in Frencine, "I am Lady Anne of Covington, and I have brought your Jean-Louis across time and space to rescue you from your plight."

There was a stunned silence, and then to Anne's shock the whole room burst into derisive laughter. "She's mad," the man next to the comtesse said scornfully. "Or she thinks we're babes who can be so easily fooled. How much does she want to be paid?"

"I don't require payment," Anne tried to say, but no one seemed to hear her over the din.

Beside her Jon said dolefully in Mesianth, "I thought it might go this way. Only Nadine and her lover ever believed that I'd been brought here by alter-power, and he disappeared weeks ago. The others all thought I was being paid to play a part."

"Who's Nadine?"

"The comtesse d'Auran. My betrothed."

Anne's jaw dropped. "Betrothed?!"

"Oh, come now, I did tell you I was betrothed. Besides, it's not a real betrothal. I did just tell you that she has a lover, didn't I?"

Had he told her he was betrothed? She did not recall, and it seemed like something she ought to remember. She knew many betrothed and married folk who had extra-marital lovers, but *their* marriages were perfectly legal. Her own to Edgar was one such case – before he was devoured by terrible lizards, that was.

But Anne could not make sense of her new knowledge that the pure, white, powdered Nadine was Jon's betrothed, so she focussed instead on the other problem. "How shall I get them to believe me? I know, I shall show them a doorway!"

"Are there any in this room?"

She checked. "Not that I can see. I must find a new one, for we cannot use the one we just travelled through. We must take them somewhere safe, but in the same time period."

"What's she saying?" someone was asking in Frencine.

Anne staunchly ignored them. "Tell them I shall be back in ten minutes," she told Jon.

He sighed, but held up his hands, all fingers spread. "Is OK," he said in Frencine to the watching crowd.

Anne sighed in much the same way. "I shall return anon," she told them in Frencine. "I shall prove to you that we can help you. You *are* in rather a spot of trouble."

Without waiting for a response, she picked up her long skirts and hurried from the room, searching for the tell-tale shimmer that would mark a remnant gateway.

But as she did so, the enormity of their mission struck her. That she would find another gateway to the correct location – well, 'twould be a true miracle.

Anne scurried from the room, reminding Jon as she often did of a small, quick squirrel. She was quite pretty, he supposed, but she lacked the essential sweetness of her sister. In a lot of ways she made him nervous.

But their situation right now made him even more nervous. He'd come back here after what had to be at least a month away, and if he'd heard Sophie-Ange right, to them he'd only been gone two days. What had he missed?

Jon considered following Anne, then smiled down at Nadine, trying to show in his expression what they intended to do. She looked confused but trusting (her usual manner when speaking to Jon), and smiled back at him sadly. "We *something something, something* dead," she said. "*Something* at once."

He stared at her in confusion, wishing once again that he understood more Frencine. He saw when she gave up, patting him on the arm with a sigh. "*Something something* Jean-Louis."

That was the name they'd given him when he'd arrived, and it had only the slightest resemblance to his real name. But then the role he'd been playing had only the slightest resemblance to his real life, didn't it? Pretending to be a prince, but on the inside knowing he was nothing like that.

Jon smiled awkwardly at Nadine again, then gave the rest of the room a brief nod before turning and hurrying after Anne.

He caught up to her not far down one of the halls off the central room. She was staring assessingly at an empty space, her dark eyes narrowed. "Look at this," she said without turning towards him. "There is a series of gateways here, and I'd vow they were made by the Eternity Stone directly as well as by Amaranthus and his ilk. But I know not where they go, and that is the central matter, is it not?"

Jon couldn't see the gateways, but he believed that she could. "So what are we supposed to do? Check every single one?"

"I do not see what other choice we have." Anne looked just as displeased with this as Jon did.

"Is this what you always do?" he asked in disbelief. "It's a bit hit and miss, isn't it?"

"Usually I don't have to *find* somewhere in particular," she muttered. "There must be millions of possible destinations. 'Twill take an eternity."

"Just start with one at a time," Jon suggested reasonably. "I'll guard you."

She rolled her eyes. "Very well. I may be a few minutes, as 'twill most likely take more than one gateway to get to another location in the same time. Ah…what year *is* it?"

"1793 AD by their calendar."

"1793," Anne repeated decisively. "I shall find another location in a similar time."

"Not a similar time," Jon tried to say. "The *same* time."

But she'd already gone, and he stood alone in the wide hall, guarding empty space.

He wasn't alone for long. Almost on cue, as soon as Anne vanished, another woman appeared. This one was slightly older – perhaps twenty or so – and quite stunningly beautiful. Madame Roelle was rumoured to be the mistress of a royal, if he'd understood correctly in his very poor Frencine.

He didn't know what brought the dark-haired, green-eyed lady out to this castle in its quiet valley, but she was always on the edge of things, not quite included by the others, yet seeming not at all bothered by her isolation. Today she wore her black hair unpowdered, and a single black jewel hung around her white neck. Her gown was blood-red, matching her smiling lips.

"*Something something something,* Jean-Louis."

Jon smiled at her awkwardly, feeling rather like a rabbit before a fox. There was something predatory about this girl, although she couldn't be more than a couple of years older than him. "No Frencine. Sorry," he replied in his best, mangled Frencine. And besides, his name wasn't Jean-Louis.

"I said," she repeated in fluent Mesianth, "we missed you these past few weeks. Where did you go?"

"I thought it was only…two days…" Jon's jaw dropped as he realised how she'd spoken. "Chaos. Are you another time-traveller, or do you have a gift with languages?"

"Both, of course." She smiled at him cheekily. "But you didn't answer my question. Where did you go two days ago? You simply disappeared."

He'd been supernaturally taken away from here just as he'd arrived. But he didn't want to tell this woman that; just because she was a traveller didn't mean she was trustworthy. He'd heard enough tales from other travellers in the Garden to know that, as well as his own experience back home.

"Who are you?" he asked instead. "Are you really the king's mistress?"

"That weak-blooded boy? I think not. But I see that you haven't heard. The king was executed last week, and we've only just received word. There's no doubt that if Chamborde wasn't so isolated, the nobles here would already be in the same position."

Jon's heart sank. The king had been executed – the others here would be desperate with fear. "The revolutionaries want to destroy the upper class," he said in dismay.

"You know, it's not just the nobles being killed," she continued in a confidential tone. "It's anyone who says or does the wrong thing. There are peasants being executed for hoarding. *Hoarding,* would you believe it? And I hear that the comtesse's common-law husband was supposed to find a way for this lot to escape to Angland – you may have missed that, what with your unfortunate language barrier – but no one's heard from him at all. One would almost think he'd died." Madame Roelle gave a careless shrug. "But that's life, isn't it? And you still didn't answer my question, Jean-Louis."

"You didn't answer mine," he countered.

The two of them stood there, almost eye to eye – she was a tall woman – and then she sighed as though giving in. "Very well. I shall tell you…" She ran her hand gently up the side of his face. There was a sudden intense pain, and then he couldn't move. There was something around his neck, something growing tighter and tighter…

"I'm learning," Madame Roelle whispered into his ear even as he silently choked, "that the more mysterious the circumstances, the more likely you'll flood me with alter-power when you die. Nothing personal, you understand."

The edges of Jon's vision began to blur, and he knew he was passing out. Surely when you died you should be able to struggle more, to make an effort? But she was killing him as easily as one would swat a buzzing fly.

Suddenly the world was brilliant white and gold, and someone was screaming. Then the tightness around his neck loosened and Madame Roelle's lovely face so close to his began to change; smooth skin bulging with wart-like lumps, green eyes turning milky, hair fading away as she *screamed*-

Then she was grasping that black jewel at her neck, and she winked out of sight, leaving Jon blinking from the bright light and with a dreadfully sore throat. There was the faint smell of burning, and Anne's worried voice in his ear. But she was babbling and he couldn't understand a word of it, even as her small hands patted his throat as though she could heal it.

"In Mesianth," he choked out.

But Anne kept babbling unintelligibly, and finally he could see that it wasn't Anne at all. It was her younger sister; very similar in appearance, but with dark hair and green eyes rather like Madame Roelle's, except filled with worry rather than murderous intent.

"Bets," he managed to say.

How had she got here? And what had she done to Madame Roelle?

"'Tis no good," Elspeth told Jon in disappointment. "You clearly do not understand a word I have said to you."

She'd known it could be a possibility; that if by some miracle she and Jon were to meet outside of the Mountain, there would be a language barrier. She just hadn't thought 'twould be *now*, when she'd had the most marvellous gift bestowed, and had just chased away a villain! She could not even explain it to him.

"Anne," he said, and she understood that much. He still had a red ring around the pale skin of his neck.

"Anne, yes?"

Jon gestured at the air, and Elspeth realised he must mean she'd gone through yet another gateway.

"What dreadful timing," she said with a sigh. "And here we are in your Frencia, not able to understand a word spoken."

Then Anne returned. She stepped out into the hall, appearing with that slight shimmer that told of a gateway in use, and with a most startled expression. "Bethie? Whatever has brought *you* here?"

Elspeth folded her arms a little defensively. "Besides saving Jon from being murdered by the evil queen? Following *you*. You needn't have left without me, you know. I can help." In fact, she just had.

Anne blinked in that way she did when she was puzzled. "Evil queen?"

"The one who almost killed us in the Other, right before we escaped and came to the Mountain. I think her name was Sane?"

"Seyen Johannis," Anne repeated in shock. "You say she was here, in this very place?"

Jon said something in his own language, and for a few moments he and Anne exchanged words, clearly explaining what had happened. It frustrated Elspeth that she would have such a barrier – but then she'd been born with barriers of birth, gender and disability. What was one more?

"What are you saying?"

Anne shook her head, her lips turned downwards. "He says that the king's mistress tried to kill him, then turned into a monster and vanished."

"Indeed," Elspeth agreed with satisfaction. "But 'twas because I fired her that she left."

"Fired her?"

Elspeth tried to explain what had happened, although she did not quite understand herself. When she'd seen he was under attack, and she'd recognised the woman at once as a younger version of the villain she'd so recently faced, something odd had happened.

A wonderful warmth had shot out from her hands like rays of the sun, and then the woman and Jon had been aglow for a moment before the woman disappeared and Jon had been freed. It was a gift called 'fire', and 'twas clearly a fire of alter-power only, but an effective one.

"I'll show you, see?" Elspeth held out one hand, feeling the warm tingle of the flame like hot water in her palm.

"What is it, Bethie? Are you pointing at something?"

"No, 'tis a sort of flame in my hand…" But 'twas evident that her sister did not see and so did not understand, so Elspeth sighed. "I shall show you later, in the Mountain. But now we must move, for 'tis clear that Amaranthus was wrong. Seyen Johannis *is* alive, and therefore we are in danger."

"But he's never wrong about things like that," Anne countered, still shaking her head. "Never. And he said she *was* dead, but it depended…"

"*When* you looked," Elspeth finished. They exchanged puzzled glances, trying to make sense of it. Either way, it did not look good. "So she *is* still a danger," she said glumly. "For 'tis evident she is alive and well. Mayhap not as well as she was before I fired her, but-"

"Bethie," Anne cut in abruptly. "'Tis a problem indeed, and I suspected that our freedom from her had come too easily. But now she has left, and we have an immediate challenge. We must find a gateway to the correct time, but 'tis a most monumental task."

When Elspeth would have queried Sane-Seyen's presence again, Anne added, "And once we return to the Mountain, we shall challenge Amaranthus on that witch-queen, have no doubt. But we must focus on what is before us."

'Twas a fair point. Elspeth put aside her lingering fear about the witch-queen and did as she was asked. "That is why you ought to have asked me to come with you," she said, unable to hide her pride at her new discovery. She held up the insect that had led her here. "Look."

Even Jon looked, for this one was not invisible, at least. The tiny beetle sat in her palm, only as big as her smallest nail, and blinking gold and green.

"What manner of thing is that?" Anne asked.

"I've been calling it a gate-bug," Elspeth replied happily. "It shone pure green and led me through the gateway to you. I trow it shall lead us wherever we need to go."

There was another quick exchange of speech between the other two, and Anne said in satisfaction. "Jon said 'tis called a sentinel, and that he was led to the Mountain by one. He never used the Eternity Stone, so they must enable people to move through Amaranthus's gateways also."

Elspeth preferred the name gate-bug, but she supposed that 'sentinel' was more dignified. Still, 'twas encouraging to know she had guessed correctly.

"By the by," Anne continued in Anglish, "with the sentinel's help we shall find our gateway, and we'll show those snobby Frogs what's what."

Elspeth let out a startled giggle. "Anne!"

"What? 'Tis not as though *he* can understand me." But when they began to move, as if to punish Anne's rudeness she suddenly stumbled on the seemingly smooth floor. She'd stepped on a silver stick about as long as her hand, and only as thick as her little finger. One end glowed white as she picked it up. "How odd. This clearly doesn't belong here."

"*She* must have dropped it," Elspeth deduced, for it had lain in the place the evil queen had stood. "'Tis without doubt a wicked thing. You must dispose of it at once."

Anne studied it, then shrugged, moving to throw it over one shoulder.

"Anne!" Elspeth frowned at her sister mightily. "Anyone might find that, and who knows what manner of harm it may cause!"

"By the saints, Bethie, who is the elder sister here?" But Anne still slipped the thing in the front pocket of her plain gown. "Now, to find the right gateway."

Bethie's sentinel/gate-bug glowed green on the dozenth gateway they passed, and Anne took a quick glance through to make sure 'twas not a fiery pit or something equally awful.

Where it *actually* led to? Well, 'twas quite a lovely surprise, but clearly only a stopping point. They'd need to use more than one gateway to find their destination.

That was the easy part. The hard part was getting Jon's friends to listen. It took true courage for Anne to return to the room where she'd been laughed at, but she did it, this time with Jon and Elspeth in her lovely, era-appropriate gown.

Anne targeted the person most likely to listen: Jon's annoyingly pure-looking betrothed.

The comtesse D'Auran looked surprised to see them back, but interested. "I thought you had given up and left," she said.

"Of course not," Anne replied briskly. "But we have found a way out, if your people are inclined to take it. 'Twill require trust and an immediate exit. Unless you have something better to do?"

Nadine's wide, light blue eyes grew even wider. "We do not. I shall tell the others, and we will come at once." She paused. "Are you a celestial?"

Everything in Anne wanted to agree in that moment, for 'twould have given her a place well above all these painted, befrilled Frencine aristos. But she shook her head. "No, but I have the ear of one who may as well be a celestial."

It seemed a lost cause for the first few moments. Jon's friends argued and wavered and in a few cases, cried; and then finally something odd happened. Elspeth had been holding the now faintly glowing sentinel in her open palm, and for the first time it flicked open previously unseen wings, the whole thing lighting up a vivid shade of purple as it took to the air. It flashed green and purple, green and purple, until it had gained the whole room's attention, then very slowly turned and buzzed its way out of the door.

There was a stunned silence, and Nadine lifted her chin. "I shall follow it," she said staunchly. "If you all wish to have your heads cut off, then do so, but I have no fear of taking this chance when it's presented."

In that moment Anne actually respected the woman. Mayhap countesses ought to stick together, hmm? But that brief respect faded back when Nadine began crying the moment they left the room.

"It's my Francois," she wept. "He went to find an escape route two weeks ago, heading north. We plan to go to Angland, you understand, but we have not seen him since. If we go now…"

"If we don't go now, then we'll face revolutionary justice just the same," snapped the older lady with the dog. Anne realised with some surprise that several of the others had followed them out here. "The rabble would be here already if it wasn't so isolated, and they'd be stealing whatever they wanted. Francois knew the risk he was taking."

Nadine nodded but cried harder, causing Jon and Elspeth to look quite worried. Anne could hear the two of them muttering about it in the background – Jon had guessed the topic of discussion correctly, but of course Elspeth could not understand him. There was only one thing to do, unfortunately.

Anne patted the woman on her befrilled arm. "Never fear. We shall find him."

The comtesse looked up, hope filling her wet eyes. "You can do that?"

"Naturally." Although Anne's fingers were crossed in hope behind her back. They *would* make it work, yes…?

But with the comtesse's agreement, the remaining aristocrats seemed more compliant. Well, not quite all aristos – there was at least one other dressed as Anne now was, and of course the ankle-biting dog. They followed Anne, Elspeth and Jon to the gateway on the other side of the castle. It sat in the middle of a plastered wall, clear as day to Anne, but no doubt unseen by the others. Mayhap 'twas curiosity that led them to follow.

"So what must we do?" Elspeth whispered worriedly to Anne. Next to her, Jon said much the same thing, except in another language.

Anne answered them both, then repeated her words in Frencine. "Elspeth, you go first with the sentinel. We must all hold hands, or we shan't get through."

The first attempt ended up with only Elspeth and Anne going through. Jon had lost grip of Nadine's hand, who seemed quite baffled by the idea of walking into a wall, and so had stopped halfway through the gateway. That of course led to Anne having to return, and some of the doubt was removed upon seeing them reappear apparently from nowhere.

In the end Anne did three trips. Three to drag the whole group of fearful, complaining aristos through the gateway and to their stopover, a small – very small – but familiar dwelling in the early twenty-first century. Anne felt a pang of homesick excitement. She hadn't been *here* in several weeks, and it felt like much longer.

"Where on earth are we?" someone asked curiously.

"Halfway," Anne replied briefly. She was looking around cautiously, hoping that the house's occupant wasn't there *quite* yet… "Never fear. No one will try to kill us in this place."

The owner of the house was nowhere in sight. Anne hadn't seen her in, oh, about two weeks? She hadn't been *here* in what felt like years.

Meanwhile the dozen Frencine aristocrats (plus servant, dog, Elspeth, and Jon, and minus Madame Roelle) looked around in confusion.

"Great Deias! What have you done to us?"

"Where are we?"

"What is that thing there? It looks evil." (One person was pointing at the tee-vee.)

"My little Chaussin needs to peepee. Now."

The last statement from the lady with the lapdog bothered Anne more than the others, so she pointed the woman towards one of the open windows. The woman's kohled eyes bulged in shock, but Anne didn't have time for that. She needed to get some order here and to find the next gateway, before Ash came in and got *very* upset.

Jon tapped Anne on the shoulder. "Please tell me you know where the next gateway is, because I'd swear that this isn't anywhere near 1793."

No, only about two centuries off.

"I shall find it soon enough," she replied airily, then switched into Anglish. 'Twas tiring changing languages all the time. "Elspeth, you shall look for the next gateway with your sentinel, yes?"

"I'm already doing so," the girl replied staunchly. Her garb had changed to a simple tunic top and rough denim skirt of the type Ash had often worn, but she hadn't seemed to have noticed the change. Anne's own garb had changed similarly, except for her shoes…

"…don't know how on earth we got here, this horrid little place…"

"…she expected me to hold him out the window! Well, I just used this odd plant thing instead…"

"…hush, she is going to tell us something!"

Anne felt mildly depressed about the chaos around her (which she appeared to have wrought herself) but then a wonderful opportunity occurred to her.

But before she could carry it out, BANG! The door slammed open, and she turned to look along with everyone else. The owner of the house stood there, clothed in that ugly garb she called pee-jays, and with a stunned look on her face.

Anne tried to look innocent. "Good morrow, Ashlea. I can explain...?"

The Other, 2597 AD

"Wait a moment," Trennan interrupted, trying to make sense of what he'd just been told. "Are you saying that the Fey are *blood-drinkers*? And the Chosen know about it!?"

"At least some of them are," Evers replied in his clipped manner, the orange light from the fire pit giving him a ghoulish air. "And at least some of the leaders do, although I won't name names at present. I wouldn't have believed it myself, boy, except that it makes sense of so much. Why people come back with those odd bruises – bruises I've had myself, as little as I'd like to feel like some kind of snack – and why others don't come back at all. Some of them, good men and women, just disappear…and we're never told why."

"We're just told to accept it," Jan added. "And we did, because it was all we'd ever known. After all, the Other is dangerous, and full of wonderful and terrible things. No one will gainsay that. Until we found this place, and it didn't seem *right* to tell those leaders when we know they can't be trusted. So many lies we've caught them in over the years. So many. But you, boy, with the volcano-"

"That wasn't my fault," Trennan said automatically, as he had many times before. But the thoughts of *blood-drinker* kept running through his head. And what lies had been told?

Evers rolled his eyes. "You can't cause a volcano, boy. All I meant is that you *ask questions*, and you see through illusion. And so here you are, and here we are."

Trennan looked down once more at the pit before them, feeling the warmth that came from it. As before, he could smell flowers and perhaps even baking bread, but the idea that it might be a trap was ever-present in his mind. "I can't do it," he said finally. "I don't trust my own eyes that this *isn't* illusion. It just goes against all common sense."

Jan sighed, sitting down beside the pit against one of the twisted sculptures of who-knew-what. "It's the Other," he said simply. "Forget your common sense. But do what you want, boy. We'll wait for Meric."

"You really think he's going to come back?"

"Sure as Hades hope so," Jan replied. "Or we'll be turned into ice sculptures of our own, in time."

A tingle of unease ran through Trennan, and he took a closer look at the nearest ice sculpture. It was twisted and blue-black/orange where the light hit it, but it wouldn't take great imagination to see it as a corpse. A drained, frozen corpse…ugh.

He craned his neck sideways, trying to make sense of it, but the closer he looked, the more it seemed constructed. Through the dark ice perhaps was some kind of wood or carved stone?

"Ruins," he announced in dawning enlightenment. "Someone used to live here." Well, of course they had. The Other used to be populated before the Fire Lord turned it into an empty wasteland…or so the Fey said.

The two knights didn't respond, and he turned to see them

descending down the rope into the pit, their armour abandoned. Jan was already halfway out of sight, and Evers was holding the other end steady. "Hey, what are you doing?!"

"Having a look for ourselves," Evers replied. "Waiting seems a waste, don't you think? Either he's dead – or soon will be – or we're missing out on something worth knowing. We're going to find out."

"But you could die," Trennan pointed out just as Jan disappeared into the orange glow. He didn't feel as alarmed as he might otherwise, the fear of moments before overwhelmed with curiosity. "Meric might already be dead."

"Got to die sometime, boy. And I'd rather burn than be bled like a stuck pig."

Trennan watched in silence as they descended, and then finally it was just him and the rope, alone in the desert of fire and ice. "Hades," he said aloud, just so he didn't feel quite so alone. "They never told me what the lies were."

Then he sat where Jan had sat, leaning back against the not-cold ice sculpture, and watched the orange glow, and thought. He thought about the little stupidities of the leadership (which all leadership had, but some were more forgivable than others) and the way Jurgis and the others had given pronouncements but never reasons why, and yes, the way people *did* disappear (including half a dozen of the kids Trennan had grown up with) and others would change…

And the Fey. Trennan thought about the Fey, and about how sharing the Other with them was like swimming in shark-infested waters. Maybe they'd ignore you, maybe they'd be curious (did sharks even get curious?) or maybe, just maybe, they'd take a bite – and then you were done for.

He wasn't sure how that metaphor worked for his mother, who'd been only a teenager when she'd gone into the Other on her own accord – not as one of the Chosen – and had come out shell-shocked and with a belly the size of a beach ball. Not long after he was born she'd wandered off again. He didn't know if she was alive. He wouldn't recognise her if he saw her, that was for sure. And she hadn't volunteered to have him, that was for sure as well.

So Trennan had darkness in his blood. Not his choice, but that was the way things had gone. He was just lucky he didn't look like so many of the other Halflings, and that someone like Coryn actually loved him…

A warm breeze wafted from the pit, bringing with it a swirl of tiny white things. One landed on his folded leg, and he picked it up curiously. It crushed between his fingers, letting out another little burst of scent. It was a petal.

"Hades," he said to himself. If that wasn't a hint, then what was? "I'll take my armour and my sword," he decided aloud. After all, he might have to rescue the three older knights.

But from what?

SEVEN
THE RIVER OF LIFE

No longer Lunden 1818 AD

Ash stepped briskly through the remnant gateway outside of (rude, sexist) Tolliver's bookstore, leaving Regency Lunden behind.

It briefly occurred to her that she really shouldn't go wandering through random gateways alone and without warning – as divers shouldn't dive alone, and so on – but she stubbornly dismissed that thought. She was grumpy and hurt, damn it, and she was going to do what she wanted to do, even if she might regret it later on. Wasn't that the whole point of storming off in a huff?

And anyway, George would know where she'd gone, and he could just darn-well come after her if he wanted to.

Unfortunately the other side of the gateway wasn't much of an improvement from the streets of old Lunden. Ash was surrounded by grey concrete studded with green and yellow moss, and what looked like litter blown about by the wind. High buildings rose up on every side, extending so high above her that they almost blocked out the sun, and with their once-bright paint almost worn off. It wasn't cold, precisely, but neither was the temperature cosy.

Ash sighed, wrapping her cloak tightly around herself. At

least she hadn't been seen coming through this gateway, right? The gateway to who-knew-where. If this was a horror movie, Ash would have been slapping herself for her curiosity overriding her intelligence.

But because it wasn't a movie, and because she wasn't a complete idiot, she pulled out her mobile phone. The reception was at one bar, so she crossed her fingers and dialled George's number.

The phone rang a few times then went to voicemail. "Hi, it's me," she said. "Obviously. So, because you apparently forgot what you promised last night, I've gone to check out that new gateway by myself. Just to have some space, because I'm not leaving you." She paused, then added, "And I do love you. Join me, if you want. Or not. Bye."

With her wifely duty done, Ash took another look at her surroundings. Then she realised she wasn't alone after all. There was a man standing nearby; Europaen in colouring, lank-haired and slightly dull-eyed; and he grinned when he met her eye. She gave him an awkward nod which he seemed to take as flirtation, because he started to move towards her.

Whoops. *No thank you…*

As casually as Ash could manage, she wandered over to the nearest building, which had black glass doors set right at ground level. Something was written in bold, shiny letters above them, but she couldn't read the script. The doors slid open as she approached and she stepped right through into darkness, a whiff of damp wind blowing at her face and giving her chills. "Hello?"

Then suddenly she was being blasted with sensations and light and conflicting sounds, all at once, like travelling through dozens of gateways one after the other. She couldn't make sense of them and couldn't grab onto a single one, and couldn't escape from it either.

Oh crap, she thought desolately in the middle of all that chaos. If she had gone through multiple gateways and couldn't retrace her steps, she could be *anywhere*…at any time. Funny, because all she really wanted right now was to go home and give her mum a hug.

Abruptly the chaos ceased, and Ash was surrounded by bright daylight. She was once again standing outside, this time on the tidy concrete of a city waterfront. The buildings here were of a familiar, glass-heavy style, with green hills visible behind and a huge drop before her leading down to a harbour. Her heart leapt. Was it…?

No, it wasn't home, she realised a moment later, but it was some place like it. Her fear now replaced by curiosity, Ash began to walk.

Lile, 2597 AD

Magdalene and Poli were waiting at the edge of the Empty Zone, just outside the faint orange line that had been painted decades before to mark its location.

Kamile drove up in her two-seater, then climbed out to meet them. "How did you get here?"

Magdalene held up her wrist to show the watch-sized band so favoured by children in particular. "We flew."

Kamile recognised it immediately even though the Fey had forbidden its use within the Compound. The girl wore a matching band on her other wrist and both ankles. They didn't look like much, but the devices called 'anti-gravity wing-bands' (or more casually, just 'wings') could literally make you fly.

The name came because when you spread your arms while wearing them, a haze of light would briefly appear between waist and wrist, like a shimmering set of wings. They were incredibly popular with the more lightweight locals. Anything more and the hover function wasn't strong enough to hold up the body. But children and teenagers especially could fly like celestials.

Wings were expensive, though. Kamile didn't know how both girls could have afforded to buy them, but she suspected they hadn't paid at all.

"Alright," she said. "Now, where shall we start?"

"I heard it was in the north-west sector," Poli ventured. "I think if we got near the entry, I could recognise it."

"What are we looking for?" Entries to the Other realm didn't usually look obvious, so could remain well-hidden for decades.

Poli shrugged a little self-consciously. "I'll know it when I see it."

Which meant she didn't know. Kamile smiled anyway. "Fine. I should be able to sense that sort of thing when I'm near it, so that should help." If it existed.

"OK," Magdalene said cautiously. "I just have one question…"

"Yes?"

"Why did you agree to come so soon? We thought that you thought this was all…you know, wishful thinking."

Kamile looked at her feet. She didn't want to tell the girls what had really spurred her here. They weren't quite children, but she still didn't want them to think less of her, or even worse, try it themselves.

"I don't know," she answered finally. "I got sick of my life as it is, I suppose. I figure that if there is something better out there, something better than the Other as I've seen it, then I'm interested.

May as well give it a try."

"That's good enough for me," Magdalene replied cheerfully. "Shall we start?"

The Empty Zone was called that because (surprise surprise) no one lived there. It was one of those wide spaces where destructive weapons had been dropped during the Great War of the late twenty-first century.

The biologically-based weapons of mass destruction had killed every living thing in these areas, and while the government now assured people that the toxin levels were too low to do any serious damage, it was still uninhabited.

Well, except for vagrants, stray animals, and people like Kamile and her two companions. People who wanted what might be in there enough to risk the danger.

They went block by ruined block, the girls at first flying overhead with their possibly stolen wings, but then realising that they couldn't see anything from up high. Kamile felt a little envy at their sheer enjoyment of the devices, though the one time she had used them in her teens (outside the Compound, of course) she'd felt very nervous. Flying was for birds and air vehicles, she'd said at the time, and she hadn't changed her mind since.

Down on the ground the going was slower, but they didn't give up. They'd been searching for several hours, with day turning into dusk, when Poli suddenly cried out, "This is it! I can see it!"

Kamile and Magdalene quickly ran to her, but Kamile stepped back in confusion when she saw Poli was standing in front of yet another half-ruined, moss-covered building. There was a closed door which perhaps had once been wood, and next to it ran a dribble of clear water from a tiny little broken pipe sticking out of the brick.

"This?" Kamile said in disbelief. "Poli, this is hardly a *river*."

The girl shook her head distractedly. "No, it's on the other side. Can't you hear it?"

Kamile wanted to say that all she could hear was the incessant birdsong that came with sunset, but then she closed her eyes and *listened* with more than just her ears.

And she heard it. A rushing sound, the sort only caused by large bodies of water and which couldn't be confused for anything else.

Next to her, Poli reached up a hand cautiously to the door. She twisted the old handle, which despite its incredible age didn't come off in her hand, and then the door swung open without a sound, and Poli disappeared. The door was once again closed, and only Kamile and Magdalene remained.

Magdalene stared at Kamile with wide eyes. Suddenly her bravery was all gone. "Do you think she's alright?"

"I don't know," Kamile replied numbly. She hadn't been able to sense this place at all. It didn't feel like the Other or the Borderlands. They reeked of an unmissable alter-power, but this was completely different. No wonder she hadn't noticed it before.

Insatiably curious, Kamile reached up to turn the handle. And the moment she did, everything changed.

The other side of the door was like another world. Kamile was standing on the grassy banks of a wide, flat river; so wide that the other side disappeared into mist. She could hear sounds from over there, like there was a party going on, and she could smell food.

But on this side there was just the long, wide shore, and the edge of the clear, clear water, reflecting the blue of the cloudless sky. There was no Other twilight here. The water looked beautiful, like liquid diamonds, but somehow it also scared her at the same time.

Ahead of her, Poli was crouched down drinking at the water's edge, and Kamile took a step towards her to do the same. But then she glanced behind her and saw that the door they'd come in through had disappeared, and Magdalene was standing wide-eyed on the other side of it.

"Magdalene."

The other girl jumped. "Kamile?" They were standing on either side of the doorway, but Magdalene had a distinct look of confusion on her face. "Where did you come from? It was like you appeared out of nowhere."

"I came to get *you*," Kamile replied. "Come on. It's worth the look. We came all this way, didn't we?"

"What do I do?" the younger girl asked in panic. "Will you help me come through?"

"Sorry, Magdalene. I'm pretty sure you have to do this one yourself. But we'll be right there! Won't it be better to come through with us now than wait out here with the mangy dogs and vagrants?"

The girl looked around in panic, and Kamile realised her joke had backfired. "Just kidding. But come on! You can do it. Just reach up and turn the handle."

As slowly as if moving through water, Magdalene obeyed, and then suddenly she was on the other side of the doorway. "We did it," she breathed, looking around in amazement.

"We did," Kamile agreed. She felt a little fearful and teary-eyed herself, even though she was already on the other side. She still had to drink the water…and she would, she assured herself, but she just needed a little time first. She would help Magdalene come to terms with where they were, and then they could walk over together – no thanks to Poli.

But when Kamile looked up, Magdalene was gone. She'd already run over to the water's edge and was talking excitedly with Poli, and then the two of them were drinking again…

Alright, then. Kamile wasn't going to be shown up by a couple of full-human teenagers. Gathering her courage, she walked briskly over to the shoreline. She wondered why she was even nervous; after all, she'd done this kind of thing so many times in the Other and the Borderlands and at the Compound. She'd lived with beings who were part of other realms. Chaos, she was one of them, partly. So why was this even scary?

The same doubting thoughts keeping running through her mind as she bent down to drink, and then a new, persistent thought popped up. *You'll die if you drink it. Why do you think you've never heard of it before? You'll die you'll die you'll die you'll-*

Kamile drank anyway, and the fearful thoughts stopped in one blessed moment.

In that exact moment, she knew this *was* the water of life. She'd never ever felt so good before: so young, so alive, so much like she belonged in this little corner of the universe. This was better than adrenaline, better than sex (especially with Aras!), better than chocolate…

She burst into tears.

Trennan was almost a full two days late, and it felt like an eternity to Coryn. No one else seemed concerned (and so she had to pretend that she wasn't either) but she was very, very worried about him.

Especially after that threat Aras had made. Oh, he'd expressed it subtly for such a big, rough man, but it was clear what he'd meant.

Things happen in the Other. Being a Halfling won't save him from that.

She never should have tricked Aras like she had. Perhaps if she'd just gone right up to him and said very honestly that she wasn't interested in him like that...then maybe he would have asked what that had to do with anything, and insisted on the handfasting anyway.

In honesty, she'd probably had no other option except to pull the trick with Kamile, not if she hadn't wanted to find herself bound to Aras for the next year. With his weird fascination for her, it was unlikely that he'd have left her alone like he had Kamile.

Speaking of Kamile, her friend had been acting very strange lately. She'd come home at midnight the night before last, and since then she'd been walking around, staring at things in the Compound as though she'd never seen them before, and then going out and disappearing again.

Coryn wouldn't think much of that as Kamile was in and out of the Other and the Compound often, as everyone was, but this time she'd barely stopped to talk to Coryn. Or if she had, she'd seemed so distracted that Coryn didn't know what to make of it.

Like this morning. Coryn had been concerned about Trennan not showing up, and she was scheduled to see Brosca again in the Other later today, and she'd started to get concerned about *that* as well. It was likely just her worry over Trennan bleeding across into other parts of her life, but she'd wanted to see Kamile, to have her 'little sister' comfort her, tell her not to worry. That clearly wasn't going to happen.

"Are you alright?" Coryn finally asked. "Did something happen when you were patrolling the borders?"

Kamile glanced up from where she was sorting through a pile of clothing. "What? Oh. Yes, a few clueless humans went wandering into the Other. I'm pretty sure they'll be dead by now."

"Oh." That would upset anyone, Coryn supposed. "So you

couldn't stop them?"

Kamile didn't answer, and Coryn had to repeat herself.

Finally the girl looked up. "No, I couldn't stop them."

"And you're really upset," Coryn persisted.

"Why would you think that?"

"You're clearly not yourself! You can't even have a straight conversation with me, and you haven't even asked about Trennan. Clearly something is bothering you!"

At last Kamile met her eyes. "Sorry. I've had a lot on my mind, but I'll tell you about it when I can. Soon, alright? Now, how is Trennan?"

"I don't know! He's two days late back from his knight's test!"

Kamile frowned. "Really? I'm sure I heard someone say he got back this morning, just before I came in here. I was going to tell you but then I...got distracted."

Coryn perked up. "Trennan's back?" She'd go to find him straightaway! Except she was trying to act less obvious – she'd better wait here a little longer. "Wait...what did you have to tell me?"

"Uh..."

"Oh! Are you pregnant?"

"Of course not," Kamile replied absently, but then her eyes widened.

"What? Is it that?" Coryn was horrified. "Is it Aras's?" Who else's could it be? Sex was pretty casual here, as long as you weren't handfasted to someone. Then for that year, you had to be faithful to them. Coryn couldn't see Kamile doing anything different.

Kamile shook her head slowly. "Coryn..." There was a long pause. "I met some girls. Most of them are younger than you, but...well..."

"Well what?"

"It's like having a gang of little sisters. I'll tell you about it sometime," Kamile said vaguely. "Soon."

Coryn stared at her for a long moment, trying to work out what she meant, and wondering if she should feel jealous that she wasn't the only 'sister'. Then she finally said, "Brosca wants to see me this afternoon."

"Oh? Isn't that normal?"

"I suppose so."

"But *you* don't feel good about it," Kamile guessed accurately. "Why?"

"I don't know," Coryn replied helplessly, anxiously twisting her ring as she had so often since Trennan had left. "Last time I saw her, things were strange, and I can't even say why. But I've been feeling like I'm spending more time in the Other than out here, and when I come back I've lost massive chunks of my life on something that, well, isn't really important."

Kamile's eyes shot open wide at that. "Did you just say that spending time with the Fey isn't that important?"

Realising she had in fact said exactly that, Coryn was horrified. "I didn't- I mean, I meant… I just meant that I'm afraid I'll come out one day and I'll be old, and that I'll have missed my whole life. I didn't mean that I don't value being Chosen…"

Her friend burst out laughing.

"Kamile," Coryn whispered. "Are you hysterical?"

It seemed the only reason why she *would* be laughing at such a thing. Coryn had worried so much over Trennan's absence (although it seemed like he was back now, hooray!!!) that she'd almost overlooked her increasing uneasiness over her time spent in the Other.

She hadn't *meant* to say that, though, because of course the Other was important, and the Fey were important! It was a great honour that she, Coryn, had been chosen by Brosca…

Kamile wiped her eyes, shaking her head again. "No. Or maybe just a little. What I have to tell you, Coryn – it's incredible. It'll change your life if you decide to believe me, and you might not even want to."

"Well…what is it? Is it something to do with those new girls?" And perhaps a hint of jealousy came out in Coryn's tone.

"Mm. Sort of. I can't tell you yet. I just need to find out one more thing, and then I'll let you know as soon as I can. Just don't go into the Other today, alright?"

Coryn frowned. This sounded ominous, and a chill of what might have been excitement was running up her spine. "Why not?"

"I can't say yet, because I'm not one hundred percent sure about it. But trust me. Go see Trennan – I'm assuming he's here, anyway – and hang out with him or whatever you young lovers do. But just don't go into the Other or near any conduits, alright? Give me until tomorrow, or even longer if you can."

"But what do I tell Brosca?" Coryn asked in dismay. "I've never just not shown up." The Fey had been offended enough over her slight lateness last time.

"If what I think is right, that won't be a problem," Kamile replied adamantly.

Coryn was desperate to know what she was talking about, but she was just as desperate to see Trennan. Tossing up between the two choices, she finally nodded. "OK, Kam. I'll do it. I'll stay away from Brosca for a while." Even though she might really be burning her bridges there.

Kamile nodded in relief, then leaned in to give Coryn a hug, resting her head on Coryn's shoulder. "You know I love you, right?"

"Of course," Coryn replied, a little flustered. While she knew that, and she felt the same sisterly affection for Kamile, they had never been overly demonstrative. She patted her friend gently on the back, and they just stood like that for a while. Then Kamile stood upright again, and she had a sheen in her eyes that looked suspiciously like tears.

"Are you alright?" Coryn asked for what seemed like the third time in five minutes.

"I'm fine," Kamile replied again. She wiped her eyes, smiled at Coryn, then said, "I have to go. I'll see you tomorrow, alright?"

"Alright," Coryn echoed.

The smaller girl finished tossing her way through the clothes on the bed, then abruptly grabbed a small pile of them, shoved them into a bag, and headed for the door. "Bye."

"Bye."

For about ten seconds after Kamile had gone, Coryn wondered if she should take a look into whatever was clearly going on. But then she remembered Trennan was back, and that idea fled from her mind.

Kamile felt like her life had been divided in two: before the River, and after the River. When she'd finally gone back to the Chosen Compound after drinking the water, everything had felt very different from when she'd left. It was her *home*, but now everything seemed different, ominous, when before it simply seemed normal.

In fact, she felt like her eyes had been opened suddenly and she could see the essential wrongness that had previously been hidden. It scared the blazes out of her, but she wouldn't have changed it for anything.

The only problem was, it had raised a whole lot of questions that she now needed answered. *Why* did she feel so uncomfortable here now? What was wrong? Who were the Fey, then, if she didn't feel like she could trust them anymore? Who *could* she trust?

She needed to talk to someone who had the answers, but she didn't know where to look.

She knew where to start looking, though. She'd been seeing the girls almost every night through their illegal hacking scheme (quite fun, actually). They were already planning mass trips back to the River; they just had to be quiet about it. The government hadn't expressly banned the use of the River, but probably only because they didn't know it was there.

Kamile was still trying to work out how she'd tell Coryn about it. Now she had an urgency to get her dear friend out of that place, and she still didn't know why. As a Halfling, Trennan needed the Other, and Kamile thought there was a very good chance that the River would do just as well as the Borderlands, if not better.

After all, it seemed to be working just fine for her so far. She just needed the perfect time to tell them about it, and she needed that last piece of information which would show for a certainty that what she suspected about the Fey was true.

Ever since she'd drunk the water, she'd felt like a new person, and the way she'd looked at things had changed as well. She'd suddenly recalled an old myth about the Other, one she'd learned about as a young child when she'd gone into the city on her own and briefly made a new friend.

The old woman Kamile had spoken to had likely died long ago, but the story she'd told had been unforgettable. It was the same as the origins tale told by the Fey, but just different enough to change everything if it was true.

It went like this:

Once upon a time the realms were unified and ruled over by a peaceful, immortal king. Even though his own people were also immortal, he still cared greatly for the weaker, mortal humans, doing whatever he could to help them.

But one day, one of the king's greatest warriors rose up against him, along with many of the immortals whose hearts had been turned away. Their wicked plan was to kill the king, steal his plentiful alter-power and take his place ruling the world.

But the coup failed, and the rebels were cast out. The realms split apart in the battle, and the rebels themselves, forced away from the life-giving power of the immortal king, became twisted, undead Creatures. They were determined to regain what they thought was theirs, and to take out their anger on the king and on the humans he cared about so much…

Or at least that was what the old woman had said all those years ago. But when the young Kamile had innocently recounted the tale to one of the adults back in the Compound, they'd told her it was wrong. They had gently explained how that myth contradicted the true story of the Fey, and that it couldn't possibly be true. If it was, wouldn't they know about it?

They themselves had been into the Other, and they knew that the beings living there weren't divided into two neat categories of good and bad. They were like humans, a mix of both, and as for undead…?

It was a horror story meant to terrify her, the adult had explained. The old woman had been confused, and Kamile should just forget everything she'd said.

The young Kamile hadn't known what to believe at first, but then she had agreed with the Chosen. She herself had met the Fey many times, and she had known that what the old woman had said just *couldn't* be true. After all, what about her Fey ponies? They too had told a completely different story.

At least that was what Kamile had believed up until she drank the water at the River. Then it was like everything about the Fey and the Other that she'd been convinced of, everything they'd told her, now seemed false and shallow. And that story of the Other, of the peaceful king and the undead Creatures, had a ring of truth to it that she could no longer deny…

There was just one thing that would confirm it. She had to *see* the Fey again, right after she'd sorted a few things out with Poli and Magdalene. In the last few days they'd planned so much. She'd told them about her own situation with the Chosen, and about her friends. Their hacking group had grown to include several others, all in similar situations to the two girls, and all in need of help that Kamile would ensure they'd get.

Kamile was certain the legend of the blood-drinkers was also closely connected. She now felt that if only she could see the Fey again, with the River's water inside her, she could see what they really were. They could make themselves look like anything, and they could say anything, but she'd see their true selves.

She now knew one thing for sure. She *did* belong here on this earth. She was supposed to exist. Even if she was wrong about the Fey and the Creatures being one and the same, she would never give up or go back to her old way of thinking. She had value, and so did the other Halflings. Deias, to think that she had considered having sterility surgery to remove her chance of motherhood forever!

Oh, and Kamile's skin hadn't been green at the River. Not like in the Other, where her Fey blood showed so strongly and she became that strange, twisted version of herself. But at the River, which she *knew* was also Other and flowing with pure alter-power, she had simply been herself. Regular human Kamile. Hooray!

Still smiling, she turned her two-seater vehicle into the

carpark of an eatery on the outskirts of the city. The plan was for her to pick up a few things to munch on while she drove to get the girls, and then they would all go back to the River again with the new ones. *Then* Kamile would go back to the Borderlands and take another look at the Fey, and she knew that once she saw them, she would be certain.

Inside, the eatery was buzzing with noise, full of people sitting and talking as much as actually eating. Kamile tapped her choices into the server-bot, then waited for the food to be retrieved. In the fifteen seconds that took, she let her gaze wander around the room, and that was when she noticed the couple. A man and a woman, both familiar as elders from the Chosen Compound, and both wearing what looked like very strange, fluffy hats.

Then Kamile blinked, and realised that she had imagined it. Both were bareheaded, and anything else must have been just a trick of the light.

Just then the man noticed her, and he lifted a hand in greeting. Kamile's food was ready, so she took it and went to say hello. How could she not?

"Hello, Jurgis, Starbright," she said politely.

If the Chosen had an official leader, it would be Jurgis, and Starbright, an attractive middle-aged woman with long brown hair, had been his friend for many years. Kamile had never liked or disliked either of them; they were perhaps a little self-important, but generally inoffensive. She hadn't spent enough time with either to notice, but with so many in the Compound she hadn't thought twice about being overlooked.

"Hello, Katherine, was it?" Starbright asked. She was wearing a dark grey cloak which had come back into fashion in general society, but which the Chosen had been wearing for centuries. Her smooth dark hair almost blended in with it.

"Kamile."

"I would ask what brings you here, but that should be fairly obvious," Jurgis said, then he laughed at his own, not very funny joke.

Kamile smiled along with him, but she was growing increasingly uneasy, and she didn't even know why.

"I know you're here to eat," Starbright inquired sweetly, "but I can sense there's something else. What is it?"

Kamile's eyes widened. Surely the elder didn't know that she was planning to leave? "I don't know what you mean," she answered as innocently as she could manage.

"Oh, never mind," Jurgis said jovially. "You just run along and do whatever it is you're doing."

"I will," Kamile murmured, but she was distracted by something she could sense near these two. Something around their heads, a sort of power that she could feel but not see.

But as she went to turn away, she saw it wispy and bright in the corner of her eye, and finally realised what it was. Her blood ran cold. She'd known that objects could carry enough power to link to certain Fey, like the drawers back in Aras's room, but people? "Elder Jurgis, I didn't realise you were a conduit...?"

"I'm a carrier," Jurgis replied kindly, but there was no kindness in his eyes. "When a human is a conduit for the Fey, we call ourselves carriers."

"Oh," Kamile said weakly, unsure of what to do. She hadn't even known such a thing was possible.

She stepped away from them, certain now that the Fey and the Creatures of legend were one and the same, because she could now see the negative energy surrounding both elders' heads. Definitely not the fluffy hats she had first thought she'd seen. She was right now in the presence of at least two Other Creatures piggybacking on these two humans in order to access the normal realm, and in light of the old lady's story about Creatures, that felt like a very, very bad thing.

"Right," she said again, almost stammering. "I'm just going to go…"

Almost tripping over her feet, Kamile walked out of the eatery and towards her nearby vehicle. She could feel the elders were watching her, and every step seemed like it was happening in slow motion. She quickly climbed into her vehicle, pressing the button for the sun roof to close, and started to drive even before her belt was on.

They'd followed her out, and she saw them watching in her multi-view camera. Starbright threw out a hand and whispered something – Kamile didn't know what, she was too far away – and for a moment it seemed like there was dust on her windscreen. But that impression didn't last, and with a brief nod she pulled away.

They watched her as she drove right out of sight, and although they'd not said anything threatening, she still *felt* hugely, massively threatened. But she'd got away, even if she had no idea what had just happened there. The only question was if she could ever go back to the Compound now.

No, she'd have to worry about that later. (And worry she would, now she knew that the elders were *carriers*!) Instead, she turned and headed for the meeting point with her 'girls', as she was now calling them, and her heart leapt at the thought of visiting the River once more. She'd never felt as alive as she did there, as when she was drinking the water, and she'd met some of the most wonderful people. She'd have to introduce Coryn and Trennan – once she'd convinced them to come, of course.

But less than halfway to her destination a sudden detour appeared on the road, preventing her from taking the usual route. Kamile frowned. It hadn't been on the two-seater's charts, but she shrugged and turned off anyway. Hopefully it would only add on a minute or two, and she was still pumped with adrenaline from what felt like a narrow escape.

That was why she ignored the incredible sense of wrongness creeping in…

Whiteside, Leister County 2013 AD

Ash stood in the doorway of her small cottage, dressed in that rather unattractive garb she called pee-jays, and with a bewildered expression on her freckled face. "Anne?" She looked around at the room full of frightened, arguing, powdered Frencine aristocrats, and blanched. "It's good to see you after so long, but please tell me these people aren't here to stay."

Anne understood her fear, as the last time Ash had unexpected time-travelling visitors, they had lived with her for six months. "Never fear," she replied breezily. "We are simply passing through on our way back to 1793."

"And this was a convenient stopping point?!"

Anne shrugged. "'Twas the direction of the sentinel that brought us here rather than my own design."

"Sentinel…?"

Anne ignored her, continuing, "But what do you mean by 'after so long'? Surely it has been no longer than a month?"

"Try three months!" Ash exploded. "Amaranthus just shoved George and I out of the Mountain, and we haven't seen any of you since. So much has happened since, and we've…well. I suppose you don't know about any of it."

Three months?! Anne was so startled by the length of time that she wondered if the gateways were badly spaced, and she'd arrived in another time than she ought. She did not know what she did not know, either.

She was just about to ask when Elspeth entered the room, triumphantly holding up the green-lit sentinel. "I found the next gateway! 'Tis outside the back entrance, although 'twas a most difficult feat to open the door. There was an odd sort of chain-lock-"

"What's she saying?" someone interrupted in Frencine. There was increasing panic in the air, and the dog began to howl.

"Now she's done it," an older lady complained. "My poor Chaussin is most sensitive to unease."

Jon tapped Anne on the shoulder. "I don't know what they're saying," he said in his own language, "but I think we'd better go."

"But Anne," Ash tried to say, and Anne gave her a kind pat on the arm.

"Never fear, I shall be back anon with explanations for all of this. But now..." She remembered that one thing, that one truly essential thing, and turned to shout at her sister. "Bethie! Lead them to the gateway, if you will. I shall bring up the rear." Then to the Frencine, "Follow her, and she shall return you home anon."

"The sooner the better," the lady with the dog muttered.

That said, Anne turned and ran for her old bedroom, the one she had used while staying here with Ash. 'Twas much the same as when she had left, except rather tidier, and she found with some relief that all her 2013 garb was neatly arranged in the wardrobe. And there, sitting on the floor of the wardrobe, were her most precious possessions.

Anne threw off the plain black slippers that had appeared upon arrival here in 2013, and slipped on her beautiful, sparkling purple ones. She admired how her small feet looked in them for just a few moments before dashing back to the lounge room, now mostly vacant of the aristocrats. The last of them were shuffling out at the back of the queue, staring at Ash's home with a mix of wonder and suspicion. 'Twas much how Anne had felt upon first arrival.

Ash, however, was standing there with that same baffled expression she'd held since they'd arrived. "Are you leaving already?"

"I fear we must," Anne replied, for she'd already noticed *where* the little dog had done its business, and wished to leave before Ash noticed also. "I shall come back to visit as soon as I am able." And then she quickly wrapped Ash in a tight hug – for she had missed the oversized, ill-mannered peasant – and ran after the others, who were even now disappearing into the cobwebbed wall outside the back door. "I took the purple slippers!" she called back into the house. "And sorry about the dog!"

"What about the…" But the last thing Anne heard before they moved through the gateway was Ash bellowing, *"Ew! It peed in my basil plant!"*

THE OLDEST ENEMY

The Mountain of Glass, time irrelevant

"I thought all things considered it went pretty well," Jon said placidly. He was sitting with the two girls in the thick grass under an apple tree, picking his teeth with a narrow leaf in the most dreadfully common manner. Or at least that was what Anne would have said. Elspeth didn't mind. After all, he was a prince, and princes might act a little commonly if they so wished.

"Considering the hundred-thousand gateways we might have got lost in?" Anne replied archly. She sat with her legs stretched out straight, her eyes fixed on the sparkly purple slippers sticking out from under the edge of her skirt, and with a very satisfied expression on her face. "And the language barrier, and the dozen ways that those Frencine aristos could have caused disaster? Yes, very well indeed."

'Twas true. It seemed a miracle that the second gateway had led them directly to the Lunden docks in 1793, only two weeks after they'd fled Frencia. Or no miracle: Elspeth strongly suspected that the gate-bu- *sentinels* did exactly what was required. Her own one had buzzed away upon leading them back here to the Mountain, but she still remembered the shell-shocked faces of the aristos, the tearful goodbyes, and the way the beautiful *comtesse* had clung to Jon as they'd tried to leave…

If not for the sentinels, mayhap they would have travelled through each of those hundred-thousand gateways, searching for the right place and the right time until their faces grew lined and they lost heart. But all things considered, 'twas a most happy ending.

Elspeth ignored her sister, instead studying Jon. His handsome face was pensive but not unhappy, and mayhap just a little darker in colour than it had been upon first meeting…? "Will you miss her?" she asked timidly.

"Who?"

"Your betrothed, of course!"

Jon smiled in that 'you don't know what you're talking about' way. He did that often with Elspeth, and she did not appreciate it. Simply being small-boned did not make her a child.

"I told you, it was a fake betrothal for the sake of convenience," he replied lightly. "It's Francois that she's worried about. Besides, I hardly knew her. Most of our conversations were mimed – I could hardly understand a word."

Forsooth, Jon hadn't told her about the fake betrothal at all. He'd told Anne who had then told Elspeth, and Elspeth couldn't help feeling irrationally hurt that he'd withheld such knowledge from her. But then nothing was rational around Jon. She was quite inappropriately in love with him – inappropriately because even if they had come from the same place and the same time period, no prince would ever marry a bastard. "I suppose not," she murmured.

"'Tis the time passing that bothers me," Anne said suddenly. "Three months, Bethie. Did you hear Ash say that?"

"Language barrier, remember?"

Anne gave Elspeth an arch look. "Ash was speaking *Anglish*, Bethie, but simply with an accent. By the by, she did say 'twas three months since she and George were ejected from the

Mountain. Three! And I could have sworn only a month had passed at most."

There was no night here in the Mountain, only endless, perfect days. They slept when they felt tired, which was not often. 'Twas no wonder that they had lost track of time. "I wonder how long it has been back home?" Elspeth mused.

"Well, we shall never know," Anne said briskly. "For I vow on my life that we shall never return to our own time. But what of you, Jon-Jean-Louis? When shall you return to your home?"

"Just Jon, thank you," he said in a bored tone, but he'd suddenly become tense. "And who knows? I don't have any control over these things. If I'm lucky, a hundred years will have passed and everyone I knew will be dead."

Elspeth understood what he meant, as going home to the same people would mean the same problems remained. "But that does defeat the purpose of going home," she murmured to herself.

But Jon's good mood was gone, and he suddenly jumped to his feet. "I've got an appointment. See you two later – and thanks for the help."

Elspeth hadn't heard of any appointment. 'Twas more likely that he wished to avoid such awkward conversations – and she *still* did not know what he fled from, or even precisely *when*. "What about you?" she asked Anne, who was still staring at her over-bright shoes with a satisfied smile. "Will you see Amaranthus now?"

"Hmm? Why would I do that?"

"The agreement to find Francois," Elspeth suggested. "Or the silver wand we found, or the reason we saw the evil queen Seyen just now…"

"The wand," Anne said decisively. "I'd vow 'tis simply a shiny piece of plas-tik, but I wish to know for sure."

And that was why they found themselves standing expectantly in the tapestry room with Amaranthus a short while later.

"Hmm," he said thoughtfully as he studied the wand, reminding her rather of Anne. "Well, it's definitely a light."

"We did know that," Anne said in disappointment, which was exactly how Elspeth felt. "Is that all?"

"Well, it is rather clever," he countered. "It doesn't require a battery. And it does do other things."

"What kind of things?" Elspeth asked eagerly.

Amaranthus smiled down at her. "This and that. But you don't need it."

"Who does, then?"

"Someone you don't yet know." He turned back to the tapestry, running his finger across the tiny threads and sending up thousands of images so quickly Elspeth could not follow them with her eyes – following the lives and *potential* of many. "But not yet. Hang onto it, Anne. If you're interested, I'll tell you when to pass the baton." He chuckled to himself for no apparent reason.

Elspeth did not know what to make of that, so she asked, "What about the woman who dropped it? 'Twas Seyen, was it not?"

"It was," he agreed, causing a nasty twist of fear in Elspeth's stomach.

"Oh, *Chaos*," Anne burst out rather rudely. "Did you not promise us she was dead? And yet here she is again, causing trouble! I'd vow the woman is an immortal!"

Amaranthus gave her a long, even stare until she finally quietened. "I've never told you an untruth," he said simply. "Seyen Johannis died in the Other, not long after your escape from her. You simply met her much earlier in her life's journey, and I cannot promise you will not meet her again."

Anne and Elspeth exchanged a confused glance. Or at least Elspeth felt confused, anyway. "So…are we in danger from her?"

"For your kind, she was a dangerous woman. People like Seyen Johannis are always dangerous, because they consider their own interests more valuable than your lives. And I assure you, you'll always find people like her. If you see her again, don't stay to chat."

"But won't she remember our faces?" Anne persisted, then her eyes crossed in confusion. "I would have sworn that when I first met her she did not know me. But then mayhap I was wrong."

"Did she get a good look at your face in Chamborde Castle?"

"I don't think so," Anne ventured.

Elspeth shook her head.

"So be sure that it remains that way." He smiled. "That means that if you ever do see her again – run into her on your own travels – you won't let her look at you for long. Especially you, Anne. Your hair is very distinctive."

There was a long pause while both girls made sense of that. Elspeth noticed that Anne had stiffened a little upon the mention of her hair. It had been the bane of Anne's life back home in 1556, for 'twas commonly believed that having red hair meant an untrustworthy character. After all, had not Judas been red-haired? And he had betrayed the Christos to death.

Anne had clearly been thinking along the same lines. "'Tis not…" she began, then tried again. "'Tis simply hair," she muttered. "I will cover it again, if I must."

"Why cover something so lovely and rare?" Amaranthus asked simply. "It would be like closing the curtains on a sunset, simply because it's neither night nor day. No, I simply meant that when you're one of my people, you might begin to become familiar to some who you'd rather not be familiar with. So I'll say the usual. Move quickly when you're outside the Mountain, and always be alert."

When you're one of my people. Anne was the one who wanted that, Elspeth thought. She wanted it too – somewhat – but mayhap not so desperately, not so quickly. She also wouldn't mind settling in a single time and living an ordinary life, one without the stigma of bastardy and disability. Mayhap with Jon…

She dismissed that foolish thought just as Amaranthus asked, "Was there anything else you wanted to know?"

Elspeth thought Anne might mention her quest to rescue Francois, but she didn't say a word. Instead Anne slipped the light-wand into one of her pockets, smiling at Amaranthus in thanks. "That is all, and I thank you. I shall wait upon your direction for the light-wand." And then she curtseyed and left through the doorway that appeared behind her as if summoned by will.

That left Elspeth alone with Amaranthus. He looked at her, one eyebrow raised. *Something you wanted to say?*

It did not startle her for him to speak straight into her mind, not in this place. But she answered honestly and aloud. "'Twas not for me to say about Francois. 'Twas for Anne, but she did not."

She'll try to keep her word to the comtesse.

"She will," Elspeth agreed. "But 'tis a difficult task, that of finding a single lost man across a whole country, and not even in one's own time. And she does not even know what he looks like!"

The comtesse had told Anne that her lover was 'a most handsome man of twenty-eight years, with melting brown eyes and golden-brown hair'; but then when Anne had relayed that to Jon, the latter had rolled *his* eyes (neither brown nor melting) and had declared Francois an ordinary Frencine-man, and balding to boot. So who knew what he looked like?

Amaranthus didn't answer, but he looked like he agreed with her assessment. She supposed *he* knew Francois's appearance.

She continued, "But I suppose she plans to use the gate-bu- I mean, the sentinels, for they led us to where we wished to go before. Is that their role, sir? That of guides?"

He turned away again, running his fingers across the tapestry once more and looking most thoughtful. Elspeth did not feel as though she was being ignored, for she knew he was considering her question.

"They may seem a sort of guide," he agreed finally, still studying the tapestry, "because they led you to your sister, and then eventually to the place you intended to go. But their main role is to protect the gateways created by my people rather than the Eternity Stone, and to keep people tidily in their own times. I expect that because you, Anne and Jon are out of time, they simply led you to each other, and Anne to a place that felt familiar to her."

Elspeth pondered that. "So they will *not* take Anne to find Francois? Should we not follow them through gateways?"

Amaranthus turned to her, smiling suddenly. "They're just bugs, Bets, for all that we give them a finer name, and they have no particular intelligence that you should trust them implicitly. You don't need to follow anything they do, unless you want to. But would you like to follow *me*? I have a task that needs doing by someone who's not one of the People, and you'd be just right...if you're willing."

Lile, 2597 AD

Coryn hurried through the meeting area of the Compound, heading for the area where the knights usually gathered. She was approaching a corner when suddenly a girl stepped out of the wall, right into her path.

Out of the wall? She must have meant from *behind* the wall.

"Oh!" The girl stepped back, dusting herself off. She was very short and fine-boned, with bright red hair, dark eyes and pale skin. Completely unfamiliar, although her ordinary Chosen clothing marked her as belonging here.

Coryn gave her a polite, impatient nod, then tried to step around her. But the redhead moved the same way, and they did an awkward dance for a few seconds until finally Coryn just stopped. "Walk around me, would you?"

The girl raised her eyebrows, then shrugged, stepped around Coryn, and trotted off. She hadn't said a word the whole time, and finally that struck Coryn as odd. But when she turned to look over her shoulder, the redhead was nowhere to be seen. It seemed that Coryn wasn't the only one in a hurry.

Coryn pondered it only for a second before moving on. Trennan!

She found him in the knight's area. He stood by a group of older men, close, but not a part of them. It was a normal reflection of his place here in the Compound. He looked up and saw her, and for a moment there was naked longing on his face before it was masked with neutrality.

"Trennan Halfling," she said, far more formally than she wanted to. "You have returned. Did you succeed in your quest?" Well duh…he wouldn't be here at all if he hadn't.

"Coryn of the Chosen. I did succeed, spending thirty days in the cold desert of the Other realm, and I am now a fully-fledged knight."

Hooray, she mouthed, and he didn't hide his smile.

"You are well?"

"I am." Then, now that the formalities were done, she added a little pertly to show some of her angst, "You're late."

The strangest expression came over Trennan's face, and he said, "Plenty of people come back late."

"Of course they do," Coryn assured him quickly. "Better late than never, right?"

"Yeah…"

She quickly picked up that there was something he wasn't saying, and that it was probably important. Taking his arm, she began chattering aimlessly about the superficial things that had happened while he'd been gone, and carefully leading him away to somewhere more private where they could really talk. There was something about him today, something almost nervous in his mannerisms that didn't fit with his usual calm confidence.

They moved to the far field, where a crop of potatoes was doing surprisingly well in spite of the soil composition, or so their head gardener always said. Trennan still seemed nervous, and that made her nervous. She smiled at him, then thought about what *she* wanted to say. Perhaps here wasn't the best place for it.

"How about a trip into the city?" she suggested brightly. "I haven't been in a while, and I *know* you haven't. We could do some VR?"

"I would love that," Trennan replied immediately, which was odd in itself. He didn't usually like VR that much, since the machines basically trapped you inside your own mind, and he usually wanted to be social after spending time in the Other. He must want to get away from listening ears, Coryn figured, and anywhere in this area wasn't really private. Conduits, conduits everywhere…

So they headed into Lile City, the unimaginatively named capital of the Secular Republic of Lile. It was a substantial journey: forty minutes in a borrowed two-seater to get to the monorail station, then another half hour on the monorail itself, across miles of farmland, gently rolling hills and through the vast Empty Zones, remnants of the Great War centuries before.

Coryn thought about how now, even the Empty Zones were beginning to blend in. Greenery was beginning to grow in them again, and several times she thought she saw movement, but they were going too fast to take a good look. They chatted about superficial things as they travelled: nothing that could be overheard and get them in trouble with either the Sec government or the very non-Sec Chosen. Their hands were loosely clasped together as they travelled. Just another young, rural couple heading into the city for a day out – their clothing and colours more subdued than those living in the city itself, but nothing to catch any attention.

Once off the monorail they began walking towards their usual VR centre, but Trennan grabbed Coryn's arm and pulled her down a side alley. There was nothing much here except the slight smell of urine and a couple of cats which fled as soon as they heard footsteps.

"I just wanted to actually talk," he said with a crooked smile.

"Yes, well, the smell of pee doesn't exactly encourage romance," she replied acerbically. But then she smiled, grabbed his face between both palms, and gave him a good kiss anyway. "I missed you. I really, really missed you."

Trennan's face softened. "I missed you too." He held her hand close against his chest, staring at her with a mix of tenderness and something that looked disconcertingly like fear.

"What is it?" Coryn asked quietly. "What's worrying you so much you'd agree to come all the way out here?"

"Wouldn't it be enough just to spend time alone with you

away from prying eyes?"

"Yes, but I can tell that's not all there is to it. Something happened out in the Other, didn't it?"

He closed his eyes briefly, then nodded. "Oh, yes. Something like you wouldn't believe, Coryn."

She caught her breath. "You weren't hurt…?" A few of the nastier Fey didn't limit their predations to females.

"No. Nothing like that. It's just…you know the three knights who were sent in to get me? Meric, Jan and Evers?

"Of course."

"They didn't come back."

"Oh Trennan, I'm so sorry. I know how you admired them-"

"You don't understand," he interrupted. "They're fine. It's *where* they are that's so amazing."

Coryn waited, but he didn't say anything else. "Well? Where are they?"

Trennan took a deep breath, then said carefully, "You know the old stories about the Fire Lord?"

He may as well have asked if she'd heard of the Other realm. She gave him an odd look, but answered politely, "A wicked, very powerful Fey that was defeated at the beginning of time, with the battle causing the rift between realms. We celebrate each Solstice that the fire still exists but doesn't destroy us." And then they put it out with huge cauldrons of water, just like they had a month ago.

"Yes. That's what the Fey told us, didn't they."

It was a statement not a question, and after a moment Coryn asked impatiently, "What does this have to do with the three knights?"

"They're with him. They're with the Fire Lord. Only he's not what they told us."

There was a long, terrible pause where she realised that he

was deadly serious, and tried to remember exactly what she'd heard about this ancient Fey. Not much, except as a child she'd imagined him as a terrible monster wielding a sharp sceptre of judgement and throwing all those who offended him into an intense fire. Childish fantasies of a creature who probably had long turned to ash (or so she'd thought), but here Trennan was saying that the Fire Lord still *existed*?

"I don't understand," she said finally. "How is that possible? He was destroyed aeons ago!"

"They didn't destroy him," Trennan repeated, his tone heavy and intense. "They just moved away from him, and not even that far, Coryn. I met him, and he's…"

"He's what?" These pauses were beginning to bother Coryn, and they weren't like Trennan. He was more decisive than this. But if he had truly met the Fire Lord…? "Wicked? Truly, hideously awful? A black-clad beast sitting on a throne of skulls?"

He shook his head fervently. "No! Not at all. He was very…*nice.*"

The moment the words came out of Trennan's mouth he knew that Coryn hadn't understood. And why should she? It was a bizarre tale even for the Chosen, for whom strange stories were something that came up every day.

"Nice?" She echoed his words. "Are you sure you even met the real Fire Lord? You know that some of the Fey love to play tricks on people."

"But even they can't create a lush garden beneath the ice," he snapped back. Suddenly the nervous excitement that had filled him ever since he'd left that place transformed into frustration. He leaned forward in that dirty alleyway, grabbing her shoulders. "I know that what I'm saying calls into doubt everything we believe, everything the Fey has ever taught us, but if you could have seen it, Coryn! If you saw what I'd seen, or spoke to him like I did, you would never doubt me. Never!"

Were words ever enough to change the beliefs of a lifetime? But miraculously, he saw the moment when she decided to listen.

"Alright," she replied helplessly. "Tell me what happened."

Trennan told her. He told her about how he'd climbed down into that orange pit, and had felt the warmth envelop him like stepping into a heated home on a winter's day. He hadn't been scared, but there'd been something inside him that had twisted and screamed and *hated* being there even while the rest of him had loved it.

He'd seen a garden lying beneath the ice, and he'd seen a colossal city shining in the impossible sunlight like a diamond. And all around had been growth, growth that never should have existed in the Other.

It was so different to the Other they'd known, that it might as well have been another realm.

And there had been Meric, Jan and Evers, acting like children. Jan and Evers were swimming in a deep river that ran alongside, and a surprisingly young-looking Meric was chatting with a tall, brown-skinned man who looked up towards Trennan with a smile. He wasn't human, Trennan had known, and he'd shone like he was lit from within.

One moment he'd been talking to Meric, and the next he'd been standing right in front of Trennan. Trennan didn't remember the details of the man's face or even if he had hair, just that he'd looked at him and it was like his whole life was laid bare, and he'd hated it. He'd still had the sword in his hand…

"Keep it if you wish," the man had said mildly. "If it makes you feel safer."

Of course that made Trennan feel foolish to have kept the thing. So he'd put it back in its sheath, studying the man with a fearful kind of interest. "Where is here, exactly? And what are you?"

"Here is the Garden," the man replied. "And the source of the River of life, among other things. And I am known by many names. Can you not guess one?"

Oh, and now it had felt so rude to ask, but Trennan couldn't help himself. He'd never been good at holding back questions. "Are you the Fire Lord?"

"Yes."

Trennan had waited for the world to go up in flames – while everything inside him screamed for him to run back to that rope-ladder – but the Fire Lord had just watched him with those knowing eyes, and what appeared to be kindness.

In Trennan's silence the Fire Lord added, "That is one name they called me, and that is a gift I still hold. Fire purifies, if used correctly. But I think what you're really asking is, am I the tyrant that split the two realms, thus causing the fractured world we know today?"

Er, yes, that was what Trennan was asking, and the same fear was twisting inside his stomach. He felt his hand go to his sword again as the Fire Lord took a step closer, within arm's reach now, and lifted his own hand. It was like Trennan's, patterned as though with bark, but even as Trennan watched, the pattern disappeared and was replaced with a bright flame, almost invisible in the full daylight.

"Touch my hand," the Fire Lord offered, "and see what you

think."

Behind him Meric was watching with bright-eyed interest and an apparent lack of fear, and then Trennan *did* pull out his sword, holding it between himself and the Fey. "Never."

The Fire Lord didn't lower his hand, instead studying the blade with interest. "Nicely made, except for the unfortunate Creature endowment."

And while Trennan pondered that comment, the Fire Lord touched his burning hand to the end of the blade. A drop of red blood appeared where the blade cut the man's skin. One second went by, then two as the bright silver metal blackened… then suddenly the whole sword was consumed by fire.

Trennan dropped it in panic but it was too late. His own hand was already aflame, and then the fire raced up his arm and covered his whole body. Someone was screaming, and it was him – although for some reason it hadn't hurt yet. He twisted in panic, stumbling towards the nearby river and throwing himself in.

The clear water closed over Trennan's head, and then suddenly the panic left. He opened his eyes, and up through the surface of the water he could see the wavery face of the Fire Lord. *Are you finished yet?* he asked, as though Trennan was a child who'd been having a tantrum.

Trennan pushed himself to his feet. The water only came to his waist, and coming up felt like being born again. That was the only way he could explain it. He had absolutely no idea what was going on, but he wasn't scared. He felt quite good, actually, and suddenly had an explanation for why Jan and Evers were swimming while fully clothed.

"What did you do?"

"Fire purifies," the man replied. "This fire destroys only evil, and you, my dear boy, were coated in the Creatures' poison since you were conceived."

"Oh." But what was a-

"Creature? I think you'd better stop thinking of them and me as Fey, Trennan Braveheart. I have a *lot* to tell you."

"But your name is Trennan Halfling," Coryn said in confusion once Trennan had finished telling his story. "Why would the Fire Lord change it?"

Trennan shrugged, feeling that same excitement that he'd had since he'd come up out of that water. He still didn't understand it all, but he accepted it because nothing bad could come from someone so good. "New name, new start."

"It's a good name," she said with a helpless shrug. "But all of this about Creatures and Fey, and the Fire Lord who doesn't want to be called Fey, only he had patterns like you do on his skin…"

"No. No, I think that he might change appearance depending on who's looking, if that makes sense."

"So he *wasn't* Wood Fey?"

"Coryn," Trennan began carefully. She hadn't understood it when he'd just explained it, so he'd have to be clearer. "He said that there are *no* Fey. That what we call Fey are actually just his own people, rebels from millennia ago, who turned on him and were cursed for it. And he said that they had turned their anger on us humans, because we were one of the main reasons that they'd fought so long ago. That the king – that's what they mostly call the Fire Lord – wanted to help humans, and that the rebels wanted to use us."

"Did you believe him?"

How did Trennan explain that when he'd heard the king speak, he'd known truth in a way which he had never imagined, that there had been no doubting his words? Just like when the sun rose, it could be seen even through closed eyelids, even someone like himself who had only ever known the Fey and the Chosen, had known the truth of those words. "Yes. I believe him."

Coryn went quiet for a long moment, and Trennan felt with dread that this must be the moment she turned on him, that she rejected him. But instead she said, "OK."

"What?"

"I believe you. I believe him, I mean," she said more firmly. "I don't know what this means for me, and for the Chosen, but I believe you."

He was ecstatic, but still… "Why so easily?"

Coryn shrugged her shoulders, giving a bewildered sigh. "I can't even name a single reason. But while you were gone, things got strange for me. I've been wanting to talk to you about it, and about what Brosca's been doing with me. Time-travel, telling the future, seeing into past lives…" She frowned. "That doesn't sound like anything out of the normal, but it didn't *feel* right, Trenn'. Everything I've seen has been making me more confused and unhappy, not less. And then…" She reached up to touch the side of her neck gently, as if it pained her. "…she did the strangest thing, and even now it's hard to think that it really happened."

"What did she do?"

She shook her head, a strange little smile on her face. "It sounds ridiculous. But Trennan, I could swear that she *bit* me on the neck, like some kind of blood-drinker. Weeks ago, but I felt like I forgot about it until more recently."

"Yeah, he said that some of the Fey were blood-drinkers."

Coryn stared at him in disbelief. "He, as in the Fire Lord King, or whatever he is? He told you that there are blood-drinkers amongst the Fey?"

Trennan nodded. It had disgusted him so much when he'd first heard it, and it still did. It had taken some time for everything the king had said to sink in. He knew it would be hard for Coryn to accept too, because she had been going to meet Brosca for many years. To hear that she was actually an enemy…? "The knights said the same thing, and he just confirmed it. He said that life is in the blood, and that was what the Creatures want. That's what they're called, Coryn. Creatures, not Fey. Calling themselves Fey was just a way to buy into some of the humans' ancient beliefs."

"Why would they do that?" Coryn whispered. She didn't know if she believed everything he'd just said – it sounded more like infighting amongst separate factions of the Fey perhaps rather than a huge conspiracy as he made out – but it was clear that the Fey, including Brosca, hadn't been honest with the Chosen. With her. "What do they gain by this?"

"Power," he replied succinctly. "That's what it all comes down to in the end, and that's what they've always wanted."

"How much did the Fire…the king tell you?"

Trennan shrugged. How to explain so much in one short conversation? "A lot."

"Then tell me. Tell me everything."

'Everything'. The world's most important conversation taking place here in a stinky alleyway, but neither he nor Coryn had given a hint of wanting to leave. He pondered her question, pacing back and forth a few times, before coming up with a simple response. "Short answer? The Fey-Creatures want to rule the world *and* the Other realm. They've started with the Chosen and the Borderlands, but to go any further into the normal they'll need real, physical bodies. They can already influence people, sort of…piggy-back, which means some people have become carriers for the Creatures. But to get their own bodies, the Creatures need the Anima chest."

"The Anima chest," Coryn repeated, understanding dawning on her lovely face. "It has a missing emblem, the spirit's blood. Brosca told me about it in our most recent session, and even

Aras asked me about it a couple of days ago. Me, as if I'd know anything about it!"

She screwed up her nose, making her distaste clear, and Trennan didn't hide his smirk. Aras might be huge, strong and respected, but *Coryn* didn't like him. Excellent. "But why would Aras think you have the emblem?"

"No, he thought *you* knew where it was, and might have told me," she countered. "Isn't that odd?" Trennan was silent, and she continued, frowning. "He was wrong though, wasn't he? You don't- you couldn't-"

"I don't have it," Trennan cut in. It shocked him, though; that Aras would ask before Trennan had even left the king's presence. Word must travel fast in the Other. But who would have told Aras? "But I do know where it is." Or he thought he did, anyway. Before he'd left the king he'd been given a task: to find and destroy the last emblem before the Creatures could get to it and cross over into the normal realm. He'd been given a series of clues that surely wouldn't be hard to decipher, once he had the time. Coryn could help, and maybe Kamile too.

Coryn was silent for a long time, standing still except for her hands which were busy twisting that ring Trennan had given her, and he knew her well enough to know that she was thinking hard, and was perhaps a little bit scared.

"Kamile said I shouldn't go to see Brosca today. I didn't know why she said it, but I was happy enough not to, because she'd been…strange lately. But Trennan," and here she looked at him with anguish in her eyes; "If the Fey *are* Creatures, and are wicked, then what does that make…"

"Me?"

Those wide blue eyes never dropped from his. "You're half Fey," she said quietly. "And…others also shared mixed blood. What about them?"

He shook his head. This was something he was still trying to come to grips with, something truly wonderful. "No, not really. What I am is human with a few extras, the king said. He said that I choose what I do and who I am, and that whoever *made* me doesn't matter, and doesn't have a part of my life unless I want them to."

Coryn looked hopeful, and she began a wavering smile. "That would be lovely if it was true."

"It *is* true," Trennan answered firmly. "I didn't have any Fey features when I was in the Garden, and I bet none of the other Halflings would either. Coryn, we don't have to do things the Chosen way! We can start over, get married for real. Oh, I want you to come meet the king, it would be amazing…"

He closed his eyes, savouring the particularly beautiful memory. "Coryn – it was unlike anything you could imagine, and nothing like the rest of the Other. That's all dead, really, just desert or ice with a few remnants of scrubby trees, or those ruins that you see occasionally. Nothing but death and the Fey. But this place was like…life. And I feel more alive than I ever have before, and like I have the potential to be anyone I want to be, and so can you. Do you want to be?"

"Of course I want to!" she agreed fervently. "But what about you? Trennan, you can't even spend a full day away from the Borderlands without getting ill. We need to stay here." She looked around her at the stinking alleyway that they'd both momentarily forgotten, then screwed up her nose. "I mean back in the Compound."

"Nope," Trennan said triumphantly. "I don't have to. Take a look at *this*." He pulled out from his fabric backpack a small vial of water. It was about as long as his finger, and inside was sparkling clear.

"What is it?"

"This, my lovely Coryn, is the water of life. It came straight from the fountains underground, and it will sustain me and *anyone like me*," he enunciated clearly, "almost indefinitely."

"Did you drink any already?"

"I certainly did, and I've never felt better. Look at me."

Coryn looked, and he knew what she was seeing. His eyes were clear and his skin was still fresh even after several hours away from the Compound. He hadn't even got the strange wrinkled fingertips that were usually the first sign of needing the Other.

"Wow," she breathed. Then again, "Wow."

"And as for the last emblem of the Anima chest, I've got the directions right in this bag, ready for us to take a look. We never have to go back to the Compound if you don't want to, Coryn."

She frowned, and he thought he must have been pushing too hard, too fast. Just ten minutes ago they were merely saying that they felt a little uncomfortable with the Fey, now he was expecting her to give up her home and everything she knew!?

"I'm sorry," he said quickly. "I didn't mean to move so fast. How about we just wait a few days until you're ready…"

"Kamile told me not to go back," Coryn blurted out. "She said something like what you're saying, but she wouldn't give me any details. She said that she just had to be certain of something…" She looked up at him imploringly. "If this is all true, we can't just leave her there. We have to tell people."

"Alright," Trennan replied, putting the backpack down next to the pile of refuse. He put his arms around his lover, resting his head on the top of hers. "Alright. We'll sort it out. Don't worry."

But even as he said it, he was wondering how on earth they would do such a thing. He'd only seen a glimpse of that world, and he knew that this went far, far further than anything he could deal with.

Lunden, 1818 AD

This, George thought grimly, had to be one of the worst days of his life. He'd had a few more terrible days than most people, having had broken engagements (his father paid the girl to leave him) failed businesses (all his money invested in one ship which sank) and even going mad (with the help of an evil, power-wielding witch who was quite thankfully dead) but…

Oh, he'd just said it to himself. He *had* gone mad, very very briefly, but it hadn't lasted, not at all. But he wasn't mad now! He couldn't *believe* that Edward would have the gall to call in those quacks, that he would betray him in such a way. What kind of brother was he?

George angrily kicked at a pebble foolish enough to get in the way, then caught his foot on the uneven cobbles and almost stumbled. He caught himself, looked around to see if anyone had noticed (they had) and then realised he'd walked all the way to Whyte's gentlemen's club. Unlike in Ashlea's time, this wasn't a euphemism for a brothel, but was a men-only establishment where the chief occupations were betting and arguing about politics.

He got as far as the door, muttering angrily to himself the entire way, then abruptly walked past. He was so dreadfully upset that he didn't think he could bear even the small talk he would be required to engage in there – and ironically, he'd forgotten what had so concerned him in the first place. Anne. He had to find some way to contact her, to warn her not to return to her own time, except bloody Edward had got in the way.

George swore under his breath, feeling angry all over again.

What truly infuriated him was that Edward hadn't spoken to him directly. He (and Olivia, most likely, but George blamed his brother) had just gone straight to those dreadful doctors from the insane asylum, as if they could decide whether he was sane or not! He felt *so* betrayed.

He could only thank Deias that Ashlea hadn't been there when the doctors had arrived. Now George knew exactly what Edward and Olivia thought of his wife, that she was a charlatan and a liar, he didn't trust them alone with her. No wonder she was unhappy here.

By Jove, that was the worst part. He'd have to admit that Ashlea had been *right*.

Right after he'd found some way to warn Anne of her impending danger, of course. George pondered the best way to do that. Unfortunately the only way he knew how to access Anne was to go from the gateway in Iversley to 1556, which hopefully was where Anne was *not*. Not the best plan, but how *did* one send a message to someone born three centuries earlier?

George turned yet another corner, then saw his familiar surroundings. He realised he had simply walked the block and was coming back to Whyte's as though that had been his plan the whole time. He sighed, then decided to walk inside after all. He needed some time to think.

"Mr George Seymour?"

He looked up from where he'd been studying his feet. A well-dressed man with a familiar face was staring back at him, flanked on either side by burly men in plain clothing. "Dr...Farnsworth. What are you doing here?"

The man flinched almost imperceptibly. "Actually, it's Dr Pennysworth," he corrected. "I was very interested in what you had to say this morning, and I was hoping for a more private place to discuss it. Away from disbelieving ears, hmm?"

George laughed aloud, but without humour. "Thank you for the offer, but I must decline."

He tried to sidestep the three of them, but the bigger men moved to block his path. "Mr Seymour," the doctor said again. "If you'd be so kind-"

George felt a wave of fury wash over him at the sheer gall of the man. He cut in, "No, I shall not be kind. Move yourself and your hired thugs out of my way or I'll call the police!"

He only realised what he'd said when Dr Pennysworth's eyebrows shot up. "Call the police?" the doctor repeated politely. "Do you mean a watchman? I don't see any nearby."

"Then I shall find some," George snapped. "Get out of my way!"

The doctor sighed mournfully, moving back. "I'm dreadfully sorry."

You should be, George wanted to reply, but that was when someone pulled a bag over his head, and he felt himself being grabbed and dragged off the footpath and into what felt like a carriage. He kicked and struggled and swore, but no one intervened.

That was when he discovered that yes, a man *could* be abducted from a public street, when it was a clearly marked Insane Asylum carriage he was being pulled into. After all, no one was going to help a madman.

TREASON AND TRICKERY

Outer Sipyria, 6000 BC

Anne stopped after the fifth gateway the sentinel led her through, slumping with a sigh onto the rough brown grass. She knew not where she was, or when; merely that the grasslands rolled into the base of vast, snow-capped mountains in the distance, and her garb had changed once more to something seeming to be made from the skin of a goat, or mayhap a shaggy lamb. Some of those animals were grazing on these slopes, unbothered by her sudden appearance. 'Twas a most primitive, barbaric place, no doubt – but at least her lovely sparkle slippers remained on her feet.

"I said I wished to go to rescue Francois," she told the uninterested sentinel in annoyance. "Not take a grand tour of space and time. Now will you take me to the man, or must I find him myself?" A foolish thought indeed, since she would not know him if she saw him, nor would she be able to retrace her steps back to the Mountain of Glass without the glowing insect's aid.

As ever, the sentinel simply buzzed in the air, flashing from black to green to purplish black once more. 'Twould not change to pure green until it found the correct gateway – whatever that meant. By now, she had asked a good six or seven brown-haired men if they were Francois, and had received nothing but strange looks in return.

With a sigh, Anne stood once more and began to trudge after the bug, then when that grew dull, simply floated through the air. After all there was not anyone else here to watch her, and therefore accuse her of consorting with dark spirits, was there? And flying was the most wonderfully freeing experience. But 'twas a short trip to the next gateway this time: the sentinel began to flash intensely green rather too near the hindquarters of a large, shaggy, placidly-chewing beast.

"That is it," she snapped at the sentinel. "I shall *not* walk into the rear end of some beast of burden. You must move!"

But the sentinel did not move, and neither did the chewing beast. Finally Anne gave a sigh that fringed on desperation, clenched her fists, and stepped through – barely a foot from having a face full of fur.

Her new location was rather nicer than the last, with a green forest to one side, an expanse of fields to the other, and what might have been the tall walls of a castle barely visible in the distance.

But what gave Anne the most cheer was that her garb had returned to the plain, dull, brown servant's gown that she had worn last time – albeit with rather prettier shoes. She even wore some kind of poofy hat covering her red hair.

Sigh. She did love her sparkle slippers.

The sentinel had disappeared from sight, which most likely meant that it thought that she did not yet require its assistance. 'Twas true, for Anne was determined not to move on until she'd ascertained the date and location from a local. Hopefully one who would also prove friendly and knowledgeable and not at all superstitious, unlike the locals from gateways number two and four.

Speaking of such locals, there appeared to be a conversation taking place not too far away. The language quickly became apparent as Frencine (tick number one). There was a man with his back to her, not old, and with brownish-blond hair (tick number two). His companion, a woman with a wide red skirt and whose face Anne could not yet see, had called him Francois. (Tick, tick, tick!!!)

"How very brave you are to venture out here alone," the woman was saying with a purr. She had one of those voices that said she was very attractive, or at least thought herself to be. 'Twas oddly familiar. "And on a rescue mission that might cost you your life."

Anne stepped back behind a tree, just out of sight. Whether 'twas incurable nosiness or good sense she knew not, simply that she wished to hear the rest of the conversation. Mayhap dear Francois had chosen to disappear.

"It will cost our lives to remain," the man replied. His voice marked him as youngish, but Anne could not see whatever 'twas about him that bound the Comtesse D'Auran so closely to his side. "I shall find someone able to clothe us and to take us to the coast, where we shall find a boat heading north."

"Angland? Your lover will forfeit her title and lands for a certainty. Have you not heard the new laws about those who dare leave Frencia?"

The man – who surely must be Nadine's Francois – shrugged in that quintessentially Frencine way. "As I said, there is no other choice."

"There is perhaps one other choice," the woman said throatily. "Will you come to see it?"

Just then the sentinel buzzed back into sight, flashing green and black as it headed right towards the two. Anne's heart leapt in alarm, thinking that the couple would see it, but the woman merely stepped aside as if to avoid it.

Then Anne saw the reason for her familiar-sounding voice, and went cold from head to toe. 'Twas Seyen Johannis, standing here in this place and looking for all the world like another Frencine aristocrat, but for the Eternity Stone which sat around her white neck like an unusual gemstone. Bethie had been right.

Anne studied her with narrowed eyes, remembering what Amaranthus had said about this very situation. Seyen was dangerous, and always would be dangerous no matter where she'd be found in her time-travel journey…and the sentinel had stopped about two feet to her left, and was glowing a steady green.

"What is this about?" Francois asked, sounding more irritated than seduced. "Do you know of a way to escape that we have not yet been made aware of?"

"Let me whisper it to you," Seyen replied, taking a step closer to him. She held something in her right hand, half hidden in the folds of her skirts, and Anne couldn't wait a moment longer.

She acted.

Ducking her head so that Seyen wouldn't see her face, she flew low and fast at the two of them, faster than she'd be able to run. She caught Francois around the waist like one of those rugby players from Ash's time, sending him skidding back into the gateway marked by the sentinel, and right through it. The last thing she saw was Seyen's shocked face as their eyes met for a split second – too slow for the other woman to react.

Whew!

That's right, you witch, Anne thought with satisfaction (and with a rather sore nose, for Francois was not as soft as the average nobleman). I *got this one*.

Lile City, 2597 AD

Trennan and Coryn had only just leaned in for another kiss when they were interrupted in the alleyway by an enforcer. "No loitering or public indecency," he told them firmly. "Ten credits each."

"We were just kissing," Coryn tried to argue, but then with a prod from Trennan she bowed her head. "Sorry, sir."

They held out their hands as the enforcer scanned the rarely-used chips embedded there, and half a second later, they were both ten credits poorer.

"Well?" the enforcer snapped. He was quite a young man, clearly still enjoying the power this role gave him. "Get out of here, then."

Trennan grabbed her hand and pulled her out of the alleyway into the more populated public streets. There was no sense getting on the wrong side of one of the bureaucratic enforcers – they had a thousand laws they could stick you with, and here in the city, they ruled.

Technically they also ruled in the Chosen compound, not that anyone noticed that. The Lile Premier was notoriously more laid back than his predecessors when it came to upholding the secular laws: his motto seemed to be that if you couldn't see it, it wasn't happening. As a result, there were dozens, probably even hundreds, of religions, spiritualist and alter-power based groups (including the Chosen) who simply operated quietly and were left alone. But to actually commit a crime on the streets? Not done.

"Kissing's not a crime," Coryn muttered under her breath to Trennan as they quickly walked away, feeling the enforcer's eyes fixed on their backs. Ten credits! That was the downside of coming to the city. Back in the Compound they didn't often use credits, and they almost never earned them except for the twenty that were automatically added to each person's account yearly by the government, a sort of limited social welfare. In truth, it would barely provide a dozen meals. How were they supposed to replace them?

"It is if they say it is," Trennan replied lightly. "Come on, let's get out of here. Shall we do some VR?"

"I suppose so. We said we would, didn't we?" She felt regret at losing even a moment with him in VR, but if they were asked what they'd been doing, she wanted to have at least a partially honest answer.

They'd made it all the way to the front of the VR centre when Trennan realised he'd left the backpack behind. "I'll go get it. I'll be back in two minutes," he promised.

Coryn waited out front, twiddling her thumbs and watching passers-by, and thinking about a fresh start in life. She'd never noticed what a good view she had of the city from here. Lile City had started out like most Europaean metropolises: just one level, with tall buildings pointing towards the sky in the very centre, and single level buildings where there was more space. But then because of the city limit rules created to preserve Lile's green spaces, the city had grown *up*.

And up, and up. Although she could probably count two dozen distinct building levels from here, there were officially only three. The ground level was where the oldest (and poorest) buildings were, and the mid-level where she now stood was mostly commercial with mid-range housing scattered throughout. The upper level was for designer stores, government buildings, nice parks and the houses of the very rich – people who could afford the sunlight.

If Coryn looked over this level's safety railing she could see the ground ten storeys below with multiple roads running through like tangled spaghetti, and even the original concrete roads on the ground far below that. Even though there were decent rails on the edge of every level and sublevel, the government had still installed safety nets below. It was too easy for someone to fall, especially with the huge number of people milling around, and of course the children with their hoverboards and anti-gravity 'wings', flitting around like birds.

The wings scared Coryn. She'd never used them, but even watching the small children was nerve-wracking. They'd take running jumps over the sheer drops between levels, then would soar up or down or wherever they wanted to go, without a hint of fear. How could they could be so young and yet so brave? Maybe they just didn't have the imagination to see how it could go wrong.

It was strange, she thought later, how she *did* have the imagination to see how things could go wrong, yet somehow she was still surprised by how things turned out…

It started when a vehicle full of Chosen girls pulled up right in front of where Coryn stood. None of them were Coryn's particular friends, but she knew all of them. They sat in one of the more unusual 'van style' multi-seater vehicles, complete with tinted windows which turned clear as the vehicle's door opened.

"Coryn!" one of the girls called through the doorway. "Come here!"

She waved back politely. "I can't," she called back.

"What?"

Oh, for goodness sake. They could come over, instead of shouting at her from a distance. Slightly irritated, Coryn walked over to the vehicle. "Hi, Maja," she said to the girl. "What are you all doing here?"

The group exchanged knowing glances. "Coming to get you, of course," Maja replied with a grin.

"Why?!"

"It's a surprise," another girl chirped. "But it's one you'll like."

Coryn glanced back towards where Trennan had gone. He was really taking too long to get that backpack. "I can't go," she said in bewilderment. "Trennan and I just got here. We were going into VR, and he wouldn't know where I'd gone."

"Don't worry," Maja said knowingly. "He's fine, see?" She pulled out one of the little discs that all the Secs carried around in the city, but that the Chosen disapproved of. Its screen displayed the inside of another vehicle, this time filled with males and with a bemused-looking Trennan sitting firmly in the middle. There was no sign of his backpack.

"We've got her," Maja told the disc. "She's balking though."

The boy sitting next to Trennan grinned. "Tell her why we're here."

"We're getting handfasted," Trennan said flatly to the disc, and therefore to her. It was the last thing that Coryn had expected to hear, and she jumped back in surprise.

"What? Why!?"

"Elder's orders," Maja said impatiently, turning the screen blank. "Now get in the vehicle before we get in trouble for loitering."

Remembering she had less than a dozen credits to her name, Coryn got in. Soon she was fixed tightly between two girls, the same way Trennan had been sitting in his vehicle. "Surely you didn't come all the way into the city just to fetch us," she suggested. "And in a multi-seater? And with a viewing disc? Where did you get all this?"

While the Chosen hadn't explicitly banned the use of such things (vehicles were necessary, after all) they certainly didn't encourage their use, especially not within the Compound.

Maja tapped the side of her nose, and one of the other girls giggled. "That's for me to know," she said cryptically. "Oh, and we did come all the way into the city. Jurgis said to make an occasion of this, since it's your first handfasting."

Coryn was still confounded. She wanted to be with Trennan, of course she did. But this was just plain strange, especially right after the conversation she'd just had with Trennan…

Impossible, she told herself. Even if somehow the Chosen had overheard what they were saying and wanted to pull them in for damage control, it still took at least an hour to get from the Compound to the city. So it must have been pre-planned. But why?

She asked. "Surely you could have just waited for us to get back and saved yourselves the trip out?"

"Don't know why," Maja replied. "Except a little bird told us that you and Trennan were starting to-" she made a face – "…you know, get attached. And of course the best cure for that is time spent together, right?"

Everyone laughed, and Coryn tried to laugh along with them. Either she hadn't been as discreet as she'd thought she was, or else Kamile had somehow let the secret slip.

Oh, who was she kidding? Of course someone had noticed Coryn's partiality for Trennan, and vice versa.

She tried to get some more information out of the girls on the drive home, but no one would tell her anything. Instead they went about dressing her in the small space the multi-seater offered. Off came her usual clothes, and on went traditional white robes with a sash around the waist. Her hair was plaited tightly with a garland of fresh flowers woven in, and another garland was hung around her neck.

Seeing herself reflected in the vehicle's shining windows, Coryn started to pick up a little of the excitement the others were displaying. She was going to be handfasted to Trennan, hooray! But she couldn't figure out why any of this was happening like it was, and that stopped her from truly enjoying herself.

This wasn't how the Chosen did handfasting celebrations. Except for major feasts like Solstice, handfasting ceremonies were always carried out with just an elder or two in attendance, plus the couple. They were such an ordinary, regular thing that people hardly got excited about them. Perhaps a little more for a first handfasting, but even then...

"Where is the ceremony going to take place?" she asked, her voice sounding very small.

One of the nearest girls rolled her eyes. "Where do all first handfastings happen? In the Other, of course."

"Of course," Coryn echoed, her heart sinking.

Damn. She'd purposely avoided Brosca today, and after what Trennan had told her, she'd been planning to make that permanent by staying out of the Other realm. What if Brosca was waiting there for her?

What did she think the Fey was going to do, Coryn scolded herself. Come at her fangs first? She looked around at the smiling, chatting girls filling the vehicle, and shook her head. She'd known these people since she was a child, and there was nothing sinister about this.

Really.

Finally the vehicle reached the Compound, and for the first time in her memory, it didn't stop in the designated space outside the gates. Instead they drove right through the gates and towards the border before stopping just short of where the lush green growth began, next to another identical vehicle.

She climbed out to see Trennan was already waiting along with two other young men. He also wore traditional white robes, but his were decorated with fresh greenery rather than flowers.

His expression was sombre, and when their eyes met, he held her gaze intently. She couldn't help smiling. If this all turned out well…they'd be together, wouldn't they? And they could leave the Compound after that, live alone in the city…

"You look very handsome," Coryn whispered. She desperately wanted to take his hand, but they weren't supposed to touch until the ceremony. "You should roll in shrubbery more often."

A ghost of a smile flitted over his face. "Are you alright?"

He hadn't even commented on how she looked, and her mood dropped. It seemed he was even more nervous than she was. She nodded. "You?"

He opened his mouth and-

"No talking until the ceremony!" someone said loudly from behind her. "Time to go, lovebirds!"

She felt two strong hands on her shoulders, pulling her away from Trennan, and then they were both being marched across into the Borderlands. She kept trying to look at him, to catch his eye, but she could barely see him past the people flanking the two of them.

Far too soon the lush greenery around them changed into trees hung with black cloud, and a mere few steps later they were in the Other. The light was as cool and dim as ever, with stones and rubble the only scenery for miles. Except perhaps now Coryn imagined that she could see the glow of the fire pits in the far distance. It brought back an image from one of the visions she'd had with Brosca, the one with fields of snow…

Up ahead was the small stone castle often used for hand-fasting ceremonies. Coryn had seen it a few times from a distance during her visits with Brosca, although had never been inside. It wasn't really much to look at, just a single hall with tall strong walls, a couple of long, narrow windows set high above the ground to let in the non-existent light, and a turret on each corner which was more for decoration than actual use.

As they reached the stairs that led up to the only entry, the door opened. "There you are!" Jurgis said cheerfully. "We've been waiting. Come along, lovebirds. The rest of you can go."

Their escorts turned to leave. Coryn looked at Trennan uncertainly. Everyone was so cheerful…so surely it was alright, wasn't it? But his expression was as uncertain as she felt, and he reached out to take her hand as they walked up the stairs, tradition be damned. She clutched it tightly, forcing a smile as they moved through the doorway. His skin was distinctly bark-like and his features a little distorted, just like it usually was out here in the Other, but a small smile assured her slightly. She wasn't alone.

Inside the castle there was just one main room, with the stone altar in the centre which was used for the ceremony. But it was who she saw waiting there that made her feel uneasy.

"Brosca," she said with a forced smile. "I didn't expect to see you here."

The Fey smiled back, her silvery hair shining like pure metal, and her orange eyes glinting. But now to Coryn they looked less warm and more like a predator's, and she felt her gut twist in anxiety.

"How could I miss the first handfasting of my favourite pupil?" Brosca said smoothly. "You shouldn't have expected anything else."

Coryn shouldn't have, but she had hoped. She shuddered and resisted the urge to cover her neck. Glancing at Trennan out of the corner of her eye, she saw his pupils were dilated with fear. Her fingers tightened around his.

The room was surprisingly crowded. There were four elders in all, including Jurgis and Starbright, the 'head' male and female elders all wearing unfamiliar red cloaks, and there was someone who Coryn had never seen before. Another young woman, a human, with a narrow crown on her head, long robes and a sleepily bored expression. She looked to Coryn like a fairytale princess, but she stood back from the others, almost ignored, and unnamed.

Off to the side she glimpsed a bundle of something covered in sacking, but she didn't get a chance to look closer before they were led to the circle in the centre of the room where the raised stone dais stood facing the altar. Jurgis stood on the dais and looked down at the two of them sternly, his earlier cheer having vanished. "Do you know why you are here, Trennan Halfling, Coryn of the Chosen?" he asked solemnly.

"To pledge my troth to Coryn of the Chosen," Trennan replied, reciting the traditional words for the first time. She saw him glance at her sidelong, and in spite of the oddness of the situation, he smiled slightly, and that dimple appeared faintly in his cheek.

Coryn couldn't help smiling back at hearing him speak those words. She said her part, mentally apologising for using his 'old' name. "To pledge my troth to Trennan Halfling."

Instead of continuing the ceremony as expected, the elders just stared at them. Then Jurgis said, "Really? Because from what we hear, you came today to tell us that you've been consorting with our enemy, and plan to bring us down."

As he spoke, one of the other elders, Jeffare, picked up an ornate knife from where it sat on a small table on the other side of the room. Coryn felt her eyes widen and her gut twist again in fear, and her fingers tightened painfully on Trennan's. This was all going so horribly, horribly wrong!

"We don't want to hurt you," Trennan replied, his voice strong even though he must be as afraid as she was. He had no weapon, little power, no way to protect them from any kind of harm. "We just want the chance to live a full life, and to know the truth about the world we live in."

"I can't make promises to either," Jurgis replied coolly, almost smiling. It was most inappropriate to the situation. "Truth, boy?"

Trennan wore that expression that Coryn knew meant he was afraid, and she heard him swallow audibly. His hand in hers became almost painfully tight, but she welcomed it. "The truth," he repeated. "That the Other isn't a dead realm, and that the Fire Lord is still alive, and that there's a world full of life beneath our feet if we know where to look for it."

"Treason," someone hissed from behind them.

Coryn didn't recognise the voice, but then it could have been anyone's, couldn't it? She was too scared to speak up, almost too scared to move, but this spurred her frozen voice into action. "It's not treason to ask questions for the good of everyone," she said very quietly, her voice almost a whisper. "You talk about treason, but is it true that you're all blood-drinkers? That you've been preying on our people for years?"

A few of the elders exchanged unsurprised glances, and Jurgis smiled. "We follow the Fey in all things."

Was that a yes or a no? Judging by the elders' lack of reaction, Coryn was taking it as a yes. And out of the corner of her eye she could see Brosca moving slowly up behind her…

Oh, Fire Lord. *Help*.

"That's it," Trennan said, and this time his voice shook. "We're leaving. Come on, Coryn."

But there was now a whole row of red-clad elders blocking the closed door, and Jurgis shook his head. He now held the knife. "We'd rather you stayed. After all, this kind of betrayal can't go unpunished. What would people think of us?" Then he gestured to the others. "Tie them up, and bring the sacrifice."

Someone grabbed Coryn by the back of her arms, wrenching her hand free of Trennan's and dragging her away to the side of the room. She screamed, trying to shake herself free, but it was like she was being held by steel cables. Over her shoulder she caught a glimpse of orange eyes and silvery hair, and a whiff of that old-book smell she always associated with Brosca...but this time it was underlaid with something rotten. "Brosca," she whimpered. "Please, you don't need to hurt us!"

"Oh, was I hurting you?" Brosca whispered into her ear. "How unfortunate." Her fingers dug into Coryn's soft upper arms, the nails digging into her flesh.

Coryn screamed, and the Fey laughed.

There are no Fey, just Creatures, Trennan had said. *And they hate humans...*

Oh Fire Lord, it *was* true. It was a nightmare come to life, but it was happening.

Forget that she'd known Brosca for years. Forget that these people had felt like family. Coryn fought with everything she had; fought to get free, to reach Trennan on the other side of the room. Jurgis had that knife...

But Brosca was far stronger than she looked, and her grip was completely unyielding from where she stood behind her. It was like a mentoring session gone wrong. That was when Coryn realised that in all of her years of 'study' here in the Other, she had never once been taught to defend herself.

Across from them Trennan was struggling with several of the elders, and as she watched he was struck on the head with a staff, knocking him off his feet. He slumped to the ground as though dazed and Coryn screamed, but Halflings were tougher than that. He recouped, spinning to the side and striking at the nearest elder's legs. He knocked the man over, leaping on top of him and grabbing for his staff, but then Starbright lifted her hands. She didn't touch Trennan, but his body raised into the air as if on strings, then went flying hard into the stone wall.

Crack. He slumped down to the ground, then tried to get up and Starbright raised her hands again…

Smash. Smash. Smash. She sent him flying against that wall over and over until he finally went limp. Then she let him fall to the floor.

Coryn was sobbing in earnest now, still mindlessly trying to get away from Brosca, but knowing even as she struggled that it was pointless. *You're like a crippled mouse among cats. You've got no chance of escape. No chance of mercy. It's only a matter of time…*

Was that Brosca's voice in her head? Coryn let out a horrified groan. How had she not known what these people were like? What these *things* were like?

"What we are like?" Brosca whispered into her ear. Her voice was hoarse, her breath hot. Her body where she held Coryn felt huge and bony, like she was wearing a suit of armour under those robes. "You're the one who turned on those who raised you."

Coryn then knew that they'd lied to her, lied over and over again. And she'd *chosen* to come out here to the Other alone? She would have wept for that mistake alone. "You *are* a blood-drinker, aren't you?" she whispered.

Even though she couldn't see the Fey, she felt the puff of breath from her laughter and then the faintest scraping of teeth against the soft skin at the back of her neck. "Just wait, sweetling. Your turn will come."

In front of them a couple of the elders carried the sackcloth-covered bundle to the centre of the room and set it on the altar. One of them pulled away the rough covering, revealing a petite, green-skinned woman, her eyes closed and her head lolling back.

Kamile.

Bring the sacrifice, Jurgis had said. And now he stood before the altar with that curved knife in his hand, his expression expectant…

"No!" Coryn screamed, feeling like all the blood had left her body. "Leave her alone! She hasn't done anything wrong!"

"That's where you're wrong, Coryn," Starbright said serenely from her place next to Jurgis. "Kamile has been visiting our old enemy's grounds. She was planning to betray us, to leave just as you were."

Had Kamile been planning to do that? "Please," Coryn begged. "She's a good person. She doesn't deserve to die like this."

Starbright ignored her, rearranging Kamile's limbs to a more comfortable looking position. A puffy set of red holes marked her thin forearm, rather like an infected snake bite.

Coryn tried again. "What will Aras say about this?"

"Aras?" Jurgis retorted. "What will he care? He never wanted her in the first place. Besides, he'll never know."

Or rather, Coryn would never get a chance to tell him. It seemed like slow motion as she watched Jurgis reach down with that knife, and Brosca whispered in Coryn's ear, "Shame she was finally pregnant…"

Then there was so much blood all around her friend's head and neck, so much it looked like someone had emptied a bucket of red paint. The elders…they were leaning in around her, leaning down towards the blood…

Coryn began to scream and scream and scream, feeling like she couldn't stop, and struggling within Brosca's grasp even though she knew she couldn't get away. The useless garlands of flowers fell across her line of sight onto the cold stone, and she felt her loose white ceremonial robe begin to fall off her shoulder, but she didn't care. She just kept screaming.

They killed Kamile They killed Kamile They killed Kamile- Blood-

drinkers killed Kamile…

Across the room she saw Trennan climbing to his feet. His face was twisted into a snarl of rage or horror, and he was holding one of the elders' metal staffs, wielding it like a sword as he staggered towards the nearest red-cloaked back. He raised it up to strike, but suddenly Brosca was there, blocking the staff with one thin hand. She'd released Coryn so fast that she almost stumbled, and she was barely gaining her footing when Brosca struck.

In one moment Trennan was staring down at the Fey, both his hands on the metal staff, and then next his head snapped backwards at an unnatural angle as she hit him under the chin, hit him with the strength that only Fey blood or alter-power could gift.

He went flying backwards towards the wall, landing with another crack, and finally Coryn was running towards him with her arms outstretched. His neck couldn't be broken, it couldn't be. That dullness to his eyes couldn't be death. She just had to touch him…

But then something hard hit her in the ankle, and she fell face forward, right into the wall next to Trennan. And just as her face would have struck the stone, something strange happened. Suddenly the wall was no longer there. Instead there was a great drop beneath her, a haze of orange and fire, and her arms were windmilling in the empty air.

The fire pit grew larger and larger and warmer and-

It was the strangest thing. Or Trennan would have thought it was strange, if he'd had the chance to think about it. As it was, he saw the Fey-Creature Brosca appear suddenly in front of him, and her arm shot out towards him as fast as a cobra strike. And then he'd heard this *crunch,* and argh, it had felt like his *neck,* but then he was shaking off the pain and going for her again. He was running on fury and adrenaline and the most incredible burst of energy, and all he could think was to STOP THEM!

But somehow the metal staff had fallen from his hands, and Trennan couldn't stop himself slamming into Brosca full-force. Into? He fell *through* her, sprawling to land on the stone floor behind.

"Illusion!" he shouted to Coryn even as he leapt up again, looking around for the true Fey, the true danger. They had to be hiding themselves, and had to have huge power if even *he* was fooled. "Watch out!"

But everything around him was fading to grey. It seemed to be becoming transparent, like a malfunctioning VR session, and he couldn't touch anyone. He grabbed for the fallen staff, but his fingers went right through it instead of gripping the hard metal. He swore. "Coryn!?"

Where was she? Was she alright? She *had* to be alright…

There she was. He saw her in the corner of that grey room, her face twisted with fear and horror – an expression he never wanted to see her wear again. And she was falling back against the stone wall as Brosca bore down on her, and then suddenly the wall opened up behind her. It was the only colour in that grey room; like a flash of orange-white firelight, like an actual fire pit had appeared right behind Coryn in the wall. *We're saved,* he thought in a moment of relief. And then she fell through into the pit, and he was reaching for her to follow her out.

Cough. The quiet sound caught Trennan's attention in the otherwise chaotic scene, and he turned to look for its origin. But something tripped him, and he stumbled, falling hard on the grey floor next to the wall. He'd landed next to someone's fallen figure, someone in pale wedding robes strewn with transparent greyish ivy. Someone with rough-looking, barklike skin.

"Hey…" The hole in the wall had vanished, and now the white-clad figure held Trennan's full focus. Ugh, it really looked like…*him*, except his neck wasn't bent back like that…

He reached up carefully to feel that his skin was smooth, as smooth as it had been when he'd gone down into the fire pit that one time. His neck was definitely at the right angle, he thought in confusion and dawning dismay. So who was that in front of him? "*Heeeyyy…*"

Cough.

This time Trennan turned towards the noise. A man stood behind him. It was the Fire Lord, and he had one hand outstretched towards Trennan. And as Trennan saw that hand, the whole grey scene around him faded into whiteness…

VIRTUAL UNREALITY

Not quite home

Ash wandered along the waterfront of the city, enjoying its cleanness in comparison to Regency Lunden, and marvelling at the masses of glass making up the buildings, the verdant green of the hills surrounding, and the barely clouded blue sky reflecting on the water far below. Gorgeous.

That was what showed her that she couldn't be home in the Southern Isles. At home several of the major cities were built on harbours, but this city was on the edge of a huge dam, over-looking the harbour from a great height. Ash wandered up to the high protective railing, right next to the sign reading, 'DO NOT CLIMB THE RAILING'. She didn't have to be told twice not to, but of course if someone was drunk or stupid enough the sign wouldn't be a deterrent.

But it was a weird place to build a city. The height alone scared her, and she was likely the only person here who could say that if she fell over the edge, she wouldn't die. She could just fly away like a bird, but even knowing that, the drop was still uncomfortable.

There must have been a mist over the water in spite of the blue sky, because when she peered out across the harbour, at first no details were visible. Then they began to appear; more hills off in the distance, misty and green-grey over the other side of the harbour.

It wasn't the Southern Isles of the twenty-first century as Ash knew it, but it wasn't too far off. Maybe, she mused to herself, just maybe it *was* her home, but in decades to come? They might have built up the city to deal with rising sea levels…but it wasn't as though she was going to ask a local what year it was. That was the best way to get either a sarcastic answer, or some very worried looks. She decided her best bet was to find a newspaper, or whatever this place's equivalent was. But whatever she did, she'd better not forget where the gateway was – or she might never get back home.

Ash memorised a couple of landmarks, glad that she was wearing trousers and seemed to fit in for once. It actually felt good to be ignored by the locals. She stood in what seemed like a large town square built on the top of the damn, all concrete with some park benches. It was ugly, but felt familiar enough for her to relax as she searched for a way down to the water.

She began to move along the edge of the dam's high fence, and as she walked the path gradually began to slope downhill. The central business district was left behind and it slowly became less city, more beach. Finally she stood level with the muted golden sand: the dam with its high railing around to her left, while in front of her flat blue water sparkled into the horizon. It was incredibly serene compared to where she'd just been, even though not far away there were children splashing in the water.

Ahhh. Lovely. There was no one nagging her, or judging her, or making her wear uncomfortable corsets. "It's practically a holiday," she mused aloud. She didn't have to do *anything* here – although she was open to helping a little, if the need arose.

She eyed the children nervously. She could swim enough to not-drown, but she'd rather not have to rush in to save them if they were struggling.

But the children seemed happy enough, so Ash walked onto the beach and just stood for a while, her boots sinking a little into the damp sand. Here she couldn't even *see* the dam, and she enjoyed the peace for a moment before an odd depression in the sand caught her eye. It was large and vaguely oval, with the water pooling in from the gentle waves.

Hmm. Curious, she took a few steps closer, then stopped in surprise as her shin hit something hard. She put her hands carefully out in front of her, feeling the smooth, slightly damp shape of something very large. What on earth…?

She moved her hands around the shape, following it right down to the ground. Now it was semi-visible, blending in with the wet sand. It seemed almost like a small whale, stranded on the beach…if whales could be invisible, that was. There was a puff of breath, and she was sprayed lightly with seawater from an unseen source, right in the face.

"Argh!" She sneezed, shaking her head. "What in Hades was that?"

"Looks like you've found something," said a nearby voice.

Ash jumped, but then relaxed immediately when she saw who had spoken. It was a boy about her age or a little older, athletic in build, with longish fair hair and a friendly grin, and he seemed about as threatening as a Labrador puppy.

She couldn't help herself smiling back, maybe because he reminded her a little of George. "I think so. But what is it?"

"It's a blue beluga whale," the young man replied cheerfully. He was speaking Southern Isles Anglish, she noted. "Ever heard of those?"

Ash shook her head. "I've heard of blue whales, and of beluga, but never the two together."

He ran his hand gently down the unseen flank, and as he did

so the area where he touched turned white. "It was stupid humans interfering that did it. About ten years back, when the whales almost went extinct in 2020, some geniuses got the idea to genetically modify certain whale species with chameleon genes, to hide them from hunters."

It sounded like something out of science fiction, Ash thought, trying to hide her jubilation at being given a date. 2030 wasn't that far after her own time. "Then it worked?"

The boy grinned ruefully. "Sort of. What it has done is make the blue beluga impossible to spot if it ever beaches itself, and believe me, they do. On the bright side, they're now one of the most common whale species."

"That's good, I suppose." She studied the length of the dip in the ground. It looked to be about ten feet long. "Do you think we can push it out? How heavy is it?"

"Heavier than you can handle," he answered. "But the tide should be on its way in, and then we can push it out. I'll wait with you, if you like."

"Oh. Thanks." Hopefully that would be soon, because as nice and cute as this guy was, she wasn't interested in staying around for long. "I'm Ash, by the way."

"Nice to meet you, Ash. I'm Seth."

The water had come in so fast it was already lapping around their feet, and these boots were showing themselves to be surprisingly waterproof. Ash perked up, then set her hands against the drying, rubbery side of the whale. "Give me a hand, Seth."

He set his against the side of the whale next to her, but even by then the waves were rushing in, somehow managing to rise quickly without being destructive. A couple of one-two-three-pushes, and the whale shifted, letting out a huffing breath, then with another it floated into the water.

"That's it," Seth said in triumph. "We've got it now."

That was easy, Ash thought in surprise. She didn't know why people complained about such things. But just then she felt a heavy weight against her legs as the water came rushing back in, and for a moment it seemed as if they'd both be knocked down under the whale's weight. "Ahhh!"

"Push!" Seth instructed. And then like trying to deliver an enormous baby, finally the whale was up and away. In the water it was barely visible, but the light played across its smooth surface, and there was yet another spray of water from its almost invisible blow hole. Ash let out a laugh and Seth laughed with her, and heedless of their clothing they followed the animal into the water, making sure it was well and truly safe.

The camouflage really was effective. She could barely see it at all, and then it was gone. A few children swimming in the blue water squealed as they were bumped by the invisible whale, and she saw one try to hang onto it and get tipped head over heels as the others laughed.

An odd job well done, she thought to herself. *Here* she was needed, not just a clueless ball and chain.

Seth spotted the smug look on her face and raised his eyebrows. "Feeling like a hero, are we?"

"Well, I can fly like a superhero," she joked.

"What a coincidence." Then he threw his hands up in the air, and shot right up out of the water...like a superhero, funnily enough.

Ash watched him open-mouthed (there were others!!) and then took off after him. Flying seemed to be easier here. Usually it was a form of exercise, requiring will and flapping arms, but now she just sped through the air. Wahoo! "Is this normal here?" she shouted.

"Nah," he said depreciatingly. "Just a few of us who are...gifted." And then he winked one bright blue eye and headed up higher over the bay, towards the low hills on the opposite side.

Ash followed, tingling with excitement. It had been so long since she'd ever done something so fun and spontaneous. Angland of 1818 was not exactly those things, not at all, but here with this almost-stranger she felt like thumbing her nose at George and his rigid rules. *Do embroidery, Ashlea. Or my mother can give you something to do.*

How about saving whales – alright, just one whale – and then flying around a beautiful harbour with a handsome boy instead?

Her conscience reminded her that George wouldn't appreciate the second part – and she sure as Hades wouldn't like it if the situation was reversed – but she dismissed it. She wasn't going to do anything wrong, and no one even needed to know she was here.

Ash wanted to ask Seth more questions (like how he'd got his gift, for starters) but he was too far ahead of her, speeding through the air faster than she ever thought she'd manage on her own, and looking like a casually dressed superhero for real.

After a few minutes he slowed to a halt, and she came to rest not far from him, grinning with exhilaration. Now they were hovering high above the green hills edging the city, with a tiny dirt road winding its way below them like a piece of spaghetti on basil sauce.

"I haven't done anything like this in a long time," she told him. "We always have to hide what we can do. It won't matter if anyone sees us?"

"Nah," he said again. "People are used to seeing the gifted. Mostly we get ignored, just like those blue beluga whales."

By the Rood, as Anne would have said. A true miracle. "Are there many others?"

"Not locally. Just me." He shot her a crooked grin. "And you, now."

Ash wasn't sure why, but she found herself blushing. "I won't be staying for long."

"Oh?"

"I just wanted a little adventure," she admitted. "To be of some use to someone." Then looking around her at the ocean and the scenery below, she added humorously, "But maybe just getting away is enough. I suppose that whale needed me, right? I was a hero to it, at least."

Seth got the joke. "If that's enough for you, then great. But if you've got a little more time…"

"Yes?"

"…Do you want to do something *really* heroic?"

Somewhere…

The grey room faded, and then Trennan was standing in what seemed like a white mist. In front of him was the Fire Lord, underneath his feet was an unseen floor, and everyone else had disappeared.

"What…what…" Trennan blinked, looking down at his now-smooth skin, then up again at the Fire Lord. The other man-being-whatever watched him with solemn dark eyes, but didn't speak, and didn't offer an explanation.

Trennan was utterly baffled. His pain was gone – in fact he felt pretty damn good – but he couldn't stop thinking of that broken white-clad figure…and how he'd ended up here.

Where *was* here, anyway? But first things first: "Where's Coryn?" he asked finally.

Safe.

The answer came immediately into Trennan's mind, and he nodded slowly. His panic was receding, replaced with a sort of calm acceptance that was really rather nice, but also seemed unlikely considering the circumstances. If the Fire Lord had said it, then it must be true.

I prefer Amaranthus.

If Amaranthus had said it, then it must be true, Trennan mentally corrected himself. There was something about the man…person…being…that just made him so very believable; that made lies seem impossible.

"Where am I, then? What happened?"

Unfortunately you were attacked by the Chosen Elders along with a Creature. It broke your neck, but I rescued you.

"You rescued me *after* it broke my neck!? Most people would call that too late for a rescue!"

Perhaps. But you would have died anyway, after seventy or eighty years. Do you feel harmed?

Trennan's eyebrows shot up at the first statement. Sure, he would have died eventually. Everyone did…

Not everyone.

Not Amaranthus, Trennan realised, and he studied the other man with new curiosity. He seemed to glow from inside, like there really was a fire in there. Not in a dragon-like sort of way, but instead like…like nothing he'd ever known before. "No, I don't feel harmed," he said finally, answering the second question. "But I'm here, and Coryn's out there, and-" Suddenly he remembered one other person who'd been in the room. One other person who definitely hadn't been rescued. "Kamile! Oh Kamile, did you see what they did to her?! What about *her*?"

Come here, and I'll show you.

Trennan moved forward towards Amaranthus's outstretched hand, and as he took it, their surroundings suddenly became clear. The white light/mist vanished, and now he could see that they stood in a vast room, as big as some valleys, and with what seemed like a colossal greyish wall running around each side.

Then suddenly they were right next to the wall, and Trennan could see that it wasn't grey at all. It was made of thousands – *millions* – of tiny black and white threads, woven together in what might be a beautiful pattern, or what might just be a big mess. "It's a tapestry?" he wondered aloud.

It's how I keep track.

"Of what?"

Everything.

Trennan didn't understand how that was possible, until Amaranthus stretched out their joined fingers to touch one spot on the wall. Then suddenly images burst out towards them, images with sound, and they were playing faster than he ought to have been able to keep up with, and yet somehow he could. And here was Kamile – oh, here she was some years ago with Coryn, who was practically a child although Kamile looked the same. And here she was handfasting with Aras, and then hmm, a couple of other things he'd rather not have seen, and then the horrible scene in the castle, and then further still.

But Amaranthus took Trennan further along, through scene after scene and person after person, until they saw how each point touched and each person affected others, and then…

"Oh," Trennan said finally. "Oh. I get it now."

And he did get it. He'd been planning to ask why Amaranthus had given him those clues for the Anima Chest, if he'd known *this* was going to happen, but he'd seen the answer to that too.

And for now, that was enough.

"So what next?"

I think we'll need a messenger.

The Compound, Lile

Coryn staggered across the border into the Compound, feeling as muzzy as if she'd slept for a month.

She hurt so much she almost couldn't feel it anymore. Heart pain, physical pain – it all blurred together until she wondered how she could even walk in this condition.

Her head was full of horrible knowledge and horrible images: Trennan and Kamile dying, the careless violence of Jurgis and Starbright, and the evil, unkillable Brosca. Oh, she wanted to kill them! She wanted to kill them, and she wanted to turn back time and save Trennan and Kamile, and she wanted this all to have been a bad dream, like the snake.

The events in the castle did almost seem like a dream now. When she'd first awoken and found herself in the bushes at the edge of the border, for a long moment she simply thought she'd had a nightmare. All she could remember was the look on Trennan's face when Brosca had struck him, and the malevolence on the Fey's. Brosca had almost looked like a beast in that moment, not a person at all. There had been something in that gaze which simply wasn't found in human beings.

The bodies, Coryn thought numbly. The Other realm never kept bodies. They'd always appear somewhere on the borders, either far more decayed than they ought to be, or in contrast, far too fresh. She needed to find the bodies and bury them. Bury her best friend, and her husband of the heart…

Suddenly overwhelmed by grief, Coryn collapsed onto her hands and knees there at the edge of the green fields tended by the Chosen. She was crying so hard that she couldn't move. She felt like she'd die.

"I didn't even stop them," she whispered to herself through the tears. "I just watched them die, then fell out the window…."

If that was even what had happened. She'd fallen through a hole of some kind, a hole in the wall, so what else could it have been? But even if she hadn't fallen, she couldn't have saved Trennan or Kamile. She'd been too weak to break free of one little old Fey, and she couldn't have saved them. She could have only died in the same way, and the fact that she'd escaped was a miracle in itself.

"*Oh, DEIAS!*" Coryn cried out that name that was forbidden by both the Secular Republic and the Chosen, wondering if such a being existed, and if so, how could they allow such evil to happen under their watch? Or maybe they just didn't care. Maybe they'd spun this world into being, then turned away towards something more interesting. Her heart hurt so much it was physical, causing racking pain throughout her whole body. She wanted to die too and end the pain.

Finally she remembered that she had others to care for. Regina, her half brother Ladon, and her other friends in the Compound: they all needed to know the truth about the Elders and the Fey. Those leaders weren't their friends. *Definitely* not their friends.

Coryn managed to look up, to see where she was. From her place on the ground she could see right over the border. Today was one of those clear days where the black-clouded forest didn't obscure the view, and she could see the castle, tiny in the distance in the eternal twilight of the Other. Here on the normal side it was bright daylight.

She'd definitely lost time. The fields had been lush with salad greens and new potatoes when she'd gone into that awful place, but now it was covered in neat rows of brassica, with a single figure weeding at the field's far end. The winter crops were already well established. Could it have been months since that awful day?

With a sort of numbed detachment Coryn realised she was still in her underwear: a pair of thin white shorts and a camisole. The handfasting robe had been left behind in the castle, in accordance with Brosca's prophecy of the future. At least she still had her own shoes.

Just then the single gardener stood upright, and Coryn knew they'd seen her. She forced herself to her feet and would have – oh who knew, run for it maybe? – when the person set down their basket and moved closer, and she recognised them.

Regina.

"Mother," she sobbed, staggering towards the gardener with arms outstretched. "The most terrible thing has happened!"

But the woman just looked at her with an odd, blank expression. "I'm sorry to hear that," she said politely. "But I'm afraid we haven't been introduced, and I'm certainly not your mother."

Coryn stopped in her tracks, dropping her hands to her sides. "What?"

"You've mistaken me for someone else," Regina continued, mild concern crossing her face. "Perhaps you've had a run-in with an unfriendly Fey. Where are your clothes, girl?"

By the Fire Lord, Regina was serious. "My clothes!?" Coryn cried out. "Mother, who cares about my clothes! Brosca and the elders killed Trennan and Kamile right in front of me! They're blood-drinkers, all of them, and I barely got away-"

"Child," Regina cut in, "as I said, I'm not your mother, and I certainly don't know any of those names. Now if you'll come with me, I'll find you some clothes, and we'll see about having you checked for injury."

Even though Regina's words weren't making any sense, and even though she couldn't shake a terrible sense of dread and unreality, Coryn found herself following the woman across the fields and into one of the nearby cottages where they kept the gardening equipment. Regina ushered her into a rickety old cane chair with a brisk smile. "Now you stay there, and I'll be back in no time."

"But-"

But nothing. Regina had gone.

Coryn sat for a few minutes staring blankly at the wall beside the open doorway, stacked with the old-fashioned garden utensils that the Chosen preferred. "She didn't recognise me," she said aloud, and she heard the confusion in her own tone. "How could she not recognise her own daughter?"

"Hello miss."

Coryn jumped in fright, and the boy in the doorway shrugged apologetically. "Sorry, miss. I was sent here with some clothes for you." He held out an armful of pale cloth: the basic 'uniform' of the Chosen. Simple, pure, and clean... but then nothing about this matched that description any longer.

Miss. "Ladon," Coryn whispered. "You know me, right?"

His blue eyes so like her own flickered over her under-clad body, and there was something in that gaze that was *not* brotherly. He glanced away. "Sorry, miss. We haven't met."

"You're my brother!" she cried, quickly taking the clothing from him and holding it in front of herself. "Is this some kind of game?"

Ladon paused, and then a strange thing happened. His features made a subtle shift…or maybe it was just his expression, but all of a sudden he looked like a different person, and a chill ran up Coryn's spine.

"I think you'll find that things have changed in the five months you've been gone," her brother said in Brosca's voice, with that same awful, gleeful expression Brosca had worn when she'd stabbed Trennan. His eyes flickered orange. "He doesn't remember you. In fact, none of them do. You no longer have a brother or a mother or friends, if you ever did. It's as if you never lived. But if you come back to me, come back to the castle, I'll change that for you."

Five months!?

Coryn stumbled backwards, shaking her head violently. She hadn't realised that a human being could also be a conduit, but that was surely what was happening to her brother right now. "Brosca, you vicious, evil *monster*. I'm not coming near you! You'll just kill me too."

"I promise I won't," the Fey crooned, and she/he took a step towards Coryn with a hand outstretched. Almost tripping over her feet, Coryn turned and sprinted away.

She'd neared the Compound gates when she realised she wasn't being chased. She still held the clothing from Ladon – Ladon who'd looked at her like she was an attractive, underdressed stranger. Like he hadn't known her at all, just like Regina.

Fire Lord. It was as if she'd lost them too. Feeling utterly broken, she quickly dressed and left the Compound. She couldn't stay here. It wasn't her home now they'd taken the last thing that mattered: her family. Now she had nothing and nobody.

She was completely alone.

They were going to need a messenger, Amaranthus knew. More than one, in fact.

He followed a tiny white thread along where it jumped in and out of other threads, taking enormous leaps across metres of tapestry and then being stitched in with others only briefly before taking other enormous leaps. He tapped the thread, and the image of a red-haired teenage girl flicked into view.

He watched for a while, unconcerned by the way Trennan was watching over his shoulder. After all, the boy had a vested interest, and now he wasn't panicking, he'd have a chance to appreciate the finer details. There wasn't a hurry, since when one stood outside of time, a plight such as Coryn's wasn't precisely time dependent.

My goodness, Anne had a lot of enthusiasm, Amaranthus mused, *even if she lacked the ability to wait for instruction sometimes.* There she was tackling Francois right through the gateway behind him (and yes, he had arranged to have that conveniently right there – the girl would have been following the sentinel for aeons, otherwise) and then somehow, miraculously finding *another* gateway just beyond that which led straight to the Lunden docks, not ten minutes after the other Frencine émigrés had been deposited. There was a little scene where Nadine squealed and cried and embraced her common-law husband, and the thoughts running through Anne's head were both proud and a little embarrassed, and then rather de trop.

What do I do now? she wondered.

Amaranthus leaned into the thread, knowing she'd hear him as a voice in her mind. *Do you want a suggestion?*

Amaranthus! Did you see what I did? {Are you proud of me?}

The last thought had been one of the quiet ones that only came from the heart, but he still heard it. *Always, dearest Anne. I always see, and I'm always proud. Do you wish for another task, dear? I*

*have one for you if you'll take it, and then you should return to the
Mountain.*

He felt her prick up with interest. *Of course.*

It's about the light-wand…

Over the harbour, not quite home

Did Ash want to do something heroic, Seth had asked from his
position high in the air.

Well, duh. Ash's heart skipped a beat at the offer. She didn't
even think about possible death or any of those other legitimate
fears that might hold her back. "Sure!"

Seth nodded in relief, then his expression grew more serious.
"There's a criminal ring around here that traffics young women
from overseas and sends them to places where no one will listen
or care if they tell their stories." He pointed at the tiny dark shape
of a car and tiny people on the road far below. "That's a pick-up
point. I need you to get those girls to the city and safety, while I
sort out the Wasp, who runs it all."

Ooh, 'the Wasp'. That was a very villainous name. And Seth
was going to 'sort him out'. Ash had no idea what that actually
meant, but she was incredibly keen to help. Maybe it was because
she was a girl, or because she had what felt like a younger sister in
Anne, but she *hated* human trafficking with a passion. "No
problem," she said grimly, momentarily forgetting the practicali-
ties of bad people with guns, and how they would react when
someone dropped out of the sky.

Maybe it was because she'd spent so long feeling bored and
ordinary, but she wasn't at all afraid. Instead she was excited and

energised. Not only could she fly, but she had this handy little ability called far-sight. Like the gift of flight, it originally came from Amaranthus, and it meant that she would be able to see what would happen if she made certain actions, and change her choices accordingly.

It wasn't quite prophecy, because it wasn't what would *definitely* happen; it wasn't fate, or set in stone. It could be changed. Mind you, far-sight hadn't shown up in a while, but she expected that it would when she really needed it. It always had in the past.

Seth and Ash quietly flew closer to the group, until finally she could make out less than a dozen figures. Now she could see they were standing next to a large four-wheel drive, as if waiting for someone else, since the vehicle clearly couldn't hold all of them. There were about five or six young women with various skin colours, although their clothing would suggest that they were from Western countries.

Standing with them were three men. Two were ordinary white men, on the bulky side (e.g. rent-a-thug), but the third looked like the stereotypical bad guy with long dark hair, elegant European features, and an expensive looking leather-jacket. Ignoring those clichéd elements (was there a villain's handbook or something?) Ash could see why girls might be tempted to listen to someone like that. He was quite handsome and a lot younger than she'd expected, and the other two were nothing to scoff at, either.

"That's the Wasp wearing black," Seth whispered to her. "I'll draw the men away, you deal with the girls."

Ash nodded, and then Seth shot off so fast that she didn't even see where he went.

Not two minutes later there was an explosion from behind the hill where they stood, where a road led to a large, white building all on its own. The Wasp and one of the other men immediately turned towards the sound, jumped into the vehicle and drove away towards the explosion, leaving the last man with the girls.

"Quick work, Seth," Ash said quietly. But now what? She flew down slowly, wondering if the man had a weapon, or if she could get to him fast enough to stop herself getting shot. Right now a little far-sight would be useful…

Just then, she clearly saw herself *flying down at great speed towards the thug, hitting him hard enough that he was knocked out clean, and she was barely shaken. Then she turned to the women and said, "We need to get out of here!"*

In a flash, Ash was back in the present, wondering why for once far-sight had come on command. Oh well…what was that saying about not looking gift horses in the face, or something? She'd take what she could get. She turned towards the group far below, took a deep breath in to build her courage, and then pulled her arms to her sides, imagining she was a hawk about to grab an unsuspecting field mouse.

The man looked up just a second before she hit him with a speed that should have dazed her at the very least. Instead it left her merely a little shaken, her knee in the now-unconscious man's stomach as he lay sprawled on the ground. Oops.

She shook herself a little, then jumped energetically to her feet. "It worked!"

"What did you do?" screamed one of the girls, a young brunette with large dark eyes. She reminded Ash of Anne's little sister Elspeth, who Ash hadn't seen since that brief time in the Mountain of Glass months before. She didn't look nearly as grateful as she ought to.

"Those men plan to sell you into prostitution and slavery," Ash told her firmly. "We need to get out of here before they come back."

The girls looked at each other in confusion and horror, and

strangely enough, none commented on the fact that she'd fallen out of the sky. Seth must have been right that people were used to the 'gifted', because in 1818 or even Ash's time, people would be freaking out – or at least be taking pictures on their phones.

Ash waited for further questions, complaints, demands that she explain herself, but the girls just fell into line as if they'd been trained for it. How convenient.

"What should we do, then?" the dark-eyed girl asked.

Good question. "Can any of you fly?"

"Of course not!" snapped one of the other girls.

Great. Now that would have been too easy, of course. What Ash needed was some way to move them out of there...

"What about that car over there?" asked the woman who'd been waiting for her husband. "We could all squeeze in."

Ash didn't know how she'd missed it – perhaps because it was light gold against the sandy road – but there was indeed a good-sized car, one of those with wide seats and a huge boot. "Can anyone drive?" She wanted to go find Seth and help him with the others.

"I can," three of them replied all at the same time.

"Well, someone do it," Ash told them, feeling an incredible confidence, but also a sense of urgency. The traffickers could be back any time, and they might have weapons. Ash had her gifts, but being bulletproof wasn't one of them. "You don't have much time."

The girls were duly packed into the car, with one of the eldest in the driver's seat and the two smallest rather comically in the boot. "Drive back to the city centre and find the police station, or whatever passes for one," Ash ordered.

"You aren't coming?" the driver asked.

Ash shook her head. "I have somewhere else to be, but I'll watch to make sure you get away."

They still paused, and Ash began to panic a little. "Go!"

"Thank you," someone called out the window, and then the car took off with a screech of tires, a cloud of dust in its wake.

Ash watched it go, noting that the thug was still unconscious, and the other villains nowhere to be seen. She allowed herself a moment to think of how she was going to rub this in George's face when she saw him again, but then remembered that what she was doing was *important*. Funny, because it felt almost like she was acting out a role. Heroine? Sure, why not?

She followed the girls' car from a height for just long enough to make sure no one tried to stop them. When it became clear that their getaway was unhindered, she turned and flew as fast as she could back towards that white building where the explosion had come from.

There was smoke coming from one side of the building, although no flames were visible. The main door was unguarded, so after a moment of hesitation Ash went right in, looking out for more trafficked girls or thug-like henchmen, or even Seth. But all she saw was endless hallways and rooms empty of people, the whole place eerily silent and white, white, white. That made her almost more nervous than if there'd been screams. Where was everyone?

Right on cue a scream broke the silence, coming from down the hall. Ash didn't see who'd screamed, but she caught a glimpse of a dark-haired man in a black jacket disappearing into a side room at the other end of the hall.

The Wasp.

A moment later Seth came flying around the corner, not touching the floor, and going straight past the room the Wasp had gone into. Just then Ash saw what made the walls so white – there was a gel-like substance, like white paint, crawling towards her over the walls. She was torn between telling Seth what he'd missed and trying to see what the goo was.

"Don't touch it!" Seth shouted at her as he flew past, reading her mind. "It's toxic!"

"But the Wasp-" Ash began, but he wasn't listening. He disappeared from sight, and then it was just her and the mysterious creeping whiteness. "Seriously?" she muttered. "You left the bad guy behind!" If the Wasp escaped then he'd surely just repeat his crimes with some other poor target. Hades, she *hated* slavery, and that's what trafficking was, just targeting the people who should be the most protected.

But she didn't have a gun. She didn't have any weapon at all past the intermittent far-sight and her flight, and she sure as Hades didn't want to get *shot*.

Suddenly (and yes, conveniently) far-sight came into play. The Wasp *had come from a room behind her and shot her in the back, and she saw too late the metal tea-tray that could have saved her-*

Ash spun in one smooth movement, grabbing the tea-tray by one silver edge and pulling it to her chest. The impact of the shot hitting the tray felt like being punched. She went skidding to the floor, falling through a doorway behind and hitting her back against the wall. Dazed, she sat there a moment before her head stopped spinning, and he came to stand in front of her.

"Drop your weapon," the Wasp ordered. His voice was clipped and smooth, and his accent vaguely foreign. He looked even younger close up – surely not more than a couple of years older than George – but unlike George, he was holding a slim black gun aimed at her head. (Oh wait, George had done that too, once upon a time…)

Ash glanced around, seeing that the room they were now in had no windows or doors, just a skylight above them. It was a dead end…and the white toxic goo was creeping in around the doorway and floor. "I don't have a weapon," she replied. In fact, all she had was the now bent tea-tray in one hand.

"Bad-" the Wasp began to say, but she never found out what was so bad. The tea-tray spun like a discus and smacked him in the head, knocking him backwards and sending his gun arm flying. A shot rang out and there was a sharp burst of pain across her cheekbone, quickly forgotten in the adrenaline rush that sent her flying off the ground and going for the gun. She turned it on him.

"Bad what?" she asked with grim satisfaction.

He went dead still, his dark eyes fixed on the gun, then looked up at her with a kind of resigned amusement. "Bad timing, I was going to say. We're both trapped in here now. What do you propose to do?"

During their fight the white toxic goo had crept in further over the walls, now barely metres from where they lay. Cursing to herself, Ash flew up onto a table, still training the gun on the trafficker. Could he tell that she didn't know what to do with it?

His lip curled into a slight smile, and he pushed himself to his feet, watching the creeping whiteness around him with alarm. "It has two rounds remaining," he said lightly. "If you're planning to kill me, perhaps you might make it quick? Otherwise this little, ah, *failed experiment* consumes all living matter. It wouldn't be a quick way to go."

Hades, the man really *was* like a movie villain, right down to the sharp cheekbones and flesh-eating experiments. Why did the handsome ones have to be evil? And he'd even given her a faint wound across the cheekbone, which she wasn't sure how she'd explain to George. But the more important issue was in front of her. "You don't deserve it," she told the Wasp, putting her full hatred of trafficking and slavery and abuse into her tone. "But unlike you, I'm not a murderer."

"I'm not a murderer," he replied seriously. "You don't know

what's really going on here."

"If you're not a murderer, then you're a slaver," she spat back. "But speak."

He looked once more at the toxic gel creeping closer and closer, then back at her. "I can't explain now – but I'm not the Wasp. I've just been playing a part."

The white gel was within two feet of him now, and Ash made a split-second decision. She threw the gun aside into the creeping goo, then held out her hand. The Wasp looked unconvinced, but what choice did he have? Ash grabbed hold of his wrist, then with all of her strength and the tightest grip she could manage, shot upwards towards the skylight. Had it been open?

It didn't matter anymore, because right then the doorway she'd come in by collapsed, and with it the roof. Up above she could see the panels coming down towards them again as if in slow motion, and there was a gap, just half a second's worth, where she swung her heavy cargo up and out, out of the collapsing building, out above the crawling toxic goo.

Now the whole building was white, white with the toxin, and for a few seconds it seemed as if it would keep spreading forever, until it consumed the whole city. But then the sludge seemed to lose its strength and stopped advancing, and the whole mess began to turn a solid dark grey, like concrete.

Ash dragged the man free of the building before losing her grip and tossing him none too gently to the ground.

"Oof!" He pushed himself to his hands and knees. "You could have been a bit more careful."

"You're lucky to be alive." She saw his hand heading for inside his jacket, and she stomped down on it hard…but not quite hard enough to break the bones.

"Ahh!"

"Tell me what's going on here," she ordered, still running on fury and adrenaline, and that too-close, energizing shave with death. "You say you're not the Wasp? Speak."

"Get off my hand and I'll speak as much as you like," he replied in a grimace.

"And let you shoot me again? Not likely."

The man looked pained, and he sighed, his voice suddenly losing its accent and becoming more ordinary. "Fine. I'm not the Wasp, I'm actually an undercover police officer. We apprehended the real Wasp three days ago, and I've been pretending to be him for the Jackson City branch of the gang." He shrugged. "Apparently I look like him. I was going to show you my badge."

Ash watched him carefully for a moment. He seemed sincere, but that kind of person would be a good liar, wouldn't he? And far-sight didn't show any warnings. "Let me see it."

He stayed still while she flicked open his jacket, slipping her hand into the inner pocket. There was a small black wallet inside, and inside that was a Jackson City Police Force insignia and an unmistakeable plastic ID card reading J. Smith, JCPF. He raised his eyebrows sardonically when he saw her expression. "Satisfied?"

So Lukos wasn't his real name, then. "I suppose so," she replied, handing him back the wallet. At this proximity she could see her reflection in his eyes, and she was struck by two things. Firstly, how *good* she looked…her hair was never normally this smooth and sleek. Good hair day, hooray! Secondly, that they really were very close – she was practically in his lap – and he really was very handsome, and he wasn't *really* a bad guy after all…

He gave her a little smile, and her breath caught. At that moment, she was ashamed to say, George did not even enter her thoughts. But something *else* did, and when he leaned in close enough that she could feel his warm breath on her cheek, he whispered, "Disclaimer."

She froze. "What?"

"Disclaimer," he said in that same warm, low voice. "Anything that happens within the boundaries of Virtual World is the sole responsibility of the user and Virtual World accepts no responsibility for any emotional or psychological harm. Do you wish to continue?"

She pushed him away, stumbling back. What on earth was he talking about? He was just watching her with that same enigmatic smile, as if he'd suggested something rather more intimate than giving her a *disclaimer*.

"What in Hades are you talking about?!"

"You were about to cross emotional boundaries," the not-Wasp replied, still smiling. "First-time users must be warned as per government regulations. Your response will be noted for future use."

"I was- I was *not*," Ash argued. She was embarrassed (because maybe, just maybe she *would* have let him kiss her) but mostly she just felt confused. "I don't know what that means," she snapped. And where in Hades was Seth when she needed him?

"Is there a problem?"

Ash spun around to see he was standing right behind her. He would have seen that whole thing, where she'd almost- almost-

She redirected that horror into anger, scowling at Seth. "What is going on here?"

His open grin didn't change. "You're in Virtual World, the premium venue for safe, virtual adventure. For your free VR trial you chose a familiar setting with a side theme of superhero/spy, as the program detected that your mind desired. Do you wish to change the setting, or continue?"

"Do I what?"

"Do you want to change the setting, or continue with this

one?" he repeated.

The setting. Virtual World… "Are you telling me this is some kind of *game*?" she choked out.

"Virtual reality or VR is the way to really experience all life can offer," Seth said brightly as if reading off a spiel. "You can be whoever you want to be, do whatever you want to do. Do whoever-"

"I get it!" Ash snapped. Suddenly it all made sense. Why everything seemed so familiar, but not quite right; why her pain and fear didn't seem as intense as it should, and why every time she'd wished something would happen, a moment later it had. She'd wanted to go somewhere familiar but not home, and had ended up in this place. And then she'd ending up 'saving' the whale and the girls, and there'd been those thugs who really did look like something off a cheap action film, and the villain who was…well, too attractive to be a real villain, and so he hadn't been.

"I wouldn't have," she muttered. "I wouldn't have kissed you."

The not-Wasp just smiled as if he knew what she was thinking, and Ash slumped. Hypocrite, much? She thought again of that last argument with George, the one where she had declared that she'd 'go somewhere she was needed', or something equally stupid. Well, she'd got it: the clean, quick version of a real fight, complete with easily defeated bad guys. In real life she would have been shot out of the sky. Hades, even far-sight had come when she'd wanted it to, and that *never* happened in real life. She now felt incredibly foolish, unfaithful, and dejected.

"You said it was a free trial?" Ash asked quietly. "How do I get out, then?"

"When your trial finishes," Seth replied brightly. "Or when you say the magic word."

"What, abracadabra?"

Suddenly the scene around her froze, then melted into greyness. Ash was standing alone in the midst of a clouded grey sky: grey below, above, on every side. Bright images flickered past in each direction, and she realised belatedly that this was what had happened when she'd first arrived. It hadn't been hundreds of gateways, just hundreds of potential programmes. And Seth? He'd never existed.

"I just want out," she said to herself. "Out, out, out- ooh."

There below her in the mist was a faint, shimmering shape. An *actual* gateway, unlike the fake programmes. It must be the one she'd come in by, she decided, and headed for it in relief. She'd go back to the townhouse, tell George that she needed a break in her own time – go back to Leister County if that's what was needed. She just couldn't stand anymore of this boredom, and the constant sniping and coldness from his family.

And then she was through the gateway, but the other side wasn't exactly what – or where – she'd been expecting.

Lile

Somehow Coryn managed to summon the motivation to travel back into the city. While the Chosen might have forgotten her, the credits remaining on her ID chip were still active. She used five of her last ones to take the monorail into Lile City, then another three to buy a solid meal.

She didn't feel hungry, but at the same time her body was screaming for her to eat something. An interesting contradiction, if she'd cared enough to notice. But she didn't care about anything except that Trennan and Kamile were dead.

It filled her mind and heart like a ceaseless car alarm, unwanted and unable to be shut off.

On the trip into Lile City she also saw a calendar-clock that confirmed what Brosca had said through her brother, even if the change of season hadn't done it already. Five months *had* passed while Coryn had been in that fire pit doing who knew what, and it was now nearing the end of 2597.

That meant that Kamile and Trennan had both been dead for almost six months, and who had mourned them? Did anyone even know they were gone, or had their very memories been wiped away from the minds of the Chosen like her own had?

It was just such a senseless tragedy. Within days of the two of them finding out the truth about the Fey (at least Jurgis said that Kamile had, and why else would he kill her?) they had both been murdered, and all their new knowledge was pointless. The only one who knew was her, and she had already proved herself useless.

Was this the true way of the world? She'd always thought that good ought to win, that those on the side of right (i.e. her own side) would emerge triumphant. But she'd been wrong. The powerful crushed the weak, and the wicked ran over the good since they weren't crippled with 'morals'. It seemed that goodness was useless without strength, and they'd had none.

Three credits was nowhere near enough for even the cheapest accommodation, but Coryn found she didn't care much about that either. After she left the monorail stop, she wandered down to the lowest levels where some of the buildings had deteriorated to the point of being rubbish tips, occupied only by the lowest members of society. It pretty much reflected her state of mind, and so she just sat herself in an unoccupied space and sobbed. She didn't move, she didn't try to go anywhere or speak to anyone. She just grieved, because her heart felt like it had been ripped right out of her chest.

It was somewhere around the second night after Coryn's escape that she remembered Trennan's backpack. It seemed ridiculous to think of it now – heaven knew it had been five months already – but she couldn't shake the feeling that it might still be there in that alley. After all, Trennan had never got a chance to pick it up, had he?

Unlikely, she told herself, and turned over to try to sleep. But her 'refound' mattress was uncomfortable and smelled strange, and she couldn't get the image out of her mind of the backpack sitting all alone in the alley for so many months. She *had* to see if it was still there. After all, it was the last piece of Trennan she'd ever have.

With that depressing thought, Coryn dragged herself up and began the arduous task of climbing the levels with a body that didn't want to do anything. A ladder here, a staircase here, until she was at the familiar park which edged onto the mid-level shopping district. It all looked much the same lit up artificially in the middle of the night, but it was eerily empty of people. That was different. Last time she'd been here at night it had been almost as busy as during the day.

After a few missteps she came across the old VR centre, and found the alley right where it had always been. Of course it was so dark that she almost couldn't see a thing, and she wondered again what on earth she was thinking. But what did she have to lose by wasting a little time here? It wasn't like she had somewhere better to be.

Coryn shuffled her way to where she thought the backpack had been, and hit her shin on something hard. "Ow!" Unwilling body or not, that still hurt.

"Shhh!" someone hissed. "Move not, nor make a sound. The curfew enforcers are coming!"

She froze into place, resisting the urge to panic over the unknown voice. Curfew? What curfew? But just then she heard the faint hum of an air vehicle overhead, skimming its way between the levels, and a bright flash of light filled her vision. In that second that the alley was lit as bright as day, and even past the spots flashing in front of her eyes she somehow saw the petite red-haired girl, crouched on top of a pile of ancient recycling bins right beside her.

Then the light was gone, and Coryn waited to be caught. There was no way she couldn't have been seen. But nothing happened, and the air vehicle hummed into the distance, and she was left standing in the pitch dark with a now silent helper.

A few more seconds went by, and then a little light flickered. It was only about as strong as a single match, but in the otherwise complete darkness it was as good as a street light. It lit the girl's face from underneath to ghoulish effect, and after a moment Coryn realised that in spite of her small size, she was older than she had first seemed. She also seemed vaguely familiar.

"Do I know you?"

The girl scrunched up her little nose. "I'd vow you do not, for when should we have met?"

"I don't know."

"Then I do not know either," the girl agreed decisively. Her accent was ordinary, but her words were strangely old-fashioned. "But by the saints, you must be more careful! Should you be caught after curfew, I'm told there would be most severe consequences."

Coryn stared at her blankly. "Since when is there a curfew?"

"Ever since the old Premier was killed and the new one decided to do things properly," she replied with a shrug. "Those are his words rather than my own."

The Premier was dead? Coryn found she didn't care. She only cared that Trennan and Kamile were dead… and now she was crying again, but silently. "OK."

Maybe the redhead couldn't see so well in the dark, because she just said, "Here, take this light. What you seek is behind the red bin."

Coryn took the offered light – rather like a silver plastic stick with a glowing end – and sniffed a little, still trying to work out what was going on. "How do you know what I'm even looking for?"

"You have friends in high places," she replied mysteriously. Then with a little more excitement, "Oh, *do* take a look. I'd vow you have about ten minutes before the curfew guard comes back around. But do not lose that light-wand! 'Tis certain you shall find it useful in the days to come."

Cautiously Coryn stared into the pile of old bins, trying to work out which was the red one. Finally she tugged it out of the way, uncovering a filthy black pile of something. Prodding at it with her foot, the black thing was dislodged and proven to be an ancient plastic shopping bag, and underneath was a familiar cloth bag, still closed with its two straps. It seemed to be in remarkably good condition; possibly because it *had* been underneath the other bag.

Trennan's bag. By the Fire Lord, that just made her want to cry even more. She forced back the tears, turning to her helper. "How did you know…?" she began, but the red-haired girl was nowhere to be seen. "Hello?" Coryn looked around, but she was still alone.

The girl's disappearance was odd, but not so interesting that Coryn would waste any more time on it. She picked up the bag, then carrying the little light-wand she headed back to the only place she knew where she could sleep…her smelly old mattress in the abandoned building ten levels below.

Good thing she wasn't afraid of heights…

Eleven

NEW PATHWAYS

Wogua, 110 AD

Anne had handed over the light-wand to the unknown girl with little ceremony, simply repeating the words she'd been given, then promptly left through the same gateway she'd arrived by. Amaranthus had given that instruction, and then had told her to return to the Mountain of Glass.

She felt buoyed up on success – with the help of the sentinel she had managed to find Francois and take him to his friends – and without even being told what to do!

Of course, this last gateway she'd travelled through had been with direction from Amaranthus. The sentinel was nowhere to be seen. Anne *did* recall the nine other gateways she'd had to use to reach this point at all, and to return to the Mountain by the same method would require quite some travel. But she was tired, and it did not sound appealing.

At this moment she stood on the outskirts of yet another unfamiliar hamlet, the whole place in shades of grey and white from the half melted snow. A flash of colour caught her eye. A sentinel buzzed past her, wings flashing green and white. Shrugging, Anne decided to follow it. Mayhap there was a faster way to return to the Mountain than simply retracing her steps.

So when the sentinel paused in front of a shimmering patch of air at the outskirts of the town, Anne followed without hesitation.

Lile City, 2597 AD

Coryn's last few credits didn't last long in Lile City. It meant about two and a half wildly expensive meals of street food, and that, to her shock, was the cheapest she could find.

"Prices have gone up with the new Premier," the vendor had told her as he handed over her rolled pancake. "Where have you been, under a rock?"

Kind of, yes. But telling him that wouldn't do her any favours. So she'd just taken the food, gone back down to her miserable little rubbish dump, and sat there for a few more days. It wasn't so bad, really. It was a hollowed-out shell of a room, with one wall missing so it was open to the elements, and stacked high with useless items belonging to centuries past. A grubby mattress hid behind piles of ancient TV sets, arranged to provide more shelter as well as hide her from anyone who might wander past.

Against one wall was a strange array of old children's toys: plastic, of course, since the more modern wooden ones tended to decay far more quickly. When Coryn had first found the room and had seen those toys so tidily placed, she'd assumed that someone was already living here. But if they had been, then they'd left, because she hadn't seen a glimpse of them in the last week.

She'd had only three small meals over six days, and she was beginning to feel like her stomach was caving in. It was hard to be numb when her body was screaming for attention, but she kept trying. Numbness beat misery – just – and didn't Kamile and Trennan deserve to be mourned properly? She didn't think too carefully about whether 'starving oneself' counted as proper mourning, but she gave it her best shot.

But she only lasted another day and a half, and that was when she found the rubbish bins. Massive, massive piles of waste dropped down from the higher levels to end up crushed and compacted in the darkness of the abandoned areas. She had thought this sort of practice had died out centuries before, but clearly not. The stench was overwhelming.

Coryn pulled out the little plastic light-wand she'd carried ever since the red-haired girl had given it to her, gently pressing the end so that it glowed. She waved it over the nearest piles, trying to make sense of what lay before her, and that was when she heard the crunch. At her foot was an almost perfect apple. It was oozing juice where she'd stepped on it, and there was a bite on the other side that was rimmed with brown, but apart from that it seemed whole and unmarred.

As if she couldn't control herself, she reached down and grabbed it, holding it up close to her face. It still smelled like rubbish and the faint scent of rot, but her unfussy stomach twisted in hunger anyway.

It occurred to Coryn that this had to be the very lowest moment of her entire life; that she had fallen about as far as she could possibly fall without being dead. She was about to eat rubbish. She was officially homeless: one of the poor, weak, forgotten souls who most of society overlooked, because it made them feel bad to know such a thing existed but still didn't want to put themselves out to fix it.

She ate the apple anyway.

That night, curled up on her mattress with Trennan's bag

sitting next to her, Coryn had the dream again. This time the massive snake chased her down the empty halls of her old home back in the Compound, getting closer and closer every second. Her legs ached with the effort of running, and her chest hurt, but there was no one to help, no one to save her.

But there was something new about the dream. This time, in that weird way dreams sometimes had, she just *knew* that the snake was sapient – not a dumb animal. More importantly, her dream self knew why it was chasing her. Brosca had sent it, and she would never stop. The snake would never stop until it had caught and consumed her.

Coryn woke with a start just as the snake was about to reach her. In the dim light of the morning all she could see filling her vision was a big, black outline, and for a moment she thought she was still dreaming. Then she realised that it was a person trying to steal Trennan's bag, and she sprang into action.

"Hey! You leave that alone!" she shouted with all the strength she could muster.

The thief jolted in surprise, turning to look at her. It was a big, burly man with a shock of dirty fair hair, and for a moment she thought it was Aras. Her blood ran cold, but then the man snarled at her and the illusion fled. This was just another poor homeless person, but there was no weakness in him.

He lifted a hand to strike her and she screamed, grabbing the bag and rolling out of the way. His blow still grazed her ear and it began throbbing, and she screamed again. "Leave me alone!"

"Just give it to me!" he roared back. He had some kind of tattoo on his neck, she noted; something like a ram's head with curling horns. His breath wasn't good.

"No! It's Trennan's bag, and that means it's mine! It's all I have left of him!"

The man reared back in confusion. "Bag? I don't want the

bag, you stupid tart. Give me the wand!"

"The wand...?" Did he mean the plastic light-wand?

That was when a small shape appeared behind the man. It was a young boy holding a broken table leg, and in the half second before he struck, Coryn saw the terror on his face. The first blow hit the man's shoulder, and he let out a roar of pain.

He turned to confront his attacker, but then a slightly older girl appeared with what looked like an old lamp base and hit him on the head. It sent the would-be thief sprawling almost on top of her, clearly dazed.

Coryn and the two children exchanged shocked stares, and then the boy stammered, "He was going to hurt you. We couldn't let him hurt you."

She glanced to where the man was now groaning, pushing himself to his knees. Oh no...

Leaping up, she grabbed the bag and stumbled off the mattress, moving towards the open entrance. "Come on, before he gets up!"

They hadn't made it the length of the street when they heard the man gaining on them. The boy let out a whimper of fear and Coryn felt for him – she was scared out of her wits too. To be attacked again? At least this one wouldn't want to drink her blood, but he was still twice her size, and furious.

Up ahead was a high wire fence, one of the kinds that used to be used for junkyards and the like. Now this whole area was a junkyard, and its high gate swung open, a thin piece of rope hanging from it uselessly. Regardless, it was a beacon of hope.

"In here!" Coryn cried. She ran through with the children, and they shut the gate just as the man slammed up against it. Suddenly full of energy and fury, she flung her body against the other side of the gate, digging her feet into the ground to prevent him following them through. The gate held, and she realised to her surprise that the man wasn't nearly as big and strong as she had first thought. In fact, he wasn't much taller than her.

For a few seconds they grappled on either side of the gate, neither side giving way. That was when Coryn noticed that the fence wasn't complete. About ten metres down, there was a sizeable gap between the fence and the wall. If he wanted, the man could just go *around* the fence.

The little girl noticed it too, and she opened her mouth to speak, but Coryn's horrified expression kept her silent. Just then the man managed to force his hand inside the gate, gaining ground, and that was when Coryn acted.

Pushing back with her whole body, she grabbed the long piece of rope that had once been used to tie the gate shut, and she quickly wrapped it around the man's wrist, then back around the gate, then around his wrist again.

He shouted in surprise and tried to pull away, but he was already caught. She wrapped it around the gate post again, tying it as best she could, then she and the children turned and ran.

It wouldn't keep him long, but it was enough for them to get away. They ran for several blocks until the buildings grew even more desolate, if that was possible, and spread apart, with large gaps between them of bare, crumbled earth. After ten minutes when it became clear they hadn't been followed, Coryn stopped. The children did too, and they all looked around them with distaste.

"We're at the edge of the Empty Zone," the girl said knowingly. "We're not supposed to come down here."

"Not supposed to come below fourth level at all," the boy said. He looked at Coryn beseechingly. "You won't tell, will you?"

"Who would I tell?"

"Dunno. Mum, maybe?"

Coryn closed her eyes for a moment of peace. So they weren't homeless. She should have guessed by their fairly new clothing, and the general air of well-fed cleanliness around them. "I don't know your mum," she replied flatly. "What level are you from?"

"Six."

Which made them on the border of mid-low level, probably edging onto mid. They would be, if not wealthy, then comfortable. "Why were you down here? You can see it's not safe."

"Why were *you* down here?" the girl returned daringly. "It's not safe for you either."

Coryn just stared at them, and finally the boy whispered, "It's our clubhouse."

"What?"

"Where you were sleeping on the mattress. That's our clubhouse, with our toys."

"But we didn't come when you were there!" the girl added in quickly.

She'd stolen a children's play area. Wonderful. "You shouldn't go down there," Coryn repeated. "Especially now. I bet that man will come back, and he'll probably take it out on whoever he finds first. If I were you, I'd do what your mum says and go back up to the fourth level." In her opinion, they were both too small to be even that far from their home. But to come down to urban ground level? Bad, bad idea.

She walked the children to the nearest staircases, former fire-escape routes, and watched as they climbed. When they reached the more solid-looking third level, they disappeared from sight. There was no goodbye, and she didn't expect one.

The wand. Coryn thought that the man must have meant her plastic light-wand, because she certainly didn't have anything else that looked like a wand on her. Either that, or he was simply mistaken…or crazy, which was completely possible. But if he hadn't been crazy…

She opened Trennan's bag to study the thing again, but couldn't find it. Panicking a little, she checked then double checked, then finally tipped the bag's odd contents out on the concrete. The light-wand wasn't there.

Coryn let out a sharp hiss of breath. It must have fallen out at some point, most likely when she was back at the 'clubhouse'. That meant her attacker could have it already, if he'd been bright enough to go back.

"It's just a stupid stick," she told herself aloud, closing her eyes. "It doesn't matter. Nothing does."

But she knew even as she spoke that it was a lie. Trennan's bag of junk-clues mattered, because it had been his, and because he'd been on some stupid bloody quest to find the emblem using those junk-clues. And the light-wand?

Well, it wasn't as if she had anything better to do than look for it. She didn't know why she was still alive while Trennan and Kamile weren't, but for her brief time on earth, she wasn't going to make things worse. And she was pretty sure that letting that man get hold of the light-wand *would* make things worse. She didn't know who he was, but in their ten minutes of interaction she couldn't say she liked him very much.

Sigh.

Coryn waited where she was for a good hour before circling very slowly (and getting lost on the way, which made it even slower) and heading back to the 'clubhouse'. It seemed completely abandoned, so she cautiously made her way back inside. She found the light-wand sitting half-hidden in a pile of old plastic toys, looking just like one of them. She couldn't even summon up the energy to feel happy about it.

She'd only just put the light-wand into Trennan's bag when

she heard a noise. She turned to see the thief was standing behind her, his face twisted with rage. He had a visible lump on his temple, and ragged fingernails on one hand. "You little witch," he hissed, only he didn't say 'witch'.

He lunged at her, and she barely had time to raise her hands defensively when he knocked her down onto the piles of refuse, landing on her with his full weight. He scrabbled at her clothes and it became apparent what his particular mode of revenge was.

That was when Coryn made a decision. She was *not* going to just let this disgusting man do what he wanted, as though her life or her body no longer had value just because Trennan and Kamile were gone.

"No!" she shouted, at the same time raising her hand and bringing the edge down sharply at his neck like a blade. He recoiled and she shoved him off, scrambling to her feet and bringing her heel down hard on his crotch. He screamed, and full of fury, Coryn raised her foot to stomp on him again, but he had rolled to his side and was retching where he lay.

Oh. That was anticlimactic, but she had never felt as powerful as she did in that moment. And that was when she made another decision: that she wasn't just going to waste away and die of starvation or exposure. Trennan and Kamile would have *hated* to see that. No, she had the clues and this…light-wand (which was probably nothing much even though the man seemed to want it, but it was *hers*) and she was going to do her best in memory of those who were gone.

She looked down at the man dispassionately. He didn't scare her anymore. "Come after me again and I'll kill you," she told him, and she meant every word.

The outskirts of Lunden, 1818 AD

"I want a solicitor," George repeated. "Now."

Dr Pennysworth leaned back in his chair on the other side of the wide desk. "I'm afraid that won't be happening any time soon. We took you with your brother's permission."

"My *brother*! I'm not a minor that I answer to *him*," George spat. "And when I leave this place…" He was going to find Edward, and there would be a reckoning.

"When you leave this place?" the doctor repeated curiously. "And how precisely are you going to do that?"

George didn't answer. They'd been over and over this for the last half hour, ever since he'd been put in this room. In chains. Chains, as though he was a madman to need restraining!

"Will you call your friends from the future?" the doctor asked kindly. "Perhaps…use a mechanical device to contact them across great distances, hmm? Or a flying machine?"

The problem was, Dr Pennysworth seemed so sympathetic. If George had truly been mad then he might have been taken in by the false sense of being believed, and tell everything. As it was, he was so tempted to…punch the man in the face, actually. How *dare* he?

"And what about your wife?" the man continued. "Will she give the same story, if she is asked?"

"Leave my wife out of this."

The other man raised his fine eyebrows. "Isn't she the one who found you in the first place, the one who, er, explained to you the mysteries of the future? Why should she be left out? It seems as though she is central."

"She didn't explain any mysteries," George snapped back in exasperation, realising belatedly that he was wrong. In fact, she'd done rather a lot of explaining: about cars, electricity, social customs… But Dr Pennysworth didn't need to know that. "Enough of this. I'm not going to say another word, and let me tell you, there will be *severe* repercussions when I get out of here!"

If he got out of here. Once in an insane asylum, it was very hard to leave. Yes, he might say he wasn't mad, but his family seemed to disagree. It was becoming increasingly apparent what a dreadful situation he was in. And Anne, poor little Anne who had no idea what dangers lay in her future...he couldn't warn her. He couldn't do anything from in here except fume.

"You keep saying that. Is there anything else you'd like to say?"

George stayed stony-faced, and after a long silence the doctor's eye twitched. "Very well. We'll speak again this evening, hmm?" He signalled to someone outside the door, and the same two men who'd abducted George earlier that day came in, pulling George to his feet. "Off to your new home, then."

As George was pulled down the halls towards the cell which was to be his 'new home', he reflected that at least there was one good thing about this. Ashlea was angry with him, and if he was fortunate, she would stay far, far away…

Somewhere

Trennan had left the Tapestry Room when Amaranthus had, following him into what seemed like a maze of glass corridors. The walls seemed to shimmer and move as he watched them, and he touched one gingerly. His fingers came away wet, and faintly shining.

The water of life trickles from the peak of this mountain, Amaran-

thus told him without looking back. *It's everywhere.*

And not a spot of mould in sight, Trennan marvelled. This was a beautiful place, one which he seemed to be seeing only a fraction of, but he couldn't stop thinking about Coryn. What he'd seen of her…time here definitely wasn't passing normally, since he felt like he'd arrived only hours before, but Coryn's thoughts clearly showed many months had passed.

"I have to talk to her," he said aloud. "She's so unhappy. She's…" Scared, and grieving, and could only see what was right in front of her, not nearly the whole picture. Not like he'd seen. He couldn't bear to see her like that.

Amaranthus didn't ask what he was talking about. *She'll see in time, once everything has played out. You know that.*

But she was scared *now*. NOW! Trennan could feel the barrier keeping him here in this place while she was in the other one. Or perhaps it was that he'd *stepped through* a barrier while she had remained behind. He knew it would be hard to go back, but it was possible. He wanted to bring her here…

Amaranthus turned and glanced at Trennan over his shoulder, one eyebrow raised. *A word in the right place, Trennan?*

A word in the right place, he agreed fervently.

Lile, 2597 AD

No one knew who truly started the tradition of mourning marks, but as it often happened in these cases, there were several different parties all claiming the honour. The truth was that it didn't matter who'd started them. Almost no one used them now, which was why when the idea flashed through Coryn's mind the afternoon after the attack, she dismissed it immediately. Normal people did *not* have blue ears.

That's what they were: deep blue designs tattooed along the upper ridge of the ear and down onto the lobe, and sometimes even on the skin behind the ear. They would be names, details of the lives of those now gone, and to receive mourning marks meant giving up on any other visible signs of grief.

The tattoos were the only signs of grief that would now be allowed, and in past times it was considered a noble choice, sort of how widows used to wear black.

Now, it was just a bit weird, and Coryn could count on one hand the number of people she'd seen with them. Mourning marks that was, not widow's weeds. She'd never seen anyone wear *those*, especially since the Chosen didn't actually have any 'widows' in the usual sense of the word.

Besides, she wasn't ready to give up on Trennan and Kamile yet. They might have been dead almost six months now, but to her it only felt like a week, and she was bloody well going to grieve for as long as she wanted. Shaking off that ridiculous idea, she went on to the next one...only slightly ridiculous. She went to the Empty Zone.

Before the almost-attack she'd felt about as low as it was possible for a person to feel. Life just hadn't seemed worth living. She'd planned to walk as far as possible into the Empty Zone, hide Trennan's bag so the Chosen would never find it, and then...

Well, the 'and then' wasn't so clear. Just stop eating, maybe, until she starved to death? Only judging by the way she'd eaten rubbish last night (yuck!) that wasn't going to be very easy to carry out.

But then that man had attacked her. She didn't know why he

wanted the light-wand or even how he'd known she had it, but the moment she'd decided to fight, and had *won*, Coryn had felt better. Not much, but definitely better. She'd felt stronger, and it was like the lever had swayed from 'kill yourself' just over the curve towards 'keep living'. She didn't quite know what that involved, but she thought it had something to do with getting out of the ground level, and finding a regular source of income.

The edge of the Empty Zone was rather like the Borderlands: easily entered without even realising. It too was incredibly barren, but instead of cold desert with the occasional ruin, it was filled with abandoned buildings, block after block of them. All in all, it covered an area half the size of Lile City again.

She didn't really know where she was going, and hunger made her slow. The adrenaline from the earlier attack was gone, as were the last of her credits. At least she still had the bag. Inside were five items, all clues to where the missing emblem was hidden – or so Trennan had said, not that they'd had long to talk about it. The only problem was that they made no sense.

There was a small glass ball with something bright inside, a curved wooden thing, a rough flat square thing, a little wire thing, and a thing that defied description. She didn't recognise *any* of them, no matter what angle she looked at them from. No wonder Trennan had never worked it out!

Coryn wondered irritably where he'd got the clues from in the first place, and whether they were even trustworthy. Then she decided that *she* didn't have to work them out, she just had to make sure that none of the Fey or the Chosen got to them.

Then there was the one other item which she'd intentionally overlooked. It was the little bottle of water; the water of life, Trennan had called it. Not that it had kept *him* alive. She had seriously considered throwing it away out of pique, but something had made her keep it. It was Trennan's after all, and that alone made it valuable.

Coryn was about half an hour into the Empty Zone when she found an old VR box. It was an antique: a blacked-out cubicle with straps for the wrists, and a strangely-shaped helmet and visor.

It was surprisingly well preserved for how old it must be, since this style of machinery had gone out of fashion over a hundred years before. Now, when entering a VR centre each person was sprayed with hundreds of micro-sensors, which combined would create the sensation of the new environment. They usually washed off in the shower, but usually stopped working once you left the centre.

Shaking her head, she moved on. She didn't know what she was looking for, but she found all sorts: stray dogs, cats, and what might have been a badger, although why it was so far from the forest she didn't know. While the Empty Zone was far greener than it had been in past years, it certainly wasn't forested enough to support much wildlife.

Then, around yet another corner, there it was. An ancient mobi-home with its wheels barely intact, the rubber looking as if it would fall off with the slightest breeze, and rust scattered down the metal sides.

But what made this mobi-home different was that it was still in one piece. Unlike everything else which had fallen to rubble, this hunk of metal and plastic still stood in the middle of its almost empty lot, leaning slightly against a half-broken brick wall as if having a rest.

Even its windows were still whole, and closer up, it became clear that someone had plumbed in the sewage and water once upon a time. This hadn't been a passing-through home.

The door was closed. That should have been a sure sign to

keep away, but like the VR box it just made Coryn more curious.

She opened the door to see the inside was in almost perfect condition, bar a light coating of dust. There was a toilet compartment with a shower, a small kitchen, and a thin plastic mattress on a bed area.

She tried the shower, and when it worked she almost cried. Who cared if the water pressure was low and the temperature frigid? To someone who'd essentially been sleeping in a rubbish dump, it seemed like heaven.

And then there was the second door. At first she didn't notice it, it blended into the wall so well, but the moment she realised what it was she couldn't take her eyes off it. There was something about it that felt familiar…

Since she'd already trespassed this much, she didn't hesitate to go through this door too. On its other side was a room. It couldn't have existed in the normal realm, because the mobi-home was far too small to fit such a thing, and the room was four times as big as the whole mobi-home including the bathroom. But it was what was inside the room that made it spectacular.

Capsules. Dozens and dozens of empty, human-sized capsules, each set upright in tidy rows throughout the room and each glowing with a faint light. The surrounding floor and walls didn't glow, but they were so incredibly clean and white that they may as well have.

Coryn peered closer at the closest capsule, trying to work out what it was made of. She had a real sense that not only was she not alone, but that this was somehow the Other…even though it must be a part of the Other that she'd never seen before.

She'd hardly gone further than the borders with Brosca, curse her wicked soul. Maybe this was one of the Other cities that she'd heard about; or even the remnants of the great civilisation that was said to have existed before the realms split.

But who cared? It felt safe, and she was *tired*. Grabbing the mattress from the mobi-home, she dragged it into the Other room, dropped it next to the door, then slept like the dead.

"Coryn."

She was sitting in a beautiful garden, next to a small rippling stream. Across the water, not ten feet away from her, sat Trennan. He looked fresh and healthy, and his skin was smooth and unmarred in a way that she'd never seen before. He beamed at her, his smile white against his brown skin.

Coryn greeted him with a happy smile, but then a moment later remembered the truth. "You're dead. What are you doing here?"

"You're dreaming," Trennan replied. His own happy smile wilted as he spoke. "You know that, right?"

"Um…of course," she agreed, confused by his tone, and dismayed that this *wasn't* real. But it seemed so real! Well, she could enjoy it while it lasted. Standing up, she went to walk towards him, but of course the stream was in the way.

"Don't cross," he warned. "You have to stay on that side for now."

"But I just want to sit with you," Coryn cried. "Just for a few minutes. It's only a dream, isn't it?"

Trennan sighed heavily, scowling. "Yeah, unfortunately. But take this seriously anyway! You are taking it seriously, aren't you?"

"Of course!" But she didn't understand what he was talking about, only that he was there, and she was here, and she wanted to be with him.

He scrubbed a hand over that smooth face. "Look…this is

harder than I thought it would be. A word in place, a word in place…I'm supposed to just say something, not everything."

"OK…"

"Coryn, you know that bag of clues I left you?"

"The clues to the spirit's blood emblem," she agreed in dismay. "I found the bag, but those clues are ridiculous. They make no sense at all. Are you sure I shouldn't just hide it somewhere?"

"You can do it," he encouraged. "You just need a word in the right place."

"How can I get that?"

"Wait…oh, but there's something else you need to see."

Just then the water rippled between them, and Coryn saw the face of a girl appear as though reflected on its surface. She was auburn-haired and skinny, with large, thoughtful blue eyes. Perhaps in her early teens. Then that changed, and there was now a dark-haired, plump girl with a dimple in her cheek closer to Coryn's age, then she changed too and there was now a fair-haired girl, again younger. The faces kept changing and moving through until she'd seen seven, and then the last disappeared and it was simply water again.

"Who were they?"

"Kamile's sisters," he answered. "Mine and yours as well, or so I'm told. They need you too…"

With those words the dream blurred and ended, and Coryn found herself lying on the plasticky mattress amongst those glowing capsules, tears running down her face. For a moment it had seemed so real, had felt bright and true as if Trennan was still alive. Damned mind, playing tricks on her – although it hadn't been good enough to add in Kamile's memory, unfortunately.

That was when she heard someone out in the mobi-home. They were almost silent, and the daylight still shining through the windows sent their shadow flickering on the walls. She could see them through the open door leading out to the mobi-home proper.

She froze, and the person on the other side seemed to as well. Then they took a few steps closer. When they came into sight they were instantly recognisable as an enforcer – one of those rule-keepers who'd fined her and Trennan for a mere kiss. The enforcer looked up straight at the open doorway, but his gaze skimmed right past her as though she wasn't there, moving to look at the ceiling and then turn back to the exit.

"Well?" came a voice from outside.

"Empty," the enforcer called back. "Looks like the toilet's been used, though. We'll have to keep our eye on this area for the next little while to make sure they don't come back."

That had been Coryn, of course, right before she'd gone to sleep. Stiff with tension, she waited for the enforcer to reveal her presence, or to even make eye contact, but they just turned and walked away. She heard the footsteps recede and then the door to the mobi-home clang shut, and it seemed like they were gone.

Coryn waited a little longer in case they were trying to trick her, but they truly had left. Why had the enforcer not given her up? It was almost like he hadn't seen her.

No, that was silly. Shaking her head, she went to use the bathroom again, then washed up in the small shower, the whole time waiting for the enforcers to come charging back to arrest her for vagrancy.

They never did.

Mortimer tapped his fingers impatiently on his leg, waiting. His VR fingers, that was. His real fingers were resting still in his real lap, in the small, rather sterile apartment he'd been living in for some time.

Here in VR, he stood at the blurred edges of a log cabin. Outside was heavily falling snow, inside was a cosy fantasy of a room, complete with guttering fire. For ambience, presumably, since here in VR temperature was what you made it.

Chaos, this was boring. Mortimer had watched this particular teenage boy more than a couple of times, since his often dark choices within VR showed real potential, but this one? Absolutely dull. Embarrassing, almost. Now if the boy would just stop kissing his fantasy girl and *pay attention…*

"You're wasting your time," came a sweet voice from beside him. "You'll never get followers this way."

Mortimer couldn't help it; he jumped. Then he felt angry because he'd been startled, not that he showed it, of course. Standing next to him was a young woman, perhaps only as tall as his chin, and with the sweet roundness that he usually found appealing in his victims. Her hair was very pale blonde, her eyes wide and blue, and the whole of it was about as authentic as this teenage boy's fantasy girlfriend.

Most people never managed more than subtle changes, but the truth was that you could look like *anyone* in VR, if you could control your own thoughts for long enough. That's why people liked it so much; they didn't have to be their own dull, ugly selves.

'She' was another hacker, of course, because in this country, there was neither the technology nor the laws to allow multiplayer VR. And judging by their choice to take on the appearance of a pretty young woman, Mortimer was guessing that they were male, in their forties or fifties, and bored. "Frock off," he told them. "This is my spot, my target. You can't have him."

The girl smirked. "You can't have him, either. Look at him. He's a dilettante. He'll fantasise about doing dark things, maybe even creep around the edges of true evil, but in the end he will never do what you're prompting him to. And do you know why?" She didn't wait for him to answer. "Because he doesn't really want to follow you or anyone. He wants power of his own. They all do."

"You're wrong," Mortimer said confidently, although her words had struck a chord with him. "Look at what he's doing now. That's hardly the work of a pure soul."

They both turned to the tableau across from them, where the boy was…well, doing something that would be illegal in all seventy-six countries, and for good reason.

"Ew," the girl said, but she didn't really seem bothered. In fact, Mortimer thought she was enjoying watching. "But still, he won't follow you."

"How do you know?" Mortimer snapped. "Who in Hades do you think you are?"

She smiled, slow and wide, and he felt something tickle at the edge of his mind. His *real* mind, not the one here in VR. "Why, I'm one of the Fey," she said sweetly. "Haven't you heard of us? Ever since the Great War caused that little weak spot between this realm and the Other, we've been kindly and thoughtfully sharing our wisdom with those humans that desire it."

The tickle in his brain turned into a fully-fledged prod, and with a jolt of fear, Mortimer unplugged, leaving virtual reality behind. He was again sitting in his rented home in front of the fire, all alone, and safe. He breathed a sigh of relief.

"You don't get to leave that easily," she whispered from behind him, and he almost screamed.

"How did you follow me here?!"

The girl looked around her curiously. "What, here?" She waved a hand, and their surroundings melted back into the scenario they'd met in, then melted again until they were standing in a desert, surrounded by massive ruins. She smiled at him. "You don't get to leave VR until I say you do."

Oh, Chaos. Mortimer knew there was a danger in using VR, but he'd been safe so many times before, he'd thought he could get away with it. "I know what you are," he said with barely a tremble in his voice. "You might make those stupid others think you're some…wise otherworldly being, but I know exactly what you are."

A Creature, without a doubt: one of those inhuman beings that inhabited the Other realm, and had been there ever since the dawn of time…and who were extremely concerned about pleasing only themselves, and beware any who got in the way. That meant very, very bad news for him, if its intentions weren't good. But when were they ever?

"Excellent. That will make this a lot easier."

"Make what a lot easier?"

The girl/Creature smiled like the cat who'd got the cream. "My proposition."

"What do you want?" Mortimer asked flatly.

"An exchange of favours," she replied smoothly. "You help me get something I want, and I'll give you what you really want in return."

"And how would you know what I want?"

"Oh, I know."

He raised an eyebrow coolly.

"You want to be immortal," the girl sang, seeming very much like the child-woman she pretended to be. "You want to be like me, able to move through the Other unharmed, and able to influence millions rather than the paltry few you manage now. To be a true *god*."

Excitement running through him, Mortimer had to struggle

to keep his expression neutral. "That's not possible."

"It is," she countered. "It is very possible, with the object I seek. This object will enable a Creature to take physical form without losing their immortality, and a human to become immortal without losing their physicality. Sound good to you?"

Ah, so that was what she…*it* wanted. To be able to move in the normal realm, instead of remaining trapped in the Other as the Creatures were. Unable to move into the normal, unable to move through time…strange limitations for otherwise powerful beings. But was there really any way around this? He'd never heard of such. "How?"

"The *how* is not important," the girl replied. "But if you help me find this object which is currently out in the normal realm, then I will also allow you use of it, and you will become like me. Unable to die."

"That sounds good," Mortimer said dubiously. "But how do I have any proof this is true?"

She waved another hand carelessly. "The proof of the pudding is in the eating."

"What?"

"You'll know it's true when you see it happen!" she snapped. "Now either you decide to do this little thing for me, which will dramatically benefit us both, or…"

Mortimer's hackles rose. He did *not* like being threatened or ordered around, even by such a thing as this. "Or what?"

Seeing that this wouldn't achieve her purposes, the girl stepped back. "Or I will find someone else who appreciates what I am offering them. I have no desire to force you, Mortimer. But you have certain skills that the vast majority of humans lack, and time is limited. There are others looking."

Mollified, he nodded. "I do, of course. I have lived many more years than most humans, and will live many more with or without your aid." He did have to admit it, though: "Your offer is appealing. What do you need of me?"

"To be my conduit. To be my eyes and ears out in the world, and to follow my directions to find the object…and the girl."

"Oh?"

The Creature recounted the details of what it wanted, and the more he listened, the more interested he was. This would be a challenge, even with the Creature's help, and he thrived on such challenges. He didn't even mind that he would essentially be its carrier at times. He would have to be oh-so-careful to achieve this out in the normal world rather than in the relative safety of VR, but what a thrill it would be to complete…

She was watching him closely, a familiar expression in her wide, pretty eyes. They were flecked with orange, and seemed better suited to a big cat than a girl. Predator, not prey.

"VR *is* safe," she agreed, not even bothering to hide that she'd again been eavesdropping on his thoughts. "Safe from your government, anyway. But the only problem with the way you use it, is that since you borrow others' experiences, you can't change anything, can you? The other human hackers can, even when it's not their own VR session. But all you do is mess up the program and make others unable to leave it. You might be able to visit virtual reality, but you can't impact it and manipulate it. Not really. Not like I can."

What was he supposed to say to that? It was true. He stayed silent out there in that cold, twilight desert, and the Creature continued, "You wish for true power and glory, and I'll give it to you if you do what I ask. Glory is such a wonderful thing, is it not? It feels like drinking a warm beverage, filling up the whole body, giving you strength."

As it spoke, the desert around them faded, and he was once again back in his house, with the VR gear still stuck to him. He heard the Creature's voice in his head, sounding very, very faint. "I know why you wish to be a god. I have been there myself, and I have more power than you can imagine. I have true immortality, and so shall you. Just do what I ask of you..."

Mortimer crooked his head curiously. Where was it going with this? Feeling bolstered by the fact that he was now truly back in the normal realm, and the Creature couldn't reach him here, he replied to the seemingly empty room, "You speak of drinks, but you can't even hold a glass in your hand without it falling to the floor. What kind of immortality is that? You might think that since you were created powerful, that you're better than me. But gods are made, Creature, by the worship given to them. Not born. And I will be a god again – I will have my power and eternal life on the blood of a million innocents if I must. It would be better for you to be my ally."

"Threats?" it whispered.

"Just a warning," he replied flatly. "I will be your ally if it suits me. But never forget we are equals."

"Of course we are. As equal as a horse and its rider..." And then at that moment as he pulled off the pieces of the VR headset, he felt a strange weight settle over the back of his neck, and the faintest echo of mocking laughter. He'd become a carrier already.

That might be true, what the Creature had said. But Mortimer knew that for all of its subservient status, a horse chose to obey the rider. If it so chose, it could also throw the rider and trample it into the dust.

He felt its laughter again, and this time he stayed silent. He could only fool himself for so long.

Twelve

SISTERS

As Coryn was heading for the door of the mobi-home she saw a small jar sitting on the bench, almost hidden in the corner. Somehow she hadn't noticed it before, but now she opened the seal and saw it was filled with strange, wrinkly little green sausages. A waft of strong vinegar tickled her nose, and she realised what they actually were.

"Ew, gherkins." But a moment later she was gobbling them down, every last one. Perhaps she had hated them before at the Compound, but now they tasted like spicy, crunchy little pieces of heaven to her empty stomach. Now that she'd decided to live, she had to take steps not to *starve*. Food was a good start.

Eating the gherkins gave Coryn the energy to take another look around the area surrounding the mobi-home. After a few minutes she went past the VR box she'd seen first thing that morning. At first she had avoided it, assuming it would have been used as a toilet for vagrants (yes, just like her, although she hadn't yet had to go that far) but finally her curiosity got the better of her.

She opened the door and stepped inside, wondering what on earth she was doing, and then after brief hesitation, slipped on the helmet and straps. It was unlikely to still work, of course, so what did she have to lose?

There was a slight buzzing noise, and then the sudden impression of cold metal hitting the back of her neck as the nerve sensors joined with her spine. For a moment she wondered if she should rip it off, just in case it was faulty (it probably *was* faulty) but then her vision blurred and she found herself sitting in a pleasant country scene, on the veranda of an old wooden house.

In front of her was what looked like a glacier moving towards her from the right, coming to meet a desert from the left. In the centre there was a blur which meant that two different VR scenes were meeting, and off in the distance, at the very edges of the scene, was a big lump of nothingness.

"I'm in someone else's fantasy," Coryn exclaimed in surprise. If it had been a normal VR session then she never would have seen those blurs, or that nothingness. It would have fixed itself as she turned her head. She could still feel that she was standing in that booth, still vaguely feel the straps on her wrists and the helmet, but it would be so easy to forget.

Just then a tall, thin, auburn-haired girl came out of the house onto the veranda. She was in her early to mid-teens, her height perhaps making her look a little older. She looked at Coryn in surprise, then suspicion. "Who are you?"

"Who are *you*?" Coryn replied automatically, then a second later the face registered as familiar. In the dream hers had been the first face visible in the stream. "Hey, you're one of the sisters," she blurted out without thinking.

"Whose sisters?"

What had the dream-Trennan said? "Kamile's," she finished cautiously.

The girl's eyes widened, then her face crumpled. "How did you know that? Have you seen her?"

"Wait, so you *do* know her?" Coryn studied the girl suspiciously. "Or more likely you're not even real, and you're just telling me what I want to hear." That was what VR did: identified what you wanted, then gave it to you through the characters and the scenes.

"How do I know *you're* even real?" the girl countered. "Tell me something about Kamile that I don't know."

"How would I know what you know?" Then realising how ridiculous that sounded, Coryn said, "She turns green in the Other."

"Already knew that," the girl said. "Tell me something else."

"*You* tell me something else," Coryn snapped back. "I have no idea who you even are." Except that she was one of the 'sisters', whatever that meant. She'd thought *she* was the only one Kamile loved like a sister.

"Alright," the redhead replied boldly. "Kamile was planning to leave her twisted little cult, but she disappeared six months ago. I've been coming here every now and then…just in case she turned up."

Well, that was sad. "I knew she was going to leave," Coryn said. "The Elders told me."

Suddenly the girl's eyes widened. "Oh stars in heaven," she gasped. "You've got to be Coryn."

"Yes. Who are you?"

"I'm Poli. I met Kamile out on the borders when she was patrolling, and we only knew each other a matter of weeks before she disappeared. The others said she must have grown too afraid of meeting with us, and that's why we haven't seen her. But what are you doing here? Did she send you?"

"I found this place by accident," Coryn admitted. "Your VR sessions aren't that secret if even I could find it." It seemed like either a massive coincidence or a small miracle. She settled for the first – someone like herself was unlikely to ever experience a miracle. Judging by her luck, she was more likely to have a meteor fall on her head.

"But Kamile," Poli persisted. "Where is she? Is she alright?"

Was she alright? Even here in VR Coryn felt a fresh stab of

grief, and her face crumpled. "No," she replied finally. "No, she's not alright."

"I'm not really surprised," Poli said some time later from where she sat next to Coryn on the porch steps. Her VR face was streaked with tears, eyes reddened. No doubt her real body would look the same, wherever she was. The mind tended to work like that.

"I thought in my heart that she must be...*gone*," the girl continued, "but I didn't want to think that way, not when there was a chance of anything else..."

Coryn wrapped her arms around her knees, pulling them into her chest. She hadn't thought she'd have any tears left after all the ones she'd cried these last few days, but her mind carried on where her body had stopped. At least now there was someone to share in her grief. "Nobody wants to think that way," she replied finally, her voice almost a whisper. "It was the last thing I'd expected. It's still hard to believe it happened."

"How did she die?"

Coryn could hardly even think about it. She certainly couldn't tell the gory details to this girl here. "The Chosen killed her. Them, and the Fey. They killed my fiancé too," she said bitterly. "They were supposed to be our friends."

"*Ohhh.* I'm so sorry, Coryn."

Coryn shrugged silently. So was she.

"But the Fey," Poli asked. "Do you mean...the *Creatures*, and the ones who follow them?"

Coryn glanced up at the other girl. There was only sorrow in her gaze, and Coryn felt like she could be honest with her. "Yes, that's what they are. I think."

"That's definitely what they are," Poli argued, and Coryn let it be. "I can't believe they killed her! *Killed* her! Oh, actually I can..." She raged on for several minutes about the incredible wickedness of such things, and when she asked how Kamile had really died, Coryn told her.

"And she was pregnant," she added desolately. "At least Brosca told me she was, although she could have been lying." But if it had been true, it was so, so tragically sad. Kamile had been handfasting for several years with no luck, as far as Coryn knew. She'd acted like she didn't care, but it had seemed to Coryn that she really did.

Poli raged on some more about the horror and injustice, and Coryn found herself feeling just a little bit better. A burden shared was a burden halved. Well, not *halved*, perhaps just one-hundredth shaved off the end. Finally Poli calmed down, and the two just sat in silence for several minutes.

"Why do you call yourself her sister?"

The redhead watched her cautiously out the corner of her eye. "All seven of us call ourselves sisters. We have no other family."

"I call her my little sister sometimes," Coryn admitted. "She's older than me, but looks younger." She paused, realising she'd spoken in present tense rather than past, and deflated. "Looked younger."

"Actually, it's because of our beliefs," Poli said suddenly. "We're like a family, and that's why we call ourselves sisters." She turned to stare at Coryn boldly. "If you pass this on to the enforcers…"

"I'm not going to tell them anything," Coryn countered. "I grew up in a Fey-loving compound, remember? I'm not exactly a model for the Secular Republic myself."

"You'd better not, because if you do, we're all dead or in prison," the other girl said frankly. "But the truth is that we're all followers of Deias."

"Who?"

"Y'know," Poli said awkwardly. "The Eternal One."

Coryn spun to stare at her. "What? Why!?"

"Because he's real. In my books, that's a good enough reason to believe."

Coryn shook her head, frowning. More like the girl wanted to believe it, so she'd decided it was true. There wouldn't be a shred of proof, though. Funnily enough, it was this foolish insistence that made Coryn believe that Poli was a real person, rather than something VR had conjured up. Except for rare glitches, VR could almost never surprise you.

"You should keep those beliefs to yourself," she told Poli. "The government can't get to what's in your head. So why take the chance that someone else finds out? You said yourself that it's dangerous."

"We went to the River," Poli continued, as if completely ignoring what Coryn had just said. She then spun a detailed story about her experiences there, and Coryn thought that she wouldn't mind checking it out some time. It wasn't as if she had anything better to do.

With a little prompting she told her own story too, ending with how she had arrived here, and leaving out the parts about being suicidal and eating rubbish. She did mention the gherkins, though. She didn't know who'd put them there.

"Did Kamile say anything about the Fire Lord?" Coryn asked. "Trennan told me that he'd met someone by that name."

"I have no idea, but I'll tell you what I do know. There's a job going at the eatery on fourth level where I work weekends. If you're interested I could probably get you an interview."

Coryn thought nothing of the fact that Poli had a job; here in Lile you could have paid employment from as young as twelve. But presuming it was real, a job for Coryn would mean credits and therefore regular food. It would also mean she'd have to act social;

act *normal* when she didn't feel normal. Even if her friends hadn't died she still would have struggled to fit in here in the city, after the upbringing she'd had.

But the thought of mourning marks flickered through her mind again, and she found herself saying, "I'm interested. But you wouldn't have a spare change of clothes, would you? I don't think rags are the best look for a potential employee."

"Of course!"

By the time Coryn unplugged from the old VR machine, she'd made arrangements to meet Poli and a few other girls in the city that very afternoon. She still didn't know how she'd managed to find their joined VR session from this ancient, battered VR machine, and Poli hadn't had a clue either. She'd called it a gift from the Eternal One, and that they were clearly meant to meet.

Coryn wasn't so sure about that. Even if there was some kind of omniscient, all-powerful being, and even if it – he – *did* care enough to intervene in people's lives, it beggared belief that he'd stoop as low as altering software if he wouldn't even save the lives of those who followed him.

Poli was a sweet girl, but she needed to grow up.

Mountain of Glass, time irrelevant

Jon turned from his seat under a spreading peach tree to watch Bets trip her way down the paved path to join him. She wore the contented expression that told him she'd done whatever it was she'd rushed off to do twenty minutes earlier.

"That was fast," he commented once she joined him. "What

did you do again?"

She wrinkled her nose adorably. "'Twas yet another odd, simple duty, Jon. I went to a rather dreadful location – ruins everywhere – and placed a pluh-gin on what looked like an extremely small guardhouse. I know not why."

"A pluh-what?"

"A pluh-gin," she repeated earnestly. "A snee-kee pluh-gin, Amaranthus called it, and said 'twould be of real use to the one who finds it. A small, metal device that had something to do with…eye-tee and vee-arr?" She shrugged one small shoulder. "So I must assume 'tis so."

Jon still had no idea what she was talking about, but it seemed too much effort to find out. "Er…good for you."

Bets didn't notice his confusion, nodding happily. "Yes, very good indeed."

Lile, 2598 AD
Two months later

Coryn studied her reflection briefly in the mirror. She didn't care what she looked like, only that the mourning marks were suitably displayed when her hair was tucked behind her ears.

They were both strange and beautiful, she mused, and the fact that they'd hurt terribly for such a short time just seemed like an echo of her time with Trennan and Kamile. Too short, and with a painful end, but never to be forgotten.

She stroked her finger along the curve of her left ear where Trennan's name was inscribed, almost illegible in its curling font surrounded by ornate fleur-de-lis. But she knew what it meant, and that was enough. She'd had the tattoos imprinted two days earlier, after weeks of saving her small income from her new job. Funny, since at first she'd rejected the idea, thinking mourning marks were too old-fashioned. Now they seemed just perfect.

"Coryn?" Guy's voice called through the bathroom door. "Your break's over."

"Coming," she called back. This job at the eatery had been just what she needed. It specialised in drinks and iced desserts, as well as the ever-present Lilluanian pancake. Not exactly thrilling, and the pay was only comfortable because she wasn't paying rent for her borrowed mobi-home, but it was steady work. Besides, having to face customers all the time meant she couldn't let herself be a solitary, depressed hermit. Even though she sure had reason to be depressed…

Oh no, now her eyes were all sad again. Slapping herself lightly on the cheeks, Coryn tried to force a smile, then gave up and slumped into a 'not horribly unhappy' expression. That would have to do. "Hold it together," she told herself. "Things to do, people to see." Clues to unravel, friends to avenge…

"Coryn!"

"Coming!"

As she came out, Guy practically ran past her on his way in. She saw the reason why when she reached the counter: the enforcer was here again. It was the third time this week.

"Hello," he said with a warm smile. "Four of your regulars, thank you."

She smiled back politely, moving to make the drinks on the multi-purpose machine. She didn't need to scan his ID chip for payment: as one of the government's workers, he drank for free. "Not all for you, I hope," she said under her breath as she turned away.

"Oh no," he called out over the humming of the machine. "Not for me. I've got a meeting."

Coryn flushed red, wondering if she was going to get slapped with a fine for slander, or something ridiculous like that. It wouldn't be fair, but she'd heard of it happening before.

The new Premier's police enforcers were nicknamed 'bureaucrats' since they upheld an unbelievable number of laws, specifying life right down to the tiniest detail. They also tended to be plainclothes, often wearing tidy suits as this one was as to blend in more easily. It didn't work, since no one else outside the highest offices wore the suits. In Coryn's opinion it just added to the bureaucratic impression…but that only lasted until they pulled out the guns.

But the enforcer didn't quote section 86, sub-section b (or whatever that might have been). Instead he smiled at her. *Smiled.* "I heard the other one call you Coryn. Pretty name."

"Er…thanks."

"I'm Daniel," he continued, unbothered by her lack of enthusiasm.

Coryn gave him another polite smile. "Hi."

"You make good drinks."

"Thank you," she said again. Then she added, "You know, you can get just as good service if you order on your link unit. A drone can bring the drinks straight to you, and you don't have to bother with coming all the way into the eatery."

"I was coming past anyway," he replied casually, that smile still stuck on his face. "Besides, it's nice to see people occasionally. Get out of the office, you know?"

Oh, so he was trying to make it seem like he was a regular worker. She didn't answer.

"So, when do you finish work?"

She glanced up at him suspiciously as she put the lid on the last drink. Why did he need to know that? "Ah…"

He looked rueful, but kept smiling anyway. "I was thinking

I could walk you home if you don't already have a ride, but by the look on your face you seem less than enthralled."

"What did I do?" she asked, deeply worried. Why would he want to walk with her? It would be terrible if he suspected she didn't have an apartment – it was illegal to live in the Empty Zone.

The smile faltered. "Nothing. I just thought you might want some company on the way home. Level four's not the safest for a girl on her own."

"But of course it's safe," Coryn said in confusion, not really noticing she was contradicting him. He didn't *seem* like he was leading up to an arrest or some serious fines. Maybe he didn't know after all… "There are loads of enforcers around here. I see you here all the time." She handed him the four drinks, stacked nicely in a reusable crate that would be picked up by one of the eatery's drones once emptied.

Daniel took the crate, seeming lost for words. For a moment Coryn worried that she'd said the wrong thing (but she could hardly have agreed for him to walk her to her illegal home, could she?) but then he said, "I'll be right there," and she realised he wasn't talking to her at all, he was talking to someone on his link unit.

Like all enforcers and government officials, Daniel had his link unit embedded in his ear and his jaw. The government encouraged everyone to do so, rather than use the more clunky attachable links, but since that meant that a person could be traced down to their very last centimetre, most tended to avoid the embedded versions. Guy (who was a conspiracy theorist) said that it was only a matter of time until embedded links became compulsory, and perhaps in this one thing he was right.

"Sorry, I'll have to leave these," Daniel said apologetically. Then without another word, he put all four drinks down on the counter, then turned and left.

A second later Guy popped his head around the corner. "Is he gone?"

"Yeah, he's gone."

"But is he *really* gone? You know they like to play tricks."

Sounded like he was talking about the Fey. And the enforcers, as annoying as they were, were *not* the Fey. "Guy, just get out here," she said in exasperation.

He took a wide step out, noticing for the first time the drinks set on the counter. "Hey, freebies. I'm thirsty."

This was one of the few situations where workers could legitimately take free drinks, and these were milk-based sweet drinks that were almost solid enough to be a food as well. Coryn took one, and Guy set himself to consuming the last three.

"He's been watching me," he told her confidentially between slurps. "I've seen him before."

"Don't be stupid," one of the regular customers called across the small room. "He was watching *her*, if anyone."

Guy's eyes widened, and he stared at Coryn. "What have *you* been doing?"

Illegal VR hacking along with Poli and others, squatting in someone's mobi-home in the Empty Zone, visiting religious sites, wallowing in alter-power… "Nothing."

"He thinks she's pretty," the customer called, and Coryn remembered that he seemed to have no sense of the appropriate. "Wanted to walk her home."

Guy stared at Coryn in horror. "He wants you to be one of *them*," he stage-whispered. "You going to leave us for a bureau-job, Cory?"

"Don't be ridiculous," she snapped. "You know I like this job." Then she added quietly, "And watch your mouth." Even though Guy seemed to be a few sandwiches short of a picnic, it didn't mean he'd be overlooked forever if he didn't curb his tongue.

More orders came in over the eatery-link, and the two of them set to work. Some orders went straight to the drones which delivered all over the fourth level, while others went to live customers, usually regulars who as Daniel said, liked the human interaction. Finally the clock reached four-thirty and her replacement came in. It was Poli fresh from school, and she looked worried.

"What's the problem?"

"I can't get hold of Magdalene," Poli replied, frowning. She was referring to one of the younger girls that Coryn had been meeting in VR over the last few weeks. "I was supposed to give her a pair of decent shoes for her interview at the Mall, but I couldn't get through to her link at all. She said she was going to a viewing at the Mall's theatre before the interview, so she probably turned her link off. It's terrible timing!"

Coryn thought of Magdalene's scruffy, worn pair of everyday shoes, and wrinkled her nose. It was hard to make a good impression while looking like a hobo – and she should know. "I'll drop them in to her on the way home," she offered. "It's the fifth level Mall, right?"

"Yes, and the ice-shop's right next to the public viewing theatre. That would be great if you could – I know her interview's in twenty minutes. Oh, and she's wearing a red jacket."

"If I run, I'll make it."

Coryn changed into her new tunic and loose trousers, the ones she'd bought with her first week's pay, then headed at a quick pace for the nearest lifts. With their help, it shouldn't take her more than ten minutes to reach the Mall.

Three minutes later she arrived at the nearest lift station to see a massive queue of what had to be a hundred people, all milling around the entryways. "What's going on?" she asked the nearest person in dismay.

"Four of the lifts are broken," the woman replied knowingly. "And there's a school trip of some kind clogging up the last two."

"Good grief," Coryn muttered under her breath, then sighed. "Where are the stairs?"

The woman pointed them out – all thirty flights leading up from sub-level to sub-level – and Coryn set off at a trot. She'd just reached the base of the first flight when she felt the hairs rise on her arms and the back of her neck. She shivered, then paused to look behind her, but no one was watching. Not even the woman who'd given instructions. It was just her imagination.

Coryn shook her head, rubbed her hands over goose-pimpled arms, then set off up the stairs.

Ash left virtual reality behind with relief, moving into the new gateway below her. There was the faint tingle as she travelled through, replaced with a warm wetness. No, she hadn't wet herself – she was underwater. She struggled for a few moments in confusion before finally breaking the surface.

Well, it sure wasn't Lunden, 1818. Damn it. But it wasn't shark-infested seas either, or the hundred-and-one other locations she would *not* want to suddenly appear in. Instead it was a place like one she'd never seen before.

Grey, grey, everywhere was grey. Ash was treading water in a big, grey swimming pool in a huge grey building. In the centre of the pool was a machine, stirring the water in strong circles, and pushing her along with it. There were others swimming too in formation against the current, although the reason *why* wasn't apparent. After a few confused moments of wishing she was a better swimmer (and getting some dirty water in her mouth, yuck) Ash managed to drag herself to the side of the pool and haul herself out, cringing as she waited for someone to shove her back in…because why else would they be swimming in this hopeless place if they didn't have to be?

No one pushed her back in; in fact no one seemed to care about her sudden appearance. She shook herself off and looked around in distaste. Her first impression of greyness hadn't been wrong: although there were patches of colour here and there, the *feeling* of grey overwhelmed it. It made her think of the inside of a spaceship: lots of metal and exposed beams, and rounded passages leading away from this room, but also that same lack of fresh, glowing life that she now found herself craving. Two minutes in wherever-this-was, and she was already desperate to leave.

A moment later Ash cursed softly under her breath as she realised the gateway was nowhere to be seen. But even if she *could* get back, she reminded herself, she'd just end up in that same virtual reality confusion, just as stuck as she'd been before.

And this was why she shouldn't go charging through random gateways on a whim. Believe it or not, she was starting to think she should have swallowed her pride…and waited for George.

Damn.

"Amaranthus, please get me out," she muttered to herself, mentally adding an apology. He might hear her, he might not. She *thought* he was keeping an eye on her just like he did the other travellers, but it was a big world, wasn't it? He couldn't watch everyone at all times.

Nearby a man sat against the wall, his legs stretched out in front of him. He was middle-aged and dressed in the same grey as everyone else, and he drummed his fingers rhythmically on his knees as he studied her curiously. "Sorry, did you say something?"

"Ahh..." How to sound not-crazy? "Can you tell me why those people are swimming in there?"

The man looked at her as if she *was* crazy. "So they'll work up an appetite, of course."

She pondered that for a moment, and wondered if she was missing something. "Right. They wouldn't be hungry otherwise?"

"Of course not."

"Oh." Ash glanced back at that swirling grey pool, and the blank determination on the faces of the swimmers inside. *She* always managed to get hungry even if she sat on the couch all day watching TV. She was hungry right now, in fact, and feeling a nagging need for a bathroom. "Is this their only choice for exercise? Couldn't they go somewhere more...interesting?"

Again that same stare, like she was a complete idiot. "Where would they go? Where in the whole world is more interesting, as you say?"

She shrugged. "Parks, even the gym...the beach. Why not go to the beach?"

"The beach?" he exclaimed. "There hasn't been a beach for centuries, girl. Don't you know where we are?"

"Uh...no? But it kind of looks like a spaceship."

The man laughed, standing up as though to walk away. "You need your programming checked. We're not on a spaceship, we're on *the* spaceship, the only one left. It's the New Earth, remember? It's all we've got now we destroyed the last one."

"Destroyed the last spaceship?" Ash asked in confusion. "Wait, what year is it?"

But he just laughed again. "Programming. Go to hall B."

He strode off down a busy hallway with a low, curved roof, passing in front of a massive poster covering the nearby wall. It caught her attention because of its vast size and how it made her vaguely uncomfortable – she didn't know why – but then she realised it wasn't a poster at all. It was a colossal window with a view of space.

It was all black, broken up with the specks of a trillion stars, and a strange purple haze. It should have been beautiful, because beauty was what Ash usually noticed when she saw the stars and pictures of the universe, but instead its vastness made her feel as insignificant as an ant on a city street.

It conveyed a kind of fear and hopelessness, and she suddenly realised why this place was so grey. Could a location carry the attitudes of those within it?

Moving away in detached horror, Ash noticed a plaque next to the window. The text read, *'The Rosmerta Window is dedicated to the founder of New Earth, Dame Rosmerta Antiochus. It shows a clear view of the remnants of the Milky Way – mankind's home for millions of years – so that all might know their place in our wonderful universe.'*

Yeah, she'd felt her place alright, and it hadn't felt all that wonderful. She stepped away from the whole thing, shaking her head. She'd seen enough. Obviously she'd gone a phenomenally long way into the future, but there was nothing to look forward to here. Nothing! All there was, was a group of people who didn't even *live* enough to get hungry…

But to get back to the remnant gateway, Ash would have to go into the pool, and that would only lead her back to her stupid virtual reality session with Seth the Imaginary. She'd have to find another, but where? She figured that if anyone had ever used the Eternity Stone to get here – that was what created the gateways in the first place – that they'd also get out as hurriedly as they could. *She* would, if she'd had the Stone. There *would* be a gateway here, somewhere…

She just had to hunt for it. Or perhaps she could use her

mobile phone, since if both she and George were close to a gateway then the reception was sometimes enough for a conversation. She could only hope it would work even outside her own time, and that it had survived its impromptu swim, of course. But when she put her hand in her pocket, she realised that she'd misplaced it.

With panic growing inside her, Ash began to retrace her steps, carefully looking over the floor. The phone could be in the swirling water, but that would be awful. It looked incredibly deep. Deep enough to hide *bodies*, if it had to. She couldn't see through it at all, let alone find a little mobile phone in there…

And that was when a girl came screaming up the hallway. She wasn't much older than Ash, but her face wore an expression of complete horror. "The ship is disintegrating!" she shouted hysterically. "We're all going to die! I can see it happening!"

Ah, *collywobbles*. No matter where you were, things could always get worse, right? Ash's eyes widened and she looked around her in shock, but nothing had changed. Same old sturdy metal everything. But then as the girl reached her, it was like a bubble of sound and shape spread to envelop Ash, and she saw the fragments of the ship's wall fall away into nothingness, and the floor roll up like a rug…

Ash stepped away from the girl in horror, and everything went back to good old depressing normal, but the fear was still evident in the girl's bulging eyes. Ash didn't know if it was illusion or insanity, but the girl was clearly feeling it.

Just as Ash would have shouted for help (and tried not to cry, because she was feeling miserable), two pillars of *something* came shooting up the hallway, quickly followed by a man and a woman in white suits.

They grabbed the still-screaming girl under both arms, pushing her back onto some kind of hovering device held between the two pillars, and then there was a flash of light. Suddenly the girl's face relaxed into blankness, and she was just a stiff figure lying on an invisible stretcher.

"Did you sedate her?" Ash asked timidly. "She seemed very upset." And that was an understatement.

"She had a virus in her programming," the man replied briskly. "This wasn't the first time she's acted out. They're almost impossible to completely remove, and they can spread. We switched her off for her own benefit, and for everyone else's."

Ash stared at the girl's still form in dawning horror. It looked more like a dead body now than a forced rest. "Switched off? You mean, permanently?"

"It was the humane thing to do," the woman told Ash gently. "She was suffering. Besides, she can be recycled now. We can put an entirely new brain into her body, give someone a new lease on life. Don't let it worry you."

Ash couldn't speak. She was feeling like she'd just witnessed a murder, and still couldn't shake how it had felt when that bubble of...of *destruction* had enveloped her briefly. She just watched mutely as the pillar-stretcher carried the girl away. A panel in the wall opened briefly, allowing the three to pass through, then closed behind them as if it had never happened.

She felt like weeping. That little incident showed exactly what she felt like this place was – a place where humanity had little value. Each individual life wasn't considered irreplaceable, but humans were just machines, needing feeding, exercise, fixing when they got broken – switching off when they got *too* broken. Not needing beauty, companionship, and purpose.

It wasn't clear what made Ash turn around then. A small sound, perhaps, or that sense you'd get when someone was watching you. But she turned and looked into the cold, grey eyes of a man about her own height, who was watching her with one of the most calculating expressions she'd ever seen on a person, ever. She couldn't help herself stumbling back in shock, but he grabbed her wrist and held her. "I know you," he said, and it was like being stared at by a snake, there was so little human emotion in that statement.

Ash tried to shake herself free. "Well, I don't know you! Do you mind?"

"Yes. Yes, I do." And he kept staring at her, at her face and her neck and her whole body, and it wasn't at all lecherous, but it was extremely uncomfortable.

But something about the man was also incredibly familiar. Those grey eyes…Ash knew them from somewhere. In Iversley 2155 one of the Nobles that used illusion had looked like that.

But it couldn't be the same person. It just *couldn't!* It would be the worst kind of luck to run into him here of all places – wherever 'here' was – and when she felt so bloody helpless. Far-sight had been no use at all, and the man seemed to have a grip like iron.

"Let go of me," she gritted out. "Now."

He abruptly let go, and she almost fell backwards, holding her wrist where he'd touched her as though it had burned. It hadn't – she didn't think – but he *had* burned her in the past. She had a decent-sized scar on her neck and other wrist from their last run-in…if it was even him.

The man narrowed his eyes at her speculatively, and then an odd thing happened. They glimmered orange, just for a moment, and the voice that came from his mouth changed. *"Why hello there,"* it purred. *"You are just* burning *with alter-power. Where are you now?"*

That didn't even make sense! Ash stumbled backwards, appalled, and suddenly his hand was on her wrist again, tight as a manacle. His eyes were purely orange now, and his other hand snapped up to press against her forehead, fingers digging clawlike into her temples.

"*Oh my,*" he said in that strange, too soft voice. "*You're not far at all.*"

"LET GO OF ME!" Ash screamed, and she punched one fist as hard as she could into the man's gut.

For a moment those fingers just seemed to tighten, his eyes brilliantly tangerine, but then he flickered. His whole form flickered in and out of view like an old TV during a storm, and then she was free.

She turned and ran.

HIDDEN STRENGTH

The Mall

By the time Coryn reached the fifth level Mall, her thighs were aching and her face was hot from the exertion, and her hip ached from where the bag with Poli's shoes had hit her with every step. She'd been wrong. There weren't thirty flights of stairs; there were forty-two. Magdalene *really* better appreciate her effort.

Coryn checked the large clock set above the entryway, and her heart fell as she realised what the delay had cost her. Magdalene's interview was starting in two minutes! She tried to contact Magdalene again on her link. But just like the last two times she'd tried, she couldn't get through. She heard noise for a brief second, as though the other end of the link was open, but then it suddenly shut off again.

Fire Lord, the girl needed to be more contactable! Didn't she know someone was trying to get hold of her?

Probably not, Coryn allowed. Or she would have answered, wouldn't she?

Coryn power-walked down the winding halls towards the ice-shop. She'd visited this complex a couple of times in the last few weeks, mostly to buy cheap clothing at even better prices. Unlike the seventh level Mall, this one was smallish and dated, its two hundred shops connected by dozens of halls, and quite a few of them now empty.

It also wasn't far from the old VR centre she and Trennan used to visit. Recently the government had tried to clean up the reputation of the fifth level Mall, hence all the empty shops, and they'd also started staging public events in the viewing theatres.

But when Coryn finally reached the ice-shop, Magdalene was nowhere to be seen. The old man running the shop hadn't seen her, either. "She'd better hurry up if she wants that interview," he told Coryn. "Punctuality is important for employees."

Coryn murmured her agreement, then stepped away, frowning. A moment later she spotted the large glass doors of the public viewing theatre, barely a hall's length away from this very shop. Hadn't Poli said Magdalene was going to a viewing? Coryn didn't think much of the viewings herself: since the dry Sec topics bored her to tears, but she wouldn't think less of Mags for attending. She would, however, be unimpressed if she'd forgotten her interview!

But then when Coryn reached the viewing theatre and glanced inside, a flash of red caught her eye. And there was Magdalene, sitting just inside the well-lit room and facing the screen up ahead as if she had nothing better to do. Her back was to Coryn.

Oh, by the Fire Lord. Coryn rolled her eyes, quietly slipping into the theatre and leaning over towards where the girl sat. "Hey Mags!" she whispered loudly.

Magdalene didn't move. The display on the screen flickered away, the podium and the rest of the theatre almost empty. Coryn didn't think twice about it. With the shoe-bag in one hand, she crept along the row of seats until she was beside her friend, then tapped the younger girl on the arm. "Magdalene!"

Finally, *finally* Magdalene turned around to face Coryn. But her movements were slow, and her expression frozen and terrified. There was something like a gob of blue jelly stuck on her cheek.

Coryn's eyes widened, and suddenly her unease was back. "Mags...?"

The girl slowly toppled sideways until she lay across the seats, her head almost in Coryn's lap. *"Run,"* she whispered.

It was then that Coryn realised the theatre wasn't empty after all. She could see slumped bodies strewn around in the aisles, and even a brightly-clad figure on the floor beside the podium, probably the session's speaker. It was fair to say they would not be speaking today, or possibly ever.

Oh, *dear*.

Coryn's breath stopped, and she began to carefully move back along the row of seats towards the door. But then as she reached the end of the row, she felt something hard hit her back. She turned slowly to see a boy standing behind her. He was about twelve years old, round-faced and smiling, and he held a weapon in one hand. It was pointed at her.

"Boo!" he said.

Then he squeezed the trigger.

The Spaceship

Ash raced away from the man with the changing eyes, her head and arm aching from where his fingers had dug in, and her heart pounding with panic.

Stupid stupid stupid stupid girl! Who just walked through a remnant gateway without checking to see what was on the other side? *Her*, of course, and she'd be bloody lucky if she didn't die this time. She'd dodged death more times than she could count, and she just-didn't-learn!

(Ash.)

She sprinted down yet another hall, then took a sharp turn around the nearest corner, almost running full force into a gaggle of pedestrians who were having some kind of intent conversation. She swerved around them, then headed for a distant metal door. Had she lost him? She must have lost him,

because she couldn't hear footsteps behind her.

(Ash!)

No, no, it couldn't be him. What had his name been, Marty? No, something less friendly – Mortimer. That was it. Mortimer, god of death. That name had stuck, as had the burns from his hands. Ash was crying as she ran, from fear and panic that this had gone so horribly wrong, and wishing desperately that she'd made a wiser decision coming through the gateway in the first place. Was she ever going to see George again?

(Ash! Wake up!)

Suddenly the man was right in front of her, eyes brilliant orange, and Ash screamed and punched him in the chest. Her hand sunk right in and there was a brief moment of blurring, what almost seemed like pixelation, before she felt the impact of the strike. "Hey-"

"Ash," he said in a young girl's voice. "Ash, wake up." He was holding her shoulders and shaking her, and scowling… But then something cold washed down her back, and the scene around her began to blur. He opened his mouth as if to speak- but then he was gone. The whole ship was gone, everything was gone, and there was only greyness.

But Ash wasn't alone.

"By the Rood," Elspeth said cheerfully. "You are most difficult to wake, and you had the most dreadful expression on your face, as though you were having a nightmare. Are you well?"

"Wha-what happened?" But even now the grey mist was disappearing, and the feeling was coming back into Ash's arms and legs. It was like waking from a very vivid dream, the sort where you're convinced it's real, and it's only reality that shows you were dreaming in the first place. They were standing just inside the entrance of a dark room full of cubicles. Some of the cubicles were occupied by blank-faced people acting out all kinds of movements, and Elspeth stood in front of her in a rather nice light blue suit of some kind, an eager expression on her pretty face. Behind her was a youngish man in a similar style of clothing, with a very tall forehead and a weird monocle-thing half covering one eye.

"You used up your trial hours ago," he answered, sounding quite irritated. "I couldn't even get you to move out of the cubicle."

Ash stared at him for a moment, the events of the last few hours finally making sense in her mind. His language was different too, she realised, and didn't seem to be one she'd heard before. "I was still in virtual reality. I couldn't get out."

Elspeth frowned, an expression of concern coming over her face. She stretched out a hand. "Ash?"

Forget dignity. Ash threw herself into the smaller girl's arms, bursting into tears.

The Mall

Pop.

Coryn looked down at where the gob of blue gel sat on the thin fabric of her overtop. She could feel it seeping through to her skin already, and within seconds she would be collapsed on the floor just like all these others. A temporary paralysis, thankfully, but looking at the gleeful face of the child in front of her, that didn't seem like a good thing.

Pop pop pop pop pop.

She felt more parapellets hit her on the neck, the face, her outstretched hands; but she still wasn't falling. She looked up in shock to meet the boy's eyes. His were green-grey and wide, and in the second it took to realise that she *still* wasn't falling over, she reached up and snatched the paragun right out of the boy's hand and threw it across the room.

She didn't wait for a reaction. She ducked around him and ran for the door. She was reaching for the exit-panel when suddenly there was a sharp, hissing sound, and the back of her hand had a dark streak that burned like fire. There was a blackened hole in the exit-panel right where her hand had been.

This was *not* a paragun.

"Try to run and that'll be your head," the boy said from behind her. His voice was strange: alternately high-pitched and deep. Not like when Coryn's brother Ladon's voice was breaking, but more like he was trying to hide something. Was he even a child? But she didn't *feel* any alter-power in use…

Coryn didn't move, except for the faint trembling of her whole body. "What do you want?" she asked, and her voice came out very small.

The boy's footsteps came closer, and she felt something cool tap the back of her neck. "The emblem, of course. Where is it?"

The emblem, the emblem! Did he mean the light-wand? That was back at the mobi-home along with Trennan's bag, and there was no way she'd let either of those out of her grasp. But how had they known to find her here? "What emblem?"

"Don't lie to me!" A solid hand grasped her shoulder,

turning her to face her attacker. He was as tall as she, and held a small black weapon in one hand, and a red light shone ominously on the end of its barrel. Red meant warning, but his young face was as smooth and cheerful as ever. "We've had this conversation before. I *know* you know where it is, and if you don't give it to me…" His voice dropped low; as low as a grown man's, and the weapon's barrel prodded her collarbone. The threat didn't need to be spoken aloud.

But his face hadn't changed, Coryn realised. With him as close as he now was, she saw that there was something wrong. In fact, the soft planes of his child's face seemed…sheer. He seemed to be wearing some kind of mask, and there was someone else underneath. "Who are you?" she whispered.

"Wrong answer." He lifted the weapon…and suddenly the lights went out.

Coryn brought an arm up to her face, feeling it strike something hard in front of her. There was a flash of red light in the darkness – the weapon discharging – but there was no burning pain. She hadn't been hit. Fueled by adrenaline, she turned and dashed away from the glass exit door with its secondary light from the hall, heading further into the theatre.

Smack. Ow – she'd found a row of chairs. She threw herself down on the ground, whimpered when she realised she'd landed on a body, then crawled further along, feeling the press of the hard chairs all along one side.

She could hear the swearing of the boy/man in the darkness; could see the occasional faint flash of red light as the weapon's 'on' light flickered; could hear the harsh sound of her own breathing. She was aiming for the other exit; because she sure couldn't stay in here. She didn't know how she'd been found, but she had, and she'd be dead or worse if the Chosen or Brosca got her back-

Coryn's hand set down on something hard and angular. She felt it a few times then realised what it was – the paragun she'd thrown across the room. She closed her fingers around the handle, then lifted it up carefully, pointing the barrel away from herself. She couldn't see the other weapon's red light anymore, but she could hear the faint shuffling sound of footsteps…

"Got you!"

Coryn screamed and pulled the trigger, hearing the pellets discharge over and over in a steady stream, hearing them hit something. And then there was a loud thump like someone falling to the floor, and she stayed frozen in that semi-crouching position; her arm still extended out in front of her.

Someone was whimpering, and it wasn't her. Then the lights flickered and turned back on, and she could see the whole theatre. Not far from her was what looked like the shooter, fallen as though asleep.

Around the room a few people were beginning to wake up, and over by the door she saw Magdalene's dark head and red jacket, the girl now sitting up. There was a *dit-dit-dit* rattling sound from outside, sounding very close – the enforcers' siren warning of their imminent approach.

Coryn forced herself to her feet and stumbled over to where Magdalene sat, the open shoe bag right next to her. The parapellet on her cheek had faded into just a faint blue spot. The effects hadn't lasted long. "Are you OK, Mags?"

"Um…yes?" Magdalene looked up at her, eyes wide. "Are you?"

Coryn shrugged tiredly. She felt like she'd just run a marathon, and in spite of what had just occurred, she couldn't summon up any energy for panic or even to think about why they'd been attacked. So she focused on what she could manage right now: "You've probably missed your interview at the ice-shop. But if you explain what happened, maybe the owner will give you another chance."

Magdalene looked down at Coryn's hand where she still held the paragun…in a room full of people who'd been shot with parapellets…and the enforcers were coming.

Damn. Suddenly exhausted, Coryn dropped the paragun and slumped down onto the next seat. "I don't think I'm up to walking," she said quietly. "But you'd better go if you don't want to be questioned." She remembered Magdalene saying that she'd been questioned before by enforcers about why she was in certain places, what she'd been doing…but they hadn't been able to prove anything. This wouldn't look good.

By the expression on Magdalene's face, she knew it too. "But…what about you?"

"I'll be fine. You go now."

Magdalene's jaw tightened. She nodded, then picked up the shoe bag and ran from the room.

Coryn couldn't help feeling abandoned. Even though it was best for the other girl to go – she had a few too many things to hide herself – no one wanted to come to the enforcers' attention if they could avoid it. At least Coryn had been off the government radar for the years she'd been living in the Compound.

But as far as she knew, Magdalene had been hacking for years, and it probably wouldn't take much digging to find out that she was anti-Sec and a traitor to the State and all of those names that the Sec government liked to use before they had people executed or locked away.

Barely a minute after Magdalene had left, the enforcers arrived. There were four of them, and three wore the black overvests that declared their profession, carrying the rather more serious efficiency rifles in their arms. Unlike paraguns, those only needed one shot to leave someone as a pile of ash.

The fourth enforcer simply wore a grey suit, looking very much the bureaucrat, and exactly like she'd seen him not an hour before, except that this time he held a small stunner and an efficiency rifle was slung over his shoulder.

Daniel, the regular drink-buyer. Was this good or bad?

"We've got a report of hostile activity and a weapon being fired," Daniel said to the room at large. "What happened here?"

There was a long, awkward silence where none of the few conscious people in the room answered. No one wanted to be the centre of attention. Coryn tried to shrink back against her chair, but then he saw her.

"Coryn!" he said in a much higher, lighter tone. "What are you doing here?"

Seriously? "It's a viewing theatre," she replied as weakly as she could manage. "I've finished work."

Both statements were true, and she could tell Daniel had interpreted them the way she'd intended. Not a hint of suspicion crossed his face. "But you've been shot!" he exclaimed. "And you're still awake!"

They were the centre of attention now, and he seemed to realise it. "Find out what happened," he ordered the other enforcers in his usual brusque tone, his cheeks flushing a little. Then turning back to Coryn he said, "I can see half a dozen parapellets on your top. You should take that off before they start to affect you."

"Mm," she murmured, moving to unzip it. He hadn't noticed the ones on her neck, then.

But he was still studying her with a furrowed brow. "Very few people can withstand parapellets. Either you're tremendously strong – or that top is thicker than it looks."

"It's the top," Coryn replied in that forcibly weak voice. She slipped it off, feeling awkward in her sleeveless undershirt, then held it at a distance. "I do feel tired, though. Um…don't you need to find the bad guy, and so on?"

Daniel looked nonplussed. "Of course. I'll just… I'll come back."

She hadn't lied about feeling tired. While she really, really wanted to up and leave, that could also make her look suspicious. *Innocents have nothing to fear* was the government line. It seemed that very few people were truly innocent, then, and she certainly wasn't one of them. And damnatus, her hand hurt. She rubbed at the burn with her other hand.

On the other side of the theatre the enforcers had gathered around the child-attacker. "Are you sure this is the shooter?" Daniel was saying, his tone sceptical. "He's been shot himself."

Another victim, a man in his sixties, sat on a nearby chair. His face still held the slackness caused by the parapellets' aftereffects. "Then he did it to himself when he heard your sirens. That's the one, I swear it. He just walked on in here during the screening and starting firing that thing. I saw him myself."

"It's true," another man agreed. He looked the same age as the first. "It's all this violent VR these days. Messing with kids' heads."

"Here's the footage," one of the other enforcers said to Daniel, holding up a small screen. "It was the boy alright. He was shooting at that girl over there when the lights went out."

Coryn cringed as half a dozen heads turned to stare at her from across the room.

"Any reason why the lights would have gone out?" Daniel queried.

Really, really good luck?

"Looks like it was linked to some sort of outage on the underground powerstation before the generator kicked in," another enforcer said. "Good timing, because the kid wasn't just shooting a paragun." He bent down to pick something up; something smaller and darker and definitely more lethal. The weapon that the shooter had dropped. "Look here."

Daniel studied it, his expression neutral, his brow just a little furrowed. "He was recorded using this?"

"Again, shooting at your girl," the enforcer said. "She was trying to escape."

Not his girl.

"That's a different level from paraguns," Daniel murmured to the other enforcers. "Although he might get lucky due to his age. But how a child like him got a weapon like this…"

"Actually," Coryn said awkwardly, and all those faces turned to stare at her again. She forced back her fear, climbing to her feet and carefully moving closer so that she could also see the shooter. He lay on the ground, his eyes creepily half-open, and that same smiling expression still fixed on his round face.

Weird. Wrong.

"His voice was strange," she said softly. "He was shouting about something I didn't understand, but his voice kept changing."

"That's not unusual for young boys," Daniel said pleasantly. "And you'd better sit down before you fall over."

She sat, all the better to keep up the illusion of helplessness. "But it was different. Could he be hiding his real face with a hologram?"

"That's illegal technology," Daniel started to say, but then one of the other enforcers pointed their stunner at the prone boy and pulled the trigger. A slim beam of white light hit him in the chest, and he convulsed. His whole face flickered like a damaged VR programme, and then he changed above the high collar of his jacket. He wasn't a tall, sweet-faced boy anymore. He was a man in his thirties with dirty-blonde hair and rough, familiar features.

The high collar of his jacket now resembled a dull black band fixed around his neck, not quite hiding a stylized tattoo resembling a ram's head with curling horns. A light flickered then died under his chin.

One of the witnesses swore, and even the enforcers looked startled.

"Well," Daniel said, and then he coughed and tried again. "This is a different story. Hiding one's identity for the purposes of terrorism is a capital offence under the Civil Securities Act twenty-five-sixty-one. Do any of you recognise him?"

The other witnesses shook their heads, wide-eyed, and an enforcer turned to Coryn. "What about you, miss?"

Oh, yes. It was the man who'd tried to steal the light-wand, back when she'd first arrived in the city. The man who'd attacked *her*, and who she'd left in a groaning pile on the ground level several months before. She swallowed. "I've never seen him before in my life."

Ten minutes later two enforcers had trundled off with the manacled, still-stunned shooter, probably never to be seen again. Daniel and the other enforcer were scanning the victims' chips, most of whom were now awake, and were sending them off to the Mall's medic station.

Coryn glanced longingly at the door with its burned exit-panel, now forced open. Escape.

Just then the other enforcer came over. "Hand, miss."

Oh. He wanted to scan her. Coryn held back, unsure of what her address would show as.

"I need to scan your chip," he said impatiently.

Coryn slowly held out her hand, the burn-side up. "Sorry," she said weakly. "I'm not thinking straight."

"That's a nasty burn," Daniel said from beside her. She

jumped – she hadn't even realised he was there. "You can leave this one, Aleks. I know her."

That was enough for the enforcer. He left, leaving Coryn unscanned…for now.

"You should get that seen to," Daniel said, nodding towards her hand.

"It's not bleeding."

"Then get something for the pain. You'll feel it more once those parapellets wear off."

They already had, even if they'd worked at all.

"OK," Coryn agreed, standing again. She picked up her now-tainted top; one of the few long-sleeved ones she owned. But at least it hadn't been her head. "I'll go see a medic, then."

"Wait. What are you going to do with that top?"

She shrugged, surprised. "Throw it away, I suppose."

"I can get rid of it," he said casually.

"OK…" She held it out to him a little self-consciously, trying not to let the pellets touch her skin.

Daniel dropped the top on the ground between them, took the efficiency rifle off his shoulder, aimed, and fired. A single bolt of very bright light hit the top, and for a moment it shone like a tiny sun before it disintegrated into fine grey ash. "Cleaner," he called, and a few seconds later along trundled a little square machine. It ran right over top of the mess, leaving the floor spotless.

He turned to Coryn, looking rather pleased with himself. "This rifle's very useful for getting rid of rubbish." Her eyes widened, and he seemed to realise he was aiming it at her foot. "I can't shoot by accident," he told her. "I have to be holding both triggers, and I wasn't. Besides, it locks itself after five seconds of disuse."

"How very clever," Coryn said weakly. All she could think of was how such things could make a human being disappear very, very quickly. "Thank you for…disposing of that." She turned towards the door, unwilling to be rude, but really wanting to get away before he asked any more questions like 'where's the paragun?'

"Coryn."

"Yes?" She looked over her shoulder.

"I'll, ah, see you tomorrow at the eatery."

She smiled politely, not explaining that she wouldn't be seeing him.

Tomorrow was her day off.

Daniel watched the girl go, her bulky bag slung over one slender shoulder. She didn't look like she had much muscle, but there must be some hidden strength there because according to the cameras she'd been shot repeatedly with the paragun – which they still hadn't found – and she hadn't collapsed.

The film stopped there, of course, because the lights had turned out; but when it had restarted, she'd been sitting on the seats by the door with another girl, and the shooter had been across the room.

Hades, she was pretty. He didn't think she even knew how pretty she was. She had that long, pale hair, and that elegant face with those big eyes which even when smiling held an edge of sorrow. He wanted to know *why*.

He'd checked out her records the first time he'd noticed her in the eatery. Coryn Regindotir had spent an unusually small amount of time in the City or in *any* major towns, if the records were correct. There was a small fine from about eight months before. It was for loitering and public indecency, jointly imposed upon one Trennan Halfling (strange last name, hmm?). That had shaken him, until he realised it probably only meant a kiss. If they'd been doing more than that, then there would have been a lot more than just a ten credit fine.

But she was almost eighteen years old, only a few years younger than him, and until last month it was like she hadn't even existed. That should be suspicious, Daniel knew, but in truth he didn't care. As long as she wasn't a spy for a neighbouring country (which he severely doubted) then he didn't care what she'd been doing.

It would be nice if she'd look at him as a person, though. It was more than obvious that all she could see was his government status, and most ordinary people found that off-putting. He didn't know why. If they had nothing to hide, then what was the problem? To be fair, there were a lot of ways that people could accidently trip up. But those things could be easily amended.

Earlier today, she was either completely oblivious to the fact he was trying to ask her out, or she was purposely pretending to be. He had to show her that he wasn't stuffy and…*bureaucratic*, and that he was worth getting to know. How he'd do that, he didn't know. But he had to try.

"I can't believe I was still in virtual reality," Ash sobbed. "It felt so *real*. It was like a nightmare!"

Elspeth patted her arm, her expression simultaneously sympathetic and confused. "There, there," she soothed. "'Tis over now."

The guy with the space-monocle looked less sympathetic.

"Speak Lilluanian, will you?" he said in another language.

"I couldn't get out of your stupid virtual reality!" Ash snapped at him in the same language, pulling away from Elspeth. "It felt like I was in there for hours!"

He drew back, affronted. "You just have to say the magic word. The intro explained that."

"There was no intro!"

"There's *always* an intro, it's part of the deal, and you're going to have to pay for-"

"The most miserable time of my life?" Ash cut in. "I didn't *ask* for the free trial. I didn't even know I was getting one, and I sure as Hades couldn't get out when I wanted to! There was just some hideous spaceship and people were getting put down for being crazy-"

A flash of guilt came over the man's face. "Oh, the Rosmerta glitch is still there? I thought we'd fixed that."

"You hadn't!" Growing increasingly angry, Ash put her hands on her hips. "What is that place, anyway? And what year is it? And what was with bringing up enemies from the worst parts of my life-"

"It's a programming error," he replied, not seeming at all sorry. "Some hacker created it a year or two ago, and it's caused- ...well, it's caused trouble, because people don't realise it's just VR even when they come out. And for the rest of it, I don't know what you saw, but *your brain* brought it into the scene, not our systems. We don't know that kind of information."

Ash felt a small hand tap her arm. "I'm sorry to interrupt," Elspeth said politely in Anglish, "but I do not understand what you are saying to this man, and I also have instructions I must give you myself. Mayhap we might adjourn outside?"

Ash was still coming to terms with the last, terrible day of her life actually being a lot shorter, and also being entirely inside her head, and was swinging between anger and relief. She looked at the small Tudar girl, and it suddenly clicked that Elspeth should *not* be here, wherever 'here' was. So she followed her outside, ignoring the man who was still droning on behind them.

Once outside, Ash saw that they were back on the street where she'd first come through from 1818. And there was the gateway she'd come through – right there, right across the street from the building with a large flashing sign. She couldn't read the script, but she'd bet ten-to-one it read something like, 'Virtual World'.

"Oh, Deias," she groaned. "What an *idiot*."

"Have you ever experienced such a thing before?" Elspeth asked.

"Well, no-"

"Then 'twould be foolish to blame yourself," she said matter-of-factly. "How were you to know where you were?"

Ash had to accept that logic. "That's a good point, Elspeth, but- wait, why are you saying that to *me*? Why are you even here?" A horrible thought occurred to her. "Oh Deias, what if I'm still in virtual reality? What if *you're* not even real? You're supposed to be in the Mountain of Glass or who-knows-where, but not *here*. I mean, this has to be at least fifty years after my own time for the virtual reality to be so good that I didn't even know I was in it, but you…"

The younger girl looked baffled. "I know not where we are. I simply came because Amaranthus told me you needed to be woken. I went through the gateway as directed, and there you were. Oh, and he also gave me a task for you, if you should choose to accept it."

Ash ran out of steam, slumping in relief. That really *did* sound like Amaranthus, and like Elspeth. "Oh. That sounds good. And thank you, by the way. I don't know what would have happened if you hadn't helped me." She kept thinking of that oh-so-creepy man with his multiple personalities and changing eyes. It had almost seemed like he'd been possessed at one point, by something less than human…

But the man had said the scenes in virtual reality were shaped by her own mind. What was wrong with her that she'd come up with such horrible ideas?

"You would have remained standing there, no doubt, until the store's owner lost patience and woke you himself," Elspeth replied matter-of-factly.

Yeah, probably. "But why did Amaranthus send you? Not that I'm complaining, of course."

Elspeth's face creased into a cheeky grin. "Oh, Ash, I have restrained myself most wonderfully, but I do so wish to tell you what I have been doing. I have been set to run errands – or that is what they call them, back at the Mountain – and I've been to all manner of places. Even-"

"Anne," Ash cut in. She didn't mean to be rude, but her mind still seemed to be all over the place. "I saw you both a few months ago when you came to my house, but not since. Is she alright?"

Elspeth closed her mouth. "Well enough. She follows a similar path to mine, but I must say does not listen to Amaranthus-"

Elspeth began to feel quite annoyed when the girl cut in yet again, blabbering on about that brief moment where they'd met in her own home with Jon's friends, and about all the ridiculous things she had seen in the confusing mind-dream of virtue-ell ree-al-uhtee, and not at all concerned about the great lengths Elspeth had gone through to get here.

Well, in truth 'twas not quite the case. Elspeth had simply followed the instructions given – followed them perfectly – and had found herself here. She rather thought that unlike her sister, if one was to simply wait for instructions, then one would waste far less time.

And she *really*, truly wanted to tell where she had been!

Instead she waited for Ash to finish speaking. The girl ended on a question as she had before, "So I suppose I could go back to 1818 now I know where the gateway is, but I don't really want to. You said there was some kind of task that needed doing here?"

Elspeth was always polite, but now she felt quite short of patience. Had Ash been so emotional and talkative last time they'd met? She thought not. So she kept her answer brief. "Find the girl with the blue ears, and tell her that the Unfading One sent you to lend assistance."

"What? What does that mean?"

"I know not! I am simply the messenger. And you do not *have* to do this, you may if you so choose-"

"No, no, I want to," Ash assured her. She began to dig through the pocket of her rather ugly breeches, pulling out a small, rectangular device. "Yay, I've still got my phone! Just give me a minute for it to turn on – I've been trying to save the battery since we don't have any way to charge it in George's time – and I'll put in notes."

Elspeth waited, but she was beginning to grow uncomfortable with the length of time spent here. On her other two travels, she had spent mere seconds in each location. One of Amaranthus's People had explained to her that 'twas best to simply give the message you had to give, and then to leave them to work it out on their own. Otherwise they'd bombard you with all manner of questions…

Ash's phone finally switched on, and she quickly pulled up the notepad setting, tapping away with her thumbs. "Blue ears…Unfading One…and what was the last thing?"

"To lend assistance," Elspeth repeated. She sounded irritable for some reason.

"Lend assistance," Ash continued, still focused on the little screen. "Huh, seems like I'm hearing that phrase a lot lately. Did I tell you what that guy said to me inside that place? Not the guy with the monocle; the one with the orange eyes. Or grey eyes. He looked like a Noble from Iversley…"

Elspeth didn't respond, so Ash looked up.

The other girl was nowhere to be seen.

"Seriously?" Ash moaned to herself. Elspeth must have taken a page from Amaranthus's book, and had left when they'd finished talking. How rude – but she must have used a gateway.

Ash looked around curiously for that telltale shimmer, but she could only see the one gateway she herself had come through; the one back to Lunden. She really ought to go back, at least to tell George what she was up to. She'd expect the same of him.

Yeah, Ash argued with herself, but she'd never asked *him* to do embroidery while she went out to have fun!

She stared at the gateway with narrowed eyes, clenching and unclenching one fist as she pondered her options. Swallow her pride… or have some fun?

Coryn walked in the direction of the Mall's medic station, but she was halfway there when she heard Magdalene's voice calling her name. "Coryn! Coryn!"

Coryn turned, and there she was, her red jacket over her arm and her young face twisted with anxiety. She wore Poli's shoes: shiny and smart and a little too big, clumping with each step as she ran towards Coryn.

"Mags," Coryn said in relief. The girl looked well, and Coryn hadn't even realised how worried she'd been. "Did you have your interview?"

"He's letting me come back tomorrow, because it's all over the news about what just happened." Magdalene came to a halt right in front of Coryn, then threw her arms around her waist. "But you're OK! What happened?" Her voice dropped low. "Were you interrogated?"

Coryn gave her a meaningful stare, then glanced around at their location. *We're in public,* she tried to express. *We're being watched.*

Magdalene seemed to get the idea, and she kept quiet until they'd well and truly left the Mall complex and were waiting near the lifts, mostly alone. "So were you?"

"No, miraculously. One of the enforcers is a regular at the eatery, and he stopped the others asking too many questions. I just acted weak and stupid, and they let me go."

"Oh. Good. What do you think that boy wanted?"

Magdalene had left the room too soon to realise it hadn't been a boy at all, Coryn realised. And so she lied again. It was for Mags' own good, she told herself. Brosca or the Chosen had found Coryn, and they only brought death and destructions. So the more distance she kept from the other girls, the better. "I have no idea."

They took the lift down a level, then paused to go their separate ways. "Wait," Magdalene said. "You left something with me." She held out the bag Coryn had given her the shoes in, this time looking almost empty.

It's Poli's bag, Coryn wanted to say, but then she looked inside. Right at the bottom, stretching the firm fabric, was the paragun they'd both been shot with.

Coryn gave the younger girl a horrified glance, and Magdalene shrugged ruefully. "I can't take it home to the orphanage. One of the older kids tried to bring in a bomb once, so there's a weapon scanner on the door."

"Of course," Coryn murmured. She took the bag. Out of everyone she knew, she probably needed it the most.

**Bethel Insane Asylum,
the outskirts of Lunden, 1818 AD**

George awoke with a start. His face was squashed uncomfortably against the stone wall of his small cell, and he had a crick in his neck, an ache in his head, and a bruised backside from the inhospitable seating. How had he even managed to fall asleep?

"By Jove," he muttered in dismay. "I was hoping this had all been a dream."

But no, he was still in the insane asylum. The one his own dear brother had put him into, and he had no way of getting out. Ashlea didn't even know he was in here. In fact, his mobile phone had been misplaced somewhere, most likely back at the Lunden townhouse.

Oh…*dear.*

So it was with desperation that George turned to the one person who might just be able to hear him even in the depths of this dreadful dilemma, alliteration aside.

"Amaranthus," he whispered hoarsely. "Are you there?"

There was no answer, but instead perhaps the sense that he wasn't quite alone. Or that could have been the headache and wishful thinking working together. Outside his cell, George could hear the faint sounds of an argument – either the asylum guards, or some poor mad soul losing their temper.

"Amaranthus?" he tried again a little louder. "If you can hear me, please respond!"

There was two seconds of silence, and then someone shouted from down the hall, "TELL HIM HE'LL HAVE TO BLOODY WELL WAIT UNTIL IT'S READY!"

"Oh, I say," George muttered to himself, taken back by both the vehemence of the shout and its timing. "Mind your language, chap."

There was no way that those having the argument down the hall could hear his quiet murmurs, although they had reduced to a more reasonable volume. He tried it one more time, very quietly. "Amaranthus…?"

Down the hall, someone shouted again, "I said WAIT! Don't you speak Anglish?"

George went very, very quiet, just as an asylum guard stomped past the barred door to his cell. He then heard them further down the hall, banging on the cell of whoever had been holding the odd part-conversation with George. "Talking to yourself again, Warrocks? That's a good way to get a cold-water treatment."

The shouting faded into snivelling, with the inmate – for that was surely what it was – muttering, "Wait, he's got to wait. He thinks these things can happen in an instant, does he? Should wait."

George slumped back against the wall of his cell, hope and confusion warring inside him. Very well.

He'd wait. It wasn't as if he had anything better to do.

Lile 2598 AD

Mortimer tore off his head set, blinking rapidly as his vision adjusted to reality once more. He was in his small apartment as always, but he wasn't alone. He couldn't see the Creature, but he could feel the connection as though it was attached to him by fine, strong threads.

"What," he snarled, "did you think you were doing?"

That girl, the Creature whispered in his mind. It sounded as though it spoke from a long way away – but it was merely the distance between the Other realm and the normal. *She was different.*

Mortimer shook his head. He was still trembling from what had just happened. He'd been inside the Mind-Killer, a VR virus he'd carefully created not long after arriving back in this time.

One of his favourites; it created a permanent link to each person who used the programme, filling them with hopelessness and despair that proved difficult to shake. If they didn't manage to shake it, then weeks or months down the track when they finally killed themselves – or so he was hoping – he'd gather their life force, their alter-power, across any distance.

Brilliant.

Except there he'd been, wandering around looking for new victims, and he'd only just spotted a likely target when the Creature had stepped in. It had shoved him out of the way, out of control of his own damned programme, and he'd been stuck watching from a distance, scrambling to get back to the programme or back to real life or back to *anything*…

"I don't care if she was different," he said finally, carefully controlling his tone. "I don't care if she was an alien or the queen of bloody Siam. This is *my* programme, and this was not part of our bargain!"

She knew you.

"What?"

She recognised you, the Creature prodded. *I touched her mind just briefly. Something about burning hands, and a place called Iversley. Sound familiar?*

Mortimer froze. Oh yes. Yes, it did sound familiar, and he'd thought for a moment she'd looked familiar too. But VR could mess with his head, and it had seemed impossible that the time-traveller was here in the twenty-sixth century. In his own little city.

If he could have seen the Creature, he'd have known it was smiling. *Let's rework our bargain,* it purred. *You get me the spirit's blood, and I'll get you her.*

The Mountain of Glass, time irrelevant

The sky was blue, the grass was soft, and the air fragrant with flowers, but Elspeth of Covington paid little heed to the beauty of her surroundings. Her attention was fixed firmly on her princely companion with whom she sat under a fruit tree, telling of her recent travels. After all, who else would listen?

"And the girl would not even hear the tidings I brought! I would have told her of how the Eternity Stone was taken from that evil witch, and how it had ended up in her own home for my sister to later find…oh. You are not listening either, are you?"

Jon blinked at her, then smiled ruefully. "Sorry, Bets. I had my head somewhere else. You were saying something about a kitchen table?"

Elspeth looked down, trying not to show how his inattention bothered her. She knew she was merely the bastard daughter of a milkmaid, and he was a *prince*. Even so, they had a friendship of sorts, did they not? She smiled back a little sadly. "Never mind. 'Twas of little import, by the by."

"I want to hear it," he said staunchly. "And I've been terribly rude not listening. Tell me about your little adventure."

'Twould be rude not to after that, she thought. So a little hesitantly at first, then with more enthusiasm, Elspeth told him about how Amaranthus had sent her to retrieve the Eternity Stone. She'd been advised not to use it, but instead to dash between two gateways as fast as she could – which was quite fast, when not hampered by heavy skirts – and snatch the thing from the air.

Elspeth had moved too quickly to even know where she had gone, except that she'd seen that girl Ash there. And then the second gateway had led Elspeth to the same little house she'd recently visited with Anne and Jon. She'd been instructed to leave the Eternity Stone on the kitchen table, and then to leave without allowing anyone to see her.

"And you did it, just like that?"

"But of course," Elspeth said in surprise. "If I did not do as instructed, then I would hardly be offered another chance, would I?" She still didn't know *why* she had been sent to do those things, but she was beginning to suspect that if she could converse at length with Anne, it might make more sense.

"And that's the difference between you and your sister," Jon announced, leaning back against the tree's trunk. His formerly white skin was now only a few shades lighter than the trunk, and the change was one of those things that made Elspeth want to ask a hundred questions. She restrained herself. "Anne wouldn't have followed the instructions exactly. She would have taken a guess and gone on to the next place, wherever *that* was. I mean, where is she now?"

Elspeth shrugged. She knew the reason for Anne's confidence, and that was growing up with knowing she was the highest of the high – except for the royals, naturally. The only way Anne could have been more confident was to have *been* the Queen of Angland, or else to have been born a male. "Finding Francois, I trow. But no doubt Amaranthus knows."

"Hmm."

And that seemed to be the end of that conversation. "What were you thinking of before?" Elspeth asked timidly. "When you were not listening?"

"Foolish thoughts." Jon looked down at where his hand lay against his white-clad knee. "How like your sister, I intend to never go home." He let out a heavy sigh. "But unlike her, I think I'll be going back sooner rather than later."

"Why is that?"
"Just a hunch. Lots of things to finish up there."

"In the future?" she asked curiously. "What kind of things?"

He smiled at her, showing straight white teeth. Forsooth, while his skin and hair might be a little darker than before, he was still most handsome, Elspeth thought. "Dangerous things. Things I don't want to talk about."

She paused, pondering whether that meant he *would* tell if she asked carefully, or whether he was politely refusing. "You do not wish to speak of them, so you will not, or you do not wish to speak of them, so you will anyway?"

Jon gave her a knowing look, one eyebrow raised. "The first one."

Oh, Saints' bones, his reticence was *most* exasperating! But not wishing to test the limits of their budding friendship, Elspeth resolved not to press for information. She changed the subject.

Lile 2598 AD

Ash had the choice to swallow her pride and go back to Lunden, 1818, or to be immature and have fun while searching for a mysterious, blue-eared girl. Bad circulation or bad fashion? Who cared!

She took the middle ground, poking her head through the gateway just long enough to ascertain that yes, it *was* the way home, then stepped back into wherever she was now.

Ash still didn't know where she was, but she looked around with interest. The buildings went up and up and up, higher than anything she'd seen before, with blocky connections between their upper levels far above her head. She still couldn't see anyone around, but she could hear the faint roar of what sounded like many, many vehicles.

Ooh, this must be a *big* city. And it was far enough in the future to have virtual reality: fingers crossed it would have flying cars too. Much more fun than smelly old Lunden, where she couldn't even go into a bookstore.

Speaking of smelly old Lunden… Ash pulled out her mobile phone and dialled George's number again. He hadn't responded to her voice message, but that didn't worry her much. Chances were he just hadn't checked the phone. But this time it just rang once then went to voicemail.

She sighed. "Hi, George. It's me again. I'm still through the new gateway, you know, the one by Tolliver's bookstore." In case he'd forgotten. She lowered her voice, feeling excitement course through her. "I've got a mission, George! It's a weird one, but I'll give it my best shot. Just…give me a call when you can, OK? Love you."

Ash ended the call, then studied the phone with a brief frown. Was there something wrong with George? The fight hadn't been *that* bad, but something wasn't sitting right…

But she dismissed that last thought, focussing on what was ahead of her. Adventure hoy!

"I," Ash said to herself, because there was no one else around to talk to, "am going to be extremely helpful."

Somewhere across time and space…

Anne followed the sentinel through the gateway, steeling herself for the shock of whatever lay on the other side. Every gateway was a little startling, for she would find herself in yet another change of garb, and with any kind of surroundings.

The air was cool here, and mayhap a little damp. The sentinel had disappeared once more – the infuriating little gate-bug – and she stood alone in a stone-built hall, light streaming through narrow windows to her left and falling onto a wooden floor lightly scattered with rushes.

She smelled the faint mixture of crushed herbs and rot indicating the rushes were overdue for a change, and suddenly she felt rather weighed down in cloth.

"My garb," she breathed. "*My* garb." 'Twas the gown she had worn upon leaving her own time, one in green and gray with a wide velvet skirt, and the usual corset that now felt unnecessarily restrictive. She quickly pulled up the skirts, noting with relief that her sparkly purple slippers were still in place.

But 'twas going to the window that showed the truth of her location. She could see only a little, but the outer bailey wall was as familiar as ever, as were the fields beyond it.

"By the Rood," Anne said in dismay. "I've come home."

Just then a maidservant came around the corner, her arms full of linen for the upstairs room, for that was where this hall led. She was gray-haired and full-figured and sour-faced, and when she saw Anne she froze.

There was no time to escape, no time to find the gateway again, nor another for that matter. "Maura," Anne said heartily. "Good morrow. I trust you are well?"

Maura screamed.

Epilogue

Mountain of Glass, time irrelevant
(but probably sometime in early 2598 AD)

"You know, I'm still getting used to how weird time is here," Trennan said conversationally. He was watching over Amaranthus's shoulder as the other being skimmed his fingers across thousands of threads, sending images flying through the air faster than Trennan could keep up with. He still tried, though. "It's been months for her, and for me it feels like minutes. Well, perhaps hours." It was hard to tell.

Amaranthus was silent, and Trennan continued, "I can see from her thread that it'll be enough. Not just my words, but everyone she comes across. It'll be enough to do what needs to be done until her time is up too."

And eventually, everyone's time was up. Trennan could wait – it wasn't as if he had any other options. But…What about him? What about *now*? Did all the people who Amaranthus 'rescued' end up trailing him around like this, moving rapidly from place to place like some kind of…some kind of…parasite?

Parasite? Not even like a suckerfish on a shark, Amaranthus said, then chuckled aloud at his own joke. That laugh was one of the few times Trennan had heard him make an audible sound, and it was startling. It also made Trennan want to laugh back, so he did.

Then Amaranthus laughed some more, then Trennan laughed. It felt good, but after a while he calmed down enough to ask, "What were we talking about?"

You were wondering about what happens to the people I rescue. Where do they go?

Trennan thought of the garden that they'd visited several times – creatively called 'the Garden' – and the colossal glass city in its centre. The water of life flowed throughout the city and surroundings, and when he was there, he'd never felt better in his life. He'd even got used to how his skin had changed. It hadn't once turned back to that barklike-appearance that he'd had since birth. But still… Was he being fussy or unpleasable to say it felt like there was something more?

You'd be correct. The Mountain of Glass, for all of its peace and beauty, is just a stopping point. For you, and for me, and for the others-…there is much more.

And then a door opened in the air in front of Trennan, and bright, golden light shone through. A moment later, as his eyes adjusted, he realised what he was looking at. And for once, words failed him.

Lile City, 2598 AD

"I can't believe you've bought an air vehicle," Magdalene said excitedly. "When are you going to take us for a ride?"

"When have you got free time?" Coryn answered. They were sitting out in the fresh air of level seven, the sun shining between the gaps of the higher levels. The area was practically uncovered, and the grass grew lushly around the bench where they sat not far from an elevator down to the lower levels.

The other girl slumped. "I'm working late for the next five

days. When do you start?"

"6 a.m."

"Oh."

"If you're working late, I hope you're not walking home alone," Coryn said worriedly, remembering the disaster of the week before. "I know the man is in prison now, but still…"

Then Magdalene did something unexpected; she blushed. "A friend from the Mall has been walking me home."

Coryn's eyebrows shot up. "A *male* friend?"

Magdalene shrugged self-consciously, and her blush deepened. "Karl is nice," she replied a little defensively. "He's fifteen, and works at the shake-palace across from the ice-shop."

"Good. I wouldn't want you to be *walking* with anyone who wasn't nice." The other girl kept blushing, so Coryn decided to give her a break. "Does that mean you can't come into the film exhibit with me?"

"I can't. I'm meeting someone."

Coryn didn't even have to ask who, because Magdalene's blush suddenly flamed up again. "*Ohh*…well, I'll see you later."

She waved goodbye, then watched in curiosity and not a little envy as Magdalene greeted a dark-haired boy at the other side of the square. The pleasure on both faces was evident, and Coryn was reminded once again of Trennan. No wonder they hadn't been able to hide their relationship, if they'd looked at each other the way these two had. The memory hurt, of course. When did thinking of Trennan not hurt?

"Coryn."

She turned and looked up towards the source of the voice, then froze.

Aras.

It was definitely him. The massive man looked even bigger when he was standing in front of her, and he was exactly the same, right down to the shoulder-length fair hair, white scar on the left side of his face, and silvery prosthetic arm. The expression on his face was different though; somehow more open, but she couldn't read it. She didn't try, because terror was shooting through her.

The Chosen must have sent him. He must be here to kill her – and she wasn't ready to die.

That thought took a split second to run through Coryn's mind, then she reached up and pushed him hard. He stumbled backwards, teetering on the edge of the platform, and after an agonising moment where his shocked eyes met hers, he fell backwards.

Really, really not the end…

The story continues in book 4, *Desert of Ice:*

Ash likes a challenge. It looks like she's got one...

So she's accidentally travelled to the massive, futuristic city of Lile, 2598 AD. But now she's been given cryptic instructions to 'find the blue-eared girl', she's going to give it her best shot. If only George would answer his phone and come join her...

Back in Lunden, 1819 AD, George is a little tied up, and severely displeased with his brother and sister-in-law. Sure, he's mentioned time travel once or twice. But is the insane asylum really necessary? Then Anne shows up in his cell with a strange weapon in her hand and a cheeky look in her eye. She also has directions for his next steps...but where has she been?

Not far from where Ash is beginning her search, Coryn is rebuilding her life after losing almost everything that matters to her. All she has left is a bag full of junk, as well as instructions to find a desperately powerful supernatural item before the wicked Creatures can do so. But then she runs into an old enemy who's more than what they seem.

Paths are about to cross in a desperate race to save a nation that doesn't even know it's in danger...

Dear Reader,

Well. My humblest apologies for finishing a novel on a cliffhanger, since I hate when authors do that to me.

HOWEVER. This is not the end.

The end of this book slides neatly into the start of the next, *Desert of Ice*, where all the loose ends are tied up.

(*Desert of Fire* was originally the first half of an oversized book called *Deserts of Fire and Ice*. But it was uncomfortably large even in draft form, hence its current format.)

The storyline was inspired by several dreams: where Trennan finds fire pits under the ice, where Kamile finds snakes in her bed, birds in a cage with a python, the two little ponies hidden in a drawer, Ash's adventures in virtual reality, and Coryn's snake-nightmare.

That last dream wasn't a lot of fun, but it worked for the story, so I suppose it was worth having. (Also, I'm wondering what's going on in my head to prompt these kinds of dreams. Too much cheese last thing at night?)

So just the usual. If you liked the book, please leave a review on Goodreads or wherever you bought it - this will help other readers find it more easily, and they'll know what to expect from reading it.

You can also check out my website mmarinanbooks.com for what's coming next.